I0788606

THE ONLY GAME IN TOWN

Geonn Cannon

Supposed Crimes LLC • Matthews, North Carolina

All Rights Reserved
Copyright © 2022 Geonn Cannon

Published in the United States.

ISBN: 978-1-952150-36-4

www.supposedcrimes.com

This book is typeset in Goudy Old Style.

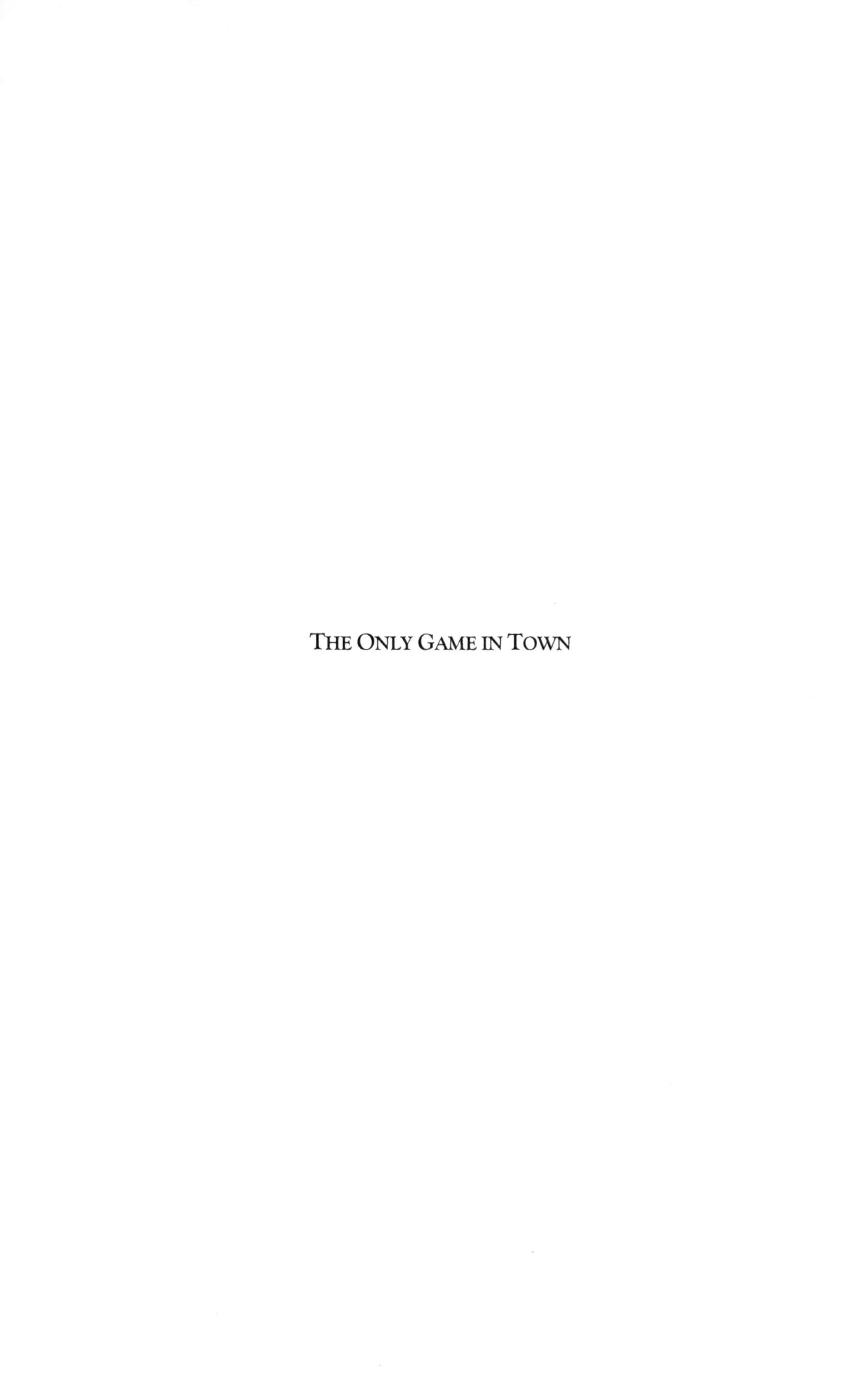

THE ONLY GAME IN TOWN

PROLOGUE

March 1916

"WHEN YOU *come to the end of a perfect day, and you sit alone with your thought...*"

Marcy Neal wrinkled her nose. The music had been playing for the better part of an hour, the same song drifting down the hall on a seemingly constant loop, but the singing was new. Worse than that, she recognized the voice. It was her savior, but also the man she least wanted to see at the moment. She closed her eyes and braced herself for a lecture.

She definitely deserved it. Bad girls got lectures, and good girls didn't find themselves sitting on an upturned bucket in a Podunk police station's broom closet listening to Carrie Jacobs-Bond echo herself on a Victrola. It would have been an uncomfortable position for anyone to find themselves in, but Marcy was tall for a woman, lanky and lean, and it felt like her knees were uncomfortably lined up with her shoulders. Her hands were limp on her thighs because her arms kept knocking into brooms and mops if she put them anywhere else.

The doorknob turned and she had to pull her feet back, squeezing in on herself. She squinted one eye closed and looked up at the man framed by the door. He was backlit by the hallway light but she would recognize that silhouette anywhere. David Buckner stuck his hands in his pockets and stuck his gut out, looking at her with a look she assumed was meant to be 'disappointing father.' She returned the stare without emotion.

"I suppose he deserved it," he said.

"Don't they always?" She stretched out her hand. "If it makes you feel better, I might not have done it if he'd been wearing his uniform."

David took it and hauled her up. "You would have," he said, "but you also might have run away faster instead of sticking around for a beer."

"I hadn't been served yet."

He sighed and motioned her to follow him toward the source of the music. Marcy squared her shoulders and brushed off the seat of her pants. She dreaded what had to come next.

All she'd wanted was a beer. A lousy beer after the game, a game she'd helped win. Didn't she deserve that? And if she hadn't been carrying her bat, the deputy wouldn't have had any reason to heckle her. "That's a peculiar looking broom you've got there, little lady. It's missing all the bristles. How do you even sweep up with that thing?"

She knew she should've ignored him. She wasn't an idiot, she knew the whole point was to make her get huffy and red-faced. But when he turned to laugh at his pals, Marcy decided she didn't feel like being the butt of anyone's joke. Not tonight. She moved closer and dropped the bat from her shoulder in a smooth, perfect arc until it was pointed at the ground. One of his friends saw her coming and his eyes went wide, but he didn't have time to utter a warning.

Marcy gripped the neck of the bat with both hands. She stuck the end under the man's stool and swept outward. The stool flew. His butt went with it, but his head went straight down and smacked the bar. His friends jumped back and then converged on him to make sure he wasn't hurt too badly. Marcy had cocked a hip and swung the bat back up onto her shoulder.

"Looks like it sweeps just fine, pally," she said.

And then she found out the loudmouth was the town deputy. Handcuffs, a quick ride back to the station, and stuck in the broom closet because the sheriff refused to lock her up in the cells with the real criminals, by which he meant men. She hadn't missed the poetic irony of being shoved in a closet with the brooms and mops, and she definitely caught the deputy's smile as he shut the door on her. There was a single bare bulb that was dim enough that she was worried it would burn out before she was released.

Now she stretched her legs with every step. She did it to loosen her muscles but also to keep pace with David, but mostly to make the walk as slow as possible. At the end of the hall, David turned and leaned closer to her.

"Just apologize, and make it sincere."

She stared at him.

"Make it *sound* sincere then, damn it."

The main room of the police station had two desks facing each other behind a longer, taller desk that separated the work space from the public. The man she'd met in the bar was seated at one of the desks. His hair was mussed and his nose was bandaged, but she could still see the massive, hideous bruise under both of his eyes. Apparently he'd hit the bar harder than she thought. She felt just bad enough that she didn't choke on her apology.

"I'm sorry, Deputy Dewhurst. I got carried away."

He pressed his lips together and jutted his chin forward. Marcy looked down at her feet, hoping she came off as contrite. Really she just couldn't look at him without laughing. She'd seen pouting toddlers make the exact same expression.

"You need to learn how to behave in public," he said.

Marcy nodded. She bit the inside of her cheek to stop her instinctive response from slipping out.

"You're lucky your husband here is willing to argue for you. I decided I ain't gonna press charges, but he's gonna keep a tighter leash on you. It'll do you good. Teach you some dang manners. Now go on, get outta here."

She lifted her head, ignoring the 'husband' comment. Whatever David had to tell this twerp to get her released was fine by her. She cleared her throat and tried to look contrite.

"I believe you still have my property."

He shook his head. "Nothing you're getting back."

Marcy's face flushed. She stepped closer to the desk. "You have my bat."

Dewhurst looked up at her. "Ma'am..."

"Marcy..." David warned.

She spun on him. "*David.*" She could look extremely severe when she wanted. She had a strong jaw, thick eyebrows, and her blue eyes could almost spark when she put enough emotion behind them. Unfortunately David had seen her rage far too often to be cowed by it, and his only reaction was to press his lips tighter together.

Dewhurst looked past her to David, like she wasn't even there. "I thought you had your wife under control."

"She's just a little–"

Marcy gave up on David and took a step toward the deputy. "Give me my goddamn bat."

Dewhurst actually leaned away from her. "You let her use that language?"

David tried to wedge himself in front of Marcy. "We don't–"

"He doesn't 'let me' do anything." Marcy stepped around the desk. Dewhurst scurried away. She spotted her bat leaning against the wall next to the flagpole. She grabbed it around the neck and brought it up in one smooth move, aiming the end at Dewhurst's face. She was very satisfied to see him cringe.

"This bat is *my* property," she said matter-of-factly, "and I'm taking it with me."

"You're a maniac," Dewhurst said.

Marcy propped the bat on her shoulder. "No, sir. I'm a baseball player. Next time you'll think twice before running your yap at one of us."

She walked to the door and left the station without looking back.

David came outside a moment later. Marcy was already halfway down the block and he hustled to catch up with her. She spotted his automobile, a yellow 1912 Garford touring car, and headed toward it as he huffed and puffed. Getting a ride in it would almost be worth all the hubbub she'd just suffered. It was a beauty, big enough to seat seven, with big bug-eyed headlights. It was open-top so everyone would be able to see them and know exactly who they were. A woman could feel like royalty riding around in something like that, even if it was a clunker he'd bought on the cheap when the company folded.

"You really do need to start behaving." He huffed and popped an unlit cigar into his mouth when he caught up with her.

"Did you tell him the same thing?" she snapped. "I was minding my business. He's the one who ran his yap and started the whole mess. I just wanted a damn drink."

He stepped in front of her and forced her to stop. "No, I mean you really need to stay in line. You're about to have a lot of eyes on you."

Marcy narrowed her eyes and crossed her arms over her chest. "What are you talking about?"

"Word just came down from on high. Baseball is officially

kaput."

Marcy's eyes widened. "Spring training starts next month. They can't do that."

"Can and did." He took the cigar from his mouth, gesturing with it. "Wilson's joined the war."

"He's running for reelection…"

"Against a Republican whose main argument is that the Democrats aren't doing enough to protect the country. He might lose a few votes from people who wanted America to mind its own business, but he's going to get a lot of Hughes supporters on his side in return."

Marcy tried not to let her imagination run away with her. "So what does that mean?"

"It means the draft. It means every able-bodied man of a certain age is going to be expected to do his part to protect democracy."

"So every man who is fit enough to play baseball is going to be overseas soon."

"Those who haven't already signed up are going to be drafted soon enough. It means, little lady, that come the first of the month, there's going to be a baseball drought in the U.S. of A. Unless there's someone to fill it. Team owners are panicking because they shelled out a ton of money on park maintenance and advertising, and suddenly all their talent is going overseas to play a different sort of game. Some of them could go bankrupt if there aren't any games to recoup their debts."

"So. Women."

"A lot of people have spent a lot of time in a lot of back rooms fighting for this, Marcy. I was one of them. We just need money and a place to play. We get to use their parks, they get a cut of the ticket and concession sales. It won't be as much as their usual earnings, but it's more than an empty park could ever earn. It's beneficial to both sides. And to the crowds, who just want to see a damn game, they won't care who is playing."

Marcy looked back down the street as if she expected to spot a newspaper to confirm what he was saying. She stepped away from him and walked in a circle, putting her free hand on top of her head as the bat bumped against her leg. David waited patiently for her to process the news and took the time to light his cigar.

"Will people come watch women play?" she asked.

He shrugged. "If they want to see a baseball game any time soon, they aren't gonna have a choice. It's gonna be you, the Negro League, or nothing."

"Are we ready for that?"

"Most of you are. We can find replacements for the ones who ain't ready or don't want to take the big step. But we're gonna have to move fast."

He started walking toward his car again. This time it was Marcy hurrying to catch up.

"Why do we have to move fast?"

"I'm not the only person who reads the *Herald*, Marcy. Every team owner in those meetings I talked about? They're all running around putting together their own teams as we speak. The same thing is happening all over the country in the other leagues, no doubt. Women ballplayers are about to become a hot commodity. If you want to replace any duds on your team, you're going to wanna get to the good ones first."

"Why me?"

"This is going to be a team of girls. I think it would go over better if they were dealing with another girl, don't you?"

"Makes sense." Marcy trotted around the front of his car to get in the passenger side. Her hands were shaking with anticipation, her mind racing.

"I'm already working on names," she said. "One in particular."

David raised his eyebrows at her. "I'm dying of curiosity."

Marcy smiled at him. "Shrikes. The Chicago Shrikes."

"You want to change the name of the team? What's wrong with Lady Yankees?"

"It's a whole new world, David. If we want them to remember us, we better make ourselves memorable."

I.
SPRING TRAINING

"FIGHT OR GET BUSY

SWEEPING EDICT TO IDLERS TO
MAKE NATION EFFICIENT
IN WAR.

IS TO BE IN EFFECT JULY 1

Order Takes Registrants Out of Deferred
Class - Ball Players, Golfers, Clerks, Bartenders, and Others,
Must Find "Useful" Employment."
- The Southern Herald (Liberty, Mississippi), May 31, 1918

CHAPTER ONE

Oswego, Illinois

"YOU'RE POUTING."

"Men don't pout," David said.

They were standing with their backs to a brick wall outside a bank. It was the first truly hot day of the month. Enough people were taking advantage of the weather that the smell of fresh-cut grass made Marcy's nose tickle. She tried her best to ignore it and focused on watching the door of the soda shop across the street. There had been a steady stream of customers in and out, but none of them were the person Marcy was waiting for. The same person David was pouting over.

"You're mad about her."

David snorted, scoffed, kicked his shoe at the pavement, and then glowered at her. "You could choose anyone in the world, and you choose Rosalind O'Brien?"

"What's wrong with her?" Marcy smirked, because she knew very well David's problems with her. She crossed her arms and waited, forcing him to say it out loud.

He sighed, started to say something twice, then finally gave up. "Rosalind's a *fucking* nightmare."

Marcy laughed. "Don't pull any punches, David. Gee willikers." She looked at her watch. "I could stand here and explain to you all the reasons you're going to want Rosalind on your team. But you already know how good she is. But we're going to stand here for another thirty seconds or so and wait for my point to be proven by itself."

"It doesn't matter if~"

The soda shop's door swung open at such a speed that it stopped him mid-word. The woman who opened it didn't touch the stoop on her way out, instead landing on the sidewalk and changing direction in a fluid full-body twist that didn't take away a lick of her speed. She was almost to the end of the block before David realized what he was watching.

"Gadzooks," he muttered.

"You've seen her play. But did you know she could do this even when no one's chasing her?"

"I..."

Marcy pointed at Rosalind's quickly-shrinking back. "She's going that fast just because she wants to, when she knows she's got a few miles ahead of her. Imagine what she can do when a home run is at stake. Do you want her on another team playing against us?"

David only stared.

She tugged on his jacket sleeve as she passed him. "Come on. The wheels give us an advantage but we're gonna wanna hurry if we expect to catch up with her."

He glanced over his shoulder, still disbelieving, as he followed her to the car. It took a minute for the engine to get started up. By the time he was on the road, Rosalind was out of sight. Marcy pointed him to the correct turn, which took them onto a dirt road.

Rosalind didn't look back as David closed the distance. She waved them for them to go around her and moved further to the side of the road. David pulled up alongside and slowed to keep pace. She glanced over and shook her head when she recognized the passenger.

"Keep driving," Rosalind said.

"You don't even know what I'm going to say," Marcy said.

"Someone got hurt or isn't living up to their potential." She didn't even sound out of breath. "You want me to join up to play while the men are at war. But I ain't interested. I'm not going to wear a cute little dress. I'm not gonna pitch underhand. I won't smile and flirt and flutter my eyelashes at the boys in the stands like a damn doll."

Marcy said, "What if I promised you wouldn't have to do any of that? What if what we're offering is real baseball, not some exhibition or spectacle? We won't have a full roster, so you don't have to worry about warming the bench. We're going to be using every warm body we've got, and we need the best warm bodies we can get."

Rosalind kept her pace. The road was long enough to keep up this slow pursuit, but Marcy could see they'd have to make a turn in just a few minutes.

"We're even changing our name. We're not the Lady Yankees anymore. We're going to be our own thing. The Shrikes."

David said, "We're not a hundred percent settled on that name."

"Don't listen to him," Marcy said. "We'll be the Shrikes. Whatever we're called, we won't be riding the coattails of any man's team. We don't have to be. For once, we're not going to be competing with the men for ticket sales or begging for attention. We're going to be the only game in town. I want to show people what women's baseball can look like, and I can only do that if I'm playing with the best. That's you, Ros."

Rosalind slowed to a walk. David stepped on the brakes and eased to a stop alongside her. She rested her hands on the top of Marcy's door and looked back the way they'd come. She jutted her chin out, brow furrowed under the fringe of her bangs.

"Shrikes, huh?"

"The Chicago Shrikes."

One eyebrow rose and she drummed her fingers on the door. "Let me think about it. Do you want to stay for dinner? I've probably got enough."

"Sure," David said. "There's probably–"

She took off running again. Marcy laughed, David stared after her.

"Is she really going to run the entire way home?"

"It's only a mile or two. Are you going to start driving any time soon? It'll be embarrassing if she gets there before us."

David shook his head and drove after her. "Okay, she can run. But I've seen her throw. She's decent at best."

"That's a lie and you know it," Marcy said. "She throws as good as anyone we already got. And she might strike out a few times, sure, who doesn't. But once she gets a hit, I'd love to see someone try to catch her."

Rosalind knew that model of car topped out at three miles an hour, five tops, so she didn't have to push herself to beat them to her house. Rosalind lived in a farmhouse with a covered porch on an acre of land surrounded by fields of tall grass. It was her oasis, her own little island from which she could see visitors coming from a mile away. There weren't many and that was the way she liked it. Peace and quiet. A normal, calm life.

She didn't need this. She had a good job at the soda shop, where she liked the owner and the other employees. It paid well. She even had a good amount of savings. And... and she wasn't entirely certain what it was for. She owned her house, and she liked it more than fine. She had no intention of moving. She didn't need an automobile, since she did her grocery shopping with Mabel and she could just run or walk everywhere else.

So what the hell was that money doing, just piling up in the bank? What on earth did she plan to spend it on? And what was she waiting for?

She heard the rumble of the engine and her lip curled in distaste. "Whatever it is I'm waiting on," she muttered to herself, "it is not coming from Mr. David damn Buckner..."

She filled a glass with water, drained it, refilled it, and went to the window to watch the cloud of dust grow larger as her first visitors in six months got closer. She ran through all the ways she could say no to what Marcy was offering. She didn't want to be rude, Marcy was a good egg and didn't deserve that. But maybe rudeness would keep her from coming back and sniffing around some other time. Then again, she didn't want her to think there was hope of changing her mind...

The car stopped in front of the house. She could see them through the dirt-shrouded windshield, talking for a good minute before Marcy finally got out of the car and started to the porch.

Rosalind filled another glass with water. Marcy knocked on the door and let herself in, smiled, and took the glass Rosalind offered.

"No."

"You said you'd think about it over dinner."

Rosalind shrugged. "I thought about it on the run instead." She looked at the door. "How come he's not going overseas with the other boys?"

"He has some kind of heart thing," Marcy said. "Unfit for duty."

Rosalind snorted. "That figures. What took him so long to get here, anyway? I'm fast but I'm not *that* fast."

"He was tempted to just go back to town. He said we had your answer. But I think you're worth fighting for. I want you on the team, Rosalind. We need you."

She looked outside and saw him puffing on a cigar. She was glad he stayed outside; she wouldn't have wanted him stinking up the house with the thing. It was as good an excuse as any to keep him outside without getting into a whole thing with Marcy about him. She had more than enough of David Buckner when she was with the Lady Yankees and he was the manager, and she had no intention of giving him a chance to continue his bad behavior.

She could've told Marcy when she left the team. Hell, she could tell her now. But she wouldn't. She couldn't, not without being absolutely sure how Marcy would react. The man was her mentor, and now he was offering her a pro-level team. Rosalind didn't like guessing where she would come out in that debate. Best to just keep quiet.

She walked to the table where Marcy was waiting. "I saw the notice and I know what Buckner wants to do. I'm not going to play some glorified softball exhibition to kill time until the boys come home."

Marcy shook her head. "That's not at all what it is. And it's not his idea, it's mine. He's just the go-between for the team and the owners. Contracts and rental agreements to make sure we have permission to use the parks. It's going to be baseball, Rosalind. No skirts. No charm school. No underhand pitching. We don't have to kowtow to anyone 'cause they need us as much as we need them. Think about how much money these owners are going to lose if the season gets canceled. With every other player headed overseas, they're looking down the barrel at a season with no income whatsoever."

Rosalind leaned back in her chair. "The season starts in a month."

"I know that."

"You think there's gonna be enough teams for a whole league in one month?"

"There are enough teams now," Marcy said. "I know, I've been playing against them. We've got our team, but we need to replace the girls who aren't serious enough to make a job out of it. We need someone like you, Ros. We need someone who cares and who has the talent to get us all the way to the World's Championship Series."

Rosalind chuckled. "A World's Series of women."

"Why not?" Marcy grinned. And damn that grin. It was enough to make a weaker woman do anything she asked.

But Rosalind wasn't weak. She got up and went to the sink. "We're still going to be managed by men. And given our marching orders by men. Men are still going to be in charge of the whole thing. And when the war ends, which could happen any day now, you know we're going to be shuffled back off to the kitchen."

"Unless we prove that we can hold our own." Marcy stood up. "When are we going to have another chance like this, Ros? You said it yourself, the war could end tomorrow. Will you be able to live with yourself knowing you could have taken advantage of this moment in history when we were literally the only option? Women are out there doing jobs we never would've been hired for otherwise. Why not ballplayer? And the only way the teams are going to stand out in places like, like, Boston and New York is if we've got the best players. We can't do it with the B-team, Ros. We need you."

Rosalind's ears pricked up, and her fingers curled on the counter. "Baltimore?"

"What?"

"Would we have games in Baltimore?"

Marcy was clearly thrown by the specificity. "Uh. Yeah, there are rumors about a team being put together there. They got a ballpark, so I'd be shocked if they didn't have a team we can play in a few weeks. What's so special about Baltimore?"

The blood was rushing in Rosalind's ears. She had to struggle to keep her breathing steady. She shook her head because she didn't want to answer Marcy's question. Her mind was going too fast for even her to keep up. So instead she pushed all thoughts of Baltimore out of her mind and looked out the window. David was pacing in front of his car, cigar poised next to his face, eyes cast on the ground.

"I don't want him in charge of me. I don't want him telling me what to do."

"Fair enough. Hell, I'll do my best to make sure you never even have to speak to him."

Rosalind took a deep breath. The things women did to chase their dreams...

"What are the uniform colors gonna be?"

"We hadn't really discussed that," Marcy admitted. "Right now we're just scrambling to get players like you before anyone else can snatch you up."

"Orange," Rosalind said. "I like orange."

Marcy bobbed her head in agreement. "Orange is a good color.

It's a great color. We'll work it into the logo."

Rosalind took a deep breath and let it out slowly. Then she held her hand out to Marcy.

"I guess you've got center field locked in."

Marcy grinned and stood up, clapped her hand against Rosalind's, and squeezed.

"We're gonna show everybody what we can do."

Rosalind pumped Marcy's arm, but she couldn't help but think about the man outside. She could almost smell the stench of his cigar smoke. She doubted he would be very pleased about her agreeing to be on the team, but maybe it would be a good thing. Maybe the Shrikes needed someone who knew what kind of man he really was, someone who wasn't scared to step in if he got back up to his old tricks. That was worth more to her than any game.

She dropped her hand from Marcy's. "So who else you got in mind?"

"We've got a few gals already who are more than ready for the jump to the big show," Marcy said. "But Dave and I are going to hit up a few other people like you. People who got tired of waiting for their chance. We're going to find them, and we're going to give the game back to them. Even if it's just for one season."

CHAPTER TWO

IONA "MOXIE" Moccia's carpetbag smacked the sidewalk directly in front of a man in a trilby. He'd been too involved with his newspaper to pay attention to the world around him and jumped back a step, stared at the bag, then twisted to look up at the same time Moxie leaned out the window to see where her bag had landed. Her hair was done up in a pompadour, and she was dressed in what looked to be her Sunday finery despite it being the middle of the workweek. She wore a pair of glasses thick enough to make her eyes look almost inhuman.

She flashed her winningest smile at him. "Morning, mister. Say, would you mind terribly sliding that trash bin over under the window?"

He looked where she pointed. A silver trash can stood next to the front steps of the building to which her window belonged. The street was empty save for the two of them. He was very clearly torn, unsure if he should mind his own business or help a potential damsel in distress.

Moxie looked back into the room and lowered her voice. "It'll just take two seconds. I'd be very grateful if you could just move it a skosh closer."

He made his decision. Tucking the paper under one arm, he marched over to the can. It was light enough that it might have been completely empty, so he had no trouble repositioning it. When it was in place, he took a step back. Moxie climbed up to sit on the windowsill, gathered her skirts, and slung her leg over and out. She had to stretch her foot to find the can, and then she took a second to make sure it remained steady and could hold her weight.

"Would you mind? Sir?"

"Pardon?" He was trying not to look at the exposed part of her stocking, his hands out to steady the can but reluctant to actually get close enough.

"Just need a little..." She got her other foot down, both hands on the windowsill for balance. "There we go."

She turned to face the street and bent her knees.

"Little help?"

"Uh. Gosh..."

He blushed as he reached up to put his hands on her hips. She put her hands on his shoulders and hopped, forcing him to take her weight or let her fall. He placed her on the sidewalk and stumbled back a step, anxiously looking around to see if anyone had appeared to witness what had just happened.

Moxie brushed off her dress before she faced him. "Thanks for the help, fella."

"What just... what did..." He pointed at the window when his words failed to produce a coherent question. "Is everything all right, miss?"

"Peachy keen."

She dropped down to pick up her bag, winked at him when she straightened up, and went to a bicycle chained to a post in front of the building. The bag went in a basket between the handlebars and she pulled up her dress enough that she could swing her leg over and settle on the seat.

"Miss, I'm not sure... I-I think we should..."

"Everything's fine." She pushed off the sidewalk with her foot and waved goodbye to him. "See you in the funny papers."

Moxie was certain he watched her the entire time she was riding away. He probably kept on staring for a while after she was out of sight, too. She didn't care. People had been staring at her for too many years for her to start caring now. All she cared about now was pedaling as fast as possible. She needed to be far enough away that she wouldn't hear her mother shouting when she discovered the bedroom was empty. If she didn't hear the shouting, she could claim ignorance, she could say she'd forgotten about babysitting her cousin Ike, just slipped her mind.

She didn't slow her pace until she reached Addison. The park was just ahead, a glorious sight framed by the steel legs of the L tracks. Just seeing the park fence was enough to make her break out into a smile. Weeghman Park, home of the Chicago Whales. Or at least it was. Before the draft, there had been talk that the Federal League was dead as a doornail, and the Whales would be merging with the Cubs. Now everything was up in the air, and the park was essentially vacant. But it didn't matter whose name was over the gates. This was where baseball lived, a steel and concrete playground with a single-deck bandstand that started at home plate and curled around until it ended three hundred feet later by left field.

Even though her thighs were starting to burn, she pedaled faster, hunching forward over the handlebars. A train rattled loudly overhead as she passed beneath the tracks, and it was almost loud enough to drown out the sound of her excited laughter. It didn't matter how many times she'd been to the park, and at this point it had to be dozens, she still felt like a little kid when it was in her sights.

She dropped her bike on the sidewalk outside the side gate, scooped up her bag, and fast-walked to the southern side of the property. She pressed her side against the wall and peered around the corner. A groundskeeper's truck was parked next to a stretch of chain-link, its tailgate open and the actual workers nowhere to be seen.

Moxie's heart began thudding hard against her ribs. This was why she'd been so irate with her mother, why she'd insisted today of all days she couldn't be expected to play the good cousin and watch the baby. Kate had been insisting this rumor was true for weeks now. She swore up and down that the new landscaper had a habit of sneaking off for a little nip before lunch, and most times he just left the gate wide open. He always came on Wednesday, and he always wet his whistle between ten-fifteen and ten-thirty. Moxie didn't know the exact time, but she knew the window was closing pretty darned fast.

She strolled along the sidewalk as casual as she liked, trying to mimic an ordinary pedestrian. Just another woman out for a casual walk, all grown-up and worried about work or bills or something silly like that. She put her hands behind her back so her bag bumped against the backs of her thighs and kept her shoulders straight as she walked. She'd even dressed up so nobody could possibly think she was up to mischief.

With one final scan of the area, she changed direction and ran through the open gate. It led to a dark and cluttered cavern under the bandstand, which afforded her a great many hiding places in many directions. She moved carefully but quickly through the storage space, sliding around crates full of things she couldn't identify and machines she couldn't imagine their uses.

Moxie froze at every sound, positive it would be someone coming to tell her she couldn't be there, that she'd have to leave. The groundskeeper's schedule, along with baseball being shut down by the government, created the perfect opportunity for exploring with very little risk of being caught. But 'very little' didn't mean 'zero,' so she still had to be very careful not to cross paths with anyone who might be haunting the same storage space.

Ten minutes after she breached the perimeter, she heard the racket from one of those blasted mowing machines start out on the grass. She hated those contraptions, but she was grateful they were so noisy now. Knowing she was safe from bumping into the groundskeeper made her bolder. She started looking for ways to explore further.

It didn't take her long to find a way up into the stands. She peeked out from a shadowy nook to spot the groundskeeper with his mower. He was in right field, as far away from her as it was possible to be without leaving the park. It looked like he was pushing a piano across the grass and it sounded about as pretty. As long as she didn't move too suddenly, he probably wouldn't see her.

Keeping stealthy and hugging a wall, Moxie found her way higher until she was in the press box. Forget any of the benches down below. This was the best seat in the house. She ran her hands over the desktop and leaned forward so she could see the whole field. The grin threatened to break off the sides of her face as she breathed in deep. Fresh cut grass wafted up from below, and she was grateful for the groundskeeper's contribution to the experience.

She dropped down into one of the seats and leaned back. She opened her bag, reached inside, and took out her glove. She slipped her hand inside, stretched the leather, and punched her fist into the well-worn center.

The park was still pretty new, and now she would know that every single home game she read about in the newspaper was seen from this point of view, written right on this very desk. She could see it now, sitting in her bedroom as they described Mordecai Brown's three-fingered knuckle ball or a save by Clem Clemens. All she had to do was time-travel back to this moment and put them on the field that was spread out in front of her. It would be almost as good as really being there.

Six years ago, her father had taken her to Comiskey Park to see an exhibition game played under artificial lights. She didn't remember the teams or any of the players, but she would never forget how magical it felt to see the whole field lit up like daytime. Everyone's shadows were sharp and dancing, stretched so long that they seemed like some whole other entity.

By the third inning, she was standing on the wooden bench eyeing every player. When her father asked what she was looking for, she told him, "I want to figure out where I'm gonna play!"

He had laughed and guided her back down into her seat. "This isn't a girl's game, sweetie."

She quickly discovered he was right. Every player down on the field was a man. But she didn't understand why that had to be a rule. Sure, they were fast, but her friend Edith could run a mile faster than any of the other boys when they were in school. And Caroline Rainy could throw a rock at a tree so hard it dropped all its apples, and she never missed. She had a feeling the only reason girls didn't play baseball is because they weren't let in the door to begin with.

When the groundskeeper drifted to left field, Moxie felt like she'd pushed her luck enough for one day. She put her glove back in the bag and snuck back out of the press box. She didn't bother to be quiet about her escape since anyone who caught her would just throw her out anyway. She found a padlocked chain-link fence with enough of a gap that she could slip through, careful not to snag her dress on it as she made her escape.

She was thrilled to find her bicycle where she'd left it. She'd been so focused on the mission that she hadn't even thought about the fact she was leaving it for any Tom, Dick, or Harry to make off with. She stood it up and climbed back on.

Maybe she could get her mother hooked on the ball games they had on the radio. If she became a fan, then she might be willing to part with the two bits and buy her a ticket. It wouldn't be nearly the same as getting to play, but it was a far step above the radio. And *anything* was better than reading box scores in the newspaper.

She took her time going home. Her mother would be livid with her, and she would spend the rest of the day imprisoned with her dumb cousin as punishment. If she had to suffer for this magnificent, magical morning, she was going to make the most out of it. She rode down to the lake, bought an ice cream, and parked to watch the waves as it melted over her fingers.

Eventually she had to face the music. She crunched the last bit of the cone, wiped her hands on her skirt, and got back on the bike.

She spotted her guest as soon as she rounded the corner. A tall woman sitting on her front stoop, leaning forward with her elbows on her knees, which were spread wide as a man would have sat. Chestnut hair just long enough that women wouldn't tut at her on the streets for being unfeminine. She was dressed in a tan-brown-orange button-down shirt and tan slacks, both of them looking like they were cut for a man but very fetching on her lanky body.

Marcy Neal saw Moxie coming and stood up to greet her. She slipped her hands into her pockets and cocked her hip at the same time she raised her chin. A smile spread across her face.

Moxie placed her feet on the sidewalk on either side of her bicycle.

"Uh-oh," Moxie said.

"Hiya, Mox." She gestured at the saddlebag. "Running away?"

Moxie shook her head. "My mother is always threatening to throw out my baseball stuff the second my back is turned. So if I leave the house, it comes with me."

"Smart. Got a second?"

Moxie looked up at the building. The curtains were drawn in their front room, but she could almost sense her mother behind it, glaring at her with brimstone eyes.

"Sure, Marcy. But let's go for a walk."

"That's probably a good idea."

She waited for Moxie to prop her bicycle against the wall and then gestured for her to lead the way.

"I think I got you in trouble with your mother," Marcy explained. "She thought you were in your bedroom and when I asked to speak with you..."

"She would've figured out I wasn't there eventually. Don't worry too much."

Marcy bobbed her head. "So I guess you're not working anywhere yet? No beau looking to put a ring on your finger or anything like that?"

"Just me and my mother and my cousin." Her father was

overseas, along with Ike's dad. "You got something that can get me outta here?"

"I might."

"Hm."

"I need a catcher."

"For what?

"Baseball team."

"Manager?"

"Me. Sort of."

Moxie looked at her.

"Officially I'm the shortstop. But the guy who is pulling everything together on the business level, that's David Buckner."

Moxie snorted and adjusted her glasses.

"He's not all that bad."

"Says you. He treats you like a kid sister."

"And as the de facto manager, I'll be the one dealing with him most of the time. You and the other girls will barely know he exists. I swear."

"The other girls got names?"

"So far, just Rosalind O'Brien."

Moxie raised an eyebrow. "She's tough. Quick, too."

"Mm-hmm," Marcy said.

"Where would we be playing?"

"Right here. Chicago. Right down the street, actually, Weeghman Park."

Moxie's skin prickled. She resisted the urge to pinch herself to make sure she hadn't fallen asleep in the press box.

"The team is called the Shrikes," Marcy continued, unaware of her reaction. "David thinks that we've got a real shot, with the men's teams being shuttered for the war effort. Baseball doesn't exist right now. The boys are having their manhood mocked for playing a game instead of fighting. So they put down the bats. Now's our chance to pick them up. Show 'em we can play the same game, the same way. We've already got the American League and the National League. And you heard of Rube Foster? He's been using the war to revive the Negro League."

Moxie snickered. "So if everyone else is doing it..."

"Why not a league for women?"

Moxie stopped, looked up into the sky, and blew out a lungful of air. "Sheesh, Marcy."

"You've got the best head for the game I've ever seen. You can play better than most. I put you behind that plate where you can help build our defensive plays, we're going to have a real shot at being the team to beat. Once you're in place, it barely matters who else says yes, because I know you can make anyone into a ball player."

"And you think we've got a shot at this really going somewhere?"

"I..." Marcy sighed and shook her head. "Everyone keeps wondering that. I think we do. But even if it turns into a miserable failure, nothing's going to happen if we don't try, Moxie. And even if we fail, maybe we inspire some little girl up in the bandstand who will decide to do what we couldn't. But that little girl needs to see us try. She needs to know it's worth trying."

Moxie looked at Marcy. "You're going to be a hell of a manager."

Marcy smiled wide. "I'm only as good as my team."

"Yeah, about that." She rubbed her knuckle against her jaw, trying to decide how tactful to be. "I know the team you've been playing with. That pitcher of yours..."

"She's already said she ain't interested in moving up. We're getting someone great."

"Someone who has a name?"

"Caroline Rainy."

Moxie leaned back. "Rainy."

"What, you don't like her?"

"No, she's amazing. I was just thinking about how great a pitcher she is. I just... thought that... the two of you..." She coughed and shook her head. "Anyway, I kind of got the impression she was through with baseball. The way she left and everything."

"I'm going to see if I can talk her into changing her mind."

Moxie blew out a long breath and shook her head. "Well, good luck. Like I said, Rainy's the best pitcher I've ever seen, man or woman. I hope you can get her."

"I'll worry about that," Marcy said. "Right now all I want to know is if I have *you*."

Moxie narrowed her eyes and then stuck out her hand. Marcy squeezed it and they shook. Moxie sighed and looked back toward the house.

"If nothing else, it'll get me out of babysitting for a few weeks."

Marcy laughed, then looked at her hand. She frowned.

"Is this ice cream?"

"Oh. Sorry." She wiped her hand on the tail of her shirt as Marcy did the same with hers. "I was bracing myself for the yelling when I got home and Mother discovered I'd slipped out for the afternoon. Kind of a last good thing before all hell rained down on me."

"Ice cream works?"

"Oh, usually." Moxie sighed. "But if I tell her I'm joining a baseball team, I'm going to have to go back and buy the whole damn soda shop."

CHAPTER THREE

CAROLINE RAINY closed one eye and lifted the baseball to the sky. The Moon was a hazy ghost hanging above the roof of the buildings next to the park even though it was a few hours past breakfast. She covered it up with the ball, held it in place, and then brought it down. It felt like she had actually just plucked the Moon from orbit. She felt the weight of it against her palm as she curled her long fingers against the seams. It was an old ball. The leather was dirty, the threads starting to come loose, but it still served its purpose. She flexed her fingers for a better grip and focused on her target.

Rainy was five-eight, though she looked like a giantess compared to the other girls trying out. And now, standing on the mound, she felt like a giantess. Her red hair was tied in twin braids that hung on either shoulder. Her jaw was set. Her spine was straight and her shoulders were square.

Sixty feet ahead of her, the batter scuffed his feet in the dirt and gave the bat a practice swing. The catcher crouched behind him, hands limp between his thighs, boredom all over his face. The other girls were lined up in the dugout to watch her along with the manager. Rainy tapped her forefinger against the seam of the ball. She inhaled, her shoulders rising along with the breath, and then she let it out slowly. She inhaled again.

And then the ball smacked against the catcher's chest protector so hard that he was knocked off his feet. He hadn't even tried to bring his mitt up for it because he hadn't been paying attention. The batter straightened up and looked down at his fallen teammate, then looked at the manager, and finally looked out at the mound.

Rainy punched her fist into her glove and brought her throwing hand up. She flashed her fingers, asking for the ball back. The catcher retrieved it and lobbed it back to her. Rainy caught it easily and assumed her position once more. She waited for the catcher to get himself back into the crouch. The batter shook his head and rested the bat on his shoulder. This time they were both paying attention. The catcher looked mad. The batter looked determined. Rainy knew they wouldn't let another one get past them easily. The smart thing to do would be pulling a curve ball, maybe a knuckler.

She put the ball behind her back. Then she brought it up above her head, she twisted and released her slowest and laziest pitch.

The batter swung far too early and ended up facing the wrong way when the ball crossed the plate and landed in the catcher's mitt.

She raised her hand to ask for the ball back, but the manager was already moving toward her at a fast clip. Rainy smiled and dropped her arm, relaxing her stance. She was surprised when someone in the peanut gallery started clapping, a very loud and sharp sound that echoed across the park. She cupped a hand over her eyes to scan the bandstands she thought would be mostly empty save for family and friends of the girls trying out. The lone spectator was sitting just above the dugout, rising to her feet and adding a whistle to her appreciation.

Even from this distance, she recognized Marcy Neal.

"Sounds like you already have a fan," the manager said when he arrived at the mound.

"Sounds like," Rainy muttered under her breath. She was still staring at Marcy. Even at this distance, seeing her again after all this time... She barely remembered where she was or what she was doing. All she could think about was Marcy, and she hated that a little.

The manager was out of breath from the short run out. He mopped the sweat off his red face. "If you can keep up that kind of speed, and keep the other guys on their toes like you just did with Pete, then I think we can make you a very attractive offer right here and now."

Rainy was watching Marcy over the manager's shoulder. She was wearing a jersey. Gray, with something written in black script across the chest. Did it say Strikes? No... SHRIKES.

"...five thousand dollars for the season. If it turns into a championship season, we can talk about a bonus, of course. We like to reward spectacular performance, you understand."

Marcy pointed at the name on her jersey. Then she pointed at Rainy.

"Sorry, Mr. Monaghan." Rainy pulled off her glove and held it out to him. "There's a better offer on the table."

"Since when?" He blinked at her, not understanding. "A-and from who? Five thousand is... is generous for a rookie player. This is going to be an unproven team, but~"

"It's a new league," she said. "There's no precedent for what anyone should be paid, and you're using that as an excuse to low-ball your players. I'm not saying it's wrong, I just want you to know you aren't fooling anybody."

"I... I, well, it's competitive among... among the... the other..."

She walked past him, not even listening to his bluster. Marcy was also making her way to the exit. Rainy estimated they would reach the fence at the same time. He trotted to keep up with her.

"Now, wait a second. If this is some kind of negotiating tactic, I want you to know I don't play those kinds of games. Hear me?" He waited until they crossed the baseline for her to respond. "Fine! Eight grand. But that's going to cut into any championship bonus you might get."

Rainy stopped. She scanned the women along the fence waiting for their chance to try out. "Danielle Forrest."

"What?"

She pointed at one of the women. "The blonde with the red cap. She's almost as good as me, and she'll be willing to sign up for five grand. It'll be a fortune for her. She'll do your team just fine."

"I... I don't *want* her! I want you!"

Rainy shrugged and started walking again.

"That's too bad, Mr. Monaghan," she said without turning around. "I'm already taken."

Marcy came down from the bandstand and waited by the fence. She muttered under her breath as she watched Rainy stride toward her. The redhead seemed to have grown in the years since they'd last seen each other, but maybe she was just thinner. Or maybe Marcy's brain had blurred some of the memories to make them easier to live with. Watching her pitch, seeing the way she moved her body, Marcy quickly remembered so much about the last time they'd played together.

"Stupid," she said without moving her mouth. "So stupid. Could've sent Rosalind. Could've had Moxie do this. But no, I had to do it myself. Stupid..."

She pressed her lips together when Rainy was close enough to overhear. The braids were cute. And she was wearing an unmarked uniform that also complimented her very, very well. When she was close enough, Marcy saw the freckles that colored her nose and cheeks.

Damn, she thought, scratching the back of her neck. *I forgot about the freckles...*

The manager had trailed Rainy all the way from the mound. "-can't just get a group of girls together and have a ball team. You need someone calling the shots! Someone who knows what they're doing. That's what you get with my team. A real chance!"

Rainy stopped in front of Marcy. "Need a pitcher?"

"Yep."

"Okay." She turned to the manager. "Thank you for the opportunity. I told you who you should pick. Hell, she's good enough, you might have chosen her over me anyway once everything was said and done. I wouldn't have been sore about it. She's great."

With that, she gestured for Marcy to lead the way out of the park. Marcy opened the gate and held it open for Rainy. When it was closed again, they started walking.

"So you're in?" Marcy asked when they'd walked a block in silence. "Just like that?"

Rainy shrugged. "We can talk salary and everything. But I figure you'll get us a good price. And you know the game so I figure you've put together a good team. You've got Rosalind O'Brien and Iona Moccia, right?"

"You've been keeping track of me?"

"I was waiting for you to show up here a lot earlier than this."

Marcy blushed. "Well. I-I was... I thought..."

"You kept me for last because you thought I'd be sitting around waiting for you to come get me."

"No!" Marcy said, and then worried there might be truth in it. "I kept you for last because I didn't want to be discouraged by a 'no' right out of the gate."

"Why would you think I'd say no?"

"You know why."

Marcy stopped and looked at her. Rainy stopped as well, turning to look back. She raised her eyebrows. Thick and perfectly arched and just a shade lighter than her very red hair. Marcy told herself not to, but she looked down at Rainy's left hand.

"Do you take it off when you pitch?" she asked in what she hoped was a casual tone.

"I don't wear jewelry."

It wasn't an answer, but it was enough for Marcy.

Rainy slipped her hands into her pockets and looked down at her shoes. "I wrote you a letter. I told you that wasn't going to be a problem if you ever needed a pitcher again."

"I know," Marcy said softly.

"Is it still a problem for you?"

"I truly don't know."

Rainy pursed her lips and nodded.

They'd known each other for their whole lives, or at least as much as they could remember. Marcy's first bedroom had been directly across from Rainy's, their buildings separated by a narrow alley. Their friendship began with drawings on the glass. Soon they were walking home from school together, doing homework with the windows open so they could collaborate on answers - Rainy was great at math, Marcy was always the better reader. They discovered baseball together, forgetting all about nail polish and makeup in favor of paper cards that still smelled of Mr. Rainy's tobacco packs they came from. It took them months to discover these men were real, and really were famous for playing a game.

They were fifteen when, during a game of stickball in an empty lot near their buildings, Marcy realized something had changed. A failed catch resulted in her left ring finger getting broken. She'd dropped to the ground with a cry of surprise followed by tears of pain. She had barely even registered what had happened when Rainy was next to her, cradling her hand, bending down to kiss the uninjured knuckles.

Marcy had been so surprised by the explosion of butterflies in her stomach that for a moment she forgot about the pain. Her tears were still flowing and her finger throbbed like the dickens, but suddenly her mind was going in a whole new direction.

"You'll be okay," Rainy said, still holding Marcy's hand.

Marcy could still remember how cool it had felt, and all she had to do was close her eyes to see the dirt under the fingernails. When her finger healed, she made any excuse to hold Rainy's hand. Walking home was when it made the most sense, but sometimes she asked even if they were just riding in the car or in the library doing book reports.

"Why do you want to hold my hand all the time?"

Marcy pulled her hand away. "I don't."

"No, I don't mind." She reached out and took Marcy's hand back. "I just don't hold hands with anyone else really. And definitely not this much."

"I just like holding your hand, that's all."

"Oh. Well, I like holding your hand, too." She laughed and swung their arms. "If you were a guy, people would think we were going together."

The butterflies swarmed back, and Marcy could barely focus on their conversation for the rest of the walk home. She was glad she hadn't said that it made her stomach do flips or that sometimes she put her hand up to her face to see if she could smell Rainy's lotion on her skin. She couldn't stop thinking about 'going together' and everything those words entailed. She wouldn't mind if people said she was going with Rainy, but the thought made her so queasy she thought she was going to throw up.

On Marcy's sixteenth birthday, Rainy leaned in and gave her a big kiss on the cheek. When she pulled back, Marcy turned her head, and their lips brushed together. Rainy giggled, pecked her lips against Marcy's, and then made a high pitched "mm!" sound and did it again with more pressure. At the end of the party, Rainy kissed her on the lips again when they were saying goodnight.

"I kinda like kissing," Rainy said under her breath, giving Marcy a smile and a wink.

Marcy only laughed nervously.

Months passed. They were still holding hands, and now they were kissing sometimes. Practice, getting used to it, Rainy said. Marcy didn't care what the excuse was. Rainy was a great kisser, and she liked the way her head got foggy while they were doing it. One afternoon they were sitting on Marcy's bed, holding hands, 'practicing' kissing, when Marcy leaned back.

"If you were a boy, or if I was, and we were holding hands, and kissing..."

Rainy's face had been flush. Her hair had been loose and hanging down in wild red threads on either side of her face. Her eyes were wide and searching Marcy's face.

"What?" she finally prompted.

Marcy licked her lips. "Well, if we were boys... I-I mean if one of us was a boy... if I was, I mean, and you were kissing me... him... this much... I think... um, wo-would you... you'd probably want to do other things, too."

Rainy brushed the backs of her fingers over Marcy's cheek. "You want to practice some other things with me, Mars?"

She couldn't bear to look up. "Yeah."

Rainy shifted her weight and pulled back the blankets. She had already taken off her shoes when she came into the apartment, so she tucked her legs up and scooted to one side of the mattress.

"Come here," she said.

Marcy laid down next to her. Rainy pulled the blanket up over both of them and tucked it around their shoulders. They faced each other on the pillows. Both of them were breathing hard, like they'd just run all the bases and kept going until they got home. Rainy smiled, showing her teeth. Marcy tried to do the same but all that came out was a shaky breath.

Rainy whispered, "It's okay."

Marcy said, "Okay."

They looked at each other while they did things under the blankets. After a few minutes, when Rainy started making strange, alarming, exhilarating noises, Marcy said, "I'm glad you're not a boy."

Rainy opened her eyes and looked hard at Marcy, and then the amazing thing happened, and they just held each other and caught their breath.

Twelve years later, standing on a street corner, Marcy realized she was holding her left hand in her right, stroking the broken finger that had started everything. Rainy noticed as well, and Marcy wondered if her brain had taken her on the same wild trip. She dropped her hands and stuffed them into her pockets.

"I want to play for your team."

Marcy looked at her. "Are you sure?"

"I just walked away from eight grand, guaranteed."

"I heard he was only offering five to his players."

Rainy grinned. "Oh, I could've gotten him to eight."

Marcy grinned back.

"Anyway, I don't imagine you're going to be able to match that price."

"Gosh. No. I didn't even think about that. We can't afford you."

Rainy smiled and rocked her head to the side. "You can. Because it's not about the money, it's about who's on your team."

"So you don't mind the fact I'm on the team?"

"Darling, that's the whole point." She put a hand on Marcy's shoulder and pulled her in for a tight hug. "I've missed you so much, Mars."

Marcy rested her hands lightly on Rainy's back, resting her cheek against the thick cotton of her uniform shirt. "I've missed you too, Caro."

"We're going to make an amazing team."

Marcy smiled and laughed despite the turmoil going on inside her.

"You bet we are. Let's go get started. We've only got a couple weeks before our first game."

Rainy nodded and stepped back. She held out her hand, fingers splayed.

Marcy, after mentally debating herself in the space of a second, clasped it in hers so they could walk away hand-in-hand, just like before. Even if nothing else between them was the way it had once been, Marcy was grateful to be playing ball with her friend again. That would be enough.

It would have to be.

CHAPTER FOUR

ROSALIND DIDN'T believe it until she was actually standing outside Weeghman Park. Even getting an apartment in Chicago hadn't made her accept the team would be real. She gave her name to the man watching the gate outside the park, and he thumbed her through. She'd spent the entire trip down cursing herself for bringing the big bag full of equipment with her. She fully expected that she'd be turned away and forced to carry the stupid thing all the way back home. Now she was a bit out of sorts.

She went directly to the clubhouse. Marcy had told her the uniforms would be waiting and cubby-holes were already assigned. She found the cubby with her name on it and, sure enough, she found the thick, high-necked gray jersey with O'BRIEN stitched across the back in big black letters. There was a big number 3 underneath the name, something she'd never seen on a uniform before but had heard rumors about. She figured that was as good a number as any and draped the jersey over her shoulder.

When she investigated the rest of the gear, she confirmed Marcy's other promise had been fulfilled: the uniform came with the same pants worn by male players. Seeing the pants made her feel better about the other things Marcy had told her about the team. Maybe there was a chance they could pull off.

She changed out of her street clothes while the room was still empty. The jersey was a little tight in the shoulders, and she didn't like the way the collar brushed under her jaw, but she could work with it. She practiced throwing to make sure the snugness didn't affect her range. When she confirmed it was passable, she fitted the cap over her hair and looked at herself in the smudged mirror over the sink.

"Damn," she said under her breath. "You look like a baseball player, Ros."

She touched the brim of her cap, nodded to herself, and went to take a look at the field. She came out into the dugout, the little cavern under the bandstand where the team hunkered during the game like soldiers in a foxhole. She took a second to observe the field without being seen in return.

The rest of the Shrikes starting lineup was already on the grass, warming up or chatting amongst themselves. Those were the remnants of the Lady Yankees, Marcy's teammates who decided to stay on and chase this ridiculous dream of a women's league. Normally they would have the big guns, and then reserves, back-ups... Most teams had a few pitchers in the rotation, six or seven catchers, and a whole slew of fielders. Right now the Chicago Shrikes had a grand total of seventeen players, and Rosalind knew that a handful of them were Worst Case Scenario alternates that Marcy was hoping would never have to play unless the game was already clinched. Maybe the ladies they had were good enough to make up for the deficit. Maybe they all had enough faith in themselves to actually make it happen. Maybe they were delusional fools who didn't have anywhere else to go.

The money being thrown around was definitely enough to make a few people deluded. Rosalind didn't think a big paycheck automatically meant getting the best players. Throw money on the ground and you just get desperate folks scrambling for it.

She was about to step out into the sun when someone spoke above her. Judging by the volume, he had to be standing just above the dugout, near the front row of bench seating in the bandstand.

"So you really think they have what it takes to be a real team?"

She recognized the second voice as David Buckner. "They can certainly fake it long enough to finish a season. And I do think they're good enough to get all the way to the end. I had one girl already on the roster, the Neal girl, I had her round up anyone she knew that we might use. She got us a couple powerhouses. The pitcher..." He whistled. "I got an angry phone call from James Monaghan about me snaking her out from under him."

"Demand is good," the other man said, his voice almost sounding impressed.

"It is when you're on the winning side. Pitcher is ours, Monaghan can suck an egg. Trust me, and trust the girl I have running the show. They'll be ready on opening day."

"They better be." A pause. "The pants... whose idea was that?"

David grunted. "Not mine. They wanted to make it feel as much like normal ball as possible. They're dedicated to actually making this women's league happen."

"Why?"

"Why else? Sixteen new teams, multiply by ticket sales and concessions, it's a whole new piggy bank just waiting to be cracked open."

The other man said, "Damn shame about the uniforms, though. You want people to show up, you put 'em in little skirts. They fly up when they run and jump, you get a little peek, yeah?"

David laughed. "Maybe some garter belts?"

"There you go! Definitely fill these seats with something to look at."

Rosalind was grinding her teeth so hard she was sure the men could hear it over their chortling. She started toward the steps to go out on the field and reveal her eavesdropping.

Before she could, the door to the clubhouse opened and Marcy came out. Iona Moccia was right behind her, both of them dressed in their uniforms.

"Hey," Marcy said. "Have you seen David? He wanted to introduce some investor to the team."

Rosalind lifted her chin in greeting, then pointed up.

Marcy looked at the ceiling of the dugout. "David?"

"Marcy?"

"Hang on, I'll come up." She was holding a ball and glove, which she handed to Rosalind as she passed. Marcy trotted up the steps and disappeared around the corner.

Rosalind looked at the gear she was suddenly holding, unsure what to do with it. She looked at Moccia, who offered a friendly smile.

"Iona Moccia, catcher." She twisted and hooked a thumb at the number on her back. "Number eight. You can just call me Moxie."

"Rosalind O'Brien. Center field." Her mind raced for something to add. "Rosalind."

Moxie nodded. "I've actually heard of you. You're great. And lightning fast to boot. Can't wait to see you in action."

"Marcy says you know the game inside-out."

"She did?" Moxie beamed. "Well, I know it as well as anyone else, I guess. But yeah, you know, I do really love it. Did you know the papers print box scores for every game? It's like reading sheet music and hearing the best symphony in the world playing it in your head."

Rosalind raised an eyebrow. "I'll take your word for it." She twisted and put Marcy's equipment down on the bench. She had heard Marcy and David talking, their voices fading as they walked away, but she still lowered her voice when she spoke again. "Do you know this Buckner guy?"

The way Moxie's face contorted was enough of an answer for her. "I've heard some rumors."

"I've got first-hand experience." She looked out at the field. "We're keeping him away from those girls."

"Wait, he did something to you?"

"No." Rosalind crossed her arms over her chest. "Back when I was on the Lady Yanks, he had a habit of showing up in the clubhouse. He would wait long enough to make it plausible. 'Oh, shoot, I thought y'all had already finished up, sorry about that.' And if you were the only one in the room, he'd find a way to linger. Strike up a conversation. I swear once he was about two seconds away from following me into the showers."

"What stopped him?"

"That time, Marcy showed up and he backed off."

Moxie snorted. "Figures. She's basically his sister."

Rosalind shook her head. "No, he doesn't see her like that. He wants her. And he doesn't want to give her any reason to think he might be a scumbag. If she never sees him being a creep, then it's our word against his. And we're not the ones who can give her a baseball team."

"I don't like necessary evils."

"Who the hell does?" Rosalind said. "But at the moment, if we want to do anything besides working in a soda shop or... or whatever you do for a living, he's what we got. We can't do this without him. So we have to be sure he doesn't get his mitts on any of these girls. You have my back?"

Moxie said, "Of course. Couldn't live with myself if something happened and I could've stopped it. You can count on me."

"Good."

"So." She crossed her arms over her chest. "What do you think? Can we actually do this?"

"Do what?"

"Be a team. Play baseball. Get enough respect that they let us keep going when the boys come home."

Rosalind sighed. "I don't like to predict things. But I'd be surprised as hell."

"Then why bother?"

"Slim chance is better than none," Rosalind said. "And maybe the fact we tried will inspire someone else to give it a go sometime. Sometimes you gotta settle for being one of the steps, Moxie. It's the only way you eventually get a staircase tall enough to get anywhere worth going."

When Marcy joined the men, David put a hand on her shoulder and introduced her like she was a prize pony. She stiffened but didn't let her smile waver. This was just part of the business and, as much as she despised it, she was a commodity in this situation.

"Ralph Sutton, this is Marcy Neal. Marcy, Mr. Sutton is the owner of Sutton Sweets. You know the name? Seven stores all around Illinois, and branching out into Indiana next summer. Ralph, Marcy's been with the Lady Yankees for about five years now. She's an absolute star. If she was playing for one of the male teams, her name would be mentioned alongside Ty Cobb and Shoeless Joe."

"She got a nickname?" The chubby guest didn't even bother to hide his leer as he looked her up and down.

"Not as yet, but we can certainly work on one." David patted Marcy's shoulder again. "Why don't we keep up this conversation while we take a little tour?"

Marcy said, "Sounds good to me."

They headed up the stairs. "Mr. Sutton is going to sponsor the team," David explained as they meandered farther along the bandstand. They were strolling along left field now, where Patty Frett and Lorna Lowell were playing a game of catch. "We get his name out there on the fences, maybe a couple of the girls can make appearances at his shop. Everybody wins."

"Do the girls get a cut?" Marcy asked.

"The girls... uh..." David looked at Sutton, then back at her. "Well, the money is going to the team, so in a way, yes, the girls~"

"The girls," Marcy said, speaking over him, "are the ones who will have to schlep themselves down to a candy shop at this man's beck-and-call, then probably spend two or three hours shaking hands and posing for pictures and signing things for whoever shows up. It seems only fair that they get a few bucks for their trouble."

David ran a hand over his hair. "We didn't really discuss that. The, um... the money would help pay your salary, Marcy. Everyone's salaries."

"For playing ball," Marcy clarified. "This is separate. Extra."

Sutton cleared his throat and slowed down. "Perhaps I should let you two discuss this..."

David held up a hand to stop him. "No, there's no need. Marcy, listen. Doing things like this helps the team. It gets your face out to the public. And if a fella gets a little crush after seeing you up close, he might be a little more likely to spend the quarter on a ticket. That's why you've got numbers on the back of your jerseys. We want the people up here to point down at the field and say 'Well, oh my gosh, that's Marcy Neal. I shook her hand down at Sutton Sweets!'"

Marcy crossed her arms over her chest and listened patiently to his argument. When he finished talking, she calmly said, "It's extra. Advertising the team, using the players as teases to draw in a crowd, that's not baseball. That's marketing, Mr. Buckner. We're not asking for anything crazy. Ten cents per autograph, two bits for a photo. It's got to be worth their while to spend their day posing and gladhanding instead of resting up for the next game."

David glared at her, his jaw working under his beard.

Marcy raised her eyebrows and waited.

Sutton looked out at the field to avoid being drawn into the conversation.

Finally, Marcy gave up on waiting for David. "Mr. Sutton," she said. "We'll put your logo on our uniforms, we'll hang the sign with your name up on the fence. We'll do all that. But if you want the players to make public appearances at your stores, it'll be an extra twenty dollars. Paid up front, cash in hand to the girls who show up."

David and Sutton looked at each other. Sutton looked her up and down. "I want you to wear different uniforms for the public appearances. More appealing. To get more foot traffic, make people pay attention. Understand?" He raised his eyebrows. "Skirts, Mrs.

Neal."

"It's 'Miss,'" she clarified. "We wear our uniforms. We're ballplayers, not dollies."

The silence hung between them to the point where Marcy was afraid David's face would literally turn into a tomato. Before he could speak up and ruin the standoff, someone down on the field shouted in happy surprise. Someone else started clapping. Marcy and both men looked down to see what had caught everyone's attention.

Caroline Rainy had come out of the clubhouse and was strolling along the path from home plate to the pitcher's mound. She looked amazing in her uniform, her hair hanging in a long single braid down the middle of her back. It was a red arrow pointing to the black 12 under her name. The inside of Marcy's chest flipped and tangled around itself at the sight of her. Fortunately Sutton and David both seemed equally transfixed by the new arrival.

The other players moved in toward the baseline. Patty Frett - number 6, second base - came out of the dugout already swinging a bat. Moxie jogged out behind her. She wasn't wearing her gear but she crouched behind home and smacked her fist into the cup of her mitt.

Rainy took her position on the mound. She kicked twice with her right foot, once with her left, and then straightened her spine. She was turned sideways to home. She held a ball in her right hand, slowly rotating it with her fingers while keeping her wrist stationary. She watched and waited until Patty was ready with the bat on her shoulder. Rainy tilted her head to one side, then the other. She brought both hands up. Five seconds ticked by.

And then she rocketed the ball sixty feet to Moxie's waiting glove at such a speed that Patty didn't even get off her shoulder.

"Shee-it," Sutton said.

Moxie tossed the ball back with a much more leisurely throw. Rainy caught it easily, took her position again, and shook out her arms. Patty took her place again. Moxie crouched.

Rainy pitched. Patty swung. Moxie rocked back on her heels as the ball sank into her glove like it was attached by a string.

"Her name is Caroline Rainy," Marcy said, answering Sutton's unspoken question. "And yes, she always pitches like that."

Sutton looked at David, exasperated. David shook his head and shrugged. On the field, Rainy threw another pitch and struck Patty out.

"Maybe your girls are just crappy at the plate."

Marcy said, "Maybe. You want to try hitting one of Rainy's pitches?"

Sutton twisted his lips. "Fifteen dollars for the personal appearances. In uniform. Cash in hand."

"That works for me." Marcy looked at David. "Shake the man's hand, David."

David's cheeks were flushed red. "You're not in charge here, Marcy," he said through his teeth, as if that would prevent Sutton from overhearing.

Marcy brushed past their new advertiser and started down the steps to join her team on the field.

"Look around yourself, David," she said. "We're in my house. I am absolutely in charge here. Keep it in mind for the future."

CHAPTER FIVE

ONCE ALL the new players were signed and present in Chicago, the team had two weeks to figure each other out before their season opener. Marcy split the players in half and had them play a game. She and Rosalind were on one team, Rainy and Moxie went on the other. When Marcy wasn't playing, she stood outside the dugout and watched the others to see how they interacted. She hadn't kicked anyone off the team when they transitioned to the Shrikes; the only players who left were those who weren't interested in making their living in the game. Those who remained were the ones she'd been hoping to keep, and she had a good feeling they would mesh well with the newcomers.

But they had to learn to trust each other. The former Lady Yankees needed to know the new players weren't ringers and wouldn't be treated any differently. She also wanted to let Rosalind, Moxie, and Rainy see the level of talent they'd be playing with.

Right field was Hildegard "Hildy" Koenig, number 4, a farmgirl who probably had the only arm that could rival Rainy's. Even from the dugout, Marcy could tell her biceps tested the limits of her new jersey. She'd have to see if it was possible to get a slightly larger size if the constriction caused a problem. She was big and tough, but not so bulky that she lumbered around the diamond. She could dive and dip with the grace of a dancer, always moving on the balls of her feet so she'd be ready to go wherever the ball went.

Her opposite in left field was Edith Mortimer, 2, was fine when it came to speed and agility, but her real power was hitting. She could hit it out of the park with stunning regularity and, once she sent the ball flying, she could tear her way around the diamond so fast that only the best arms had a chance of tagging her.

And the basemen...

She wrinkled her nose. "Is there a word for first, second, and third players?"

Moxie, who was waiting for her turn to bat, was caught off-guard by the question. She looked at Marcy and then out at the field.

"You mean the basemen?"

"Base*men*," Marcy said. "There's not a single man on the field. Why should I call Ida, Patty, and Lorna men just because that's what the position is called for the men? I mean good lord, the fact anyone would call Ida any kind of man."

Moxie covered her giggle with her hand. Ida Coe was a petite blonde with a strong jaw and bright baby blue eyes. She looked like a Kewpie doll except for the fact the girl was busty as all get out. She hadn't been able to button her first uniform jersey because of how blessed she'd been in that area. Marcy tried not to be distracted by the girl's figure, but it was hard when she cut such a gorgeous silhouette.

"Well, you're right, no one will ever confuse Ida for a male. And basewomen does sound peculiar. But I guess that's only 'cause it's not exactly common. If we're changing everything else, I figure we might as well change that, too."

"Basewoman," Marcy considered, then nodded.

The three basewomen - Ida Coe at first, Patty Frett at second, Lorna Lowell at third - were all carried over from the Lady Yankees, so she was very familiar with their skills and limitations. They were good enough that she wasn't concerned about David keeping them on the payroll. But she wanted to be sure they meshed with the new players. Talent didn't mean anything if the actual players didn't get along or cooperate.

"What do you think of them?" Marcy asked.

Moxie said, "They're a good team. I can see why they want to give this whole thing a try. Most of them are good enough to make it."

"Most of them?"

"Some rough edges," Moxie said. "I don't want to name any names. But this is the first time any of us have played together. It's going to take some time before we really mesh."

"We've got two weeks," Marcy reminded her.

Moxie nodded. "I know. It'll be enough. We might not win the first game, mind you, but we'll figure it out. The girls out on the field right now have been dreaming about this moment their whole lives. Most of us never thought we'd ever get a chance. We're not going to let it slip through our fingers."

"Good." She bumped Moxie's arm with her elbow and nodded at the plate. "You're up."

Moxie adjusted her cap and headed to the plate. "Wish me luck."

"Luck," Marcy said.

Moxie managed to get on base, but she was tagged out by Lorna on third. Once everyone had a chance at bat, Marcy called the game and told everyone to head home and rest.

"We're going to be back here tomorrow," she shouted as they drifted off the field. "We've only got a handful of days before those ladies from St. Louis get here, and I want to make their visit as miserable for them as possible."

She followed them into the clubhouse and took her time changing back into her street clothes so she could eavesdrop on their conversations. Rosalind and Patty seemed to have discovered a mutual interest in crochet, though Marcy couldn't even imagine Rosalind holding a hook. Moxie, Edith, and Ida were talking about the best dance halls in town and which one they should hit first.

The team left in clusters, Hildy offering dinner at a nearby restaurant to any out of towners who might not know the best hot spots yet. She got enough interest that it soon morphed into a full team outing. Marcy was relieved to see that her hand-picked choices weren't being treated as intruders and told them she'd catch up a little later.

She finished getting ready after everyone else had left. She brushed her hand over the jersey hanging in her cubby hole, smiling at the fact they were so, so close to playing a real game. She was almost to the door when she heard Rainy's voice.

"Anyone still out there?"

"Just me. Where are you?"

"Treatment room. If there's a cup of water out there, I'd sure appreciate it."

Marcy searched for and found a jug of water and a cup. She took it into the treatment room, which was little more than a closet with a padded bench and a bed where injured players could stretch out. Rainy was sitting on the bed in her uniform pants. Her jersey had been removed to reveal a sleeveless undershirt, definitely a men's shirt judging from the cut. She had a towel wrapped in ice held against her right shoulder.

"Oh hell," Marcy said. "You didn't overdo yourself, did you?"

"No." Rainy took the cup of water from her. "I'm just making sure I take care of it from the get-go so nothing does go wrong. I haven't pitched regularly for a while, and now you're going to have me doing it every day until the game. I don't want to let the girls down just because I'm sore."

Marcy said, "I'm such a taskmaster. Poor dear." She walked around to the other side of the bed so she was behind Rainy. "The least I can do is help keep you limber. Scoot back a little."

Rainy shifted on the bed and looked back at her. "This is typical manager stuff, huh?"

"Oh I wouldn't know. I've never really paid attention to what managers do. But I've got to keep my players happy."

"In that case, let's see what you've got."

"I think you know what I've got, Miss Rainy."

She caught a smile as Rainy turned away. "It's been a while. Refresh my memory."

Marcy flexed her fingers, rested her hands on Rainy's shoulders, and began rubbing. She had massaged Rainy many times in the past, both before and after her feelings started becoming something more. She worked her fingers into the muscles and moved her thumbs in wide circles on either side of Rainy's spine, digging in just enough to loosen the muscles.

"Oh, yeah. I remember this," Rainy grunted.

"Yeah?" Marcy said softly.

"Mm-hmm." Rainy's head rolled forward. "God, you're a magician."

Rainy's hair was still in a braid, so Marcy was granted the full sweep of her neck, the pale skin with its varying freckles. She brushed her fingertips over a cluster as if she was trying to wipe the color away. She knew the freckles very well. Some were pale pink, some were almost brown, while others were practically red ink. She once said that it looked like Rainy was covered in fall leaves, and Rainy had blushed and caused all the freckles on her cheeks to change colors.

"God," Rainy grunted again. "That really does feel good."

Marcy muttered, "Good," and moved her hands lower. She used the heels of both palms to dig in, and Rainy hunched her shoulders in response.

Marcy stared, transfixed, at the way the cotton of Rainy's undershirt moved with the pressure of her fingers. She thought of nights in her bed on sleepovers, Rainy hugging the pillow as Marcy straddled her waist and rested her whole weight on Rainy's shoulders. Those nights had always led to the clothes being tossed aside, to laughing and kisses and hands between thighs. Sweat and gasping and tongues on necks...

She realized she was leaning in to kiss Rainy's neck with enough time to stop herself, but she didn't. Her lips brushed across the skin warmed by the sun. Rainy tensed, then relaxed and rolled her head to the side, giving permission without saying anything. Marcy closed her eyes, half-wishing she'd been told to stop, but she went forward. She parted her lips and licked, then kissed, and she was transported back to her bedroom. Back to the hotel rooms they'd shared when they barnstormed games in southern Illinois and across Indiana.

Her hands, victims of muscle memory, followed Rainy's ribs around to her front. She felt the sharp intake of breath Rainy took and held. She cupped Rainy's breasts and kissed her neck again, letting her lips slide up to nibble on her earlobe. She suddenly wished she had untied the braid, pulled it free, so Rainy's hair could be falling over her eyes and her cheeks, veiling her whole face.

"Your hands are on my breasts, Mars," Rainy whispered. "I've missed that."

"Me too," Marcy said.

Rainy turned her head and suddenly they were kissing. Rainy leaned backward and Marcy strained forward, the bed still between them. Marcy's brain tried to figure out a way to climb up onto the bed without moving her hands or breaking the kiss.

"Scoot back," she said against Rainy's mouth.

Rainy did as she was told. Marcy kept one hand on Rainy's breast and slid the other down between her legs. She cupped Rainy there, spreading her fingers and pressing down with the heel of her hand like she'd been doing during the massage. Rainy lifted her hips in response and grinded down on Marcy's hand.

"I want your mouth on me," Rainy said.

"My mouth *is* on you."

"You know what I mean, Mars..."

Marcy could hear another version of her in her mind, like a second person locked in a glass box, yelling that this was a Bad Idea, that it could only lead to heartache in the long run. But she was already moving around to the front of the bed. The voice got quieter when Rainy lifted her hips and Marcy helped her tug the uniform pants and underclothes down. Marcy dropped to her knees and put her head in Rainy's lap.

How many people knew she had freckles here? How many people had seen or kissed them, these little spots that hardly ever got to see the sun? She dragged her tongue across them and then turned her head to press her mouth hard against the spot she'd forced herself to not think about for the past few years. She wrapped her arms around Rainy's legs, her hands shaking when she rested them flat on her hip bones. Rainy grabbed one hand, placed the other on the back of Marcy's head, and she held her in place as she rocked her hips forward.

"Yes, Mars. I thought I remembered how good you were..." She exhaled sharply and shakily. "You're so much better..."

Marcy forced her eyes open and looked up. Rainy's nipples were hard against her undershirt. She pushed her free hand under the cloth, reaching to cup her breast. She pulled back, lightheaded, as if she'd somehow gotten drunk and the decision-making part of her brain had gone to sleep. Her lips, wet, were parted and all she could smell was Rainy's arousal, and all she could do was lean forward, leading with her tongue, and continue what had caused Rainy to start making those noises.

"Don't stop," Rainy whispered, her voice rushing out on heavy breaths.

Marcy wondered why she would stop, why she had ever stopped. She pulled her hand free from Rainy's and reached down. It was difficult to get her pants open with just one hand, but she managed it enough to reach inside. Using two fingers on herself and her tongue on Rainy, she flicked and teased Rainy's nipple with two fingers, both of them moaning, gasping, thrusting their hips in a matching rhythm.

She sensed Rainy's orgasm was imminent when her lower body started moving forward in short shoves, thrusting upward against Marcy's mouth.

"Please, Mars, please, Mars," Rainy whispered. "Oh it's been..."

A door shut somewhere close. Somewhere damn fucking close.

Marcy threw herself backward and shot to her feet. She wiped her hand roughly over her mouth, wiping again at her chin with the back of her hand. She looked over at Rainy, who was frantically pulling her clothes back into place. They exchanged a look and silently agreed that Marcy would buy them some time. She buttoned her pants, still throbbing between her legs as she walked out of the treatment room.

She came through the door at the same time David Buckner entered the clubhouse. He blinked and stopped short, as if he hadn't expected to find anyone there.

"Marcy? I thought you left ages ago. The rest of the team went out somewhere."

"Mm-hmm," Marcy said. "I think Hildy put something together." She ran her tongue over her lips. She could still taste Rainy. Was she blushing? She felt hot. Was she sweating? She decided to avoid his implied question and ask her own. "What are you doing down here?"

David said, "Caroline Rainy wasn't with the team when they left. I wanted to make sure, uh, everything was, uh..."

"Everything's fine." Rainy came out of the treatment room. Her uniform was back in place, though she hadn't buttoned the jersey. "Marcy was just making sure I didn't overdo it with my arm. You know, trying to run a marathon when I haven't even jogged for years."

David smiled. "Right. And, uh, I assume...?"

"Fit as a fiddle," Marcy said. "Nice and strong."

"Great. Okay, uh, good to hear it. And if there's nothing that needs to be done, um, I'll leave you ladies alone."

"Thanks, David," Marcy said.

He waved as he ducked his head, hurrying back the way he'd come.

Marcy waited until she was sure he'd left before she relaxed.

Rainy, arms crossed over her chest, stared at the door he'd gone through. "Huh."

"What?"

"I don't know. It just sounded a bit like he came down here assuming he would be catching me alone, that's all."

"He wanted to make sure everything was okay."

Rainy shrugged. "Sure. But it's the clubhouse. A women's clubhouse. He didn't even knock or announce himself before he barged right in. Does that sit right with you?"

Marcy laughed and went to her cubby hole. "He's a little absent-minded, but that's nothing. You're starting to sound like Rosalind."

"Oh? Why? What does Rosalind say about him?"

Marcy sighed. She regretted bringing it up. "It's nothing. There was a misunderstanding when Rosalind was on the Lady Yankees."

"A misunderstanding."

Marcy turned and leaned against the wooden frame of the cubbies. She matched Rainy's crossed-arm pose. "There was talk of Rosalind getting a bump in pay. She asked for a little extra, and she was playing well enough that it wasn't the craziest idea. David implied it was a done deal, but he wanted to talk with her first. Knock out all the dents, understand? It's a contract. It's a lot of money going to one person. He wanted to make sure she was really worth it. That she was sticking around for the long haul."

Rainy said, "How'd that talk go?"

"Badly. She said he grabbed her rear end. She slapped him and left. After that, any talk of raising her salary kind of went mum. Eventually she left the team altogether."

"You don't think that's a little strange?"

Marcy shrugged. "David says it was a normal talk. I don't have any reason not to believe him."

"Do you have any reason to think Rosalind made it up?"

"No," Marcy admitted. "All I know, though, is that I've never seen that side of David. He's always been a stand-up guy as far as I've seen."

Rainy twisted her lips.

"Look, all we know for sure is that he wanted to give Rosalind more money but maybe someone higher up balked at the last minute. And maybe he was just trying to pat her on the back and his hand landed a little lower than he meant for it to. And just now, all we know for sure is that he was coming down to check on you."

"And you're fine with that? Him 'checking on' a player when she's alone in a room with only one exit?"

Marcy lifted her hands and let them drop. "I don't know what I'm supposed to do about it, Caro. Give him a babysitter? Hang a bell around his neck? He's going to be around the clubhouse. That's just a fact. I can talk to him about knocking and all that stuff. Because you're right, that's definitely a misstep. But I don't think we should jump to any conclusions about him being a creep based on this."

"Okay," Rainy said softly. She dropped her arms and went to her own cubby.

Marcy watched Rainy gather her things and stuff them into a duffel bag. "Um. S-so... uh. Maybe we can go somewhere more private and talk about what we were just doing. Maybe finish things."

Rainy zipped up her bag and slung the strap over her shoulder. "Maybe another day."

"Sure," Marcy said, trying to hide how crushed she felt.

Rainy stopped at the exit and turned around. "You need to think about David Buckner, though. And you need to ask yourself how much we need to know for sure before we actually do something about him."

She turned and shoved the door open, disappearing through it before Marcy was able to come up with a response to that.

CHAPTER SIX

THE NEXT two weeks were dedicated to practice and preparation for the season opener. Marcy focused everything on the team and shut off any thoughts about Rainy. She also built a wall around David Buckner and questions about his behavior. He was a good man. Maybe he lost his senses a little when it came to women. He was a single guy, Rainy and Rosalind were both beautiful. Was she really going to risk all this to yell at a guy for some fumbled flirting? It seemed like both women had dropped the subject. David hadn't made any further unexpected appearances in the clubhouse. She hoped that meant the situation was moot.

She had a harder time forgetting what had happened just before David threw a wrench in her reunion with Rainy. Some nights she lay in bed and relived the massage in the treatment room, savoring the memory of everything that came after. Rainy seemed to have forgotten anything happened. She was completely focused on the game, on keeping her arm in shape, and building rapport with the other players. Marcy was glad she wasn't forcing a conversation; she had no idea what on earth she was going to say if she was forced to put her thoughts into words.

Today, there was only one thing on her mind. She hoped it was the same thing on the mind of every other woman wearing a Shrike jersey.

The St. Louis Firebricks had come in on the early train. At that moment, there were a dozen women from Missouri occupying the guest clubhouse at the stadium, and Marcy was itching to sneak down the hall and see what she could find out about them.

She tried to distract herself by lingering over breakfast and reading the newspaper from front to back, but she still ended up pacing her apartment and staring at the clock as it ticked, ticked, ticked, one second to the next, the minute hand sticking in place for so much longer than made sense. She did her exercises. She gathered all her dirty clothes, decided she didn't have time to do any laundry, and left the pile on her divan. Finally she grabbed her coat and bag and hurried out into the day.

Marcy was the first member of the team in the locker room. She was changed and waiting on the bench when the other girls started drifting in. Rainy met her eye and nodded a greeting. It was the most they'd interacted since the day in the treatment room. Marcy instinctively licked her lips. Rainy lifted her eyebrow and smiled. Marcy blushed and looked away.

When the team was all there, Marcy checked the time. Then she stood and clapped her hands to get everybody's attention.

"Okay, ladies. Listen up. I know we've had a lot of fun out there the past few weeks, but now it's time to get serious. Now it's gonna matter every time we walk out on that field. 'Cause if we can show people a game, a *real* game, they'll start taking us seriously. But only if we change their minds. Only if they see a team of ballplayers out there, no matter what we wear off the field.

"But you're not going to worry about them. You're going to forget those people are even there. All you're going to focus on is those ladies in the other clubhouse. Those St. Louie whoever-they-ares. We're going to show them that this is Chicago, and we are the Chicago Shrikes. This is our backyard. And we ain't going to let anybody come in here and hand us a loss the first time out. You know that field like the back of your hands. You know this game as good as any man who's picked up a bat. So we're going to go out there and show everyone. How's that sound?"

The women cheered and applauded. They rose to their feet and left the clubhouse like there had been an evacuation order. Marcy and Rainy brought up the rear and watched as their team hit sunlight and spread out to take their positions. It was almost one in the afternoon and the sun was high enough that their shadows were short and squat.

Rainy pushed the brim of her cap up on her forehead and turned to scan the bandstand. "Oh, my."

Marcy's heart leapt as she looked, expecting a huge crowd to justify Rainy's response. Her spirits and smile fell when she saw that Rainy's utterance had been for the opposite reason. There were barely thirty people in the stands, spread out far enough that the number seemed even more pathetic. Marcy looked along the whole length of the seats and saw maybe a grand total of two hundred spectators, very few of which looked like they were eager to watch a ball game.

"I don't understand. Ida, Patty, and Hildy spent the past two weekends at Sutton Sweets signing autographs and handing out free passes. And David literally stood on a street corner giving people coupons."

"So you're saying some of these people didn't even pay to be here?"

"No, no," Marcy said. "Because, um, he handed out around three times as many tickets as there are people here. There's a chance *none* of these people paid to be here."

"Jesus," Rainy said under her breath, then headed out to the mound. "Not exactly an auspicious start to the Shrikes season, is it?"

Marcy pressed her lips together and jogged to her shortstop position. The other players had also noticed how empty the stands were. It would've been hard not to see the vast expanses of empty bench wrapped around the stadium. Those who were there didn't even bother to clap when the team appeared on the field. She was glad she'd given them the speech about ignoring the crowd, because at the moment even she felt like just turning around and going home.

Marcy kept her spine straight and planted her shoes in the dirt, kicking to make divots to symbolically mark her station.

The St. Louis Firebricks wore dark grey uniforms with pinstripes, the team name written across their chests in script so scarlet that it looked black from a distance. She wondered what a firebrick was, and why someone thought that would be a good idea for a team name. The letters had to be squeezed so tight to fit on the jersey that it was probably unreadable even from the best seats in the house.

One of the Firebricks strolled from the dugout with her bat swinging easily from her left hand. The umpire straightened up and shouted, "Let's play ball!" and tugged his mask down over his face. He was the only man on the field. She scanned the Firebrick lineup to confirm that was true, and then took a second to appreciate the fact. A group of women, *only* women, were about to play a game of professional baseball. She felt the goosebumps on her arms and flexed her fingers to ease them a bit, rocking her weight from one foot to the other.

It suddenly mattered very little to her how many people were in the stands. The game was what mattered, even if no one was there to see it.

Rainy looked around the diamond to make sure everyone was ready. Her gaze lingered on Marcy. Marcy gave her a wink, and the corners of Rainy's mouth tightened in a smile that no one else would notice. She turned her head to look at the batter, giving Marcy a great view of her profile. She eyed Moxie behind the plate. She nodded once and then the machinery of her body went into motion.

Caroline Rainy pitched the ball. It streaked sixty feet and cracked off the end of the bat wielded by Gladys Brady, flying high into the air as Rosalind O'Brien and Hildy Koenig ran to intercept it. Hildy got to it first, scooped it up off the grass, pivoted at the waist, and rocketed the ball back the way it had come. Gladys Brady charged around first. The ball landed securely in Patty Frett's glove at second, and she stuck out her arm to tag it against Brady's shoulder before she could touch the base. Gladys Brady was declared out by the umpire. Marcy took a deep breath and let it out through her nose.

The inaugural season of the Women's National League had officially begun.

There were no runs until the third inning, when Lorna Lowell sent a ball sailing low across the foul line. It was low enough that it impacted the edge of the base itself and shot straight into the air, confounding the Firebricks' third basewoman to the point where she could only stand and watch as it arced out of her range. It was ruled fair, and Lorna ended up on second. When Edith Mortimer batted next, she sent the ball on a trip to center field and Lorna headed home. Edith scored a run herself a few minutes later when Moxie hit the ball into the bandstand, taking the game to 3-0.

In the fourth inning, Marcy was on second base waiting for her chance to make a run for it. She glanced at the second basewoman for the Firebricks, eyeing the team name written across her jersey.

"Can I ask you a question?" Marcy asked.

"Sure." The other player didn't take her eye off Ida at the bat, who had just gotten her second strike.

Marcy had her knees bent, legs spread slightly wider that shoulder-width, leaning forward in anticipation of running. "What is a firebrick?"

The other player smirked. "Honestly? I'm not sure. It has something to do with clay mining. It's big in St. Louis." She worked her jaw. Ida was struck out and headed for the dugout. Rainy came out to take her plate at home. "What's a shrike?"

Marcy said, "It's a kind of mean bird."

"Oh." She rocked on her feet. "I thought it was a mistake on the schedule. I kept expecting someone to say you were the Strikes. Or the Strikers or something."

"Nope."

"Mean birds," the second basewoman said.

Marcy nodded. "Yeah."

"Okay." The other woman nodded back.

Rainy hit the second pitch. The ball went to right field and Marcy raced to third. She didn't think about where the ball was, who had caught it or where they might be throwing it. She kicked dirt over the base when she passed, stomping her foot down on it hard when she changed direction. She could see movement on the field, a Firebrick with her arms up and then bringing one down in a manner that indicated she was holding the ball. Marcy put on an extra burst of speed. She pumped her arms. The ball was thrown home.

Marcy bent her knees like she planned to slide. The catcher lunged. Marcy pivoted and juked to the right, twisting her body around the catcher's fist. Marcy's feet left the ground and she made sure she slapped home plate with her hand as she came down hard.

"Safe!"

Marcy rolled onto her back and smiled, looking past the angry catcher to see Rainy had ended up on third.

"Where'd they get you," the Firebrand catcher said. "Taking some time off Broadway?"

"Wait 'til you see my high kick," Marcy said.

Rainy scored a run after that, and the next three innings they kept the score at 5-0. The Firebricks got lucky in the eighth, narrowing the score to 5-3.

As they went into the last inning, Firebrands batting first, David suggested letting some of their alternates finish out the game. Marcy agreed and stayed behind as the others took the field, taking the opportunity to step from the dugout and look at the spectators. The crowd was still as pathetic as it had been at the beginning of the game, but that was actually good news now. It meant nobody had left. One man seemed to be doing a crossword in the newspaper folded on his lap, but at least a handful of people seemed to be giving the game their full attention.

Rainy joined her and brushed the dirt off Marcy's jersey, sweeping her hand over the shoulder and down her arm.

"Heck of a move you made earlier, Mars."

"She was in my way. And then she wasn't." She shrugged. "No big deal."

Rainy chuckled and looked at the crowd with her. "Could have been worse, I guess. Wouldn't have been any fun playing for completely empty seats."

"I suppose," Marcy said. "Maybe they'll tell their friends and we can actually get some paying spectators next time."

"That would be nice. Anyways, it gave us a chance to get the kinks out. Next time we'll be ready for a real audience."

Rainy hooked her thumbs in her belt loops. "Would you want to come over to my place and celebrate when we win?"

Marcy was quick enough to stop herself from looking over in surprise. She maintained her cool and watched as their relief pitcher struck out a Firebrick.

"Don't jinx it," Marcy scolded. "We're only two runs ahead. Firebricks could come around."

"Then you can come over to my place and we can drown our sorrows together."

Marcy said, "Sounds like you just want me to come over to your place."

Rainy rocked her head to the side. "Well, the last time we were alone, we didn't exactly finish things up. And I feel bad about not following up on that. But now that the season is rolling..."

"Might be a good idea to focus on the games," Marcy said.

"Sure..."

Marcy let the silence hang between them. She casually looked down at Rainy's arms. They were sheened with sweat, glistening in the sunlight. The muscles looked like they had been carved in wood and then covered with a thin varnish. She swallowed the lump in her throat and looked out at the field again. The Firebricks put a player on first, followed by a strike out, followed by another hit. The player on first went to third, and her teammate ended up on second.

Rainy tensed, hugging herself tightly. "They could tie it up right here…"

"And we'll have a chance to pull ahead," Marcy reminded her.

Rainy shook her head, jaw tight and eyes focused on the relief pitcher. "I should be out there."

"You did your part. You kept them from scoring for almost the entire time you were out there. We gotta save your arm for when it really matters."

"Lucille is a good pitcher."

"Not as good as me."

"She doesn't have to be. Not against this team. Have faith in her, and have faith in our fielders."

Rainy's jaw bounced and stayed clenched. Her eyes didn't move from the field as the next batter stepped up to the plate.

Another strike out. The next batter could end the game. Marcy turned so she could see the crowd in her peripheral vision. The crossword guy had put his paper away. The chatter had died down.

"They're paying attention."

"What?" Rainy said.

"The crowd. They know this could decide the whole game. They're watching."

Rainy twisted around to look. "Do you think that means something?" she asked.

"It means they're invested," Marcy said. "At least for right now. We gave them a good game."

Rainy nodded.

There was a pitch, a swing and a miss. The players on base were antsy, inching farther away from safety. If the player on third tried to make a break for it, and if the player on second followed, Lucille would have to decide where to throw in the space of a second. She eyed the player on third. She looked at the batter.

She pitched. The batter swung. Missed. Strike two.

Marcy lifted herself up onto her toes. "One more," she whispered. "Come on, Lulu, close it down for us."

Lucille bent forward. She lifted her right foot off the dirt and leaned far to one side.

The ball flew.

CHAPTER SEVEN

RAINY LAUGHED and whispered in Marcy's ear that she had neighbors. Marcy cared, of course she cared, she didn't want anyone to get suspicious and make a fuss. But at the moment she lacked the ability to do anything about it. She was being loud. She was making the bed loud. The mattress groaned and creaked underneath her with each thrust. And the headboard, though a sturdy support, tended to smack the wall every time she rocked forward. She wasn't going to stop thrusting, not until she achieved her goal, and she was close. She was very, very close.

Marcy stared down at Rainy. Her eyelids were heavy but they never dropped completely. She never closed her eyes or looked away. Her face shone, the skin flushed almost red enough to obscure her freckles, and her lips parted with soft, rhythmic 'huff-huff' breaths as she lifted her hips to meet Marcy's thrusts. Her bottom lip was full, plump, so kissable, and Marcy bent down to do just that. Her tongue slipped into Rainy's mouth and then ran along the bow-shape of her upper lip before she sat up again.

Rainy was underneath her, propped up on two pillows with her shoulders against the rocking headboard. She had one leg hooked around Marcy's hip and the other was between Marcy's thighs. They were both naked, both sweating, and Rainy's sheets were tangled around them like chains made of fine cotton. She dug her knees into the mattress and dropped her hand from the headboard to Rainy's shoulder. She squeezed her thighs tighter and arched her back, baring her teeth for a growl that turned into a shaky sigh of release when she finished.

Her arms suddenly went weak, her spine failed her, and she slumped down, letting Rainy guide her into a comfortable position. Rainy brushed her fingers through Marcy's hair. Marcy kissed the curve of Rainy's breast.

"I might check out in the fifth if we're going to celebrate every win like that."

Marcy smiled. "If you do that, we might not be celebrating wins at all."

Rainy kissed the top of Marcy's head. "Maybe we'll have more fun taking out our frustrations after a loss."

"Maybe," Marcy said with a smile. "Let's not find out any time soon."

She hadn't expected the fire that surged through her when Lucille got her third strike. The Shrikes officially had one in the win column, and against a team who had made them work for it. They could be proud of this victory.

She had been shaking when she followed the team into the clubhouse. She could barely remember all the hugs, the laughter, the backslaps, but she could still feel the sheer joy that filled up the room. She'd found Rainy and gripped her bicep hard enough to hurt. She pulled Rainy aside and leaned in close to whisper into her ear.

"I need you to take me home. Now."

"Are you okay?" Rainy asked.

Marcy tightened her grip. "I need you."

"Oh," Rainy said, understanding.

She remembered every second of the train ride across town, itching to sit in Rainy's lap, to kiss her or even just hold her hand, but she didn't want to do anything that might make the other passengers suspect what they had planned. She felt all of them already knew, even though a quick scan of their faces proved they didn't even know she or Rainy existed. They were all in their own little worlds and two fidgety ballplayers in casual clothes barely even registered to them.

They started undressing each other just inside the front door. Marcy had pushed Rainy against the wall and just barely managed to prevent herself from ripping the clothes off of her. Luckily the apartment was only one room, so they didn't have to go far to reach the bed. Rainy was naked by the time she laid down, and Marcy took off the last bits of her own outfit before she climbed onto the mattress to straddle Rainy's waist and begin her work.

Now she wasn't even sure how much time had passed. She caught her breath and traced lines over Rainy's chest, transported back to those nights they'd spent crowded together in her bed, trying to muffle the sounds of their giggles by pressing their face into each other's shoulders or arms. Even if her parents heard something, they would just knock and say, "Go to sleep, girls! Now!"

"I feel like I could just fall asleep now," Marcy said.

"You're more than welcome."

Marcy chuckled and cuddled closer. "Don't tempt me."

Rainy took a deep breath and curled her arm around Marcy, hand flat on her shoulder. "I've missed this so much."

Marcy opened her eyes. She wanted to respond to that with the truth, with the anger she'd been insisting for years she didn't have. *You're the one who stopped it,* she wanted to say. *You're the one who got scared. The one who ended things because you felt safer with a man.*

She didn't have to find any willpower to hold the words in, because there was a knock on the door before she could say anything. Rainy stiffened under her, and Marcy grabbed for the sheet in a futile attempt to pull it up over them both.

"Neighbors?" Marcy whispered.

Rainy shook her head, uncertain. "Who is it?"

"It's Moxie."

They looked at each other, confused, and Marcy scooted to the edge of the mattress. She dropped down into the space between the bed and the wall as quietly as possible, taking the sheets with her. She draped herself with them like a shroud as Rainy got out on the opposite side of the bed. She cursed herself for being so lazy. She didn't remember if they'd told anyone they were leaving, or where the team might be right now. What if there'd been a celebration where their mutual absence had been noticed? She doubted anyone would jump to the right conclusion, but still. Stupid.

"Just a second," Rainy said.

Marcy could only guess what she was doing; probably grabbing a robe and fixing her hair, checking the mirror to see how flushed her face was. Marcy tried to melt into the carpet. She rolled onto her side and pulled her knees up in an effort to make herself as small as possible. She squeezed her eyes shut as well. It probably couldn't hurt.

The apartment door opened. "Hey, Moxie," Rainy said, feigning breeziness. "What's going on?"

"You hightailed it before David's grand little gesture. In honor of winning the first game of the season, he gave each of us a five-spot. You know, because we won by five runs. Cute, huh? I volunteered to bring yours to you."

"Oh. Thanks. Thank you, that's very kind of you."

"No problem. You were on my way home."

Rainy said, "I appreciate the effort. What about Marcy's?"

There was a pause. "What about it?"

Marcy pressed her hand against her face. *Damn it, Caroline.*

"Did... I-I don't, um... it's just that... um, her place isn't far from here, right? No. I don't know."

"Are you accusing me of trying to steal Marcy's money?" Moxie sounded more amused than offended.

"No! No, not at all. You're as honest as they come. I know that."

Moxie said, "How'd you even know Marcy wasn't there when the money was handed out, anyway?"

Just say I came home with you for drinks, Rainy. They know we're friends, goddamn it, just tell her I'm in the bathroom or something!

"Oh. W-was she not... there? I thought she was."

"Then why'd you ask?" Moxie sounded more confused than angry. "Caroline, is everything okay? You look weird."

"I'm fine."

Moxie exhaled sharply and said, "Oh, my God. Don't tell me. He came here, didn't he? Son of a bitch, I knew he left too damn quick!"

"Wait!"

There was a banging noise as the door bounced into the wall. Moxie had clearly shoved her way past Rainy into the apartment.

"Where is he?" she asked.

"Where is who?" Rainy sounded on the verge of panic.

"Fuckin' Buckner! He handed out the money and when I said you'd left, he couldn't have gotten out of there fast enough." The bathroom door opened. "Is he here? It smells like sex in here. Look, is he making you do something?"

Rainy stammered. "I-I-I don't... I'm..."

Marcy couldn't take it anymore. She sat up and pulled the sheet off her head, which caused her hair to twist and tangle around itself.

Moxie was standing in front of the bathroom door, brow still furrowed in anger but lips slowly parting to make a "Whu~" sound.

Rainy was by the divan, her hair pinned back but already falling loose. She had indeed wrapped herself up in a robe, but it gapped enough in front to reveal she wasn't wearing anything under it. Moxie looked between them as her brain caught up with what she was seeing.

"Huh." Moxie blinked hard. "Oh... Uh."

Rainy moved closer. "Moxie, it's just a thing that happened, all right?"

Moxie looked at Marcy. "I thought you were screwing Rosalind."

Marcy pulled her head back. "Ros? Why on earth would you think that?"

"I dunno," she shrugged. "Probably 'cause you're the only two women like this I've ever met." She looked at Rainy. "Well, three now."

"No, I'm not..." Rainy cleared her throat and looked down at her feet. "No, no. It's not like that."

Marcy felt all the good emotions of the afternoon flutter away from her like frightened birds. She wrapped the sheet tighter around her chest and got to her feet.

"I should get out of here."

Moxie moved toward the door. "No, hey, whoa, I'm... Don't, uh, don't run away because of me. I'll just head out. And don't worry, my lips are~" She mimed locking her mouth with a key.

"No, I really need to leave." Marcy was already gathering her clothes with the hand not holding the sheet up.

Rainy held out a hand to her. "Mars, wait. Let's talk."

"It's fine," Marcy said, not looking at Rainy.

Moxie was at the door now. "I'm going. Sorry for, um... s-sorry."

She let herself out, closing the door quietly.

Marcy kept her back to Rainy as she straightened and untangled her clothes.

"I know what I said," Rainy admitted quietly. "I was scared. Of what she thought. Or of what she would tell people."

"But did you mean it?"

"Did I...?"

Marcy looked over her shoulder. "She implied you were queer and you almost jumped out of your skin."

Rainy flinched and averted her eyes. "Because I'm not like that."

"Sure." Marcy tossed the sheet back to the bed and started getting dressed.

"Mars..."

"No, I believe it. You never go down on me. Did you even realize that? You barely do *anything* to *me*. You don't mind being there when I'm doing stuff, or when I do it to you, but when it comes time to return the favor, you might as well be a firm pillow. And normally, I'm fine with that. I still get off just fine, and just looking at you naked is enough to get the wheels turning. But a little effort wouldn't go unnoticed, Caro. I want more. I want to have sex *with* you, not nearby you."

Rainy kept her eyes turned away. "I thought you missed me. I thought that's why you wanted me on the team."

Marcy sighed and tried to fix her hair. "I wanted you on the team because you're a great pitcher, Caroline. And because I like you. I still want you on the team. This..." She gestured between them, and then at the bed, and flipped her hand up in frustration. "I thought I was going to resist this. But I guess I'm not as strong as I thought I was."

"We don't have to stop. Moxie said she wasn't going to say anything, and~"

"It's not about Moxie. It's about the fact you still can't admit who you are."

Rainy paced away from her. "I like men, too. I-I prefer men, honestly."

"No," Marcy said. "No, I've known women like that, and I've seen you with men. Different animals. Remember Nicholas? You could barely stand being in the same room with him, let alone holding his hand. I know you want to be with me. You want to be with me as much as I want to be with you. But if you're not willing to admit that to yourself, then... then I'm not wasting any more time waiting on you."

"Wait."

Marcy stopped at the door. "Can you admit you want me?"

"Yes. Marcy, I want you. Come back to bed, please."

"Can you admit what that makes you?"

Rainy took a deep breath. "I'm not."

Marcy shook her head, disappointed. "I deserve to be with someone who knows who she is. Do me a favor, Caroline. The next time we win, just hump your damn pillow."

She left the apartment, slamming the door behind her.

CHAPTER EIGHT

THE CHICAGO Shrikes were scheduled to play the Firebricks again the following day, and once more on Saturday. Rosalind understood why the games were stacked so tightly together. It allowed them to make up rain delays, and it saved the teams from crossing back and forth all over the country multiple times per season just to fill their quota of games for the season. The end result was that the players got more time to rest, but God almighty, did it feel exhausting in practice.

She was surprised by Marcy and Rainy, though. They'd both been playing the game long enough to have expected and prepared for this sort of thing, but they were more out of sorts than anyone else. Rainy let three runs get past her in the first inning. In the second inning, a pitch was returned straight to her. When she tried to throw the runner out at first, she misjudged and sent the ball flying high into the stands. The Firebricks got two more runs from that.

Marcy wasn't doing much better. Slow reactions and sloppy throwing made her close to useless and created a huge blind spot on the field. Rosalind couldn't even be happy that the crowd was quite a bit larger than it had been the day before, since it just meant more eyes were seeing them play like chumps.

They ended the second inning down 6-0, and David made the call to swap Rainy out. Marcy was also replaced, which emptied their replacement bench to a worrying degree. Losing their top two players took the fire out of everyone else, who started making their own dumb mistakes. Lucille did what she could, but by the seventh inning, the score was 2-10. Rosalind could see Marcy and David arguing by the dugout, a fight which resulted in Marcy throwing her cap in the dirt and storming into the clubhouse.

She remained there for the rest of the game, which they lost 14-2. Rosalind slumped off the field, tired and dejected and wondering what the hell had happened to the team that had been so joyous and victorious the day before.

David was already mid-speech by the time Rosalind reached her cubby. "–another chance tomorrow, but you've absolutely got to come through this time. This is your home town crowd. You're going to need to get them behind you if there's any chance for the Shrikes to become something. It's not going to happen if you let the Firebricks stomp all over you."

Rainy was sitting on a bench in front of her cubby. Her jersey was unbuttoned to reveal the undershirt beneath. "Thanks for the pep talk," she grumbled. "Now how about you get out of here so we can start washing that game off us, huh?"

David moved toward the door. "Think about what I said, ladies." He scanned the room. "Where's Marcy? I think she and I need to have a one-on-one talk."

"Marcy left," Ida Coe said.

David and Rainy both lifted their heads at that. "What do you mean 'left'?" David asked.

Ida shrugged and hooked her thumb toward the door. "I was down here icing my knee because of the fall I took when that Firebitch tagged me. When she stormed off during the seventh. She changed into her street clothes and kept on going. Didn't even seem to notice me. She looked damned angry, though."

"Well, that's fantastic." David shook his head and slumped out of the room.

The women looked at each other, no one willing to be the first to break the silence or even move. It was Rainy who finally took the initiative and stood up, stepping over the bench and stripping out of her jersey. Everyone else took that as the permission to finish changing as well. Feet shuffled on the concrete floor. Hangers rattled against metal rods.

"Thought you were supposed to be a ringer."

Everyone stopped moving again, turning toward the bench where

Patty Frett sat staring at Rainy's back. Rainy didn't turn around to look at her.

"We only needed a new pitcher 'cause Nancy decided she'd rather start a family. Didn't think we'd be trading so far down."

Moxie said, "Now, come on. We all have bad days now and then."

"That wasn't a bad day," Hildy said, "that was a damn travesty."

"Did she trip you in the fifth?" Moxie said. "Edith, was she the reason you swung like the ball was fucking invisible? And Lucille, lord almighty, don't get me started on that triple play you handed them on a damned silver platter. Rainy pitched like she's never held a ball, but we got her out of there quick-like. The rest of it was on us."

Rainy finally faced the room. "Thank you, Moxie, but Patty was right. I set the tone. I threw everyone else off." She scanned the faces of the other players. "I apologize, ladies. It won't happen again."

There were a few murmured comments in response, mostly accepting the apology. Rosalind wondered how many of them were just going along to end the fight before it escalated. Hurt feelings and throwing blame around could taint their performance tomorrow. Right now they were starting the season on even ground... 1-1. Losing again would dig the hole deeper and make the bad moods fester. They had to beat the Firebricks in the third game or she was worried the Shrikes would fall apart before they even got off the ground.

When Moxie wrapped herself in a towel and went down the hall to the showers, Rosalind silently got up and followed her. "Hey, Moccia. Hold up."

Moxie turned and raised her eyebrows. "Everything okay?"

Rosalind looked over her shoulder to make sure no one had followed them. "I wanted to let you know I appreciated you throwing water on things back there. I was afraid they were ready to start throwing punches."

"They probably were," Moxie said. "Who knows? It might actually have helped release some tension. Lots of big emotions right now. But I know Rainy's better than her performance today. She's..." She suddenly clammed up, tensing her shoulders and crossing her arms as if she was trying to physically hold herself back. "Never mind. I just know she's dealing with stuff that doesn't have anything to do with the game."

Rosalind narrowed her eyes. "What stuff?"

"It's not worth mentioning." Moxie waved her off. "But I think

Rainy learned her lesson. She's going to keep it off the field. Tomorrow will be a whole different story."

Rosalind moved closer and lowered her voice. "Do you know something, Moxie?"

"No." She held eye contact with Rosalind, then raised an eyebrow. "And if I *did*, I think someone like you would appreciate my ability to keep my mouth shut."

"Someone like…" She realized what Moxie was implying. It would explain their absence when David handed out the bonuses the night before, and why they'd both started playing like uncoordinated children. "Ah, shit. They didn't."

Moxie shrugged and started backing away. "I don't know anything. I'm just going to hit the showers before all the hot water is used up."

"Thanks, Moccia."

"Sure thing."

Rosalind fumed as she went back to her cubby. She'd known Marcy and Rainy had a sexual history, but she'd assumed it ended when Rainy originally left the team. She'd left to get married, Rosalind thought. At least that was the story she'd heard at the time. When she showed up to join the Shrikes, there was a distinct lack of a ring on her finger or a new surname. But she never would have thought Marcy would be stupid enough to risk this experiment on a roll in the hay. And if they were already having the kind of problems that affected the game…

She dressed as quickly as possible, deciding to skip the shower. She needed to figure out where Marcy had gone, track her down, and smack some sense into her.

Marcy had traveled all over Illinois to put this team together, to give them a shot at making history, and Rosalind wasn't going to let her throw it away over a woman.

Marcy ordered another coffee and stared down into the cup, unsure of how she'd finished the first without realizing. Her brain was too busy analyzing and tearing apart her shitty performance in the game. David had told her she was playing like an amateur. She'd blown up at him, even though he was absolutely right. She hadn't played so horribly since she was a kid. That was also probably the last time she'd acted like such an idiot about Caroline Rainy.

Rosalind slid into the booth across from her. Marcy sat up

straighter and furrowed her brow at the other woman, who signaled the waitress to bring her some coffee. She had changed out of her uniform into a peach-colored blouse and dark slacks. She looked almost like a schoolmarm if it wasn't for her fierce expression.

"How did you find me?"

"I asked Rainy where you were most likely to go. She said your old ballfield." She pointed out the window. "Thanks for sitting where I could see you from the street."

"It wasn't intentional."

They fell silent as the waitress put a mug down in front of Rosalind and filled it. She offered sugar and Rosalind declined.

"So I guess you started up again."

Marcy narrowed her eyes. "I don't know what you mean."

"Moxie told me. Not in so many words, but enough to get the gist if you know history. Fooling around with someone from work is never a smart idea. Especially if you have history with the person. Especially if you've got as much on the line as we do."

"I know that. We both know that."

"Then what the hell are you thinking?"

Marcy sighed and wiped a hand over her face. "I was thinking that I'm in love. And just being near this person is enough to make me stop thinking normally. We work well together, you know? When it works, it works. And we're good. But then..."

She sighed and looked around to see if anyone was close enough to eavesdrop. The booths around them were empty, but she still lowered her voice and leaned across the table.

"I said 'I love you' when we were on the Lady Yankees. I was willing to wait for her to say it back, but eventually I gave her an ultimatum. I wanted to know where we stood. It didn't have to be love. I just felt like I needed to know for certain. And she vanished. She just..." She snapped her fingers. "Gone. For three days. And she came back with some pretty boy in tow."

Rosalind nodded. "Nicholas. The fiancé."

"Well, not at first. But eventually. Yes." She sneered. "He always treated the team like we were kids, you know? Like we were on display at the carnival. He said our uniforms were cute. He actually called them 'costumes.' And Rainy would laugh along with him like he'd scooped her brain out of her head. He eventually proposed. Rainy could quit 'fooling around' with us and go be a good little housewife."

"Looks like that didn't happen."

"Looks like," Marcy said.

"And then you recruited her for the Shrikes and the two of you..."

Marcy hung her head. "Like magnets dropped on a table. She still refuses to admit she wants to be with me. She refuses to..." She ran her tongue over her bottom lip and squirmed on the seat. "When we're intimate..."

Rosalind held her hands up. "I don't need to know any of that stuff."

"I wasn't going to give you details," Marcy said, rolling her eyes. "But it's very much a one-way street with her. I'm the one doing all the work, every time, and eventually I wonder if I'd be better off just staying home taking care of myself."

"Well, I think we've all been with people like that. What snapped the camel's back this time? Just Moxie catching y'all?"

"That, and Rainy's reaction to it. She acted like she'd been caught throttling me." She could feel the tears building behind her eyes and refused to let them out. She looked out the window and hoped the sunlight would give her an excuse for any moisture Rosalind might notice. "I can't be with someone like that, no matter how much I might feel for them."

"You deserve better, absolutely," Rosalind said. "But you also can't let that shit get in the way of the fucking game. Understand? If it comes down to you or Rainy, she's the better player and you'd be a lot easier to replace. Sad to say it so blunt, but it's true. Buckner might have something to say about cutting you, but he wants a team that proves women can play the game. He'll get rid of you if it helps the greater good."

"The greater good," Marcy mumbled under her breath, then shook her head. "You're probably right. About all of it, about David agreeing and the team being more important than whatever's going on between me and Caroline. I won't let it interfere with the game again."

Rosalind nodded. "That's all I ask. What about Rainy?"

Marcy shook her head. She had no idea what to say.

"Well, putting aside the team and everything. You're truly crazy about her right?"

"Yeah."

Rosalind tapped her fingernail on the table as she put her thoughts in order. "She has every reason to be confused and scared.

It's not a little thing to admit you want something that could destroy your whole life. She might not even be able to admit it to herself, let alone anyone else. Give her time if she's worth the work."

"She is," Marcy said quietly. "I'll talk to her. We'll sit down like grown-ups and have a conversation. Try to figure something out. She believes in the greater good, too. We can be professionals."

"Good. Because I don't want to lose to these clay smackers again."

Marcy smiled. "Thanks for the talk, Ros."

"Any time." She lifted her mug. "Thank you for the coffee."

"Who said I was paying for that?"

Rosalind raised an eyebrow and took a sip.

CHAPTER NINE

RAINY ONCE thought there was no worse feeling than her entire team blaming her for a loss. It didn't take long for her to realize it felt infinitely worse to know they were right. No one had been playing their best in the second game, but Rainy had set the mood. She made the Shrikes doubt themselves and gave the Firebricks the confidence to dig deep. It didn't matter that her performance had been clocked early and she was replaced before she could do even more damage. She'd already shaken the others enough that there was no way they could pull themselves out of the spiral.

The game was a pyramid. Physical and mental fitness joined together by talent. If any part of that got knocked, the other two went haywire and it didn't matter how good you were or how long you'd been playing the game. And she'd taken a wrench to everyone's mental anchor.

When she arrived in the clubhouse for the third and final game against St. Louis, she could feel their blame settle on her shoulders as she went to her cubby. No one said anything overt, but conversations ended and tones became hushed. She changed into her uniform in silence and then turned to face the room.

"Today is going to be different."

Ida, Patty, and Hildy all turned to face her as if they had rehearsed the move. One by one, others looked at her as well.

"I'm sorry I let you down yesterday. But I was brought onto this team for a reason. I'm going to spend the rest of the season showing you what that reason is." She started toward the exit. "I'll be out there warming up if anyone wants to join me."

She didn't look back, but she heard someone rise off the bench and follow her. The first player was followed by another, then another. There was a bag of balls next to the door to the field and she bent down to scoop one up without breaking pace. She squeezed the leather, ran her fingers over the thick threads, and passed it from one hand to the other. It was dirty and beaten up and a few of the seams looked like they were about to pop loose. It was used and abused and perfect. It felt like it had been formed to fit her palm.

They emerged into the sunshine as a team, suited up and ready to make up for their poor performance the day before. Rainy tried not to look at the bandstand but she could tell the attendance remained sparse. That didn't matter. Word of mouth took time to spread and she would've been flabbergasted if their performance the day before had prompted anyone to buy a ticket. Unless, of course, they were hecklers eager to see a disaster unfold in front of their eyes.

She chuckled and shook her head.

Moxie, walking next to her, glanced over. "What's the joke?"

"I was just thinking, we sold this many tickets to people who presumably support us. I wonder how many we would sell if we went after the folks rooting against the idea of a women's league. 'Come see the dames make fools of themselves,' you know? It doesn't matter what got their butts on the benches once the game starts. Ticket still get sold. No refunds."

Moxie laughed and shook her head. "I'll let you sell Buckner on that one. Quick game of catch?"

"Sure."

They moved a few feet apart and Rainy tossed the ball to Moxie in a lazy arc. The other players jogged, stretched, swung a bat, or did their general warmups near the dugout. The Firebricks were in the outfield doing the same warmup exercises.

After a few minutes, Moxie caught the ball and straightened, looking past Rainy to the clubhouse entrance. She caught Rainy's eye and nodded for her to look. Rainy turned and saw Marcy standing just inside the threshold, still in shadows and making no move to come out.

"Think you should go talk to her?" Moxie said.

"It kind of sounds like you think I should."

Moxie shrugged and pivoted on her heel. She whistled to Lorna Lowell and lined up to throw to her. "Third base, think fast!"

Rainy didn't watch to see if Lorna caught the ball. She jogged back across the grass. She ignored how Marcy tensed when she saw her coming. When she stopped, she kept a safe distance between the two of them. It was demarcated by the sun, Rainy's side, and the shadows on Marcy's.

"Did Rosalind talk to you?" Marcy asked.

"No." Rainy frowned and searched for the centerfielder. "Does she need to?"

Marcy shrugged. "I don't know. She came and found me yesterday. She gave me a talking-to about my behavior during the game yesterday."

"*Our* behavior," Rainy corrected. "I got in my head. I wasn't thinking about the game at all. You might as well have had a goat out there pitching."

"We might sell more tickets."

Rainy couldn't help but smile. "Everyone loves a gimmick. I, um, I was just telling Moxie about, uh, if we marketed tickets to people who don't like us. We can tell 'em it's a chance to see us falling flat on our faces."

Marcy looked intrigued. "It might cause problems with hecklers. But I think that might not be a bad idea. No point in only playing to the believers. Let's try to convert some souls at the same time. Their money spends the same no matter why they plunk it down."

"Sure," Rainy said.

"I'll mention it to David. I'll be sure you get credit."

Rainy shrugged. "That's not necessary. I was just goofing around."

"It's still your idea. I'll make sure he knows." She uncrossed her arms and hooked her thumbs in her belt loops. She pretended to be fascinated by the activity on the field. "How do the Firebricks look?"

"Overconfident."

"We got 'em just where we want 'em."

Rainy laughed quietly. "Yeah. We should've beaten them yesterday."

"We'll beat them today." There was no hesitation or doubt in Marcy's voice.

"Yes we will."

Marcy nodded once, determined. "We're teammates. We... behave like teammates should. We take care of each other. We support each other. And we draw the lines we've got to draw."

Rainy said, "I think that would be for the best."

"Mm-hmm." She came closer, stepping into the sun. "So are we okay?"

"We're okay. Come on. Let's go redeem ourselves."

Marcy smiled and followed her out onto the field.

The Firebricks were determined not to go home as losers. They came out hot in the first inning, scoring two runs despite Rainy delivering fire with every pitch. Marcy wanted to warn her that trying too hard was almost as bad as being careless. Both approaches would result in stupid mistakes. When the Shrikes got their turn at bat, Hildy set up their turning point by getting on base. Moxie followed her, and then Ida Coe pushed Hildy to third.

The bases were loaded when Rainy stepped up to bat. It was her chance to make amends for her lousy pitching the day before. Marcy watched from the batter's box, holding her breath as she clocked Rainy's cold stare at the other pitcher. Her jaw was tight. The bat was steady on her shoulder. The Firebricks pitcher, a dark-haired farm girl named Nell, shook her head at their catcher. She shook her head again. Then she dipped her chin and assumed a pitching position.

Marcy saw the corners of Rainy's mouth curl up. She adjusted her posture. She flexed her fingers on the neck of the bat.

Nell did the windup, brought her left leg up, and then stretched it out behind her as she launched a knuckle curveball.

Rainy slid her inside foot toward the outside and straightened her spine as she brought the bat around. Wood cracked leather and sent the ball sailing, sent the Firebricks scattering, sent Hildy toward home. Rainy loped toward first in no particular hurry, because even without looking she knew where she'd sent the ball. There was a strange sound of the few people in the crowd inhaling at once, followed by another crack of wood as the ball landed in the bleachers.

Hildy crossed home. Then Moxie, then Ida, and then Rainy in no particular hurry. She casually tapped home plate with the toe of her right foot and stepped around the Firebricks' irritated catcher. Only then did Marcy hear the crowd: a scattering of applause, laughter, chattering from people with a lot of empty space between them.

Rainy passed Marcy on her way into the dugout. "That'll put butts on benches, huh?"

Marcy laughed and nodded at the bandstand. "Looks like you took them off the benches, too."

Rainy grinned and headed down to where the team was waiting. She was greeted with back claps, handshakes, and tugs on her braids. Marcy grinned, added her applause to the crowd's, and then jogged out to the plate. The inning wasn't over yet, and she was eager to see just how big of a lead they could build before the Firebricks went back on the offensive.

In the second inning, Rainy struck out the first two Firebricks without breaking a sweat. She got the third out when the third batter hit the ball straight back to her. Moxie watched it all crouched behind home plate, thrilled to have the best seat in the house for the comeback performance. She was the only one who heard the grumbling of the Firebricks as they came up to bat. She was the only one who saw their faces as the ball smacked into Moxie's glove without getting anywhere close to the bat.

"Tough luck," Moxie said to one of them as she tossed the ball back to Rainy.

"Stick it in your ear."

Moxie smiled and dropped back down, hooking her fingers in the mask to straighten it.

Rosalind scored their fifth run, followed a few minutes later Edith got their sixth. The Firebricks seemed to read the writing on the wall. By the fifth inning, when the Shrikes were up by seven, Moxie could almost see their motivation flow from the dugout like a physical cloud. A few of them still batted as if they intended to single-handedly turn things around, but there was no doubt what would happen by the seventh inning stretch.

Moxie felt a little bad about sending the ladies home as losers, but she would've felt infinitely worse if they'd opened the season by losing to strangers in their own house.

The unfortunate side effect to their domination was that a lot of the crowd decided the end of the game wasn't worth watching. Moxie was in the dugout at the top of the ninth and shook her head at the vast stretches of empty benches.

"You'd think they would stick around and get their whole quarter's worth."

Rosalind shrugged. "Maybe they're running out to tell all their friends."

"Fat lot of good it'll do us in Detroit." They were hopping the train as soon as the game finished so they'd have time to settle in before they had to play. Everyone already had their bags packed and waiting in their cubbies. "Hopefully they'll remember us when we come home."

The game ended with a score of 12-4, and Moxie figured that would be enough to keep them in Chicago's hearts while they were out on the road.

David was already waiting when the team surged into the clubhouse. He looked like the cat who got the canary, clapping his hands loudly and beaming with pride as the women went to their cubbies.

"Fantastic game, ladies! Just fantastic! I'll get out of your hair in a second, I just needed to grab Rainy for a second."

Rainy had already unbuttoned her jersey to reveal the undershirt beneath. She frowned at him, her hands hovering near the buttons as if debating whether or not to do them up again. "Me? Why?"

"It's a surprise." David backed toward the door. "Come on."

Rainy hesitated, then followed. She lightly grabbed Moxie's elbow as she passed, pulling her along. Moxie didn't fight and fell into step next to her. Strength in numbers and all that.

David glanced back once they were in the hall. He was visibly surprised to see Moxie. "Oh. I actually just needed Rainy."

"Oh," Moxie said without inflection. "Well, I'm already here."

Rainy said, "I don't mind her tagging along."

David clearly didn't like it, but he didn't force the issue. He faced forward and continued down the corridor to a clear area that led to an exit. The doors were open and two men were standing on the sidewalk chatting to each other. They stopped and stood up straighter when they saw David coming. They were dressed in shabby suits, unshaven. One of them was holding a notepad, and the other reached into his jacket pocket for one.

"As promised, gentlemen," David said, holding his arms out to frame Rainy. "Caroline Rainy, our lucky number 12."

Rainy slowed and eyed the men like they were predators. "What's this?"

David pointed to the men in turn. "Ronald Waffle and John Carmel. One is from the *Daily News* and the other is from the *Journal.*

They want to talk to the woman that not only threw an amazing game but got the first grand slam of the Women's National League."

"Oh." Rainy looked at Moxie as if hoping for a rescue. "Is that really necessary?"

"Yes," David said before either reporter could answer. "We always welcome the chance to have the team profiled in not one but two prestigious papers with very high readership numbers." He raised his eyebrows at Rainy to make sure she got what he was saying.

"Right." She cleared her throat and stood up straighter. "Sure. We can talk."

The men took a step forward, pencils poised, and began firing questions off at her.

"Now is that Rainy with an -ey or an -ie? Turn around, sweetie, is it on your blouse?"

"How long have you been playing ball?"

"Did your father teach you how to throw like that?"

"Maybe your brothers? How many brothers did you grow up with, honey?"

"You got a man waiting at home?"

"What does your man think about you playing professional ball?"

"Is your man overseas, sweetheart?"

Rainy instinctively took a step back, raising her hands. "Hold on. Wait, just..."

Moxie stepped between her and the men. "Hiya, gents. You're going to have to be just a little more focused here, all right? Now, our girl here just pitched an amazing game, and she's still a bit buzzed from that. You keep throwing questions at her, she's bound to try swinging her bat at a few of 'em. Might get a few extra runs out of it." She smiled big and winked. "Now give her a second to breathe and you'll both get a nice solid piece from her."

Ronald, or maybe it was John, pointed a pencil at her. "Who is this?"

"Iona Moccia," she said, and then spelled it for them. "Number eight. Catcher."

Rainy put a hand on Moxie's shoulder. "And apparently my bodyguard." She forced a laugh, Moxie echoed it, and the men joined in. "But she's absolutely right, gentlemen. I'm sorry. I'm still in game-brain. If I could just have a few minutes to myself I'd be more than happy to give you an official and much more coherent interview afterward."

David cleared his throat. "Caroline, these men have deadlines to meet."

Moxie said, "And your pitcher needs to breathe after winning that game for us. I don't think ten minutes is too much to ask, Mr. Buckner. The men want suitable quotes, I'm sure. Let's just let her unwind and then she'll give them as much time as they need."

David sighed and tossed an apologetic look at the reporters. "Sure. Uh, I'm sure they would like to try some of the, the, the refreshments that the park offer."

Moxie nodded and put an arm around Rainy to guide her back to the clubhouse before David could give them any dirty looks behind the reporters' backs.

"Thank you for that, Moxie," Rainy said once they had put some distance between them and the men.

"Hey, no sweat. I know you can take care of yourself, but Ros and I decided that no one on this team is going to spend any solo time with that man if we can prevent it."

"Smart. Has anyone actually accused him of anything?"

Moxie shook her head. "No. I think that's why Marcy is still willing to work with him. It's all weird feelings and, you know, questionable behavior. He can explain everything away, which is sketchy enough to raise an eyebrow or two. Anyway, if the man's got nothing to hide, there's no reason for him to object about a buddy system."

"I still appreciate it."

"Any time. We need to make sure the rest of the girls know, too. Might as well get that out of the way now, huh?"

Rainy nodded as they re-entered the clubhouse. Everyone was present, all in various levels of undress. Rainy cleared her throat to get everyone's attention, and Moxie stood in the doorway to keep lookout.

"Ladies, can I have your attention for just a second? There's something we need to address before we head out on the road..."

CHAPTER TEN

MARCY HAD been fuming since Rainy's big overblown speech after the game.

She hated herself for being angry but, at the same time, she didn't appreciate Rainy holding that impromptu team meeting to cast aspersions on David's character. She knew that Rosalind had a bad feeling about him. Moxie seemed to share it, and now it looked as if they'd recruited Rainy to their way of thinking. She couldn't believe how quickly the others had just gone along with the idea of the 'buddy system.' No one ever being alone with their manager? Was that even feasible? If he was pure as the driven snow, a bunch of women treating him like a monster was bound to make him irritable. And an irritable man was as dangerous as anything else out there in the world.

The hectic rush to get to the train station after the game saved her from getting caught in any awkward conversations with her teammates. Once they were aboard the train, she slumped down in a seat separate from the other players and pushed her cap down over her eyes.

An hour into the ride, someone sat down next to her. She knew without looking that it was Rainy, and she knew Rainy didn't believe Marcy was really napping, but she still kept her chin down and her arms crossed over her chest.

"If he's not going to do anything anyway," Rainy said under her voice, "then it shouldn't matter if there are witnesses around."

Marcy took a deep breath and let it out slowly. She kept her voice equally low. "You're punishing him for something he ain't even done."

"So you're saying we should wait until he gropes Lorna? Or convinces Patty that the quickest way to a pay rise is to spend some time on his office couch?"

Marcy sat up and used a knuckle to push her cap higher on her head. "Saying these things, putting ideas like that in the heads of these girls... They know I helped him build this team. We're practically partners in the thing. You start whispering that girls get treated nicer for fucking him, what are they going to think about *me*, hm? You consider that, Caroline? Suddenly I got half my team thinking I put out."

Rainy twisted her lips. "I hadn't thought of it that way."

"Clearly! And the fact he didn't pull any nonsense with me is enough evidence that he's kosher."

"Oh balderdash," Rainy said. "You don't believe that. You've known him for years, so maybe he doesn't see you as a potential victim. But Ida, Patty, Hildy... and these girls you brought in for the second string are eighteen, nineteen years old. They're fresh out of their mama and daddy's house and they don't know they can stand up to a man in authority or even tell them he's making them uncomfortable. You know how many of them call me 'ma'am'? Too damn many."

"Well, I'm not going to prosecute a man over what people are worried he might do."

Rainy shrugged. "Do what you want. But I'm encouraging everyone to buddy up. I'd rather make him feel uncomfortable than put any of these girls in a situation where they can't say no."

Marcy pulled her cap back down over her eyes. "Just don't come crying to me when he responds to you treating him like a leper."

Rainy got out of the seat without responding to that.

At some point, Marcy's ruse became reality. She was aware that she'd drifted off, the activity on the train fading into a quiet hum as if it was all happening behind a curtain. When she woke, someone else had taken the seat next to her. It only took one whiff of his cologne to know it was David. She kept still for another few minutes and tried to determine how close they were to their destination. She finally gave up and lifted her head.

"There you are." David had a newspaper on his lap and passed it to her. "Guy in the dining car had that. There's a sports section." He poked the page. "Thought you might like to see how our next opponents stacked up in their season opener."

Marcy fought back a yawn as she unfolded the paper. "Why not. I'm sure they're doing the same thing with us." She skimmed the page. "I don't like their name."

"The Detroit Pros?" David said. "What's wrong with it? Nice and succinct. And there are worse things than being known as the Professionals."

"That's not what it's short for." He looked confused. "You really don't know? Prohibitionists. They want to ban alcohol."

David raised his eyebrows. "Oh. That would explain why there are such strict rules about concessions."

"Mm-hmm," Marcy said, still scanning the box scores. "They sound like a hoot."

David tilted his head to the side. "Does that work against us or to our benefit?"

"How could it do either?"

He shrugged. "If they're having drinks after the games, there's a chance they show up with hangovers. Makes 'em slower and easier to tag. But if they're sharp and we're the ones who stayed up late the night before..."

Marcy said, "We'll just have to make sure we're sober for the games and hope for the best." Something in the paper caught her eye and she took a second to read the full paragraph. "Holy smokes. This can't be right. This says they beat Cleveland twenty-nil on their first game."

David nodded. "Yep. The next game was a little closer. 12-1. And I guess they barely tried in the third game, because they only got eight runs. But the other team stuck with a goose egg."

"At least they're trending downward." Twenty runs in a single game, though? She examined the box scores carefully. It was unbelievable, and a very bad omen. She couldn't imagine only scoring a single run across three games when their opponent was throwing out double digits. "Are they really that good, or are the Cleveland Hawks just stinkin' rotten?"

"Right now I'm hoping for the latter. But we should be prepared for anything." He twisted to look back down the car, then patted his pockets. "I'm going to go find a window so I can have a cigarette. Care to join me?"

Marcy shook her head. "I'm going to go over these box scores."

"There will be time for that when we get to Detroit."

"Now's the time to get the facts," Marcy said. "Once we're in town, we can use those facts to figure out a game plan."

"Good luck," he said as he got up out of the seat.

Marcy sighed and shook her head. She read the numbers and let the first inning of the first Pros-Hawks game play out in her mind's eye.

"Thanks, Dave. We're gonna need it..."

Heavy gray clouds rolling in from the east hit Detroit at the same time their train arrived. David feared any kind of storm might cause a game delay, but the resulting showers weren't enough to do anything but make the field a little muddy. David and the manager of the Pros had a meeting and decided conditions weren't bad enough to justify delaying the game. So after a restless night in a hotel, the Shrikes headed down to Navin Field for their first of their next three games.

The lousy weather hadn't kept away the fans. Either Detroit was much more supportive of women playing baseball, or there were just fewer options on a dreary Friday afternoon. Whatever the reason, the seats behind home plate were packed full of spectators. There were still wide, empty sections behind right field, of course, but there were more than enough people in the bandstand to make a ruckus. It was inspiring to see.

The Pros, however, took away any hope Marcy had gained from the size of the crowd. Her first opinion of the Detroit team was that they were monsters. They were giantesses with hands the size of mitts and powerful jaws, women who lumbered and lurched from the dugout like ogres woken from a long hibernation.

"Well," Rainy said as she watched their new opponents mill around on the field. "Look at the bright side. Maybe this means they'll be slow."

They weren't slow. And they weren't gentle, either. When their first basewoman tagged Edith, she did it by smacking her on the shoulder so hard her entire arm went numb.

One of the stories in the newspapers had mentioned the Pros were intimidating enough to 'make even the toughest male player quake in his cleats,' but she hadn't expected anything like these beasts. The Shrikes scored two runs in the first inning. The Pros doubled it when they stepped up to bat. Ida Coe got their only run in the second inning, and the Pros increased their score to seven.

In the fourth inning - 3-9 in favor of the home team - Marcy scanned the Shrikes dugout and saw a dozen women who looked like they'd been to war. Marcy herself felt exhausted when she thought about the fact they weren't even halfway through the game. *And we've got two more days of this ahead of us.*

They had replacements ready to go, but they all looked terrified of being asked to step in. Marcy motioned for David to step aside with her.

"They're murdering us out there."

"Yes, I think everyone is quite aware of that fact."

Marcy looked out at the field, where Rosalind was about to bat. "If we lost these three games, we've still got almost the entire season ahead of us."

"What are you saying, you want to throw this series?"

"Not throw it," Marcy said. "We'd still try our best to win. But we're being run ragged trying to keep up with these gals. All of us are being forced to give a hundred and thirty percent. I'm suggesting we drop it down to... to maybe sixty percent. Save something for Cleveland when we get there."

David scratched his thumbnail over his top lip, considering it. "It would be better if you hadn't lost the game at home," he said. "Four losses in your first six games is a terrible record, Marcy."

"We might win a couple of these games even at half-steam," she said. "Especially if the Pros start getting lazy in response. They might be inspired to put in their second string, and we could stand a chance against that roster. But there's no point in killing ourselves for the exact same result."

He sighed and waved a hand. "Put in the backups. Let them know the strategy is just to put numbers on the board, not necessarily to overtake."

Marcy nodded and went back to the team and reported the new tactic. Moxie and Lorna were literally relieved to be relieved. Edith, who was still icing her shoulder, was sent to the showers to sit out the rest of the game. Rainy made her way over to Marcy.

"So we're just going to let them whip our asses?"

"We're going to lose this game no matter what." She looked at home plate in time to see Rosalind get a third strike. She winced. "We're going to take a hit on this, but at least we won't be completely drained for Cleveland."

"And what if Cleveland is even tougher?"

"They're not. I read the box scores and the articles. We've got a chance against them."

Rainy twisted her lips. "Well, if nothing else, I can keep their score from getting too insane."

"No. We're putting in Lucille."

"The hell we are."

Marcy said, "You need to rest your arm."

"I'll rest it against the crappy team we're playing next," Rainy said. "Right now we need the best we've got. I understand subbing out the batters, but this is just me. I can keep them off the bases."

Marcy kicked at the dirt, arms crossed. "Caro..."

"Don't Caro me. You're the manager and I'm the best chance your team has of winning at least one of the next three games. Don't put me on the bench."

"Okay. For this game. But if I see you start to lag--"

Rainy cut her off. "Fair enough."

Patty Frett struck out, ending their time at bat and returning them to the field. Rainy squatted down next to the bag of balls, dug around, and withdrew one that looked more battered and beaten than any of the others. She tossed it in the air, caught it effortlessly, then threw it into her weak hand. It smacked hard against her palm as she climbed out into the gentle rain.

Marcy followed her and couldn't help but be inspired by the sight, a hero striding out to her mound, a soldier ready to win the entire damn war for her team.

RAINY IN THE RAIN

Samuel Champlin, *Detroit Gazette*, April 16, 1916

NAVIN PARK, DETROIT.

"Our local fans will have to excuse a bit of a switch-up from our usual focus. We'll have plenty of columns to talk about our Tigers once the war is over, and the brand-new Pros have shown us already that they're worthy of our attention in a great many articles, but today I must talk about the spectacle that happened on the field yesterday, and to do that I have to heap praise on our current enemies, the Chicago Shrikes.

"It was the bottom of the fourth, the score 9-3 in favor of our Pros, when the rain began falling like a bad omen. The girls from Chicago had clawed their way for those three runs, no question, but a gambling man would question whether they'd get many more. But then Caroline Rainy emerged from the visitors dugout as if she'd been summoned by the storm. Cap low, back straight, left hand weighed down by a ball that seemed to weigh a hundred pounds, she took her position on the mound.

"And that, my friends, is where things took a dramatic turn for the worst for our beloved Prohibitionists.

"Number 12 threw nine pitches in a row, and our girls hit nary a one. Three strikes and the shortest inning in recent memory came to an end. I could see the shock and confusion on the face of manager Stevie Robertson even from my perch in the press box."

"The rain kept falling as the fifth inning started, and the Shrikes sent out

a fresh crop of batters to give their starting line-up a breather. They managed to put two runners on base, but Janice Griffin wasn't about to be shown up by another pitcher and kept the score solidly at three and nine.

"And so it would remain for the rest of the game! The Shrikes never got another run but Caroline Rainy made darn sure the Pros didn't build on their lead. If old Ernest Thayer had been in the crowd that day, he would've forgotten about that has-been Casey and focused instead on the monolithic batter in the brown and orange uniform.

"Red braid hanging over her shoulder and rain dripping from the brim of her cap, Rainy threw the high cheese, a knuckler, she threw fast and slow, straight and curved, and our faithful Pros couldn't keep up with her. By the seventh inning, every other player in both dugouts had lined up to watch to see if she was going to tire out or meet her match. Robertson even sent in Tacoma Mary Camp to try and break the spell, but Rainy served our girl her first embarrassment at the plate.

"Despite their pitcher's efforts, the rest of the Shrikes weren't able to rally in the final innings. The score remained 9-3 when the towel was thrown. My friends, believe me when I tell you I've never seen a winning team so despondent, or losers so exuberant, than I did when that game was done and dusted. But I know the girls from Chicago gave our Pros a lot to think about for their next face-off this afternoon, and I know without question I'm going to be there to see what happens.

"I suggest you be there, too!"

CHAPTER ELEVEN

RAINY COULDN'T move her right arm. She'd woken before dawn and rolled over onto her back, fully aware of the dead weight attached to her torso. She stared at the ceiling and flexed her muscles in an attempt to make the arm do something, anything, but it remained stubborn and stiff. She listened to the gentle snoring of Hildy and Rosalind, her roommates, and squeezed her hand into a fist. The effort made her wince. She relaxed her fingers and clenched her jaw and folded them again, squeezing hard, digging her nails into her palms.

The room gradually filled with light. Hildy woke first, sitting up on her cot across the room and running her hands through her hair before she stood up. She pulled on a dress and pinned her hair back. She stretched and stood up, noticing Rainy was awake.

"I think the hotel has a free breakfast," she said under her breath. "Want me to bring you something back?"

"No, thanks."

Hildy nodded and left. Rosalind was also stirring, probably woken up by Hildy leaving. Rainy pushed herself up as best she could with only one arm, leaving her other resting heavy across her lap.

"Ros."

"Mm." She was still lying on her side, facing the wall.

"I need you to go get Marcy."

Rosalind rolled over. "What's the matter?"

"Nothing's the matter. I just need to talk with her, that's all."

Rosalind got out of bed and put on her robe. "Did you throw out your arm?"

Rainy shook her head. "I just overdid it a little. Marcy will know what to do, just go get her. I think she's staying with Ida and Moxie." She hesitated and then added, "Tell her to bring some ice."

"Damn it," Rosalind said, but she left the room without delay.

Five minutes later, Marcy appeared. She was wearing a full pajama set with the pinstriped blouse buttoned all the way to her throat. She climbed onto Rainy's bed without hesitation.

"Damn it, Caro."

"Ros already said that," Rainy informed her. "Just give me a quick rubdown. Loosen things up. I'll ice it, and I'll be better in time for the game."

"The game is in eight hours." She gently prodded the muscle between Rainy's shoulder and her neck. "If you hurt yourself just so we could lose the game anyway..."

"It was worth it," Rainy said. "Those arrogant hometown girls learned a lesson yesterday."

"Yeah, make your opponent mad enough, they'll put themselves in the hospital just to spite you. How humiliating for them."

"I'm not going to need the hospital."

"No, not now," Marcy agreed. "But if you think we're starting you today, you're nuts."

Rainy had been staring at the foot of the bed. She whipped her head to look at Marcy so quickly that it sent a spasm down her spine. She hissed and stiffened.

"Be careful!" Marcy scolded her.

"You're not serious. Do you really think Lucille can hold off those monsters?"

The door opened again and Rosalind came in. She held out a towel wrapped in ice, and Marcy took it with a quick thanks.

"I think I'd rather have three losses on our scorecard if it means we get to keep our pitcher."

Rainy licked her lips, clearly holding back the true depths of her anger. "I'm just a little rusty. I haven't been playing regularly. The games in Chicago and now this... my arm just needs to get used to the schedule. I can't do that if you smack me on the bench every time I have a little pain."

Marcy pressed two fingers into Rainy's shoulder and made her yelp and twist away from her.

"That's not a little pain. Ros, can you go to the front desk and ask them if they have any aspirin?"

"Sure."

She headed out again, leaving them alone. Marcy sighed and began to massage Rainy's shoulder. "You didn't do your exercises last night, did you?"

Rainy rolled her eyes. "Who are you, my mother?"

"Well, someone has to stay on top of you."

They both realized what she'd said and fell quiet. Marcy kept massaging the tired muscles, moving one hand to the back of Rainy's neck. Rainy grunted and dropped her chin to her chest.

"That feels great."

"Can you lift your arm for me?"

Rainy slowly brought her arm up, stopping with a hiss when her hand was chest level. "That's improvement, at least."

"I like the optimism."

Rainy closed her eyes and focused on Marcy's fingers. "I'm going to miss this."

Marcy's massage paused. "This isn't going anywhere. This is just a teammate helping another teammate. That's all."

Rainy looked at her. "So you did this for Edith, too? Her arm is probably still pretty sore after getting tagged the way she did."

"She was feeling better by the end of the game," Marcy said. "Besides, her arm isn't as important as yours. If you insist on pitching today's game, we've got to make sure you aren't doing permanent damage to it."

"Okay."

"That's all this is."

"Okay," Rainy said again.

Rosalind came back into the room before Marcy could say anything else. Her assertion that the massage was totally platonic collapsed when she pulled her hands away as soon as the door opened. Rosalind didn't react to the site of Marcy sitting on Rainy's bed or the way she jumped, too excited by whatever had happened while she was downstairs. She had a bottle of aspirin, which she handed to Rainy, and newspapers under her arm that she gave to Marcy.

"Rainy's in the papers."

"Well, that's to be expected," Marcy said. "I suppose they could have just ignored us, but it's a good sign they're writing up the games."

"Not just the games." Rosalind opened one of the papers and pointed. "Rainy specifically. Look, that's a Detroit paper, and the story is all about how amazing Rainy is."

Rainy leaned over to look, wincing when she put pressure on her arm. "That can't be right."

"I guess they got bored of covering their own team," Rosalind said. "There are only so many ways you can talk about them being amazing."

"Rainy in the Rain," Marcy read. "It's poetic. And putting attention on you is a good way to get people interested. Look at Honus Wagner and Ty Cobb. You could be the next Cy Young."

"The first female Cy Young," Rosalind amended.

"I don't know if I want that. I just want to pitch."

Marcy said, "Well, if you want to pitch for more than one season, it might be good to embrace this sort of thing." She noticed the other paper. "What's that one?"

"Our hometown rag," Rosalind said. "They did a whole interview with our gal after our last home game. It ran this morning, too."

Marcy whistled. "Two articles in different states on the same day. You might not have a choice about becoming famous, Caroline. When our baseball cards come in, you can sign a bunch. We'll have giveaways during the game. Two bits for an authentic Caroline Rainy autograph!"

Rainy made a face.

Marcy folded the paper and climbed off the bed. "We should let you rest. Lift your arm again?" Rainy did as instructed, and it came up a little higher than before. "Okay. We'll keep checking on it. But if you're not at a hundred percent an hour before the game starts, we're using Lucille."

"Fine," Rainy said.

They hustled out, leaving behind the Detroit paper. Rainy stared at it, then reluctantly picked it up and turned to the sporting news. "Rainy in the Rain," she said under her breath, shaking her head. At least there weren't any photographs. It might not be so bad being famous if it was restricted to when she was on the mound. Once she took off the uniform, she was anonymous as anyone else on the street. She tossed the paper away so she wouldn't be tempted to read and re-

read the article.

"Anything for the team," she said as she settled carefully back onto her pillow.

The liniment and exercise combined to get Rainy's arm back to normal by lunchtime. She mimed throwing in her hotel room a few times before she found Marcy to tell her she'd be ready for the game. Marcy insisted she demonstrate a full range of motion without twinging or grimacing. When she successfully pulled it off, Marcy reluctantly agreed to let her pitch. "But you're bottom of the starting lineup. You don't bat unless you absolutely have to."

"Fine by me."

She continued to stretch and warm up, determined not to repeat the worry of that morning. By the time they left for the park, she was calm and confident. David had arranged for motor bus to transport the team to the game so they could arrive in style. Rainy found the contraption alarming. The thing looked like a streetcar with a driver's bench bolted to the front of it, horribly unwieldy and terrifying when it took a corner and leaned so far to the left that she was positive it would topple over. Her feelings of calm and confidence were replaced by a twisted knot of anxiety in the pit of her stomach.

That knot tightened and doubled in size as soon as the park was in sight, and she spotted the cluster of people surrounding the entrance. Her first thought was that they were protesting the game, trying to prevent anyone from getting into the park, but then she realized people were being let through the turnstiles.

"What's going on?" she asked under her breath.

David, riding with Marcy in the seat behind her, thought she was talking to him. "That's what a sold-out game looks like."

"Sold out?" Rainy looked over her shoulder and met Marcy's eye. "The game can't possibly be sold out. You're kidding."

"I don't kid about that sort of thing," he said. "Marcy told me you saw the paper this morning. These people realized something pretty quickly when they showed up for the first couple of Pros games. Their girls are unstoppable. And there's nothing more boring than a game where you know in advance who is going to win. So ticket sales slumped on the third game. They dropped even more for yesterday's game, although that might've been partially due to the weather."

Rainy was amazed to think that crowd was what counted as a slow day for Detroit. "So what changed?"

"We changed!" David said. "We gave them a challenge."

"We lost," Rainy reminded him.

He shrugged. "But we made them fight for the win. You kept them at bay. Who knows what's going to happen today? This crowd is either going to see an underdog come out on top, or their hometown team is going to take home a victory. No matter what happens, it's not the sort of game you sit out. Don't get me wrong, though. I don't expect anyone in this crowd is actually rooting for you. But I don't think they're going to form a mob if you win, either."

Marcy said, "And if we win, imagine what the crowd will look like tomorrow."

Rainy turned around to face forward again, slumping down in her seat. She flexed her fingers and made a fist, trying not to feel the pressure.

When they got to the clubhouse, she focused on her uniform. It was freshly laundered, but she brought it to her face anyway and breathed in deep. When they first started playing as the Lady Yankees, they sometimes went five or six games before the uniforms got washed. She swore she could still smell the sweat, dirt, and grass in the fibers even after they'd been cleaned. Smelling them reminded her of every pitch, every run, and every error of the day before. She actually kind of preferred that, she discovered. A clean uniform was a reminder that whatever happened before was in the past.

Once she was dressed, she found the bag of balls and sorted around all the unmarked, undamaged balls to find one with some scars on it. She hated a perfect ball. It was too clean, too perfect. It didn't know how to fly right. She found one with just the right amount of wear and tear and carried it with her out to the field.

Nothing prepared her for the sound. She'd been to games played by male teams, of course, and she'd heard the shouting and cheering and the rumble of thousands of voices all speaking at once. In those cases she had been part of the noise, inside of it, building it with everyone else. Stepping out of the clubhouse it quickly became apparent that being in the center of the hum was a whole different animal.

She wished it was a home game. She greatly preferred starting games in her proper post, in the center of the field on her raised hill of dirt. She had a few minutes before the game started so she left the dugout and started walking across the grass. She would just get her cleats dirty, reacquaint herself with the view, and then she'd go back and wait for their turn to come.

Rainy was halfway to the mound when the first jeers reached her. They didn't register at first but, as more and more people picked it up, she realized they were directed at her. And it made sense. She was an invader, an enemy soldier, and to their eyes, she had crossed enemy lines. She didn't slow down, though. To turn back now would have sent all the wrong messages to both the Pros and their crowd. So she kept walking.

"*Rayyyyyyy-kneeeee...*"

The chant started behind her, in the bandstand above right field. It spread like a wave, raising in volume as thousands of Detroiters dragged her name out so it lasted almost ten seconds.

Rainy stepped up onto the mound and planted her feet. She stood up straight and turned to face the crowd. She rolled her shoulder with perfectly painless fluidity. Not a twinge of the morning's paralysis remained. She felt like a whole new woman. She gripped the ball with four fingers on one side, her thumb on the other hemisphere.

The crowd's chant continued. "*Rayyyyyy-kneee...*"

She pinched the brim of her cap and tugged it lower over her eyes. She cocked her hip and tried to pick out individual faces. If they were people, they wouldn't be intimidating. People weren't a crowd or a mob, they were just fans who had paid their twenty-five cents to see the game. A man with a bushy white mustache and wild black eyebrows. A man with a high forehead and a flat top haircut, a boy with acne and glasses, a woman who wasn't joining in the chant but had a self-satisfied smirk on her face.

The jeering grew louder the longer she stood there. Other Shrikes players had gathered in the dugout, watching. The Pros were there, too, just watching. Arms crossed, talking amongst themselves.

Rainy didn't want to be a celebrity. But the articles had stuck the knife in, and this stunt would only push it deeper and twist the hilt.

So be it, she thought. She took off her cap and lifted it high above her head, swinging it in a wide wave as if she was royalty greeting her public.

"*RAYYYYYYY-KNEEEEEE!*"

She dropped the cap back onto her head and jogged back to the dugout at a leisurely pace. The crowd booed and shouted incoherently at her but she just kept her head down and ducked down the steps to where the rest of the team was waiting.

"What was that supposed to be?" Marcy said.

"Pitcher's mound is my territory," Rainy said, unaware she was going to say it until the words were out of her mouth. "I just wanted to make sure they knew it."

Marcy smiled and shrugged. "Works for me. Arm?"

"Arm's good. Arm is perfect." She looked out at the field. "Let's get out there and make these Pros look like amateurs."

CHAPTER TWELVE

SWEAT STUNG Rainy's eyes but she blinked it away. Her arm hurt, but so did everything else. There was a low-level throb in the small of her back, and her thighs felt like iron. She was pretty sure her braid was coming unraveled but she didn't dare check it. She had more important things to worry about. Like Number 8 inching her way onto the third baseline. Like Number 4 directly ahead of her lifting a bat and waving it in a slow orbit. Like the sixteen thousand residents of Detroit - David had told her the count last time she was in the dugout - screaming for her to get knocked down a peg.

It all depended on this pitch. A strike would end the game and the Shrikes would win by one point. The best case scenario with a hit would be Number 8 scoring a run and forcing extra innings. But if it was a home run, or if Number 4 was fast enough, they could snatch back a victory at the last second. They would be heroes. Rainy worked her jaw and stared into the batter's eyes. Two teams hopes came down to her and this other woman, someone whose name she didn't even know.

Moxie signaled a pitch. Rainy shook her head. Moxie flipped out two fingers to change her suggestion, and Rainy shook her head again. She knew what she was going to throw.

She lifted one shoulder, then the other. She lifted one foot behind her and then smacked it down hard, digging the ball of her foot into the mound. She split her fingers across the top of the ball, two and two along the seams. When she pitched, the first two fingers of her hand pushed down to give it a curve.

The ball spun toward Number 4 in slow motion, giving her just enough time to track its movement and predict the point of impact.

The bat came down.

And the ball curved sharply to the left as if Moxie had pulled it to her glove by a string. It landed with a satisfying and heavy thud, and Number 4 almost twisted her legs into a bow as she swung at the empty air where a fastball would have ended up.

That was strike three in the bottom of the ninth inning. The Shrikes had just beaten the Pros, nine to eight.

Moxie shot to her feet and threw the ball straight up in the air as she ran to the mound. The Pros hitter threw her bat to the ground in a fit of pique. Moxie slammed hard into Rainy and knocked her back a step, but Ida Coe and Patty Frett hit her from behind. And then Rosalind, Lorna, Hildy, the whole team was packed around her, holding her up even as she struggled to keep her feet on the ground. She laughed and patted the back of someone's head, allowing herself to be crushed by their enthusiasm.

It was possible she didn't touch the ground until she was back in the clubhouse. She wanted to tell them to put her down. She hadn't won the game alone. Moxie was responsible for three of the runs all by herself over the course of the game. Patty, Hildy, and Rosalind had gotten the game off on the right foot by getting three runs in the first inning. Rainy's first pitch was during a 3-0 game, and the Pros got four of their runs off her, giving them an early lead.

Everyone had done their part to ensure their success. Winning by one meant that every single run mattered. She went to her cubby and stood on a bench, whistling to get everyone's attention.

"We won by nine points, and we didn't get a single one of them because of my pitching. We got them because of Patty, Hildy, Rosalind, Moxie, Ida, and Marcy. And the Pros only got eight runs because of everyone else building a damn wall around that field. Lorna, where's Lorna?" She scanned the faces and pointed at the third basewoman. "Number 3 thought she was going to take a leisurely stroll home, didn't she? But thanks to you, where'd she end up?"

Lorna hooked her thumb over her shoulder in an exaggerated umpire gesture. "Outta there...!"

The gathered team cheered.

Edith had worked her way to the front of the group. She handed Rainy a paper cup of water, and Rainy lifted it above her head in a toast.

"To the Shrikes!"

Rainy downed the water, crushed the cup, and tossed it toward the trash can as she hopped down onto the ground. Her speech had the intended consequence and the other players were all focused on congratulation each other on their accomplishments. Rainy grinned and slipped away from them into the hall, making her way to the shower.

She unbuttoned her jersey in the hallway and was shrugging it off when she got to the showers. Marcy was sitting on one of the benches with her back against the tiles, already in an undershirt and her dirt-stained uniform pants. A towel of melting ice sat on her right knee. Rainy paused with the jersey halfway down her arms and, after a moment of consideration, shrugged it back up onto her shoulders.

"Hey," Marcy said. "Where's your buddy?"

Rainy pressed her lips together. "Why aren't you with the rest of the team?"

Marcy patted the towel. "Twisted my knee sliding into second that last time. Nothing major, but David thought I should take care of it."

"Are you okay?"

"Mm-hmm." She gestured around the showers. "And look, I managed to be all by myself with David Buckner and nothing terrible happened to me."

Rainy scoffed and shook her head, taking off her jersey after all. She tossed it onto the bench and unfastened her belt.

"It doesn't hurt anyone to take a little precaution."

"If we treat David like a predator when he hasn't done a damn thing wrong–"

"Yet."

"*Ever*, then we run the risk of making him feel unwanted and unnecessary. He backs away from supporting the team, the Whales decide they don't want to help set up the Women's League, this whole house of cards collapses."

"If the whole thing is built on letting men do whatever they want to us behind closed doors, then I don't think it's worth it."

She finished undressing and went into one of the shower stalls. She started to close the door, but Marcy blocked it with her hand and stepped inside. Rainy put her back to the wall and Marcy stood in front of her. She was apparently unaware of Marcy's nudity.

"David isn't like the other men you've dealt with."

"I'm sure you can find women to say that about every man who's ever been caught with his hand on the wrong butt."

Marcy squeezed her eyes shut, her face twisted in frustration. "Okay. Okay, for the benefit of the doubt, say David *is* secretly a creep. He's never actually done anything to anyone. Can we just... can we just appreciate the fact he's managed to keep his hands to himself? He got us this far. We wouldn't be standing here if~"

She gestured at the floor and, in doing so, realized where they were standing. Being naked in front of Marcy in any context was arousing, and Rainy crossed her arms over her chest to hide the fact her nipples were hard, but the goosebumps on her arms were a decent telltale sign on their own.

"Maybe..." Marcy tried to turn away, but the stall wasn't wide enough to allow it. She ended up with her hip pressed against Rainy's, and they both went stiff. Marcy swallowed the lump in her throat. "Maybe we should put this conversation aside for now."

"Yeah. Probably should."

Marcy put her hand on the door but didn't open it. "You played an amazing game today."

"Thank you."

"You okay? Your arm, you, um... y-you sore...?"

"No, I'm fine. I'm okay."

Marcy nodded and her hair fell across her face. Not reaching up to tuck it behind her ear was the hardest thing Rainy had ever done. She put both hands behind her back to make sure neither went rogue and did it themselves. Marcy opened the door and practically fell out into the main room. She pushed the door shut, and Rainy reached out to flip the latch to lock it.

She waited until she heard Marcy's footsteps fade to silence before she slumped against the side of the stall and covered her face with both hands. After a moment to let the arousal fade, she reached out and twisted the cold water tap as high as it would go.

Moxie was still buzzing with energy after she took a shower and changed into her street clothes, so she borrowed a bicycle from someone who worked at the park and took a quick ride downtown. She planned to just go a mile out and then come back, but she spotted a tavern sign and decided to make a pit stop. She wasn't much of a drinker usually, but the game she'd just left deserved a celebration. The entrance to the bar was in an alley. Not the sign of a hugely reputable establishment, but she'd never really liked the reputable places anyway.

She left the bike next to the door and went inside, found a stool, and motioned to the bartender for service. Someone had left a newspaper on the bar and she pulled it closer. German airships were continuing to bomb London, and the French and Germans were still fighting in Verdun. She hated reading news like that and feeling even a smidgen of relief, but it meant that the games could continue. Baseball would, for at least one more week, belong to them.

"Hey." A man whistled to get her attention. "You at the end, with the Coke bottles on your face."

Moxie lifted her eyebrows and lifted her chin so she could see him through her glasses. He was almost painfully thin and his receding hairline made his head look like the top of a turkey baster. The man narrowed his eyes and pointed a finger at her.

"You were one of the players, weren't you?"

"I'm just having a drink, pal," she said.

The man shoved away from the bar. His stool wobbled behind him. "No, I ain't your pal. And you *are*. You're one of those Chicago girls. You're one of the Shrieks."

Moxie rolled her eyes. "It's not a hard word," she muttered.

"Who do you think you are, coming down here and mocking our Pros that way?"

"I'm not sure you understand how sports work. See, one team is always‑‑"

The man shoved her shoulder hard enough that she had to grab the bar to stay on her stool. The beer sloshed out of her bottle and onto her fingers.

"I ain't gonna have a little girl explain sports to me. We invented sports, sweetheart. Y'all are just the dancing monkeys they're using to justify keeping the grass mowed until the real players get back."

Moxie turned slowly on her stool. "Because all the real players are overseas right now."

"Damn straight."

"All the real men are fighting for God and country, not playing a game."

"God bless America," the man said, smiling smugly.

Moxie tilted her head to the side and scanned up and down the man's body. "So what does that make you? The drunk guy picking fights in the local bar when the 'real' men are all serving?"

A couple of other men in the bar chuckled. Her opponent's cheeks reddened. "I..."

"I'm guessing you weren't a ballplayer before the war, either. So I'm just curious where~"

He took a swing at her. Moxie was shocked by the escalation, but not so surprised that it slowed her down. She hunched her shoulder to deflect the blow, which ended up being a hard slap against her temple. She threw herself off the stool and brought up her fists, prepared to finish what he'd started. But the man behind the bar was already shouting at them.

"Henry! Cut it out, now. You just hush up and sit down, finish your beer. Miss, maybe you oughta leave."

"Maybe I should." She dug in her pocket and tossed a coin onto the bar.

She kept her head up and her pace steady as she left. She didn't want any of the men, but especially Henry, to think she was running away. Her heart pounded against her ribs and she could feel the start of a tremor in her hands as she walked fast toward where she'd left the bicycle.

She was almost there when something wet slapped against her back, right between her shoulders. She spun to see what it was and caught a fist on her chin. She tripped over her feet and stumbled backward, clattering into a pair of trash cans as her feet were tangled in a black bag sitting between them.

"Stupid whore."

It was Henry again. She brought her arms up and made an X in front of her face, and he responded by slugging her in the gut. She doubled over and he grabbed a handful of her hair.

"You were the catcher, huh? Maybe I should mangle these hands up a little~"

Moxie threw her whole body into his. She didn't weigh enough to do any damage, but he was knocked off balance. She stomped the heel of her shoe down on his toe, wishing she was still in her cleats, but he howled in pain just the same. She squirmed away from him and stooped to pick up the first piece of detritus she saw. Sadly, it turned out to be a sodden corner of a cardboard box. She gripped it tight and hurled it into Henry's face.

"Oh god, it's a dead mouse!" she shouted.

Her lie worked. He screamed and twisted to get away, slapping his hands at what he believed to be a rodent. Moxie started to run but slammed into a solid mass, a warm body. The obstacle gripped Moxie's shoulders with both hands and squeezed tight enough that Moxie knew she wouldn't be able to squirm free. She had just enough time to think *oh shit* before the person holding her spoke and revealed herself to be a woman with an accent that indicated she'd been born south of the border.

"Henry Potts. What in the blue blazes do you think you're doing?"

"Ah hell," he grunted, breathless but defeated. "Look, Celia—"

Celia cut him off. "I'm not looking at anything you have to offer, Mr. Potts. Now get the hell out of here 'fore I decide your wife needs to know you're hanging around Elijah's harassing women."

Moxie had gotten her feet back under her and turned to watch Henry slink away. When he was gone, she looked up at her savior. She jerked back when she realized she recognized the woman. Her hair was pinned back and she'd changed into a dress, but just a couple of hours ago, Moxie had been standing on second base next to this woman.

Celia looked down at her and raised a thick eyebrow. Her eyes were heavy-lidded but it made her look more amused than sleepy.

"You okay, sweetie?"

"I…" Moxie frowned. "You're a Pro."

Celia grinned. "Number 2, Celia Torres, at your service. I know you're a Shrike, but I didn't memorize all your names."

"Moxie. Um, Iona Moccia."

"I like Moxie better." She nodded toward the street. "Sorry about him. Don't know what gets into these fools. It's bad enough you made us look like fools at the park, now you're gonna tell everyone our fans are trash."

"Well, I don't think I have to tell anyone about this." She cleared her throat and tugged at the collar of her polo shirt. "I admit that I'm a little surprised you bothered to save my keister, though. We're supposed to be enemies."

Celia grinned and rolled her eyes. "Oh please. Leave that trash on the field. Right now we're just two women who want to play baseball, and that puts us on the same team once the uniforms get put away. And I'm not going to stand by and watch a lady get beaten up just because she's from another town."

Moxie said, "Well, I appreciate it. A lot. I probably got in over my head there."

"Oh, you seemed to have it under control." Celia turned back toward the bar. "Come on. Let's go back inside and I'll buy you a drink. Celebrate that amazing win y'all got away with this afternoon."

Moxie followed her to the door and then realized the discrepancy. "Hey, hold up a second. You're a Pro. I thought that was short for Prohibitionists."

"It is. But that's just the name chosen by the guy who signs our paychecks." She shrugged. "We get paid to play a game we love. For that, I'll wear whatever the hell you want on my shirt."

"You know what, Celia Torres, I think I'm taking a shine to you."

"Peachy," Celia said. "Because we could always use a catcher if you're looking to defect..."

Moxie grinned and opened the door, letting Celia lead the way inside before she followed.

CHAPTER THIRTEEN

SIXTEEN HOURS after leaving Elijah's bar, Moxie found herself standing next to Celia again. Her left foot was on second base, her right foot stretched out so far that she was positioned almost like a crab, shoulders low and forward. She was watching home plate, where Edith had just arrived and was getting into position to knock the ball out of the park.

"You okay?" Celia said under her breath.

"Just fine," Moxie said without turning to look at her. She hoped by keeping her face forward the second basewoman wouldn't see the color in her cheeks. "You?"

Celia chuckled. It was a low, heavy sound, and it made the hairs on the back of Moxie's neck stand up. The feeling wasn't entirely unpleasant.

"Well, sure, *I'm* okay. But it wasn't my first time at Elijah's. So I kind of had an idea about what to expect. From your reaction, it seemed like maybe you were caught off-guard."

Their pitcher threw, Edith swung. Strike one.

Moxie focused on the game taking place in front of her. She rubbed circles over the knees of her uniform pants, the cotton warm against her palms. She didn't let her mind take her back to the night before, to the drink Celia bought her 'to steady her nerves,' or the drinks Moxie had bought them both as a thank you. She didn't think about Celia leaning in, or how her lips had felt on her neck.

Her heart thudded, but that was just because her adrenaline was spiking. Her body was preparing to run, to get to third or maybe home. She was buzzing with exercise and exertion, not from the memory of her fingers curling around the collar of Celia's blouse to keep her from pulling away.

Edith swung at another pitch, stamping her foot on the ground before she squared up next to home plate again. Strike two.

"We don't have to talk about it," Celia said. "I really do just want to be sure you're okay."

Moxie nodded her head. "I'm fine."

Nothing had happened the night before. Maybe her pants had been unzipped by someone else's hand, maybe she'd forgotten to zip up when she left the bathroom. Maybe Moxie's head was swimming from all the alcohol, and thoughts of Marcy and Rainy and what she'd caught them doing. And maybe it just felt fucking fine to have someone's mouth on her neck and someone's hand snaking into her clothes.

And if someone's lips are on your skin and their hand is pressing against your underwear, and if it's been over a year since anything like that had happened to you, then orgasm was only a hormonal reaction.

Her face burned as she thought the word. Because thinking it made her relive it. Sitting in a booth, in public, close enough to other people that she could smell their cologne and perfume mingling. A near-perfect stranger pressed hard against her side, rubbing her and whispering encouragement in her ear. The buzz of feeling her climax building, and building, and then crying out so quietly that no one in the bar even turned their heads to see what had caused it.

The catcher retrieved the ball and lobbed it back to their pitcher.

"I just want to be sure I didn't take advantage." Celia was speaking in a rush, her words slurred a bit since she was trying not to move her lips too much. "That's to say, I know I took a bit of advantage, and I apologize. But at the time, it seemed like what you wanted but over the past few hours I was worried maybe the drinks~"

"I did," Moxie interrupted. "I wanted it. At the time. I..." She hated saying what she was about to say, but she wanted to put Celia's mind at ease. "I wasn't so drunk that I wouldn't have stopped you. Do you follow me?"

"Yeah." Celia sounded relieved. "Thanks for saying."

Moxie nodded. "Don't know what that means for *me*. But it's not your problem."

"No, I guess not. But if you want to talk~"

The bat cracked off Edith's bat and sailed high into the air and the Pros scattered in pursuit.

Moxie charged to third, eternally grateful to Edith for the excuse to run from the conversation as fast as possible.

Marcy let the water cascade over her face to wash away the dirt from her last slide into home. Her whole right side felt like she'd raked it across coals and she was terrified to look down to see how red the skin had gotten. There hadn't been any actual scrapes that she'd seen, which she considered a blessing, but boy did it sting. But it had been worth it.

Her lips curled into a smile. Those last few seconds of the game were seared into her mind's eye. She hoped they never faded. The taste of dirt in her mouth as it stung her eyes. The grunt of the Pros catcher followed by the sound of a baseball hitting the leather of her glove. The smoothness of home plate under her palm, quickly followed by the smack of a ball between her shoulder blades. That interminable pause where it seemed like thousands of Detroiters were holding their breath along with everyone on the field, waiting to hear, waiting for the verdict from the umpire...

"*SAFE!*"

The roar of the crowd had been tinged with rage. After six innings stalled at 5-5, neither team willing to give an inch, Marcy had finally broken through the unbreakable Pro defense and scored a home run, taking their score up to six, handing the Pros their second loss. Marcy had stayed on the ground, suddenly worried about how they would safely get out of the park.

"Come on, Neal."

She reluctantly looked up and saw the Pro catcher standing over her, hand extended. Marcy gripped her forearm, and the beefy woman hauled her to her feet.

"No hard feelings?" Marcy said.

The Pro catcher shrugged and looked up at the crowd. "Maybe it would hurt if we lost to a lousy team. I don't feel too bad losing to y'all."

Marcy considered it and then nodded. "You have a point there."

The catcher slung her arm across Marcy's shoulders and turned her around so they could walk to the dugouts together. She'd seen the other Pros on the field offering their hands to Shrikes players, and she hoped the people in the crowd took the hint. They weren't enemies, not once the game was over.

"We're probably going to see each other in the playoffs if you keep playing the way you have been," Marcy said.

"You better be scared, Neal. Next time we'll be ready for you."

Now, in the shower, the park seemed eerily silent. The crowd couldn't possibly have cleared out so quickly, but at least they weren't banging on the clubhouse door demanding blood.

She finished showering and stepped out of the stall to find Moxie sitting on one of the benches with her back to her. She was still in her uniform. Marcy wrapped herself in a towel.

"Hey, Mox. I'll be finished in a second."

"Okay." Her voice was flat. "Can I ask you a question that might be, uh…"

"You can ask me anything. What's on your mind?"

Moxie took a deep breath. "Rainy is… she was married to a man, right?"

"That might be something you need to talk to her about."

"No, I know. That's not really what I want to talk about." She put her hands on her knees and sat up straight, then stretched. "I did something. With a woman. I've only ever done anything with men. And I like it. I like it a lot. But I… liked what I did with the woman a lot, too."

Marcy sat down next to her on the bench. "No one says you have to pick."

"Don't I, though?"

Marcy shrugged. "Like you said, Rainy was with a fella. And you know that ain't always how she chooses. I've known plenty of women who played both teams."

For some reason that made Moxie flinch and look away. Marcy chuckled and put a hand on her shoulder.

"So to speak. Don't feel bad. Just take the time to figure out what you're thinking, and what you're feeling. Whatever you land on, that'll be just fine."

"Thank you, Marcy. That helps."

"You're welcome." She started to get up, then stopped and looked toward the door. "Is it someone on the team? You don't have to name names. But if it might affect the game~"

"No, it's no one on the team."

Marcy relaxed. "Good. And you don't have to worry about me blabbing to anyone. It stays between us."

"Thank you. Same goes for what I know about you and Rainy."

Marcy nodded and held out her hand, pinky finger extended. Moxie smiled and hooked her own pinky around it. They squeezed and then pulled away from each other with a snap to seal the agreement.

"See you in the clubhouse." She stood up and retrieved her clothes to start getting dressed. "Train leaves at five-forty five in the morning."

"Who are our next victims?"

"Cleveland Hawks."

"Think we've got a chance against them?"

Marcy shrugged. "Who knows? But after the game we just played, I feel like we could take on the whole league and come out rosy."

"From your lips," Moxie said.

Marcy smiled and started dressing. The Hawks were mostly unknown to her, a completely new team created when this Women's National League idea started brewing. That meant they were all rookies, with no experience playing so many games back to back to back. And according to the papers, they'd lost big to the Pros. Marcy didn't want to be overly confident, but their season was currently 4-2, and she didn't see them slowing down any time soon.

***

The next morning, the groggy and grumpy Shrikes gathered together on the dark platform. Rainy hated being up this early. The air was damp with rain, and it felt like dew was forming on her skin as they waited for the train to roll up. She hugged herself against the early morning cold and paced to the far end of the platform, standing under a flickering light inside a cast iron cage. She hoped the bulb would provide a little extra warmth, but it was too weak to make much of a difference.

The station behind them was empty even though the lights in the waiting room were on. The porter had vanished, leaving his post eerily empty.

"Liminal space."

Rainy turned to see Moxie standing nearby. She looked just as frozen as Rainy felt. Moxie smiled sheepishly and gestured at the empty station.

"It's one of those places where the world stops, you know? In a half hour or so, this place will be busy as heck. A couple hours ago, it was probably full of people, too. But right now, we're smack in the middle. It's like, um, being on stage before the curtain goes up."

"Oh." Rainy looked over the empty room again. "I kind of like it."

"I do, too." She shuddered and looked down the tracks again, as if the train was sneaking up on them. "How's your arm? And back and shoulder and..."

Rainy grinned. "All fine. I learned my lesson after the first game."

"Good. Good."

They stood quietly in the halo of the street lamp. Fifteen minutes later, the train to Cleveland rolled in.

They boarded and found their seats. While their bags were being stowed, David appeared at the front of the car. Rainy pulled a face and scanned the seats until she found Rosalind. They exchanged a look as David whistled to get everyone's attention. He had a wooden box tucked under his arm and he patted the short end of it like a drum once the conversations died down.

"Good morning, ladies. And don't worry, you'll have plenty of time for a beauty sleep as we scoot around Lake Erie. But before we get underway, there's something I want to give to y'all."

"Another bonus?" Ida Coe shouted, prompting laughs from her seatmates.

Edith said, "Half a sawbuck doesn't go as far as it used to, Mr. Buckner!"

He chuckled and shook his head. "Not this time, gals, not this time, but I've got something even better." He balanced the box on the back of a seat and opened the top. "I've been promising you this since the season started, and they're finally in. I am proud to present you with the very first set of Chicago Shrike baseball cards!"

There were murmurs of excitement, and several of the girls leaned forward. David pulled the cards from the box and held them like he was about to deal a game of poker.

"Patty, Lorna, Hildy, Rosalind... here you go, ladies. Find yourself and pass them along." He handed the deck to Moxie. "Fans are going to have to mail in for most of these, but some of them are going to be in Cracker Jack boxes starting next week."

The deck reached Rainy. She didn't have to shuffle very far before she saw her own face staring back at her. She slipped it out and passed it along.

The portrait showed her from the waist up, hands on her hips, head turned to reveal her profile as she squinted to something to her right. Her hair was in twin braids on either shoulder. Her cap was pushed high up on her forehead so it wasn't shadowing her face. She was standing against a cherry-red backdrop that almost matched her hair. CRACKER JACK BALL PLAYERS was written above her head, and the portrait was captioned "RAINY, Chicago - Shrikes."

Ida's voice broke above the hum of excited conversation again. "Hey, why do they need to know our measurements?"

Rainy furrowed her brow and flipped the card over. Sure enough, right there next to her position, birthdate, and hometown, it listed her measurements.

"Where'd they even get them?" Ida asked.

David said, "You girls are the ones who insisted on having your uniforms specially-made. You especially, Ida... We, we just thought it was, um, a fascinating... statistic."

"Male players don't have their height and weight listed on *their* cards," Hildy said. "Why do the fans need to know how big Ida's chest is?"

David sighed and ran a hand through his hair. Rainy looked at Ida, who had dropped back down into her seat. She had her arms over her chest and her head down, looking like she regretted bringing it up.

"I'm sorry we didn't run this by you ladies. But the fact is, even if you tried rejecting it, the company insisted. You wouldn't have won the argument. They might have gotten so annoyed they cancel the whole project, and then the Shrikes would be the only team out there not getting the publicity. This is just the way it is."

There were grumbles of surrender as the cards kept getting passed around. Rainy got out of her seat and made her way down the aisle, crouching down next to Ida's seat. The blonde kept her head down but looked over at her, raising an eyebrow.

"Are you okay?" Rainy asked.

Ida shrugged. "It was nice, for a change, to feel like people were paying attention to *me* and not to..." She cut her eyes down toward her chest. "We were supposed to be treated like the guys. We had uniforms like the guys, not sexy little skirts. I just thought maybe I could do something I enjoy and it would be about me. But I guess David's right. It's not worth fighting about it."

Rainy twisted her lips in irritation. "Maybe he's right. I don't believe he is, but in this case with the cards already printed up and on the way out into the world, maybe it is too late to fight. But that means you should fight harder next time. And there's going to be a next time. And you won't be fighting alone. I guarantee it."

Hildy, sitting beside Ida, said, "Well, he *did* apologize."

"And then he got his way," Rainy said. "If it happens enough, he'll stop asking all together." She took the card from Ida's hands and flipped it over. She poked her finger against the measurements. "Remember how it felt to see that the next time he tries to take away our options and say it's for the good of the team."

Ida nodded. "Thanks, Rainy."

Rainy nodded and patted the girl's knee. She got up and returned to her seat to discover Marcy had moved to sit next to her. Rainy sat down and faced forward.

"I heard some of the speech," Marcy said when the train started rolling. "It was good. You might have made a fighter out of her."

"I hope so."

Marcy looked down at her own card. Rainy looked and saw that Marcy's portrait was just her head and shoulders. Her chin was angled up, and her hair was center-parted so it fell on either side of her face like curtains that had been opened. She was frowning and it made her look far more severe than her normal expression.

"I guess I should be glad they didn't ask us to pose like pin-up girls."

Marcy chuckled and lowered her voice. "Although, to be a complete hypocrite, I wouldn't mind having a few of those to look at."

Rainy couldn't help but laugh at that. She sighed and slid down in her seat, resting her feet on the basket of the seat in front of her.

"Wake me when we get to Cleveland."

"Yes, ma'am."

Rainy closed her eyes and settled into the seat as best she could, letting the hum-rumble of the engine lull her to sleep as the train rolled off into Moxie's liminal spaces.

II.
SEVENTH INNING STRETCH

"It's the athletic girl that takes the front seat to-day, and no one can deny it. I only wish that some of our rich sisters would consider the good they can do with only a small part of their wealth and start something like an A.A.U. [Amateur Athletic Union] for girls and bring out healthy girls that will make healthy mothers."
- Ida Schnall, 1913

CHAPTER FOURTEEN

MARCY WOULD never have believed she could sleep on a train. The crush of other passengers, the constant noise and motion, the steam. But after two months of traveling exclusively by rail, she'd discovered she had a natural ability to pass out anywhere. They'd taken a train from Detroit to Cleveland, where they completely shut out the Hawks. Four games, four wins. They had six wins in a row when they boarded the train to go all the way back home to Chicago for a series against the Kansas City Pinks. They lost their first two games, taking the wind out of their sails in a spectacular way, but they came back after being rained out and won both games in a double-header.

Then it was back on a train, trekking east again, all the way to Maryland. Marcy knew she would've been a crazy wreck if she hadn't figured out a way to sleep on a train, so she made it work.

She heard the whistle announce their arrival in Baltimore and opened her eyes. Her head was resting on the window, the glass freezing, and she saw the city flashing by. There was a heavy weight on her chest and she turned carefully to see Ida Coe had fallen asleep using her shoulder as a pillow. At some point during the journey the girl had slipped down enough that they looked like they were sweethearts. Marcy lightly patted Ida's knee.

"Wakey wakey," she whispered.

Ida twitched, then rose up and stretched her arms over her head. "Gosh. Sorry about that, Marcy."

"I don't mind being a pillow for a friend," Marcy said. "How'd you sleep?"

"Pretty well, I guess." She put her hands on the arm of her seat and twisted at the waist until there was a pop in her back loud enough that Marcy heard it. She sighed, put her hands on the other arm, and repeated the twist. Another loud pop, followed by another sigh. "I'll never get used to sleeping in a chair, though. It ain't natural, and as far as I'm concerned, it ain't real sleep."

"I hear you," Marcy said, even though the girl seemed to have been sleeping well enough to leave a little drool on Marcy's shoulder. She ignored it. "But we're in Baltimore for over a week. Plenty of time to luxuriate in the hotel beds."

Ida rolled her eyes. "I keep getting the rollaway. My back hates that center bar!"

"You can room with me. I'll make sure you get a real bed."

"Aw. You're the best, Marcy."

Marcy smiled and bumped Ida's arm with hers. She climbed off the train onto the platform and was startled by David appearing at her side as if he'd been conjured.

"We really ought to hang a bell around your neck," she said.

He ignored her. "How long is it going to take you to get settled at the hotel?"

"I don't know. It depends. I'd like to take a proper nap." She looked at him, suspicious. "Why? What have you got planned?"

"Fella from New York is coming down and wants to do a profile on the team. Manhattan doesn't have a team, so they've got no dog in the fight. It would be a straight character piece. He wants to talk to a couple of the players. I thought you'd be a good choice."

She rolled her eyes. "You mean you thought I'd be least likely to tell you to take a hike."

David shrugged and looked at the women scurrying over the platform, retrieving their bags and stretching out kinks from the long train ride.

"Sometimes it seems like you're the only one of these girls who actually knows we're running a business. We've gotta promote ourselves! Yourselves. You've gotta promote *yourselves*."

"We are! They all are. Rainy and Ida are signing their cards left and right. We've got a schedule for going to local Sutton Sweets stores to make those silly public appearances. And all of us were glad-handing the crowd after all our home games. We spent two hours running around the field and then we had to stand there and greet people for another hour before we could get out of our uniforms and clean up. Don't say we're not doing our parts."

David put his hands on his hips. "Okay, okay, you're trying. I'll admit, you're trying. But this is big. This is a New York paper, Marcy! It gets national coverage, suddenly the Chicago Shrikes are being talked about from coast to coast. There are other teams out there, you know. Teams in Phoenix and San Fran, up in Seattle. And if you make it to the end of the road, you're going to be facing one of them for all the marbles. I want them to know and fear Caroline Rainy before that happens. I want them to be so scared they can't swing straight!"

She couldn't help but smile at his enthusiasm. "Fine. Okay. I'll talk to the reporter."

"At the field, in uniform."

Her smile vanished again. "We don't even have a game today!"

"They want it for color! They want a photographer to--"

"Oh good God."

"--get some action shots," he raised his voice to drown her out. "And unless you want them running around the field during the game, this is the best way to get 'em. Cracker Jack cards are one thing, but we need to put names to faces. We need people to know their Marcys from their Moxies, their Rainys from their Rosalinds."

"There's no mistaking Rainy," Edith said as she walked by. "Who else has hair that red?"

David laughed. "Well, when they have color pictures in the paper, we'll be sure to get Rainy in them. But for now it should be you and a couple other girls." He looked to see who was still nearby. "Moxie, Ida, Rosalind... whoever you think would be willing."

"I'll ask," Marcy said, "but no promises."

"I can only ask you to ask," David said, bowing forward in a not-quite sarcastic way. "Thank you, Marcy."

She grumbled a response and slung the strap of her bag over her shoulder. Ida came up behind her and put a hand on her shoulder.

"I'll go with you."

"You don't have to," Marcy said. "I can tell him I looked for you on the way to the hotel but you slipped away from me."

Ida smiled. "I appreciate the offer but nah. He made good points.

We need to get our faces out there. Right now we're just girls playing baseball. They might have a harder time sneering at us if they think we're real people."

"You're a smart cookie, Ida Coe."

"Thanks, hon." She winked one baby-blue eye and smiled, giving herself dimples. "Don't let it get around. I got a reputation to protect."

Marcy joined the team on the trek to the hotel. She spent the trip asking Moxie and Rosalind if they were up for the charade, and they agreed so she wouldn't be stuck doing it alone. The car David had gotten for them waited so they could drop off their bags and unpack their uniforms. The driver looked surprised when they piled into the backseat with the garment bags on their laps. He turned around to face him, his arm draped over the back of his seat. He couldn't have been more than seventeen, all eyes and ears to make up for the fact he barely had a chin.

"Oh, gosh. I think Mr. Buckner expected you to be in uniform for the ride to the park."

Marcy narrowed her eyes. "Why would you think that?"

He looked flustered. "Well, uh." He pushed up his cap to scratch his scalp. "He told me to be sure I went real slow. And he might've told me to blow the horn if there were a lot of people on the street."

Marcy clenched her jaw. Rosalind shook her head and said, "The blockhead tried to make a little parade out of us."

The driver said, "I don't mind waiting if you want to run back inside and–"

"We're fine the way we are," Marcy said. "And don't bother with any of the theatrics Mr. Buckner mentioned. Just get us to the park, please, with haste."

He tucked his cap back into place and twisted back around in the seat. "Yes, ma'am." He started the ignition and the car rumbled away from the curb. After going a block in silence, he cleared his throat. "And I just wanted to let you ladies know, um, I'm a real big baseball fan. I'm real excited to see the game tomorrow, even if you are girls."

Marcy forced a smile so big it made her cheeks hurt. "Well, aren't you sweet."

She didn't know if he picked up on the sarcasm in her voice, but he shifted uncomfortably in the seat and hunched forward as if he was anticipating a blow to the back of the head.

The rest of the ride was spent in silence.

"We pray there will be peace..."

The ball hummed toward Marcy. She swung a wide arc, missed, grunted. She tapped the end of her bat in the dirt and replaced it on her shoulder.

"...and we pray our boys will all come home safe and sound."

She swung at the next sailing ball. Another miss. She narrowed her eyes and stuck out her chin. She shifted her weight from one foot, then the other, and then planted her cleats firmly in the dirt in anticipation of the third pitch.

"...But we pray neither happens tomorrow."

She swung, the bat cracked against the rawhide of the ball. The bat dropped and she was off like a shot to first base.

Rosalind, their stand-in pitcher for this exhibition, straightened and pushed her cap up with a knuckle to follow the ball's arc across the field. Moxie and Ida were both running after it but, fast as they were, it was clear Marcy could round the bases before either of them got back to her with the ball to take her out. She slowed down to a trot and crossed home as if she was out for a casual stroll.

The reporter raised an eyebrow and offered a quiet round of applause as he came closer. He was an older man, stooped and so thin that his clothes draped over him. But he had sharp eyes and spoke with a reassuringly deep voice that sounded like it should be coming from a much younger man.

"Impressive swing," he said, "but I hope you're a little faster than that when it really counts."

Marcy shrugged. "No point in tiring myself out when it doesn't count, right?"

She looked out on the field. The photographer was using a box camera to photograph Ida.

"I suppose that's a good point," he said. "It's really something to see you ladies playing real baseball. Actual baseball, I mean, not the sort ladies usually play."

"We're more than capable of playing the same game men play. We can swing the bat just as hard, we can run just as fast. There's no reason not to let women play the game."

He gestured around them. "Well, right now you're using the park of a minor league team for your game. And back home, you're using the Whales park. Is that correct?" He gave her a comical shrug. "What does happen when the boys come home and you suddenly don't have a park anymore?"

"We'll figure something out," Marcy said, filling her voice with more certainty than she felt. "Maybe we can claim squatters' rights, hm? Make the boys earn the park back. I think the Shrikes could hold their own against the Whales. What do you think?"

He chuckled and shook his head. "Hard to say, Miss Neal. I suppose we'll see tomorrow, hm?"

"Are you going to be in the crowd?"

"I might, I might." He squinted out over the field. "I do enjoy the game. And you ladies seem to have a handle on it."

"Gee, thanks, mister," Marcy said flatly.

He chuckled and slipped his pencil into the wire spiral on his notebook. "Sorry, Miss Neal, but I meant it as a compliment. Good luck tomorrow. The Starlings are tougher than the name implies."

"They'd almost have to be, wouldn't they?"

He laughed louder at that and touched a finger to his brow in a salute as he turned and strode away. Marcy retrieved her bat and lifted it with one hand, then let it fall and swing alongside her leg. She hadn't planned on those two strikes. She had been hoping she would be able to make a run before she had to finish the thought, which she hadn't actually put any thought into at all. She decided in the end it didn't matter what she said. The reporter, whose name she'd already forgotten, would probably just focus on their makeup or the way their butts looked in these 'cute little uniform pants.'

Rosalind came down off the mound and joined her by home plate. "Rainy's going to think I'm after her position."

"It's good for people to know they can be replaced," Marcy said. "Keeps everyone on their toes."

Rosalind cleared her throat. "Actually, on that topic. I was wondering if I could miss the game tomorrow."

Marcy was surprised, but then she remembered Rosalind's mysterious inquiry about Baltimore when she was first recruiting the team.

"We can probably rotate up one of the reserves," Marcy said, already flipping through a mental file of names. Nell would probably jump at the chance. "Is everything okay?"

Rosalind nodded, but wouldn't meet Marcy's eye. "Sure, everything's fine. There's just something I gotta do, and I don't want to be all tired and sweaty from the game when I do it."

"Makes sense. Let me know if you need anything."

"Will do."

Marcy watched her go. She tried to quiet her brain and stop it from spinning. Rosalind, like every member of the team, had a right to privacy and to keep her own secrets. As long as it didn't affect her playing, Marcy didn't see any reason to pry.

Still, it did vex her a bit. Rosalind looked positively spooked, and it took a good decade off her looks. Rosalind was a tough cookie even on bad days but just now she had transformed into a nervous teenager. She couldn't help but wonder what might've had that effect on such a normally stoic dame like Rosalind O'Brien.

CHAPTER FIFTEEN

THE NEWSPAPER in Rosalind's lap was folded to the sports section. It had been in the seat when she boarded the streetcar. Originally she'd just planned to move it to another seat, but then she recognized Marcy in the small photograph next to the article. She stared at the headline to avoid looking out the window. CHI GALS LOOKING FOR BIG DIAMOND by Otis Fellows. She had tried to read it several times but her brain wouldn't focus long enough to make sense of anything. She finally determined he hadn't said anything too bad or embarrassing and put the whole thing out of her mind. With nothing else to distract her, she crossed her hands on top of the paper and leaned back against the headrest.

She honestly didn't know what she was doing. It was madness, temporary insanity. But the second Marcy mentioned road games, the idea popped into her brain. And once it was there, well, it was impossible to ignore it. There was no way she'd ever have been able to afford a trip to Baltimore on her paycheck at the soda shop. But as a member of a baseball team, all she had to do was be patient and some old man in an office that reeked of cigars would pay the way for her.

And now she was here. She was a ballplayer, which by itself was something she couldn't quite believe, and she was riding the bus to an address she'd seen once on the back of an envelope she received over a year earlier.

The whole endeavor was going to be a waste of time. She just knew it. So there was no reason to be anxious about what was waiting at the end of this streetcar ride. The only thing she had to look forward to was disappointment and irritation.

"Federal Street!"

The streetcar slowed down at the driver's announcement, and several other passengers stood up. Rosalind took a deep breath and got out of her seat as well. She swallowed the lump in her throat and dropped the paper back where she'd found it. She waited until it was her time to disembark and followed the trio of men in suits out onto the sidewalk.

She had a slip of paper in her pocket and she slipped it out to re-read the address. She looked at the houses up and down the street and was horrified to see they were all identical. The same cookie-cutter lawns, the same two-level steps leading up to copycat front porches in front of houses that varied from each other only in the tiniest, most superficial ways.

"Gadzooks," she muttered under her breath.

"Can I help you, miss?"

She turned toward the voice. A man in a fedora was smiling at her from a few steps away. He raised his eyebrows, prompting her to answer. She wasn't used to men approaching her like this, in that chipper, helpful way. She usually dressed to dissuade anyone from getting too close. But at the moment she had done away with her slacks and men's shirt for a bright yellow dress borrowed from Ida. She'd even done her hair and put on far more makeup than she would ever have worn in everyday life. Ida had also helped her figure out just the right shade of lipstick the night before. Now here she was, five seconds in stockings and heels, and some Joe was flirting with her.

Then again, she *did* need help...

"I-I suppose you could. I'm looking for 2807..."

His smile widened and he stretched an arm out to point. "You were almost right on top of it. That's the one, right there."

She smiled her gratitude to him. "I suppose I could have taken a second to look around before I troubled you."

"No trouble at all." He touched the brim of his hat, then hurried along on his way.

Rosalind looked up at the house he'd indicated. She didn't feel like herself at all, what with the hair and the heels and the damned bag she now held with both hands. The dress was borrowed from Ida, the heels from Edith, and the purse belonged to Hildy. They had packed them along for the rare nights they weren't playing in the hopes Baltimore had a vibrant night life. They probably thought Rosalind was using them to troll for a husband of her own. Rosalind didn't want to know what kind of husband she'd attract in Ida's dress, which was baggy on top and way too tight in the hips. She felt like a poorly-packed sausage. But she'd come too far to turn back now.

She wet her lips, grimacing when she tasted the lipstick she'd smeared on. She decided that the sooner she got it over with, the quicker she could be back with the team. She looked at her watch. The game would be starting about now... it killed her not to be there with them.

There was movement at the front door of the house which inspired her terror. She snapped her head up as the curtain in the arc of glass fell back into place. Rosalind held her breath.

The door opened.

Daisy Compton stepped out.

Perfectly porcelain skin, hair just as inky black as it had ever been, currently styled into a chignon with a wave that fell across one eye. Her dress was yellow, like she was trying to live up to her name.

Rosalind exhaled sharply and tears popped into her eyes. She hadn't realized until that exact moment how certain she'd been that Daisy was dead. But here she was, standing on her front stoop looking like she was the one who'd seen a ghost, like it was taking all *her* power not to start running. Rosalind knew she could beat the streetcar to its next stop. And to be perfectly honest, she'd done what she set out to do. She'd confirmed Daisy was still alive. She could go back now, there was no reason to actually speak with her.

"Hello," Rosalind said, raising her voice to be heard from the sidewalk.

Daisy blinked like a trance had been broken. She looked east down the street and then took a step back over the threshold.

"W-would you like to come in?"

There was a fence between the sidewalk and the steps. Rosalind put a hand on the gate, but hesitated.

"Is he home...?"

Daisy shook her head. "Please, before anyone sees you."

Rosalind felt ashamed. Of course that was Daisy's concern. Nosy neighbors, probably friends of hers, who would ask about the mystery woman standing in front of their house.

She opened the gate and walked up the steps. Daisy took a step aside and waited to come into the house behind her.

The foyer smelled like cinnamon, a sharp but not unpleasant scent, and not the one she'd been expecting.

"What are you doing here, Ros?"

She stepped around Rosalind and glared hard at her. Life had snapped into her eyes as soon as the door was closed, and she was no longer the posed mannequin that had been frozen on the stoop. Her voice had been sharp and angry when she asked the question, and it cut through Rosalind's fear and worry as well as her relief to see Daisy alive and well.

"You stopped replying to my letters."

"Well, I..." Daisy looked down at her hands. She worried the nail of her right thumb. "I ran out of things to say."

"Then you could have said that," Rosalind said. "You could have told me to stop writing."

Daisy shook her head. "I didn't want that." Her voice was meek and small. "I hated it when the letters finally stopped coming. Even though I understood why you gave up."

"I thought you were dead. I hoped you weren't. I prayed you weren't. But after the fifth or sixth letter without hearing a peep in return, what else was I supposed to think."

"I got married," Daisy said, sweeping her hand around to indicate the house. "Married people are busy. I-I just, I didn't have the time..."

Rosalind tensed. "I know full well you got married."

Daisy looked away.

Rosalind glanced toward the parlor, the dining room. "Where is he?"

"Not here. He's..." She chuckled. "He's actually down at the pool hall listening to the game. He invited me to go, but I didn't want... I-I can't hear..."

Rosalind nodded. "I understand."

"I hear you're doing well. The Shrikes, I mean. Even Robert is impressed, and he wasn't keen on the idea of women playing at all. You're starting to win him over."

"I'm elated," Rosalind said flatly.

Daisy flinched and looked away.

Silence fell over them. Rosalind could hear a clock ticking somewhere in the house. She crossed her arms over her chest and looked down at her shoes. Edith's stupid high heels, which pinched her toes.

"I just wanted to make sure you were alive. I didn't intend to talk to you or even interrupt your life at all. I just needed to know for sure, is all. And now that I do, I also know you ignored my letters on purpose, so I guess, um, I guess I can go~"

"No!" Daisy lunged forward, then immediately took a step back. "Please. Ros. I didn't stop responding because~" She growled low in her throat and turned her back on Rosalind. "The things I wanted to say to you, I couldn't bear anyone reading them. Not even you. And what if my postman managed to get the envelope open and read it? What if Robert found the letter before I could get it into an envelope?"

Rosalind couldn't help wondering what Daisy had planned to write that would be so scandalous.

"But I kept all your notes," Daisy admitted. She smiled wryly. "I folded them up real tight and I put them in the drawer with my lady things. Robert wouldn't go in there with a gun to his head. I read them sometimes when he's at work. You said such lovely things."

Rosalind didn't expect how much it would hurt to be in the same room with her again. Her heart was pounding and she couldn't catch her breath. It was like she was having a panic attack.

"I think I need to go," she said, turning to the door.

"No! You just got here. Please, Ros. I've missed you."

"You had your chance." The amount of venom in her voice surprised her.

Daisy flinched. "I know. But I... I wasn't... I..."

Rosalind held up a hand. "You don't owe me an apology."

"Don't I?"

Daisy took Rosalind's raised hand in both of hers, pressing her thumbs into the palm. A spike went into Rosalind's heart. Her fingers curled down. The fingernails were blunt, and miraculously clean. She'd taken care to scrub them with soap before she left the hotel. She hadn't borrowed any polish, though Ida had offered. Now she regretted it.

Daisy brushed her thumb over the backs of Rosalind's fingers. "I can't give you what you came here for."

Rosalind's eyes burned. "I know. I mean, no. I didn't come here for anything. I just wanted to see you. To know for sure. I didn't..."

"Shh." Daisy bent down and kissed the back of Rosalind's hand.

Then she took a step back until her shoulders touched the wall. "I can't give it to you. But you can take it."

Rosalind blushed. She looked down Daisy's body, taking in the dress and the long legs and the smell of perfume and...

"Daisy, I don't know~"

"It's okay. He won't be home any time soon. You could do anything and no one would ever know. Except for you. And me."

Rosalind swallowed hard. She took a step forward. Daisy pressed harder against the wall.

"You should go upstairs," Rosalind said.

"No," Daisy said.

Rosalind put her hands on Daisy's cheeks and tilted her head back. "Please go upstairs."

"Only if you follow me up."

"Daisy..."

"I've missed you saying my name."

Rosalind closed her eyes and rested her forehead against Daisy's. "I can't."

"No, *I* can't." Daisy linked her fingers with Rosalind's and brought her hand up. She pushed up Rosalind's forefinger and then guided it to her mouth. She ran the tip of it over her bottom lip, then leaned forward to take it onto her tongue. She sucked slowly and looked at Rosalind's eyes until the lids rose and they saw each other.

"I can't," Daisy said again. "But I won't stop you."

Rosalind took her hand from Daisy. She held eye contact as she reached down and started pulling up the hem of Daisy's dress. She brushed the back of her hand over Daisy's thigh. She wasn't wearing stockings, and her skin was warm.

Daisy bit her bottom lip. Rosalind slid her hand higher. Daisy made a quiet noise in the back of her throat and leaned forward.

"Oh no," Rosalind whispered.

"Please," Daisy sighed.

It was all Rosalind needed. She moved her hand higher and leaned in to kiss Daisy's lips.

The pool hall wasn't far from the house Daisy shared with her husband. Rosalind walked the distance in less than ten minutes. She barely remembered leaving the house. She was still weak-kneed and lost in a loop of sensations and actions and scents, tastes... She didn't have a destination in mind when she set out. But then she saw a sign and felt drawn to it.

She walked into a haze of cigar smoke and a hum of conversation. Men's laughter. The far end of the room had a platform set up with a telegraph machine in front of a large posterboard with a picture of a baseball diamond printed on it. Rosalind weaved through the tables and ignored the men to focus on the chits of paper dotting the diamond.

It showed the top of the seventh, the Shrikes' most recent turn at bat. The operators only got updates twice an inning, so she could see their entire attempt at one glance. 8 MOCCIA had scored the first run, taking the Shrikes up to five. Then 5 COE and 4 KOENIG struck out. 7 NEAL saved the day by getting on first, and then 1 LOWELL pushed her to third. Marcy and Lorna both scored runs before 11 MARTIN struck out.

Rosalind felt a pang of guilt that it was her replacement who ended the inning for them. But according to another note hanging on the corkboard, the score was currently 7-2 in favor of the visitors. The last two innings would have to be spectacular for the Starlings if they had a chance of a comeback.

She went to the bar and tapped one of the men on the shoulder. "Pardon me."

He turned. He had closed-cropped black hair and a face that looked like it had been drawn by an advertiser. Perfect eyes, perfect nose, sharp jawline. He was made for pictures, and he smiled like he knew it. Rosalind, of course, recognized him immediately. She'd seen him twenty minutes ago in a framed photograph on the mantle while she fucked his wife against the coffee table.

"Uh oh, fellas," Robert said before she could ask her question. "I told you this would happen. You start letting gals play the game, they start infesting everything connected to the game, too. It's a slippery slope!"

"Why did you marry him?"

They were lying next to each other on the living room floor, sweaty, mostly clothed but with the vital parts exposed. Sweating, breathing heavily. Rosalind's hand on Daisy's thigh. Daisy's hand between her own legs, protecting the unbearably sensitive part of her.

"He could give me a home."

"I could've given you a home."

Daisy closed her eyes and shook her head slowly. "Not together. Not like this."

"Okay. So. You wanted a home. Why him?"

"He's kind. Successful. Very handsome."

"There are a lot of men like that out there."

Daisy rolled onto her side and looked at Rosalind's profile. After a long time, Rosalind turned her head to look back at her. She raised an eyebrow, still waiting for an answer to her question. Daisy cupped Rosalind's exposed breast and brushed her thumb over the nipple.

"Because his name is Robert. And that gives me a second to save myself if I start to say a different name when he's fucking me."

Robert laughed and slapped Rosalind's arm a little harder than absolutely necessary. "Sorry, sweetheart. I'm just joshing you. You better get used to that if you're going to hang around here." He turned back to the bar and pulled a bowl of pretzels closer. "Are you a fan of the Starlings?"

"The Shrikes, actually. Hopefully you won't hold that against me."

Daisy throwing her head back, the flush of red spreading over her chest as she ground her hips down against Rosalind's thigh. Daisy's hair a mess of tangles that covered her eyes like a veil.

"It takes all kinds," Robert said. "No one takes these girl games too seriously. It's just a lark. Killing time until the real players come back."

"Does he fuck you like this?" Rosalind asked, lips wet from Daisy's sex.

"Never," Daisy gasped, then put her hand on top of Rosalind's head and pushed her back down.

"Just don't root for them too loudly in here," Robert continued.

"Sure," Rosalind said. "I thought I might stay for the rest of the game. See who wins."

Robert looked at the corkboard. "I'd say it's pretty much a done deal at this point. But who knows? If they keep going, maybe our local gals will have a trick up their sleeve."

Rosalind had been distracted by the mental image of Daisy in her husband's bathroom, a tub of water on the counter, bent over to wash evidence of their affair from her thighs. It took her a moment to register what he had said.

"Sorry, pardon? If they keep going...?"

"They might stop the game, 'cause of what happened." He looked at her and realized she didn't know what he meant. "I thought that was why you came in here so late in the game."

Rosalind shook her head. *I was late because after the fifth orgasm I gave your wife,* she took her time evening the score. But now that he mentioned it, she was a bit surprised the game was only in the seventh inning.

"I haven't heard anything. What happened?"

Robert picked up his mug and, casual as anything, said, "Caroline Rainy might've killed one of our girls."

CHAPTER SIXTEEN

RAINY'S HANDS wouldn't stop shaking. She stared at them, tried to will them to stop, but that only increased her distance from the action. The floor went blurry around them. She could hear the rest of the team talking but it sounded like they were all muttering into tin-can phones, their words vibrating over pieces of string between them. Rainy clenched her fists but that only made the shaking more noticeable.

She could still hear the crack, the way that poor girl's head snapped back, the blood. Almost a perfect arc of red following her as she fell. And then the utter silence of the crowd. Thousands of screaming fans hushed in an instant. The moment was so surreal that goosebumps had risen on Rainy's arms even though it was a hot day. She stared at the girl on the ground as the other Starlings ran to her, soon obscuring the sight as they crowded around her.

Someone touched Rainy's shoulder, and that was how she realized she was about to fall over. The person touching her had actually caught her, was holding her up.

"...okay... get ... look at me, baby."

Rainy turned her head and saw Marcy's eyes. "Mars?" she said.

Marcy said something and pushed her. She was forced to walk or fall down. The next thing she knew, the sun was out of her eyes. Then she was being sat down, and something cold and wet was on top of her head. It dripped down over her temples.

"...said a word since... worried..."

She suddenly wondered if the game was over. Who was pitching? Lucille? She sat up straighter and the towel flopped off her head, tumbling down her back. Marcy and Moxie were standing in front of her, and they stopped their conversation to look at her.

"Caro?" Marcy said.

"Is she dead?"

Moxie started to say something, but Marcy cut her off. "No. She's not dead."

Rainy was focused on Moxie. She was pale and looked frazzled. "You were right there. You saw it. Is she... was..." She pressed her lips together and narrowed her eyes, as if she was trying to send the question from brain to brain without putting it into words.

"It was pretty bad, Rainy, I'm not gonna lie. The pitch hit her square in the face. And when she fell, I don't..." She flinched and shook her head. "But she was crying when the team shoved me away. So that means she was still alive."

"Okay," Rainy said softly. She hung her head again and nodded. "Okay."

Marcy sat down on the bench next to Rainy. "David is out talking to their manager right now. They don't know if they're going to end the game or power through. If they decide to keep going, I'm putting Lucille in for you. I don't think you'll fight me on that."

Rainy shook her head and put her hands over her face.

"Okay," Marcy whispered. She stroked Rainy's hair. "I'm sorry, baby."

She didn't know how long she sat there crying before the door to the clubhouse banged open. She jumped at the sound. Marcy's hand tightened on her shoulder as she made a quiet calming sound.

"The show must go on," David said. "And I need at least one of you out there, because with Rosalind playing the ghost, the reserve tank is running dry."

Moxie said, "What happened to the girl?"

"The girl?" David almost seemed confused for a second. "Rita Hicks. She'll be fine. It'll whistle when she breathes for the rest of her life, but otherwise..." He laughed.

Marcy said, "For God's sake, David. We were afraid she was dead."

"No. She's getting patched up right now. It'll probably end up going great for her. She gets to be the hero when she gets patched up and walks out for her next game. The papers are probably already writing up stories making her an icon. Her nose will never be the same, but that's her own damn fault. People in the crowd, and the ump, all confirmed that she was crowding the plate. And her own teammates said she has a habit of using hit-by-pitch as a trick to get herself on base. Take it as a compliment, Rainy. She didn't think she'd be able to hit anything you threw so she decided to get hit *by* you."

Rainy lifted her head to glare at him. "Go fuck yourself, Buckner."

He looked surprised, then angry, and then he lifted his hands in defeat. "I'm not going to fight. But I really do need players out there. Everyone agrees to go ahead and finish the inning and right now I don't have a catcher or a shortstop."

Marcy looked at Rainy, who nodded at her. "Go on."

"Are you sure?"

"Go," Rainy said.

Moxie reached out and rested her hand on top of Rainy's head. "We'll come find you after the game."

"Thanks," Rainy said softly.

David went to the door and held it open for Marcy and Moxie. Once they were out, he let the door close and went back to Rainy. He crouched in front of her.

"Are you going to be okay for tomorrow's game?"

She sniffled and shook her head, going for the honest answer. "I don't know."

David sighed and looked at the floor. "We need you, Caroline. Lucille is a fine pitcher, but there's a reason she's a reserve. And your name is plastered all over the paper. You're the one people want to see when they buy a ticket to a Shrikes game."

"I know the team is counting on me."

"Yeah. And you know who else is counting on you? Rita Hicks. What happened was entirely her fault. And I guarantee she's going to consider it worth the price of a busted schnoz if it means she got into your head. We're slaughtering these folks. And if we've got you throwing, we're going to keep slaughtering them for the next few games. So they're counting on you taking this personal."

Rainy nodded. There was sense in what he was saying.

He patted her knee. "You can sit out the rest of the game. Of course you can." His hand was still now, but it remained on her knee like a dead weight. "Besides, it's not like it's going to make much difference for them at this point. But I want your guarantee that you'll be back out there tomorrow. Can you do that for me?"

"I'll be out there." Rainy tried to make it sound like she meant it.

"Attagirl."

He squeezed her knee, then moved his hand so that it rested more on her thigh. He leaned forward and slightly rose up out of his crouch, putting his other hand on her cheek.

"Hey, stop–"

"Shh," he said, and then pressed his lips to hers.

Rainy swung her foot up between his legs, but the angle was wrong and she only kicked air. He moved closer to her and kissed her harder, so she went for her backup plan. She backed up, pushed her ass off the bench, and let gravity pull her away from him. A bonus effect was that it brought her leg up higher and she finally landed a kick to his crotch. He bent double, grunting, as Rainy retreated on her hands to increase the distance between them.

The clubhouse door swung open again. "I forgot I had your cap in my pocket." Marcy stopped and stared at the situation in front of her. She tilted her head to the side, her face expressionless. "David?"

He chuckled nervously and rubbed the back of his hand over his mouth. He was still standing oddly, probably due to the pain in his crotch.

"This is embarrassing," he said. "Caroline and I have been, um... we've been kind of flirting back and forth since the season started. I was trying to comfort her and I think I moved a little fast for her."

Marcy came closer, moving like she was in slow motion. "Flirting..."

David chuckled and shrugged. "Typical man, I suppose. I picked the wrong time to, ah, to take things further. But I thought she needed a little extra comfort. And given the fact she's been coming on to me from the first day, I just–"

Marcy punched him in the face.

It was such a sudden, untelegraphed blow that he stumbled backward more out of surprise than pain. There was nothing slow about Marcy's next moves, as she punched him again, and a third time. She grabbed a handful of his shirt when he started to fall and pulled him back up to punch him once more. He slapped at her arms and she let him go with a shove, which forced him to fall down.

By the time Rainy got on her feet, Marcy had started kicking him. He was curled in a ball under a bench, but Marcy was unrelenting.

"Mars, stop. *Mars. Stop.*"

"Fucking fucker, fucking fucking fucker, fucking..."

Rainy wrapped her arm around Marcy's torso and physically moved her, the heels of her cleats dragging across the floor. She slammed Marcy hard against the wall and got in front of her, close enough that her face would be the only thing Marcy saw.

"Look at me. Look at me, Marcy."

The blue eyes shifted back into focus, the pupils shifting as the rage faded. She was still breathing hard, nostrils flaring, lips puffing out with each exhale. Rainy could feel the heat emanating off her skin.

"I defended him."

"I know, baby. I know." Marcy's hair had fallen into her face during her tirade. Rainy brushed it back and tucked it behind her ear. She let her fingers brush over the ridge down to the lobe. "I'm okay, though. He didn't do anything."

David was coughing on the floor behind them. "Marcy." He coughed again and then spit, groaned. "I'm sorry if I led you on..."

Rainy turned on him. "Shut the fuck up before I let her go, motherfucker."

David actually cowed away from that threat. He held up his hands to prevent any further violence. "I don't know what kind of sisterhood thing I got in the middle of~"

"Get out.," Marcy said.

"Right. Probably the best if I..." He started to stand up and grunted, pressing a hand against his gut. "I'll give you ladies a little space."

"Not out of the room." Marcy gently pushed Rainy out of her way and walked toward him. David, proving he wasn't a complete idiot, retreated to maintain the distance between them. "Out of the park. Out of Baltimore. Out of the fucking profession. Go back to Chicago. Resign. Find a new line of work. You are no longer employed by the Shrike organization."

David scoffed. He smiled, wincing when the skin of his split lip pulled. "You're crazy. You don't have the power to do that."

"I have the power to make sure every one of these women refuses to play until you're fired."

"The front office will have to decide what's easier to replace,"

Rainy said. "A successful team or a useless manager. Marcy has been doing the bulk of your job anyway."

David glared, blood dripping off his chin. "This is insane. You're both insane. I was just trying to comfort a player who~"

"We know what you were trying to do." Marcy's eyes were wild. She hadn't blinked since she walked into the room. "I ignored it. I explained it away. I protected you. But I'm done. If you don't get out of my sight immediately, I swear I'll walk out that door and pull every single one of our women off the field. And we won't lift another bat until you're gone."

"You'll hear about this," David said, moving gingerly toward the door.

Marcy said, "I'm sure we will. You run home and tattle on yourself."

David slammed through the door so hard it smacked the wall. The clubhouse was suddenly silent and empty of tension, and the change made Rainy lightheaded. She put a hand on Marcy's shoulder for support.

"I'm going to regret that," she said.

"It had to happen."

Marcy turned to look at her. "Oh, I don't regret that it happened. I'm going to regret not waiting until Rosalind was here with a tub of popcorn."

Rainy laughed, and Marcy stepped closer and wrapped her in a hug. Rainy's laugh turned into a sob, and she clung to her.

"Are you okay?" Marcy asked softly against the collar of Rainy's jersey.

"I will be," Rainy said. "Thank you."

Rainy pulled back and kissed Marcy's cheek, then her lips. Marcy started to pull back, but Rainy whispered, "It's okay," and kissed her harder. She wanted to erase the feel of David's mouth, that sloppy and disgusting pressure, with something she chose. It took Marcy a few seconds to reciprocate. When she did, she moaned quietly in surrender and wrapped her arms around Rainy's waist to pull her close.

"I've missed you," Rainy whispered.

"Caro..."

"I love you."

Marcy tensed and pulled away from her. "Don't say that right now. Now after..." She gestured at the bench. "Or..." She swung her arm in the direction of the field. "Don't. Don't say it *now*. Not after everything that just happened."

Rainy said, "But I want to say it now."

"Great." Marcy bent down to pick up Rainy's cap, which she'd dropped when she realized what she'd walked in on. She dusted it off and placed it on Rainy's head. "But I mean it. Don't tell me now."

"When? When can I tell you?"

Marcy smiled sadly. She cupped Rainy's cheek and leaned in to kiss the corner of her mouth.

"Tell me when we win the Series."

She let her hand linger for a moment longer, then dropped it and walked out of the locker room.

***

Rosalind returned to Baltimore with too much on her mind to process the past twenty-four hours. Everything that happened with Daisy had felt like an ending, but she was terrified to close that book. She was terrified of what might happen to Daisy if she persisted. But what if she just walked away? Could she leave Daisy with that man? Then again, she had chosen that life for herself. It wasn't Rosalind's place to save her, if that was even what Daisy would want.

That all would have been enough to distract her for an entire trip, but she also had to worry about what happened with Rainy and the player who had been hit. Would the team be fined? Would there be criminal charges? Assault? No, it certainly wouldn't go that far. But what if the other girl was really hurt? That might twist anybody, and Rainy was kind enough to feel responsible. Would it affect her performance? Had they just lost their star player? It was a disgusting thought to have when Rita Hicks might be seriously injured, but Rosalind didn't know her. She could only spare empathy for the people she actually knew.

When she got back, she discovered there was more to be concerned about. She'd run into Moxie in the lobby of the hotel and got a quick, breathless recap of what apparently happened in the locker room. "David finally fucking did it," she said, eyes wide behind her glasses. "He went after Rainy. Marcy caught him. Knocked his lights out! Hildy said she saw him and he had blood all over the bottom of his face."

Rosalind had been too stunned to ask questions, but her joy at David Buckner being out of their lives was tempered by horror for the implications of what it meant for the team. It was basically the final nail in their coffin, unless Marcy pulled some miracle out of her cap in the next few weeks.

There was nothing she could do about any of the various crises, so she went up to her room. She traded her dress for her own clothes, sighing with relief as the she slid into the cotton, and washed the makeup off her face. She carefully checked the dress for any stains or damage, remembering how frantically Daisy had worked the buttons, before she zipped it back into its garment bag and carried it down the hall to Ida Coe's room.

Ida took so long to answer the knock that Rosalind was about to give up when the door finally swung open. She was wrapped in a fluffy hotel robe, and her hair was as wet as if she'd just stepped out of a thunderstorm. Her face was also completely scrubbed of makeup, probably the only time Rosalind had ever seen her look so un-put-together. She thought it might actually have been an improvement.

"Hi! Sorry. I was washing my hair," she said unnecessarily.

"Hi," Rosalind said. "I'm sorry. I was just returning.. sorry, I just realized that I probably should wash it before..."

Ida waved off her apology. "That's no trouble. Did you have a nice day?"

"I don't know," Rosalind said, putting a full stop between each word. "I think I need time to process that. But your help was very much appreciated."

"Sure! We might be playing a boy's game, but we can still look pretty doing it."

Rosalind forced a smile, but apparently didn't pull it off. Ida's own smile faded and she tilted her head to the side.

"Hey. You okay?"

"Yeah. Long day. Lots of travel time, tires you out."

Ida nodded, but it was clear she didn't buy it. She folded the garment bag over one arm, smoothing it down with her other hand.

"Do you want to come in and talk? Or I can throw something on, we can go get a drink somewhere? Talk?"

Rosalind's smile was genuine this time. "I appreciate that, Ida. But I don't think it's the kind of thing talking will help. Thank you though. Very much."

Ida said, "Sure. The offer stands if you change your mind." She patted the garment bag. "Thanks for bringing this back. Let me know if you need to borrow another sometime."

"Will do. Have a nice night."

"You too, Rosalind."

CHAPTER SEVENTEEN

THE SHRIKES left Baltimore with two more wins, and two more losses, to their record. David had been correct about Rita Hicks. Though she definitely wouldn't be allowed to play, she walked out onto the field in full uniform with the rest of the team to wave at the crowd. She was so heavily bandaged that it really could have been anyone wearing her jersey and no one would've been able to tell. But the home crowd roared and cheered for her, and the Baltimore Starlings played like they were seeking vengeance. Rainy might have been able to rein them in but, as good as Lucille was, she couldn't read the batters as well.

The Shrikes lost that game, and the next, but redeemed themselves by closing the series by eking out a win. Rainy hadn't played in any of the three games after the incident, but she suited up for each one and watched from the dugout.

When the team came off the field after the final game, too relieved by their win to properly celebrate, Rainy pulled Marcy aside and told her she'd be ready to pitch when they got the Philly.

"Are you sure?" Marcy asked. "I don't want to rush you."

"I felt ready today," Rainy said, glancing to be sure they weren't being overheard. "I wanted Lulu to get a win before I swept back in and took over again."

Marcy smiled. "That was considerate of you. I'll make the change on the roster. And welcome back, Caro."

Now they were back on the road, and Marcy was starting to dread stops further down the road. David had arranged for their hotel in Philadelphia well in advance, but she had no idea about Brooklyn. Then there were travel arrangements to get them to New York. Not to mention home again. Was she expected to pay the expenses out of her own pocket? And if she did, would the front office of the Whales reimburse her after David got back and spun his version of events? There was a chance the whole team could be washed out.

She didn't tell any of the others about her fears, though she had a feeling Rosalind had intuited most of it when they filled her in on the game she missed. She hadn't offered any advice and, honestly, Marcy was in a foul enough mood that she wouldn't have received it very graciously. She didn't want solutions. She wanted to sit in her frustration and worry for a bit to see if her brain figured out the answer on its own.

Their first day in Philly, Marcy bought a newspaper and sat in the lobby of their hotel to read about the ladies they'd be facing the next day. The Philadelphia Belles. It was a cute name, and they seemed middle of the road in terms of talent. Not the best, but it wasn't going to be a cakewalk. Their last four games had been against the Brooklyn Breakers so the coverage gave her insight to them as well. And they were a much more worrisome team.

She put thoughts of the Breakers out of her mind. If Chicago cut the cord on them, the Shrikes weren't getting any further than the current series anyway. No reason to borrow stress they might not have to cash in. They would focus on the game. Four more wins against the next team on their schedule would go a long way toward proving their worth to the home office.

When she finally went to the room she was sharing with Moxie and Rosalind, she discovered she couldn't stop her brain enough to sleep. She kept thinking about Rainy. The kiss. Rainy and David. Her knuckles were still sore. She'd been given so many opportunities to prevent that from happening. So many warnings and red flags, and she'd defended him. She'd dismissed her friends and their concerns. She'd approached Rosalind and Moxie separately to offer apologies, but both insisted she had nothing to apologize for.

"We know why you wouldn't listen," Rosalind said. "We understand. You were just refusing to see it for the good of the team. We can't be mad at you for prioritizing."

She didn't know how that was supposed to make her feel better. She'd put the team ahead of the safety of women. Ida and Edith and all those young girls with a predatory asshole roaming the hallways. How many of them had he 'accidentally' walked in on? And if he'd chosen someone besides Rainy to go after first, how would that situation have gone? Would she have believed him when he claimed there was mutual flirting?

Her mind tossed around these thoughts for the entire ride to Philly and followed her to the hotel. Word about the team's tenuous future had spread through the train like wildfire. It was a morose bunch who gathered in the lobby to check in. Marcy gave them David's name and cringed, waiting to be told the rooms had been canceled or the bill was due, or~

"You're all set, Mrs. Neal," the clerk chirped. "You've got the whole west wing of the third floor. If you'll wait a moment, we'll have some bellboys assist with the bags."

Marcy was so relieved she completely overlooked the 'Mrs. Neal' and thanked the girl for her help. She stepped away from the counter.

"Oh, one more thing, Mrs. Neal. There's a telegram waiting for you."

"For me?"

Marcy returned to the front desk as the girl went through her file. It could only be bad news from someone she didn't want to speak with. The clerk handed the paper across the counter. Rainy had noticed Marcy was lingering and made her way over to see what was holding her up. Marcy had already finished reading the short message and held it up for Rainy to see.

"Who is Lorraine Waldron?"

Rainy's eyes flashed with obvious recognition. She snatched the telegram from Marcy and read it herself, brow furrowed.

"She's inviting us to a party," Marcy summarized. "We just spent all day on a train. Why would we ever go to a party?"

"Because Lorraine Waldron asked us to."

Marcy raised her eyebrows. "Why, pray tell, would that matter?"

"Why wonder what women of worth wear," Rainy sang in a chipper, high-pitched voice. "We're wearing Waldron!"

Marcy stared at her. "What is wrong with you?"

"Waldron Department Store, goofus. You've heard of Montgomery Ward? Sears?"

"Sure. I've seen the catalogues."

Rainy shrugged and thumped the telegram with her finger. "Waldron is right below those two, only because it's not national. But it's swanky, it's Chicago, and Lorraine Waldron is currently the woman running things. Henry Waldron is in his nineties and both his boys are in some European foxhole. A lot of people are saying she's been running things for a lot longer than that, but they finally made it official."

"What's she doing in Philadelphia?" Marcy asked.

"Who *cares?*" Rainy put her hands on Marcy's shoulders and turned her around, guiding her toward the elevators. "If we want to put any kind of dent in Chicago, we need money. We need support. We need someone like Waldron."

Marcy let herself be guided. "Fine. But I'm not wearing a dress."

Rainy patted her shoulder. "It's at the Green's Hotel, Mars. If we're getting through the front door, a dress is just the first step."

Marcy always felt dowdy and odd in dresses, but Ida's borrowed dress made her feel downright matronly. It wasn't just that Marcy was five inches taller than their first basewoman, or that Ida's chest made the bodice ridiculously baggy on Marcy's frame. It was down to the fact that just walking into the lobby, she was aware that the outfit was decidedly less expensive than anything any of the other ladies present were wearing. She brushed at her sleeves and tugged at the hem and tried to hide behind Rainy as they approached the front desk.

"Don't fidget," Rainy scolded.

"Easy for you to say. You look like a model no matter what you're wearing."

Rainy shook her head. Her hair was down and curled, and it bounced off her high cheekbones in a way that Marcy felt just proved her point. Her borrowed dress didn't fit any better than Marcy's, but somehow she'd managed to make the extra material look intentional and flattering.

The clerk smiled at them as they approached. Marcy could see in his eyes that he expected them to say they were lost.

"My name is Caroline Rainy and this is Marcy Neal. We've been invited to meet Mrs. Lorraine Waldron."

He looked at them both and then cleared his throat, bowing his head to look at the logbook. After a moment he looked up again, and a line had appeared between his eyebrows.

"Did you say Caroline Rainy? Like the girl ballplayer?"

Rainy inhaled deeply, but managed to refrain from letting it out as a sigh. "Yes, sir. That's me."

His jaw dropped and he grinned at her. "Well, I'll be!" He laughed and shook his head. "My wife's gonna get a kick out of this! I told her you gals dressed up just like anyone. Look at you, out here all gussied up."

Rainy cleared her throat. "Mrs. Waldron...?"

"Oh, yes, right." He pointed to the left. "Down that hallway. Just follow the sound of voices."

"Thank you."

They left the desk before he could think to ask them to sign something. His directions proved to be enough, because they could hear the party even from the lobby. It was taking place inside a large dining room where people were loitering around the tables and chairs. Marcy eyed the pillars throughout the room, decorated by golden statues, and took an extra step behind Rainy.

"You can't hide back there forever," Rainy said over her shoulder.

Marcy hooked her fingers in Rainy's belt. "Watch me."

A young woman in a stylish bob made her way over to them, lifting her chin and looking a question at them.

"Caroline Rainy and~"

"Marcy Neal!" The girl gasped and clapped her hands together. "Oh my goodness. This way, this way." She started walking back the way she'd come, but she remained twisted at the waist to look back at them. "We've been waiting for you all afternoon!"

"Oh. The telegram said~"

"You're on time, don't worry! We're just impatient and we've been looking forward to this ever since Mrs. Waldron had the idea. Oh, I'm Lillian, by the way. Wonderful to meet you, just wonderful."

She led them to a table in the back of the room. A woman in her sixties seemed to be the only person in the whole room actually sitting. She wore a black gown with sheer white sleeves, and her silver hair was gathered in what looked like a solid orb underneath a black hat. She had just taken a sip of her coffee when they reached her table.

"Mommy," Lillian said, striking a pose next to the table. She held her hands out to frame the women behind her. "The ballplayers have arrived!"

"Mm!" Lorraine Waldron put down her coffee cup and dabbed at her lips with a napkin. "Splendid. I would ask which is which, but I have your Cracker Jack cards. And who could forget that hair! I expected it wouldn't be so red in real life but look at you!" She waved away the people who had gathered around the table. "Go, go. I need to talk to these girls privately."

Lillian successfully shepherded everyone away from the table, and Lorraine gestured for Marcy and Rainy to sit across from her.

"Hello, girls."

"Hello," they said nervously.

"You're probably very confused. And honestly, I don't blame you one bit. I'd be confused, too, but my brain hasn't caught up with my body yet. It doesn't even know I'm in Philadelphia because I arrived here about three hours ago. Before that, I was in Chicago."

Rainy nodded. "We know. We shop at your store all the time."

Lorraine looked down at their dresses. "No, darling, I don't think you do. Those dresses aren't mine, and they're definitely not yours. But I appreciate you making the effort."

Marcy shifted uncomfortably. "With all due respect, ma'am, if you're looking to advertise with the team, we're not really in a position to~"

She shook her head. "No, I'm not interested in a little patch on your uniforms. Although now that we mention it... yes, that might be a lovely addition. But we can discuss that later. Yesterday afternoon, I was in the front office of the Chicago Whales. It's not important why. Business things. Boring things. When all of a sudden this *man* bursts in. Screaming about women using terms even I won't use. I follow the papers enough to know about this Women's League. And while I'm generally not a sports fan, I do respect what you ladies are doing. My daughter Lillian is the real fan. She'll probably be embarrassed by this, but she's the one who has the Cracker Jack cards.

"So I knew the man who busted into the meeting was David Buckner, and I knew he was talking about your team. Unmanageable! A train wreck! More economical to just set your money on fire! He was desperate to convince them that the best thing to do about the Chicago Shrikes would be to just cut anchor and let you sink."

Marcy sank back in her chair, arms crossed over her chest. She'd been dreading that, but to hear that it actually happened was devastating.

"I don't know what the fat cats would have done if I hadn't stepped in. Maybe they would have believed his story. But I've been following the season… not by choice, really. Lillian talks incessantly about you girls and some of it elbows its way into my brain against my will. But I spent the train trip learning everything I can about you. You're good! You have a chance at the pennant, maybe the whole Series."

Marcy said, "Yeah, but if we don't get backing, we don't even have a shot at getting to Brooklyn. Hell, we won't even have the cash to get home."

"You'll get to Brooklyn," Lorraine said. "And then back to Chicago, and then to… Kansas City, or wherever is next. Honestly, you girls play so many games! You must be *exhausted*."

"You have no idea," Marcy said.

Lorraine shook her head. "That kind of dedication deserves rewarding. Therefore, I am happy to reveal that I am the new owner of the Chicago Shrikes."

Marcy looked at Rainy, who seemed frozen. "I'm sorry?"

"The Whales front office didn't seem invested in you," Lorraine said. "It was just a money thing for them, so I made an offer. We'll be renting their ballpark for a flat fee, rather than sharing in ticket sales and concessions. I'll provide your travel and lodging when you're on the road. Miss Neal, the newspapers tend to believe you've been managing the team. Is that correct?"

"Yes, it is," Rainy said, answering before Marcy could demur.

"Well, you're doing a damn fine job. I don't see any reason for that to change."

Marcy sat forward again. "Why are you doing this? It's going to cost you a fortune."

Lorraine grinned. "Darling, I *have* a fortune. And this isn't even going to make a dent in it. I'm doing it because I want you ladies to succeed or fail on your own merit, not because you couldn't afford train tickets. The money isn't doing anybody any good sitting in a vault somewhere. I want to put some good out into the world while I still can. That's the main reason, anyway."

"What's the secondary reason?" Marcy asked.

Lorraine took a moment to take a cigarette from a gold case. She lit the end, took a drag, and then held it between two fingers and watched the smoke rise. Finally, she leaned back and answered.

"When a man shows up with a face like that, and then claims he can't work with the women around him…" She smiled knowingly. "Well. Most women can figure out what that means. Is she okay?"

"Who?"

Lorraine looked at Marcy like she was dense.

"She's fine," Rainy said.

"Good. That's very good to hear. A lot of times, the women, they can't say anything because they assume people will believe the man. Or the man has some sort of leverage over the woman. It's easier to just pretend it's not a big deal and try to move on." She glanced down at Marcy's hands. "My, my. Are you okay, Miss Neal? Your hands look about as rough as that raving lunatic's face did."

Marcy covered her healing knuckles with her other hand. "Yes, ma'am."

"Good." She winked and sat up straighter. "Now, I don't know the first thing about baseball. But I know about traveling and I know about hotels. I can make sure you get where you need to be, I just need someone to tell me where that is and when you should be there. Lillian is going to be more than happy to serve that purpose. That is, if we have an arrangement."

Marcy looked at Rainy. "We may need to discuss it with the other players. But I can't think of a reason they'd be against it. Especially if the option is the team going away, which I think is our only alternative."

Rainy said, "Actually, I've gotten to know them pretty well since the season began. I think only one of them is going to have a question."

Lorraine raised her eyebrows as she awaited the question.

"Ida's going to want to know if this means she'll get a discount at your store."

Lorraine laughed and slapped her hand down on the table. She leaned forward, winked, and said, "Win a couple more games for me and we'll talk. Win the pennant and I'll let Miss Coe go on a shopping spree that will make her head spin."

Rainy looked at Marcy for her vote.

Marcy just smiled and extended her hand across the table.

"Welcome to the Shrike organization, Mrs. Waldron."

Lorraine smiled and raised an eyebrow. "Welcome to the Waldron empire, Chicago Shrikes."

They shook.

III.
THE PENNANT RACE

"If this first suffraget (sic) team is a success, it is likely that more of them will be organized in other large cities of the country."
- *Rock Island Argus*, (Rock Island, Illinois) 5 May 1913

CHAPTER EIGHTEEN

MARCY LEFT the clubhouse and went up into the stands, amazed at how vast and empty they seemed without a crowd. They were home in Chicago, at Weeghman. Their home ground. It felt like years since they'd been home. Her apartment felt like a place she'd left behind a long time ago. It certainly didn't feel like home. After the past five months, home had come to mean train stations and sleeper cars, hotel rooms with three or four other women snoring and keeping her awake, parks that were almost the same but always different enough that it was clear they weren't at home.

But Weeghman wasn't really home, either. The park belonged to the Whales. Lorraine Waldron was allowed to rent it simply because it was more lucrative to the owners than letting it stand empty. And they were definitely earning their keep. She didn't know the exact attendance numbers, but the stands had been getting more and more crowded with every game. The last time they'd played at home, it looked like any other baseball game in the history of the park.

They were winning over the crowd. They were proving their worth. But while the war still waged overseas, she knew it would eventually come to an end. She *wanted* it to end, obviously. It was terrible that so many people were fighting and dying so far from home. They deserved to come back to their lives. But for those select few whose lives took precedence over hers... what about them? What happened when the men came parading back home and wanted their parks back? What would happen to the crowds when they actually had a choice?

"I thought I'd find you out on the field."

Lillian Waldron had snuck up on Marcy while she was distracted. She smiled an apology when she realized her approach hadn't been noticed.

"I like coming up here when I have a chance. It seems so huge when you're down there on the field. And when you're running after a fly ball. But up here..." She chuckled and shrugged. "Okay. It still seems pretty big from up here, too. But you can see more of it at once."

Lillian crossed her arms and looked out as well. Marcy pretended she was still looking as well, but in reality she shifted to watching the other woman. Lillian was a dynamo. She knew baseball inside and out, and she'd been following the Shrikes from their first game of the season. Marcy couldn't help but think about the fact the team wouldn't even exist now if it hadn't been for Lillian talking her mother's ear off about the potential of the Women's League. They owed her everything, but she never acted like a savior. She acted more like someone who had seen a locked door and decided to hold it open for them to walk through.

Lillian realized she was being watched and looked at her. "What?"

"I didn't say anything," Marcy said.

"Mm-hmm. You say nothing pretty loud, Miss Neal."

Marcy laughed. "What does that even mean?"

"You know full well what it means."

Marcy shook her head. "I'm just glad your mother decided not to drop us after we muffed it so hard out east."

"You know how much she believes in you."

"I believe in us, too," Marcy said. "I put all my eggs in this basket, and even I was starting to question if we were at the end of the road. Who wouldn't have?"

She still hated thinking about their premiere performances in Philadelphia and Brooklyn. No one had been playing like themselves, least of all her. She wanted to blame it on the stress of the David revelation and being distracted by the Waldrons sudden arrival in their lives, but she knew it wasn't anything that simple. They were just playing like they'd never touched a ball before, like they didn't know which end of a bat was up. Rainy suddenly couldn't throw straight.

Rosalind got confused about where to throw when she needed to tag a runner. And Marcy made so many errors she was wondering if it was morally ethical to keep herself in the games.

In the end, they miraculously won two of their five games against the Philadelphia Belles. But a week later when they arrived in Brooklyn, they entered the darkest week of the team's existence.

Five games against the Brooklyn Breakers. Four in a row, one day off, and then a final match-up, and the Shrikes had lost them all. Their best outing had been the third game, when they scored four runs. It was a pathetic number to serve as a high-water mark. Their scores, though pathetic, served as proof that the team was trying. They were just coming up short on every measure. It was humiliating.

Lorraine Waldron would've had every right to cut and run. Marcy kept waiting for the telegram to arrive, which definitely didn't help her focus on the games. When she finally couldn't bear the wait any longer, she sent the telegram asking flat-out how much longer they could expect to be a team.

"*At least a season, the same as every other team in this league,*" the reply said. "*My husband didn't get rich by turning tail at the first sign of trouble. You don't give up on a ball team just because they lose some games. You've got time. I look forward to your recovery.*"

The support made Marcy tear up, not that she would ever admit it to anyone. She was just glad she'd read it when she was alone.

And the belief was well-placed, because they followed up that atrocious string of games with a winning streak. They swept the Kansas City Pinks the next time they faced them. They won half their next games against the Detroit Pros, all but confirming they would end up racing each other for the pennant. From that point on, the Shrikes had found their stride. Losing some, but always leaving a city with more games in the win column.

Marcy patted Lillian's hand. "I have a feeling you had something to do with convincing her not to lose faith. Thank you."

Lillian dipped her head bashfully and shrugged. "Well, I'm just so impressed by everything you all are doing and accomplishing here. I was so excited when I heard the league was being formed, but I don't have a lick of athletic ability myself. I get tired just watching other people play. So I had to find some other way to be part of it. I got lucky that my hometown team is also the best."

"I didn't know you were from Detroit."

"Fresh," Lillian laughed. "Those ladies are tough, for sure. But I know who I'm rooting for in the pennant race." She turned her hand over under Marcy's and looked down. She brushed her fingers over the pads of Marcy's. "Goodness, your fingers are so rough."

Marcy started to pull her hand away. "Oh. I'm sorry."

"No, don't be." She held on so Marcy couldn't get away. "I like it. My hands are soft. Lazy hands, my daddy used to call them. He grew up on a farm, so he had different ideas of what counted as hard work. But even though I don't agree with him about that, I have to admit I feel self-conscious about how soft my hands are."

"You shouldn't be." Marcy stroked Lillian's palms. "Women are supposed to have softer hands. Soft and... supple..."

Lillian inhaled sharply. Marcy was holding her breath.

After a second too long, Marcy cleared her throat and pulled her hand away too fast. She smiled and tucked her hair behind her ears, and Lillian turned to look out at the field again.

"It's probably going to be nice playing at home again."

"Mm-hmm," Marcy said. "Even if it doesn't really feel like home. It's a rented field that we're just keeping warm until the real owners can use it again. The boys are coming back, it's only a matter of time."

"Sure, but it's going to be a while," Lillian said. "I read in the paper that German agents blew up a munitions factory in Jersey this summer. Wilson's not going to take too kindly to that. I wouldn't be surprised if these parks are still vacant next season. But you're doing more than just keeping the wheels turning. You're proving that a Women's League can bring in fans and money."

"Let's say we succeed at doing that. If the whole country agrees that women can play baseball and all our teams get to stick around after the war ends, where are we going to play? We don't have our own parks. And given the choice, I think three-fourths of our so-called fans would still prefer to go see a Whales game than supporting us if we're in the same town."

"Then we'll find another town for you. There are lots of places all over the country who would love to be home to an established team. Indianapolis, maybe. Madison. Who knows? The team is the important piece of the puzzle. As long as the players are there, everything else is going to fall into place. Trust me. And trust my mother's bank account."

Marcy said, "Well, those are two pretty rock solid things to have faith in." She turned around and looked at the benches. "You and your mother have attended games here at the park, right?"

"Yep. The last one we saw was, um, the Philly Belles and the Baltimore Starlings."

"Oh, the Starlings?" Marcy was distracted from her original question. "How is Rita Hicks?"

"Milking her injury for all it's worth," Lillian said with a scoff. "Someone at the *Tribune* suspects she blew the whole thing out of proportion for sympathy."

Marcy said, "She looked pretty hurt."

"She looked pretty *bandaged*," Lillian said. "The bandages are gone, and it's hard to tell anything even happened. I wouldn't put it past a publicity hound like her."

Marcy felt a brief flare of rage for Rainy. She'd put herself through hell for hurting that girl. Sleepless nights, loss of appetite, crying jags on the train... If the whole thing had been based on a lie, Rita Hicks would be officially on Marcy's shit list.

"Was that what you wanted to ask?" Lillian prompted.

"Hm?" Marcy squeezed her eyes shut and shook her head like she was erasing a blackboard. "Oh. I was just wondering if you had reserved seats."

Lillian nodded. "Oh, sure. I'll show you."

She took Marcy's hand so casually that they were halfway around the bandstand before Marcy thought to consider it odd. She let herself be led to the section directly behind home plate, high in the stands where the benches gave way to individual seats. Lillian stopped and gestured at the first two next to the aisle.

"This is where we watch the games."

Marcy slipped past her and took a seat. Lillian followed her lead and sat down next to her, crossing one leg over the other. She pointed down at the field.

"And that's where you'll be tomorrow."

"Mm-hmm," Marcy said. "Will you be here cheering me on?"

Lillian nodded. "I'm going to be at every game."

"Well, sure. You get a discount on the tickets."

Lillian laughed and patted Marcy's knee, then let her hand rest there. Marcy put her hand on top of it. Lillian's fingers spread out slightly, and Marcy slipped her fingers into the gaps between Marcy's. She looked down at their now-linked hands because it was a better alternative than seeing Lillian's face.

"You look really nice in your uniform."

"Thank you. I think it's really important that they're not very different from what the men wear. We're playing the same sport. We should be dressed the same."

Lillian nodded. "Yes," she said, sounding distracted.

"Do you really have my Cracker Jack card?"

Lillian laughed. "Oh gosh. Yes. Is that embarrassing? I have Rainy's, too. And most of the rest of the team."

"It's not embarrassing," Marcy said. "It's flattering. If you want to bring it to a game sometime, I'll autograph it for you."

"Really? Maybe you could come by the house and sign it."

"Whatever is easiest."

They sat silently for a while, listening to the wind whistle through the open bowl of the park. The overhang shading their seat had a row of American flags planted along its peak, and Marcy could hear the fabric rippling as she brushed her thumb over the side of Lillian's hand. Lillian didn't seem to mind having her hand held. Marcy didn't mind holding it. And neither of them seemed too bothered by the idea of sitting in an empty bandstand to watch a field where nothing was happening.

"You know," Lillian said after a while, "I never took you for one of those girls who just casually holds hands with her friends."

"I'm not," Marcy said.

Lillian took a deep breath. When she let it out, her mouth spread into a smile. "Good. I'm not, either. It's not always the easiest thing in the world to admit that."

"Well, I'm glad you told me," Marcy said.

"Me too."

They could figure out what exactly it meant another time. For now, Marcy was content to just enjoy the weight of another hand in hers.

When they finally left, Marcy took the L train home. The apartment was cold and alien to her, but she was still glad to be there. It was her space, all hers, and she didn't have to share the bathroom with anybody. She took a long shower, probably earning the irritation of her neighbors, and stayed undressed as she went into the bedroom. It didn't matter, there was no chance anyone would barge in. She stretched out on top of the blankets of a bed she wouldn't have to share with Ida or Moxie. It was almost like being released from prison, she assumed.

Staring at the ceiling, she thought about holding Lillian's hand. Her soft... supple... hand...

She bit her lip and closed her eyes.

Then, before she could get too carried away, she jumped up from bed and threw on the first clothes she found. She didn't bother trying to make an outfit. She just needed to be covered enough to leave the house.

Once she was decent, she left and hurried down the street to the L station she had just left. She spent the trip mentally preparing what she wanted to say, what needed to be said, and how she was going to say it.

Forty minutes after she'd been lying on her bed with a hand on her thigh threatening to move elsewhere, she knocked on Rainy's apartment door and took a step back.

Rainy answered, dressed in a T-shirt and shorts. Her hair was down for a change, wild and wavy from spending so long in braids. She squinted at Marcy with one eye while she rubbed the other with the heel of her hand.

"Mars, what the hell. I had just fallen asleep."

"I want to kiss someone else."

Rainy dropped her hand, frowned, and blinked. "Okay..."

"I wasn't sure where we had landed. I didn't know if we were over, or just~"

"Come in here." She grabbed the sleeve of Marcy's sweater and pulled her into the apartment. She checked both ways down the hall and then shut the door. "That's not the conversation we should have in a hallway. Do you want something to drink?"

"No, I'm probably not staying that long. Unless you think I need to stay that long, so we can talk. I just didn't want to do anything, even in my head, before we talked about it."

Rainy sat down on the sofa. "In your head? You mean you haven't even done anything with this other person yet?"

Marcy shrugged. "No. I mean, yes. We held hands."

Rainy grinned. "That's adorable."

"Hey, I'm trying to be respectable. I don't want to two-time you!"

"Okay, okay. I'm sorry." Rainy sighed. "I don't think we should do anything while we're playing on the same team. It can only screw things up. So I guess that means we're not together for as long as the team is around. And we both assume the Shrikes are going to be around for a while, right?"

Marcy nodded and sat on the arm of the recliner across from the coffee table. "And if we weren't playing on the same team, it would be because one of us was traded. And then we'd be rivals."

"And living in other cities."

"Yeah. Most likely."

Rainy leaned back. "Shit. I hadn't thought about it."

"Me neither. I just assumed we would eventually~"

"Yeah. I did, too."

Marcy chewed her bottom lip. "I didn't go looking for someone else."

"I know," Rainy said. "Who is it?"

"Lillian Waldron."

Rainy looked surprised. "Oh. She always seems nice."

"Yeah." Marcy blushed.

"She has your Cracker Jack card."

Marcy chuckled. "Shut up."

Rainy looked down at her hands and fiddled with her thumbnail. "I just want you to be happy, Mars. That's all I've ever wanted."

"Same. I love you, Caro."

"I'm not supposed to say it until we win the Series."

Marcy shrugged. "You can say it now. If you~"

"I love you, too."

Marcy shuffled her feet awkwardly. "So what happens now?"

"Now..." Rainy stood up. "I go back to sleep. You go see if Lillian feels the same way about you. And then starting tomorrow, we start working toward getting our pennant."

Marcy smiled.

It sounded like as solid a plan as any.

CHAPTER NINETEEN

MOXIE SAT in the dugout between Rosalind and Rainy. The pitcher was leaning forward, elbows on her knees and hands over her mouth. Their centerfielder was slumped back with one hand over her eyes as if she couldn't bear to watch any more of the debacle happening out on the field. Moxie thought about covering her ears to complete the picture, but she didn't want to discourage anyone who might happen to look over and see them.

Marcy was at bat. Two strikes against her, bat poised in anticipation of the next pitch. Striking out now would end the eighth, and they'd go into the final inning with the Detroit Pros leading them by three.

The problem was that they were too evenly matched. The only difference was the Pros defense, which had apparently taken lessons from their previous matchups. Their pitcher seemed to have made it her life goal to never let the Shrikes touch a ball. And the few times they managed to get a hit, the Pro outfielders seemed capable of flight and split-second decision making. Ida, Rainy, Rosalind, and Edith were all struck out before they even got to third base. Lorna Lowell and Moxie were responsible for the two runs they'd managed so far, but it was hard to feel proud about that given the reality of the situation.

Rosalind dropped her hands, forcing herself to witness the last pitch. Rainy leaned back and smoothed her hands nervously over her thighs.

"We've still got another chance," Moxie said.

"Bottom of the ninth," Rosalind said.

"It's going to be tough as it is," Rainy said, "and if they get more runs, we might as well throw in the towel and save everybody some time."

Moxie said, "Don't talk like that."

There was the pitch. Marcy swung.

The catcher rocked back on her heels with the ball cradled in her glove.

Strike three, and that was the end of the eighth.

Marcy swung her bat away as if it was to blame for her performance. She stalked back to the dugout and muttered, "Motherfucker," under her breath as she grabbed a cup of water. She splashed the contents into her face, crumpled the cup, and hurled it against the back wall at a speed Rainy should have been jealous of.

"They're going to slaughter us," Ida said.

"Going to?" Marcy said. "You look at the scoreboard lately?"

Rainy stood up and stretched. "We've still got a chance. I'll hold them off from getting any more runs, then we just have to get three more runs to force an overtime. We get four, we win."

"That's all, huh?" Marcy scoffed and took off her cap. "We might as well just give them the pennant now. Save everyone the trouble."

"Let's just see how this inning goes."

Moxie slipped on her mask and chest protector as she headed out onto the field. She crouched behind home plate, glanced toward the Pros dugout, and fought the urge to swear out loud.

Celia Torres strode toward her wearing a casual smile, bat hanging from her left hand. It was Celia's first time at-bat in this game, and Moxie had been hoping she was injured or sick. She wasn't hoping for anything major, to be sure, just something that would keep her from playing the entire time her team was in Chicago. The first couple of innings had made her hoping she'd gotten lucky.

It seemed she wasn't lucky after all.

"Hi, Iona," Celia said as she took position.

"Number 2."

Celia clucked her tongue. "So formal. We're just playing a game here, Moxie."

"Yeah? What game is that, exactly...?"

Celia laughed and put the bat on her shoulder. Rainy was watching her for a signal. Moxie brushed the backs of her fingers over her chest protector, then tapped two fingers in the dirt between her feet. Rainy frowned and tilted her head to the side. Moxie signaled *Yes*, and Rainy gave a subtle shrug as she adjusted her stance.

"I had a dream about what you did to me at Elijah's," Moxie blurted.

The ball thudded hard into Moxie's glove. Celia had swung a second too late, the sound of her bat followed by a quiet chuckle.

"Oh, we're going to play like that, huh?" Celia said.

The umpire cleared his throat and shifted his weight from one foot to the other. Moxie looked at him from the corner of her eye without turning her head. Moxie returned the ball to Rainy.

Moxie's signal: *Screwball.*

Rainy nodded.

"I decided I want you to do it again," Moxie said as she caught the second pitch.

"You're cruel, you know that?" Celia said.

Moxie tossed the ball back. "Why? I'm just making conversation."

"You shouldn't distract the batter. It's against the rules."

"Oh, look at you, Celia Torres. Suddenly a rule follower."

Celia laughed. "I'm going to enjoy humiliating your team in their own house."

"It's only fair," Moxie said. "We spanked you in yours. Oh, speaking of spanking..."

Strike three, and Celia was out. She flipped her bat, shook her head, and turned to Moxie as she walked away. "Next time, I'm wearing ear protectors."

Moxie winked at her from behind the cage of her mask.

The umpire said, "If you do whatever that was to all the batters, you Shrikes might actually have a shot."

"There are only so many hours in the day, man. Let me have a fresh ball for my girl out there."

The umpire tossed her the ball. Moxie rubbed it on her pant leg like it was a fresh apple, then hurled it to Rainy...

...who caught it in her right hand. She walked a tight circle around the mound of dirt that made up her kingdom. One out. Only two more to go, and then they'd have a chance to make things right. Keeping the Pros at five runs was the only thing she could do to help the team. If she did that, she was confident they could get the three runs they needed in order to even things up. Maybe they could even get four and win at the last second.

She tossed the ball in the air and caught it. She did it once, twice, thrice, then held it against her hip as she looked toward home. Number 8 was batting now, Ann Howard. No problem. The Pros were getting overconfident now, putting in their reserves. They were playing this like they already had it in the bag. Rainy looked at the scoreboard. 5-2. She looked at Ann, she looked at Moxie. She just had to get the ball past one little woman with a stick.

Rainy pitched. The bat cracked, it soared in a high arc over the diamond toward Rosalind...

...who tracked it coming. Her body moved without her telling it to. Time slowed down as her cleats tore across the turf, legs pumping, arm outstretched. The ball landed hard in her glove and she closed her fingers around it. When her left foot hit the ground again, she used her whole body to pivot and change direction. In her mind's eye she saw the field, saw Number 8 running from second base to third, and she threw directly to...

...Lorna Lowell's whole palm stung when the ball hit it, but she didn't think about that. She threw her foot toward the base and touched it just before Number 8 made contact. Ann Howard stumbled and tripped but managed to remain upright as she slowed to a trot, hanging her head and changing direction to return to her dugout. Lorna grinned and lobbed the ball back to...

Rainy, who clutched it like a trophy. She lifted her chin and kicked at the dirt under her feet.

Two outs, one to go.

Patricia White approached the plate with her bat wielded as a weapon. She looked as if she planned to use it on Rainy's head. Rainy just smiled at her and shook out her arm like she was cocking a weapon of her own. The leather was warm against her palm and she rotated the ball until she felt the seams under her fingertips. She tilted her head to the left, then the right, and watched Moxie for the signal. There were signals that most every other catcher in who had ever played baseball knew. Then there were the signals Iona Moccia had come up with herself.

Moxie drew an X over her heart and then placed the tips of her first two fingers in the dirt.

Rainy grinned. *Make her wait.*

She adjusted her grip and threw a change-of-pace. The ball sailed leisurely toward the plate, and White swung far too early and missed it completely.

Moxie signaled for another just like it. Rainy nodded and threw another lazy roll. Again, White's bat whistled as she swung at something that hadn't reached her yet.

Rainy already knew what Moxie was going to signal, so she looked at White. The woman's eyes were small dark coals under heavy brows, and her bottom lip pushed up so high that it seemed to touch her nose. Moxie was going to tell her to throw a fast one now, take advantage of White's expectations. Someone who had just been fooled by two changeups would expect a third one and swing accordingly.

Rainy nodded to Moxie without bothering to look at her signals. She took a deep breath. She held the ball behind her back. She counted to three, and then she threw the slowest pitch she knew.

The bat came off White's shoulder as fast as it had the first two times in anticipation of a fast pitch. She'd been expecting a trick, tried to outthink them. The result was a ball landing in Moxie's outstretched hand like there was no other possible place for it to have gone.

Strike three, and three outs.

Moxie shot to her feet and jogged out to the mount, slapping Rainy hard on the shoulder as they walked off the field together.

"You ignored me! You nodded but you ignored me!"

"Should I apologize?"

Moxie laughed. "I'll let it slide this time."

Marcy clapped as Rainy entered the dugout. "Excellent work, Caro. Cut them off at the knees."

Rainy shrugged. "I did my job. Now it's up to y'all to get three runs."

"We need four to win," Rosalind said.

Rainy winked at her on her way into the clubhouse. "I'll take care of that one."

In her cubby, she dug around until she found the tub of her liniment and sat down on the bench. She unbuttoned her jersey and shrugged out of it, wincing as she rotated her shoulder. Once her shirt was out of the way, she opened the medicine and began applying it. She wasn't hurting terribly, and she would certainly be able to bat when her time in the lineup came around, but she found it worked better when she did it as quickly as possible after she left the mound.

The clubhouse door opened and Lillian came in, hurrying halfway across the room before she realized someone was there. She stopped in her tracks, looked at Rainy, and then quickly looked away.

"Oh! Caroline, I'm sorry."

"I've still got my undershirt on. It's fine. What are you in such a hurry about?"

"I..." She frowned when she got a good look at what Rainy was doing. "Are you hurt?"

Rainy shrugged. "I always hurt. This makes it better."

"Can you reach?"

"Yeah. But if you're willing to help me out..."

Lillian glanced at the door, then came over to Rainy's bench. "What do I have to do?"

"Just use the applicator." She tapped the spot on her shoulder. "Around about there."

"What is this stuff?"

"Just liniment. Absorbine Junior." She chuckled. "The original medication was for horses. Never thought I'd be using horse medication."

Lillian said, "Well, this league treats you all like workhorses, that's for sure." She put down the applicator. "It would certainly explain why someone might have said something they didn't mean."

Rainy frowned as she stood up to put her jersey back on. "What are you talking about?"

"What did Marcy say to Otis Fellows?"

"Heck if I know," Rainy said. "Why? That article came out ages ago. I read it. It was fine."

Lillian sighed heavily. "Well, it would seem there was something he left out. Mother has friends at the *Tribune* and he gave her a heads-up. There's going to be a story about the Shrikes in tomorrow's early edition. Specifically about Marcy."

Rainy's blood went cold at the possibilities. "What-what's it... gonna say?"

Lillian caught the panic in Rainy's eyes. "Not *that*," she reassured her in a quiet voice. "Apparently Marcy said something at the end of the interview that David Buckner convinced Fellows to leave out of the article. It seems Mr. Buckner called him up again recently and said it was okay to go ahead and print it."

"Marcy's not exactly the most tactful person in the world, but I can't imagine she said anything too troublesome."

"According to Mother's source, she was asked her thoughts about the war. She apparently replied, *We're obviously not hoping for peace any time soon.*"

The blood that had drained from Rainy's face came rushing back, burning her cheeks and ears. "Oh hell. That's not going to go over well."

"So you believe Marcy would actually say something like that?"

Rainy considered it. "I don't know. I think maybe Mr. Fellows paraphrased something she said off the cuff to make it sound worse. But it's true. If the war ended tomorrow, this whole league would probably be toast. But none of us want the fighting to go on any longer than it has to. We don't want any more people to die on either side."

"The nuance doesn't really translate to print."

"Right," Rainy said. "So what does this mean?"

Lillian shrugged. "This story comes out tomorrow. And when it does, every person in this park is going to be booing her the entire time she's on the field. So we won't put her on the field."

"No..."

"Mother wants it done immediately."

"You can't do that," Rainy said. "We can't beat the Pros without her. They'll be guaranteed the pennant."

"I'm sorry, Caroline. I fought her on it. You know I did. But Mother is insistent that winning with Marcy Neal on the field is worse than losing."

"You can't do it in the middle of the game."

"I have to. I'm sorry, there's no way around it. Effective immediately, Marcy is benched."

CHAPTER TWENTY

THE SHRIKES came from behind with a tremendous ninth inning streak that gave them four runs, ending the game in a 6-5 victory. Despite that stunning upset, the lead story in the Sports section the next day was Marcy's quote about the war. The next day when the team arrived at the park, they were met by a mob carrying signs declaring the team anti-American. Another crowd accused them of being war profiteers who were getting rich off the fighting and dying. Rosalind glowered at the dueling screamers as she passed between them, and a reporter caught a picture of her sneering in the direction of a woman who was later identified as a war widow.

Marcy looked at the photo from an armchair in the Waldron penthouse. Lorraine was out for the evening, and Lillian had invited her over for dinner as an apology for benching her and also as an escape from the insanity. Marcy was grateful for the company but she couldn't get comfortable in their lush home. She was in an armchair that threatened to devour her, and every other piece of furniture looked even more dangerously plush. The carpets were so thick that footsteps were nonexistent, something Marcy was surprised to discover made her anxious. She didn't like the idea of anyone sneaking up on her.

"The food is almost ready." Lillian came back into the sitting room from the kitchen. She clicked her tongue when she saw what

Marcy was reading. "Don't pay attention to that claptrap. They yell at Wilson for not getting into the war early enough, then they threaten his re-election when he does get us involved. They're never satisfied. They just like to yell."

"It makes me sound like a warmonger." She looked up at Lillian, who was dressed in a long black dress and a blouse that shimmered between silver and white. Her hair was pinned back with a curl hanging down over her right eye, and the look was completed with a wide black necktie. She looked amazing, and made Marcy feel positively dowdy in her slacks and man's shirt. "You really should let me do the kitchen things. I look more like the hired help anyway. You don't want your makeup to run."

Lillian laughed and waved her off. "You're my guest, I invited you." She sat in the armchair across from Marcy's, her hands resting comfortably on either arm as she draped one leg over the other. She looked like a queen settling into her throne. "Besides, you don't seem like the type to be offended by a little runny makeup."

Marcy smiled. "No, ma'am." She leaned forward and rested her elbows on her knees. "I'm just antsy is all. It feels all sorts of odd that the Shrikes had a game today and I wasn't on the field."

And what a game it had been. Eighteen women pounding each other for almost three hours. The final score was a stunning 1-2, the Pros coming out ahead with a second run in the fifth. The crowd had already been meager due to the article and the protestors, but by the ninth inning the bandstand looked like it had been evacuated.

Lillian said, "Let's take your mind off of it. How many more games are there against the Pros?"

"In this series?" Marcy said. "Two. We have to win both of them if we're going to stay in the pennant race. I don't think it's going to happen."

"What happens if it does?"

Marcy tried to envision the schedule. "Then we have four games against the Brooklyn Breakers, which will be even worse than this series was. They're absolute monsters. We've only beaten them a handful of times. They humiliate us every time we play, even when we come out on top."

"And then you win the pennant?"

"If we beat the Pros in the next two games, and *if* we manage to play better against the Breakers than we ever have, then yes. We will win the pennant for the league, and we'll go up against whoever wins the pennant for the western division. Last time I looked, it was either going to be the San Francisco Phoenix or the Sacramento Sentinels. My money is on San Fran."

"They're probably looking at us, terrified about facing the Shrikes."

Marcy said, "We'd have a much better chance if your mother would allow me to play." Lillian started to answer, but Marcy cut her off. "Enough time will have passed by the time we get to Brooklyn. Hell, they might not even get the story out there. You know New York. They only care about the shit that happens in their own city."

"I'm trying. It's not personal, Marcy. She's not angry, she's being strategic. She doesn't want a player on the field who is going to get booed every time she shows her face. When the story dies down, you'll be back where you belong."

"What if I ask nicely?" Marcy said. "What if I begged?"

Lillian laughed. "I can't imagine you begging, Marcy Neal."

"I can beg."

Marcy slipped out of the chair and onto her knees. She clasped her hands in front of her. "Please, Mrs. Waldron. Please let me play."

Lillian put her feet down on the floor, legs apart. She smiled and hooked her finger. "Come here, Miss Neal."

Marcy walked on her knees to the chair. Lillian leaned down and brushed the back of her fingers over Marcy's cheek.

"Will you be grateful to me, pet?"

"Yes, ma'am."

"Good."

Lillian leaned in. Their first kiss was so brief that Marcy only tasted lipstick before Lillian was pulling away. She made a quiet sound of protest and leaned forward, and this time Lillian's mouth stayed on hers. Marcy put her hands on Lillian's thighs. She squeezed and then pushed her palms higher, skimming the slick material over her skin on her way to Lillian's hips.

"I'm not sure where to put my hands," Lillian said without taking her lips away from Marcy's.

"My hair," Marcy said.

Lillian moved her hands to the back of Marcy's head under her hair and went back to the kiss with renewed passion.

Marcy lost herself in the kiss until the smells coming from the kitchen became too strong to ignore. She pulled back and kissed Lillian's cheek.

"Should you go check on the food?"

"Damn." Lillian put her head down on Marcy's shoulder. "Yes. Don't go anywhere."

Lillian got up and hurried to the kitchen. Marcy stood up and smoothed her hands over her clothes. She heard a clatter of plates and silverware, followed by Lillian quietly swearing, and debated whether she should offer to help. She was about to ask if everything was under control when she heard the keys in the front door.

Lorraine swung the door open, bent down to pick up her suitcases, and carried them over the threshold. She jumped when she saw Marcy by the divan.

"Miss Neal! What a surprise. I assume you're here to see Lillian."

"Uh, yes. She invited me over f-for a talk about my benching."

Lorraine ran her eyes up and down Marcy's outfit. "You certainly dressed to impress, dear. Well, it worked. I'm impressed."

"Thank you," Marcy said.

"Who are you talking to?" Lillian came out of the kitchen and stopped on a dime when she saw the answer to her question. "Mother. You're not supposed... I thought..." She reached up to touch her hair. "I-I only planned for two people for dinner..."

"Oh don't worry about me, darling. I ate at the station. A dreadful meal, but it's put me off the idea of food for at least twelve hours." She looked at Marcy. "And I'm afraid my decision is final. At least for the home games. The fans are out for blood after what you said, and I don't want my girls being booed the entire time they're playing a team like the Pros."

"I understand," Marcy said. "Lillian explained that to me quite clearly."

Lorraine nodded. "Good. Well, I'm not going to intrude on your girls' night. I'll just settle in with a good book and let you talk out here. No business talk, though. Just two friends. Can you promise me that?"

"Yes, ma'am," Marcy said.

"Good. Lovely to see you, Miss Neal." She tilted her head and narrowed her eyes at Marcy. "You do look fantastic, my dear, but you should ask Miss Coe for tips about makeup. Your lipstick looks like a child applied it."

Behind Lorraine, Lillian put a hand to her own mouth and quickly tried to rub away any smudges of her own lipstick.

"Yeah it's a... it's something I could definitely do better on."

Lillian hurried to help her mother carry the suitcases to her bedroom, tossing an apologetic look over her shoulder as they left the room. Marcy laughed, chuckled, and tugged at the collar of her blouse. It was a good thing the food had started burning, otherwise Mrs. Waldron might have walked in on a whole different kind of girls' night. Marcy wondered how long she would be benched if Lorraine had caught her tearing off Lillian's underwear with her teeth.

She shivered at that thought, both the mental image and the idea of being caught, and went to see what she could do in the kitchen to salvage dinner.

Despite saying she would leave them alone, Lorraine appeared in the dining room fifteen minutes into the meal insisting they ignore her as she prepared a snack. There was no question that the mood had been effectively ruined, so Lillian and Marcy both invited her to join them for dinner. They didn't talk about Marcy being benched, despite her multiple attempts to bring the topic around, and she eventually decided to drop it.

The next day, Marcy showed up at the park in uniform just in case there was a slew of injuries and Lorraine to change her mind. It had been raining since dawn. Not enough to force a delay, but enough that people might slip on wet grass or mud, the ball might go wild, any number of mishaps could get her in the game.

The protestors were still there by the clubhouse entrance. Today they were joined by a man she recognized as a reporter by his suit, his thick-framed glasses, and the way he was hunched forward to protect a pad of paper in his right hand. He was talking to one of the protestors and nodding emphatically at whatever was being said.

Marcy walked up behind the reporter and jabbed his shoulder with two fingers. "Maybe you want to hear what I have to say."

He turned, looked her up and down, and immediately straightened up. "Hey! Number 7 herself, Marcy Neal. You're really willing to give a statement?"

"Are you willing to write down and print what I actually say?"

He held up his pencil as if that was proof. Then he tapped the tip against his tongue, and leaned toward her in anticipation.

Marcy hadn't prepared anything but she said the first thing that came to mind. "My words in the other article were taken out of context. I never asked the country to go to war. I didn't ask for men's baseball to be suspended. And I certainly don't want a single life to be lost. Caroline Rainy and Ida Coe and Lorna Lowell, and every other woman on every team in this new league are just doing the same thing as women in munitions factories and the Red Cross and everywhere on the home front. We're keeping the country running. My earlier statement came from frustration that it took such ridiculous extremes to give us the opportunity."

He raised an eyebrow as his pencil flew across the page. "So if the war ended tonight, and all the men got on the first boat home, would you ladies step aside? Let them have their ballpark back?"

Marcy grinned wide and winked. "Maybe we'd play them for it."

She walked away as he scribbled the last response. Rainy had arrived and was leaning against the clubhouse door waiting for her.

"I liked that last line," Rainy said as they walked inside together. "Maybe a little cocky."

"Let's hope it doesn't kick me in the keister like last time."

"Either way, you gave them something to use besides 'Rainy in the rain.' I swear, every time there's so much as a cloud in the sky during a game..."

Marcy laughed. "That's your fault for having such a great name. It's every lazy journo's dream."

"Maybe I should change it."

"You could always get married again." She expected a laugh, and looked over when it never came. Rainy's lips were pressed together in a tight line. "Hey, I'm just kidding around."

"No, you weren't," Rainy said.

Marcy sighed and put her hand on Rainy's elbow to guide her closer to the wall. She looked to make sure no one was around before she spoke.

"We haven't really talked about that, but I guess we have to. It hurt when I found out you got engaged. Especially because of how I found out, and who it was to. But I'm not mad about it anymore. You came to your senses and we got back together, and we found out that we're probably not meant to be. So I'm not~"

"I didn't come to my senses," Rainy said.

Marcy frowned. "Of course you did."

"He left me. We never went through with getting married. There were things he expected from me, and I was willing to do them. I enjoyed doing them. But not often enough. Or enthusiastically enough. I don't know. So he finally got fed up and left me for someone else."

"Oh. I'm sorry, Caro."

Rainy looked up. "Are you? You got what you wanted."

Marcy shook her head. "No, I didn't. Sure, I was giddy when I saw you were available. And I was more than happy to pick things up where we left off. But all I ever wanted was for you to be happy. I just thought that meant the house and the husband and all that jazz."

"I'm happy when I'm with you. And that's the honest truth. I know what I said the other night. About you and Lillian. I meant it. I really did. I guess it's like what you said about Nicholas. You being happy is more important than what I want."

Marcy looked down at her hands, fiddling with her fingernails. "If I walked away from Lillian right now, what would you do?"

"I won't ask you to do that."

"I know, but if it did happen. Would you be willing to run around? Keep secrets? With everything we've got at stake right now?"

Rainy shook her head. "I don't know, Mars. I don't think I would. We've got one chance at making this league work, and at being the team who takes it all home. We could be set for life if we come out on top this season. I-I don't think it's right to risk that."

"Right." Marcy sighed. "And I hate that I have to agree with you."

"And you have a chance with Lillian. You should at least give that a chance. See where that goes. Don't bring me into it at all. Just do what's right for you."

Marcy rubbed her hands over her face. "Maybe what's right for me is waiting for you to be ready."

"I don't know when that will be."

"I know."

"I don't know if there will ever be a time when what I want and the game~"

"I know." She took Rainy's hand in hers. "But you're worth waiting for. Even if you never show up."

Rainy smiled, but there were tears in her eyes.

They stepped away from each other when Rosalind came into the corridor. She was in full uniform, taking long strides, but she slowed when she saw them.

"Everything okay, ladies?"

"Everything's fine," Marcy said, rubbing the back of her hand against her eye.

Rosalind decided to accept the lie. "Well, come on, then. We've got a game to win."

Marcy smiled and followed Rosalind out to the field, walking backward to keep an eye on Rainy.

"You heard the woman. Let's go show the Prohibitionists what professionals look like."

Rainy chuckled and jogged to catch up.

CHAPTER TWENTY-ONE

"IT WAS *a cool Fall day when the Shrikes hosted their final game against the Pros, a lake breeze sweeping across the field before the first inning got underway. Each team had two losses and two wins under their belt for this series, and this final game was the dealbreaker. Whoever lost this time was out of the race for the pennant, and every player on both sides obviously had that thought in their minds as they took the field.*

"From way up here in the press box it was easy to forget we weren't watching a normal game of baseball. The long red braids of Caroline Rainy, standing tall and proud on center stage, whipped every time she fired the ball. Rosalind O'Brien slid into third base in the third inning and spent the whole rest of the game with a red-brown stain all down the right side of her uniform to remind everyone in the stands of how fiercely she was playing the game.

"And fierce she had to be, because the Pros were certainly living up to their moniker! Pitcher Anna Stewart had an allergy to the ball and threw in a hectic, unpredictable style that had our local girls' heads spinning. Constance Ferguson was a triple threat between hitting, fielding, and speed. She was solely responsible for three of the Pros runs by the sixth inning.

"Both teams traded the lead like a hot potato. Tied up at the end of the second, 3-3. Tied after the third, 5-5, a score that stood until the seventh inning, when the whole game turned on its head. Because the top of the seventh inning was when the Shrikes threw a five-foot-eight brunette wrench into the works and sent Marcy Neal out onto the field.

"Neal, a source of controversy for her statements over the war, hadn't been seen on the field for the past two outings, and her absence was sorely felt. Her arrival was marked by a cacophony from the crowd. Boos and cheers in equal measure, though this reporter believes the joy drowned out the anger by just a smidge. She approached the plate and assumed the position as if she hadn't been gone at all. Stewart marked one ball and two strikes against the dark-haired shortstop, but Neal didn't give her the satisfaction and sent the last pitch soaring so high I could have caught it in my hat.

"Neal's home run pushed Ida Coe off her base, and the score was finally a little more lopsided at 7-5. There was no booing from the home crowd at this point as Neal jogged around the baseline in a manner that looked very much like a victory lap. She took off her cap as she passed home plate and continued on toward the dugout, waving it in the air toward the crowd as she acknowledged their forgiveness for what she'd said in the papers.

"After that, there was no catching up for the Pros, despite their best efforts. Two innings later the game ended with a Shrike victory, 10-8, and the Pros season came to an end. But there is no shame in the loss because even a Chicago devotee can't help but admit the Detroit gals put up one heck of a fight. And it was because of their efforts that made winning taste that little bit sweeter.

"I admit I was as skeptical as anyone when these ladies swept in and took over parks across the country, but I grudgingly admitted that any game was better than seeing the fields get overgrown and abandoned. Folks, I am here to tell you that from where I'm sitting, the game is only as good as whoever is playing it, and the Shrikes have kept baseball alive in the Windy City."

- Frederick "Math" Mathison, *Chicago Tribune*

"There's a fucking Pro outside asking for you," Edith said as she came into the clubhouse.

Moxie looked over her shoulder but only saw a blank wall behind her. "Me?" Even though she knew who it probably was, even though the color rising in her cheeks likely told everyone what it was about. "I don't know any Pros."

"She seems to know you," Edith said as she started changing out of her uniform. "It's Number 2, if that helps. Torres."

"Good hitter," Lorna said.

"Damn good hitter," Edith confirmed. "Don't mind saying that now that we don't have to play against her again."

The other players cheered, and Moxie took the opportunity to slip out.

She found Celia halfway between the home and visitor clubhouses, still in uniform and looking completely at home, one shoulder against a support beam.

"What are you doing here?"

Celia smiled and pushed away from the beam. "Good game today."

Moxie grimaced, unsure what to do with that compliment at this particular time. She looked over her shoulder to make sure no one had followed her.

"I'm not sure the rest of your team will feel the same way if they catch us talking."

"Relax. No one saw me slip away. It's been hard not reaching out while we were in town. But I figured you probably wouldn't fraternize with the enemy anyway. But now that the series is over, I wanted to know if I could take you out to dinner."

Moxie was shaking her head before the question was asked. "No. No, I'm sorry. I've been thinking about everything that happened in Detroit, and I don't... I'm not..." She took off her glasses so she wouldn't have to see Celia clearly. "I don't think I want that."

"Oh."

"I know I teased you during the game, and I'm sorry, but I~"

"You don't have to be sorry. It's okay." Celia sounded disappointed, but not upset. "I guess I understand that. We're in town until tomorrow, and I think you leave for Brooklyn right after that...?"

Moxie nodded.

"Okay. The invitation stands. We're staying at the Blackstone Hotel. You know it?"

"Of course I know it. But I'm not going to-to do~"

"I know," Celia interrupted. "Room 513. Just letting you know. So you'll know." She started to back away. "You really did play an outstanding game today, Iona. If nothing else, I wanted to be sure someone told you that."

Moxie blushed deeper, her face almost on fire. "Okay. Y-yeah, okay."

Celia laughed. "You're welcome."

"What? Oh! Thank you."

"See you next season, Moxie."

She watched the blurry woman walk away and then put her

glasses back on. She returned to the clubhouse as slowly as possible. She wanted the time to think about the invitation and what it meant. She knew what dinner would have led to. And she didn't want that. She *didn't*. Did she…? She had to admit there was something like disappointment growing in her chest. But if she'd said yes, then she would be the kind of person who said yes to invitations like that.

A person like Rainy or Marcy or Rosalind. And weren't they all swell…? They were some of the best women she'd ever known, in fact. Why shouldn't she want to be like them? It would be an honor to be like them.

When she got back to her cubby, she caught Rainy's eye. The pitcher, strands of hair stuck to the sweat on her still-red face, raised her eyebrows. "Everything okay?"

"Uh-huh," Moxie said. "You played a good game today."

Rainy grinned. "I'm not alone in that."

Another cheer went up. Someone whistled to get attention, and Lillian climbed up onto a bench. Moxie hadn't even seen their new benefactor's daughter arrive, but she looked to have been hanging out next to Marcy's cubby. The cheering died down and she turned at the waist to scan the room.

"Mother has asked me to extend an invitation to the entire team to a dinner tomorrow night at the Blackstone Hotel. Bring your family, your significant others, anyone who wants to cheer you on to the pennant is welcome to come. The Waldon family is footing the bill, so definitely bring your appetites as well! Wonderful performance, ladies!"

She started another round of applause.

Moxie faced her cubby so no one could read anything into her reaction. Why did it have to be the Blackstone? Of all the hotels in Chicago, of all the ballrooms, it had to be one downstairs from the snake in the Garden. She took off her glasses and took a towel out of her cubby, pressed the cloth to her face, and breathed deeply in the hopes it would help clear her mind.

Marcy had to wear a dress. That was very firmly asserted by Lorraine Waldron. "If you need to buy one, just go to our store and tell any associate who you are. They've been told to extend a line of credit to any Shrikes." Marcy reluctantly went to the store and allowed the chirpy women who smelled like powder treat her like one of their dolls. She told herself it was for the greater good. A nice dress would be a reusable resource, and they couldn't just keep borrowing things from Ida.

She didn't know what made her dress beautiful or how the hell it could cost the number on the price tag. It was just a black dress with a high collar and no sleeves. It was too tight, which the saleswoman said was because it actually fit her perfectly, and she wanted out of it as soon as she put it on. Whatever the reason for the existence of the dress, she didn't mind too much as long as the money wasn't coming out of her account. She did ask Ida to help with her hair and makeup - "The bare minimum," she insisted, "the least you think I can get away with at this sort of shindig." - and had to admit she looked better than she ever had.

Marcy felt like there were spotlights on her when she walked into the Blackstone ballroom. Heads turned, examined her, then looked away. She'd been prepared for the humiliation of staring, but the shun of indifference caught her off-guard. She tugged at the collar of the dress, resisted the urge to pluck at her hips, and was mindful of every step she took in her heels.

Rosalind was standing by a table of drinks in a pair of slacks and a wrap-around blouse. She didn't even bother to hide her smile but she waved Marcy over.

"How'd you get away with pants?"

"No one said dresses were mandatory."

"That was literally the only stipulation Lorraine Waldron made."

"Oh. Oops." She had a napkin folded in one hand, unfolding her fingers to reveal a pile of small pigs-in-blankets. "Horse dor-vehs?"

"I'll pass." Marcy scanned the room. She saw a few other Shrikes looking equally gussied up, some of them almost recognizable in their finery. "I should have just said to hell with it. Some women just aren't built for this kind of frou-frou."

Rosalind looked past her and raised an eyebrow. "And some definitely are."

Marcy was already regretting it as she turned to see who had just arrived. She knew in her heart who it would be and braced herself, but nothing could have prepared her for the sight of Caroline Rainy.

Her dress was strapless, midnight blue, with black lace on the bodice. Her hair was up but a handful of ringlets fell in artful curls to frame her face. She was stopped awkwardly on the threshold of the ballroom, one hand against her stomach while the other hovered near her face as if she wanted to pull the brim of a cap down over her eyes.

Marcy reached for Rosalind's hand without looking, grabbed a tiny sausage, and crammed it into her mouth.

"You're with the Waldron girl, right?" Rosalind said under her breath.

"Shush. There's nothing wrong with staring."

"Drooling, though..."

Marcy swept a hand over her chin and forced herself to look away. "Speaking of Lillian, have you seen her around anywhere?"

Rosalind shook her head and scanned the room. "I saw Lorraine earlier. She looked like she was inspecting the troops. Making sure we're all in the proper uniform."

"What did she say about yours?"

"Sighed. Heavily."

Marcy chuckled and patted Rosalind on the arm. "I'm going to see if I can find Lillian."

"Good luck."

Her first stop was a waiter carrying a tray of champagne. She plucked one for herself and took a slow sip. There were some perks to this sort of shindig.

The room wasn't particularly large, but there were so many people and waiters and tables set up that it felt like navigating a labyrinth. She meandered through the crowd, smiling to people who made eye contact with her and staying in constant motion to prevent any potential conversation. She had no idea who most of the people were. Supporters of the team? Baseball fans? People from the Whales front office? Maybe they were just pretty rich people invited for the sake of looking pretty and being rich.

She spotted Lillian between two columns and started working out a way to intercept. As she got closer, she discovered Lillian was surrounded by a crowd of men. She was about to make her presence known when the voices sharpened into words and she could make out what was being said.

"~proven they can play the game. It's all technical. Rules and mathematics and that sort of thing. They can't compete against men, but they don't have to. Every player on the field is equal."

"I can't argue that. I simply have a problem calling it *women's* baseball. When I look at those players, I don't even see women. Women are like you, Lillian. Soft and gentle. These women are brutes! Their arms are too muscular and they stomp around like stevedores. Some of them still have curves in the right places~"

"Ida Coe!"

The men laughed.

"But it doesn't matter how you gussy them up, they're hardly *women*."

"And they're certainly not men."

"Certainly not!"

"The worst of both worlds, really."

Marcy's face would have burst into flames if it was physically possible. The conversation up to that point had been infuriating enough, but the last interjection had been given by Lillian, who had been joining in the laughter during the rest of the conversation.

Marcy took a deep breath to calm herself down before she started walking again. She stepped into the circle and watched the faces of the men as they realized who she was. A few of them had enough shame to look away from meeting her eye, uncertain about how much of what they said had been overheard. Lillian's eyes were frozen wide, and her smile looked painted on.

"Gentlemen, may I introduce you to our secret weapon, shortstop Marcy Neal?"

They offered pinched smiles, fake greetings. One of them offered his hand but Marcy ignored it as she carefully examined all the men.

"You." She pointed to one with a walrus mustache. "How fast can you run?"

"Pardon?"

"If I challenged you to a race right now, how far would you get before you collapsed? Your face would be redder than those strawberries on the refreshment table."

He blinked in shock at her. "I-I don't see what—"

"You." She turned to a young rake-thin man with a receding hairline. "How many times could you throw a ball before you couldn't move your arm? And how many of those pitches do you think would actually make it sixty feet to home plate?"

Lillian stepped out of the circle. "Marcy, let's go for a walk."

"Rosalind O'Brien can run laps around any of you. Any man in this room! And you all know that. And you would rather attack our femininity than admit you can't beat a girl at your own game. There's no reason women can't play baseball. The Shrikes and the Pros and the Breakers are proving that. And if we have to prove our worth when the Whales or the Cubs or the White Sox get back from the war, then we'll absolutely do that."

The rake-thin man pointed a finger at her. "Hey, Marcy Neal. You're the one who was in the paper saying you'd play the men for the right to use their park."

"I meant every word, too. I'd put Caroline Rainy's arm against Joe Benz any day of the week."

"Caroline Rainy has never pitched a no-hitter."

"And Benz didn't pitch one in his first season, either."

One of the men smiled condescendingly. "So you're saying we have to make allowances for your girls rather than compare them equally."

Marcy returned his smile with an extra dose of smugness. "I'm saying that by the time the boys come home, they'll be at least one whole season out of practice. Us 'girls' will just be hitting our stride. So if anyone is going to be getting sympathy points, it won't be the women."

Lillian handed her drink to the man next to her and now used both hands to guide Marcy away from the group.

"I think you've had a little too much, Marcy, let's get you some fresh air."

Marcy let herself be led into the crowd. "What's the deal, Lillian? I thought you were having a grand old time razzing us before I showed up. Don't let me ruin your good time."

"Darn it, Marcy, you can't be foolish enough to act like this. You know how these things are done. It's how you get ahead in this world. Those men have influence. They have power. You think guys like that want to do business with Mother? Or with me, once I've taken over. I've got to show them I'm one of the boys."

"I'm not one of the boys. I'm sick of aiming low just to stroke their egos." She pulled free of Lillian's grasp. "We're going to play like women and they're going to have to deal with it."

When she stormed out of the ballroom, Lillian didn't pursue her.

CHAPTER TWENTY-TWO

EVERYONE IN the ballroom witnessed Marcy's departure. First there was a hush, and then a wave of whispers and barely-concealed chuckling. Rainy hadn't even seen Marcy up to that point in the evening. She had been trying not to move too much because moving would require her to breathe and the dress was determined to suffocate her. She smoothed a hand over her stomach again and was reminded of the stupid lace, which snagged on her fingernails even though she'd trimmed and filed them for half an hour.

Moxie appeared at her side. Moxie's dress made her look like an old woman, most likely because it had probably been borrowed from her actual grandmother, and her hair was slicked back with some kind of gel that reflected every light in the room. Her coke-bottle eyeglasses were the only recognizable thing about her.

"What do you suppose that was about?" Rainy asked.

"I don't know," Moxie said, "but Lillian isn't following her."

It took Rainy a moment to understand her implication. "Well, I'm not going to follow her."

Moxie shrugged. "Seems like somebody should." She looked Rainy up and down, whistled. "You clean up real good, Miss Rainy."

"Stop it." She looked at the exit again. "Do you really think I should follow her?"

"I don't have an opinion, really. I'm just going by that look on your face and telling you what you already know." She stepped around Rainy. "As for me, I'm going to go track down those little wiener things Rosalind had..."

Rainy watched her go. Then she looked at the exit again. Finally she sighed and put down her drink on the nearest flat surface.

She made it as far as the lobby before she found the woman she was looking for. Marcy was sitting on the stairs that led down into the main floor. Her shoes were sitting on the step next to her, and she was covering her face with both hands.

"Storming off works better if you have somewhere to go." Rainy sat down next to her and took the opportunity to toe off her shoes as well. "Are you okay?"

Marcy dropped her hands and let them fall limply in front of her. "I was excited about her. I thought we could make it work. She understands the game. She knows how much it means to me. Or I thought she did."

Rainy sighed and stretched her legs out. "Giving her the benefit of the doubt, you know that's just the game *she* has to play. Right? She's in business. Probably nine out of ten people she deals with every day is a man. She's got to lower their guards."

"That's exactly what she said."

"Because it's the truth."

Marcy pushed her hair back out of her face. "That doesn't make it feel any better."

"I know."

"I just want someone I can trust not to be two-faced, you know? I don't want to hear her talk and wonder 'is this what she really thinks? Or is it what she says in private? Which one is the lie?' I want someone who lets me know where they stand without question or, or, or gray areas."

Rainy nodded. "That's not much to ask for. You deserve to know you can trust the person you're with." She drew her knees up and rested her arms across them. "For what it's worth, I'm sorry for being such a mess with you. Telling you how I felt and then backing away and then showing up engaged to a man. You didn't deserve that."

"You were confused. I was pushing you to give answers when you didn't even know the questions yet."

"Maybe," Rainy said. "Either way. I'm sorry."

"I'm sorry, too."

Rainy ran her stockinged feet over the carpeted stairs. "I always thought the best times of my life were when I was playing ball. But that ain't really true. When I decided to try out for the Women's League, I didn't have that… I didn't… there wasn't a spark. I didn't care if I got picked or not. And then I saw you up in the stands and I wanted to play. I didn't care what team it was for. The happiest times in my life have been with you, Mars."

Marcy put her hand down on the top step. Rainy looked down at it, then moved the shoes and covered Marcy's hand with hers. After a few minutes, she squeezed and began the complicated process of standing up without ripping her dress.

"Come on," she said.

"Where are we going?"

Rainy offered her hand. "We're going to walk around the hotel."

"Why?"

"Because moving forward is always better than just sitting around like a lump on a log. And we could start walking to the train, but there's a chance we might feel like rejoining the party once we've gotten this angriness out of our systems."

Marcy was unconvinced.

"Okay, it will be easier for Lillian to find you if you just keep sitting here."

That one did it. Marcy raised her hands. Rainy took them and helped Marcy stand up. She collected their shoes, handed Marcy's to her, and then gestured vaguely to the left. The hallway in that direction seemed longer, and she hoped they could wander for a while before they were forced to turn around to find another path.

"What about you?"

Marcy said, "What?"

"You kept playing after I left. Was it still fun?"

"Sure. Yeah. It's the game. I love the game." She looked down at her feet. Rainy stayed silent. "No. It was a chore and it became a job. I started getting into scrapes, starting trouble. The number of times David had to bail me out of some backwater jail because I'd gone looking for a fight…" She chuckled. "I would take my bat with me to bars to make sure the guys there knew who I was. If I'd had one of these jerseys with my name on it back then, I probably would've worn it."

They reached the end of the hallway and turned around to go back the other way.

"I wish I'd been there to see that."

"I wish that, too," Marcy said quietly.

Rainy put her hands behind her back. She could hear the party had gotten back on track, laughter and loud voices mingling into a single noise the echoed up and down the halls.

"I'm glad you're here for this," Marcy said when they turned the next corner. "None of this would mean as much without you by my side."

Rainy grinned. "Although it might have been fun if we were on different teams. The Breakers sent a telegram back in the first weeks of the season."

"They didn't!"

"Yep. Offered me the same price as David plus an extra grand."

Marcy laughed. "Well, I'm glad you didn't take it."

"Me too. But that means you owe me a thousand bucks."

Marcy patted her hips. "Shoot, I don't have pockets. Remind me later."

Rainy laughed and lightly poked Marcy with her elbow.

They reached the end of another hall, but this one had doors on either side. One was marked EMPLOYEES ONLY, but the other had a small window set just above the handle. Marcy quickly moved ahead and peeked through the glass.

"Oh my goodness." She tested the handle and smiled over her shoulder at Rainy. "Come on."

"Wait, what is it?"

Marcy was already inside and didn't bother to enlighten her. Rainy looked over her shoulder to see if anyone was watching them, then she hurried through the door without bothering to check where she would end up. The room was easily fifteen degrees cooler than the hallway and fifty percent darker. The reason for the temperature change was the large five-lane swimming pool that dominated the space. The lighting was because the pool was obviously closed to the public.

"I don't think we're supposed to be in here."

Marcy had gone to the edge of the pool to look down into the water. "I've never seen one inside. I knew they had them, of course, but... how much do you think it costs to fill it?"

"I shudder to think." Rainy reluctantly moved closer. "I don't understand the purpose of having one indoors. Isn't the whole point to feel the shock of cold on a really hot day? You swim to cool down and get some relief."

"Because it's fun!" Marcy bent her knees and swept one foot through the water, creating a wave. "Oh my gosh! That is so chilly."

"Stop it!" Rainy looked back at the door. "You're going to get us kicked out."

Marcy shrugged and walked further along the edge of the pool. "So let them kick us out. We were going to leave anyway."

Rainy crossed her arms over her chest. "Marcy Deborah Neal. We are leaving right now."

Marcy slowly turned to face her, eyes wide and eyebrows so high they were almost obscured by the wave of her hair. "Did you just use my middle name, Caroline Francine Rainy?"

"We can't be troublemakers. Do you want Mrs. Waldron to put you right back on the bench? Because she will, if you cause a ruckus."

"Oh my, we wouldn't want to cause a ruckus."

She dipped and swept her foot through the water, this time splashing a bit on the hem of her dress. Rainy noticed the previous splash had caused Marcy to leave one wet footprint in her wake. It would dry quickly, but what if someone happened to come through before that happened? They'd know someone had been in the room. Someone with large but slender feet. Beautiful toes...

"Mars!" she hissed. "Stop it! Come away from there and stop messing around."

"Just come feel how cold it is!"

Rainy said, "I don't care."

Marcy sighed and straightened her knees. "Honestly, Rainy, you can be such a~" She put her foot down too close to the edge. The ball of her foot slipped, her arch went over the edge of the pool, and she was thrown entirely off balance. She swung her arms like she was in a flicker show, her mouth wide open as she tumbled. Rainy ran faster than she had ever run in a ballpark but she was still too slow. Marcy was in the water by the time Rainy reached the edge.

"Marcy! Can you swim?"

Marcy, spluttering, broke the surface, and swept her hands over her face. "What?"

"I asked if you know how to swim!"

"Of course I know how to swim!" Marcy bobbed like a cork, her dress spilling and floating all around her like ink. Once she was upright, the water came to just below her shoulders. "You were there. We learned at the same time."

"Oh. Right." Rainy looked around for something she could offer for help. After failing to find anything, she crouched down and offered her hand. "Here. Come here, grab my hand."

Marcy floundered. "The dress is... it's weighing me down. It feels a hundred pounds heavier."

"That's because you just filled it with water!" Rainy scolded. "Can your feet touch the bottom?"

"Yes."

"Okay, just walk to me. I'll pull you out."

Marcy waded forward and held her hands out. Rainy took her hands and had a brief overwhelming memory of all the other times Marcy's hands had been in hers. Hundreds of touches, squeezes, caresses, filled her brain in the space of a breath, and her muscles momentarily forgot what task they were supposed to be doing. Her legs and back relaxed just as Marcy tried to pull herself up.

Rainy had time to shout, "No!" before she fell, but she was underwater before she fully realized what had just happened. She had managed to twist to one side first so she hadn't fallen directly on top of Marcy, but now she was wrapped and swathed in the great wet curtains of Marcy's dress. The trap was made worse when Marcy twisted around to try and help her but only succeeded in confusing Rainy's sense of up and down.

After a few desperate seconds of splashing, Rainy broke the surface back into the air. She breathed deeply and clung to Marcy, who was now holding her upright.

"You're okay, you're okay," Marcy was saying.

Rainy opened her eyes. "You *brat!*"

"Me? I was just doing what you told me to do!"

Rainy wasn't interested in hearing logic. She smacked the water and sent a wave over them both.

"You pulled me in!"

"You said you were going to pull me up!"

"I was unbalanced!"

"That's not *my* fault!"

"You always do this. You always drag me into your messes!"

Marcy laughed. "And you enjoy every minute of it!"

"I... I don't... I..."

They bobbed up and down for a few seconds, staring at each other. Marcy was a pain in her ass, trouble waiting to happen, an accident factory. But she was also the reason they were being paid to play baseball. She was the reason Rainy had gone to Detroit and

Philadelphia and Boston, the reason she had a playing card, the reason she'd heard thousands of people chant and cheer her name. Marcy was chaos, but maybe life needed chaos to be worth living.

She cupped Marcy's face in her hands. The smile faded from Marcy's face as she finally recognized the look in Rainy's eye.

"You're with~"

Marcy shook her head as much as Rainy's grip would let her. "No I'm not."

"Does she know that?"

"I don't~"

Rainy cut off the last word by kissing her. Marcy clung to her, throwing herself against Rainy so hard that Rainy's feet slipped and she fell backward. Luckily she remained upright and they just drifted, floating, kissing, holding each other, both of them trying to keep above water but not really minding if they went under now and then.

CHAPTER TWENTY-THREE

MOXIE TOOK off her glasses in the elevator. She looked for somewhere to put them, realized she couldn't see anything without them, and put them back on. She tucked her hair behind her ears. She hated her dress. It was the nicest thing from the trunk of her grandmother's clothes. She wished she could have taken something from her mother's closet, but she would have noticed it missing. That would lead to questions. "Why do you need to look nice? It's just going to be a bunch of girls." The dress had looked nice enough at home, but the closer she got to Celia's floor, the more she felt like a child.

She should have bought her own dress. She could certainly afford it. She could have looked like Rainy. Well... no. Nobody could have looked like Rainy. That was some kind of magical spell.

The elevator door opened and she considered waiting for them to close again. She could ride back down to the lobby and flee the building. Celia would never know she'd come this far. And there was no shame in coming this far just to change her mind. A person could change their mind, it wasn't unusual. Especially with something like this.

The doors started to close. Moxie yelped and jumped forward, bumping her hip and shoulder and the doors as she escaped the car. Damn things never should have been electrified. An operator would have let her stand there as long as she needed to. Of course maybe that wouldn't have been such a good thing. If an operator had been holding the door, she might have stood there all night long trying to make up her mind.

She reached up to her glasses. "Stop it," she snapped at herself as she dropped her hand to her side. Every floorboard creaked under her feet, announcing her progress to every room she passed. And of course 513 had to be at the end of the hall, so she had to pass by the room of every single Pro player before she reached Celia's room. But she didn't slow down and she didn't hesitate. She brought up her fist and knocked just underneath the 5. Her hands immediately went to the collar of her dress, to her glasses, her hair.

The door opened. Celia, dressed in pajamas that looked very soft with her hair pinned back, smiled. She kept one hand on the door, as if she was just grabbing room service.

"Do you think Mrs. Waldron chose this hotel on purpose?" Celia asked by way of greeting. "Rubbing it in our faces?"

"I don't know." Moxie's voice was smaller than she'd ever heard it. She hoped it sounded stronger to Celia. "I don't think any of us knew where you all were staying."

"You did," Celia pointed out.

Moxie looked down the hall toward the elevators, clocking her escape route.

Celia laughed softly. "I'm glad you did."

"Me too. I guess. I mean, I d-don't know how I feel about it. But I'm here now. And I'm not going to leave. Probably. Unless you want me to." She winced. "Should I go?"

"I don't think so." Celia stepped back and opened the door wider. "Do you want to come in?"

Moxie said, "You look like you were getting ready for bed."

"You can join me."

Moxie's mouth went dry. "Oh."

Celia waited a few seconds. Then she dropped her hand from the door and walked into the room. Moxie watched her go, then stepped into the room.

She shut the door behind her.

The room was only lit by one lamp next to the bed, but it didn't need much more than that. It cast a yellow glow over everything, and it turned the shadows burnt-orange. Celia picked up a bottle that she'd had on the dresser and carried it to the bed. She sat down on the edge of the mattress and casually draped one leg over the other.

"How was the party?"

"Annoying." She shrugged. "You know how that sort of thing is. People with money parading you around like you're paper dolls."

Celia deepened her voice. "Look at them, they're almost like real ball players!"

"Exactly!" Moxie said. "Marcy gave a couple of them a piece of her mind, though."

"Mm. She's got cheek, that one."

"Yeah."

Celia took a drink from her bottle. She was watching Moxie very carefully, and Moxie was very aware of the scrutiny.

"How come they call you Moxie?"

"You know my name."

"Sure. But there's got to be something more to it than that. Nicknames like Moxie don't just happen. And it's not a straight line from Moccia. So? Who started it?"

"Gosh. That, I really don't know. It was probably one of the girls I used to play stickball with. You know I grew up on the same block as Rainy and Marcy. It might've been one of them who first used the nickname. Most likely, actually." Her eyes lit up at a long-forgotten memory. "My grandma didn't like me playing boy games. Mainly because there were usually boys playing. I'd come back all dirty and scraped up. She would always try to keep me from going to play. She would lock me in the room if she even heard Marcy's voice on the street.

"It happened one day when we were supposed to play these boys from across town. A real grudge match. I had to be there, it was a pride thing. But grandma told me to stay home and be a good girl. Read and do my homework. She had an old armchair right beside the front door so there was no way I could get past her."

Celia smiled knowingly. "So you went out the window."

"I've gone out a window or two in my time. But I thought I had to be sneakier that first time." She smiled and sat down on the bed next to Celia. "I went down to the basement where our building had a coal chute."

Celia laughed and slapped her knee.

"I showed up covered in coal dust. I must've looked like a shadow that peeled off the sidewalk. And someone..." She pictured the moment in her mind and smiled, nodded. "Marcy. It was Marcy.

She clapped me on the shoulder and she coughed when a big ol' plume of coal dust went up. And she said, 'Well, kid, you definitely got moxie.' After that the name stuck."

"Well, it's fitting."

"Nah. It means fearless. And I'm definitely feeling more like an Iona than a Moxie right now."

Celia shifted her weight so she could face her. "Well, maybe I can be the fearless one."

Moxie looked at her. Celia hesitated just long enough that Moxie could move or turn away or say no. But she remained where she was, eyes open, lips parting just a little before Celia's lips touched them. The kiss didn't even last for ten seconds before Celia pulled away, tucking her bottom lip into her mouth. She started to say something but Moxie kissed her again before she could get any of the words out. Emboldened, Celia leaned into Moxie, their hips pressed hard together. When Moxie opened her mouth to gasp in surprise, Celia took it as an invitation.

When Moxie's head cleared, she put her hand on Celia's chest and gently pushed her back. Celia leaned away from her but left her hand on Moxie's leg.

"We don't~" Celia started.

"No, no, I want to." She licked her lips. She couldn't look at Celia now, though her eyes had been open throughout the kiss. "I hate how I look in this dress. I think if I'm going to remember what happens next, I shouldn't be wearing it. For the sake of the memories."

Celia smiled. "Sounds reasonable. Stand up."

Moxie stood and turned her back. Celia stood as well, and Moxie stiffened as she began undoing the buttons. The hands paused.

"Still okay?"

"Mm-hmm."

The unbuttoning resumed and the dress became looser. She pulled at the front and slipped it down her arms. She shivered when Celia's hands brushed her hips to help guide it down her legs. She was standing in another woman's hotel room, lips still tender from kissing that woman, in her underwear, and she was... fine.

Celia's hands rested on her waist. They felt heavier and hotter than they could possibly be in reality. Then Celia bent down and kissed the curve of Moxie's neck where it curved into her shoulder, and Moxie melted. Celia held her up easily and continued to explore the soft skin behind Moxie's ear with her lips and tongue.

"We don't have to do anything to each other," Celia whispered.

"We don't?" Moxie sounded half-asleep even to her own ears.

"We don't," Celia said. "We can just do things to ourselves. We can finish taking off our clothes, then we can get in that bed together and touch ourselves."

Moxie's ears burned. "That sounds really nice."

"I think so, too."

She turned around and kissed Celia, her hands going for the buttons of her pajama top. Celia put her hands on Moxie's hips and walked her toward the bed without breaking the kiss. The top was discarded and Moxie felt warm skin under her hands. She explored without looking, cupped a heavy breast, moaned as she found the nipple with her thumb and teased it.

They broke the kiss just long enough for Celia to grab the blankets and throw them back. While she was doing that, Moxie stepped away from her and took off her underclothes as quickly as possible. The room felt suddenly very cold, so she climbed into the bed and scooted to the far side so Celia could join her. She was still shaking, but Celia looked a bit shaky as well. They faced each other with only a thin strip of mattress between them.

"I don't know how to start," Moxie admitted.

"You just start." Celia said. "Just like normal. Like this."

Celia put one hand on her own neck and slid it down, across the smooth brown skin of her chest, teasing the dark nipple, resting it between her breasts before traveling lower. Moxie knew Celia was staring at her, but she couldn't take her eyes off that hand, those fingers, that skin. She didn't even realize she was moving her own hand, but she pressed her palm against her thigh and bent her knee. When she looked up to meet Celia's eyes, Celia smiled at her.

"I think you know where it goes from here."

"Show me anyway."

They both looked down. Moxie touched herself, but she was focused on the way Celia's hand moved. She used her middle fingers, and she moved her hips as the muscles in her forearm flexed. Moxie watched, hypnotized, lips parted as if she was in a stupor. She had crouched behind home plate and seen this body twist and flex and wondered what it would look like under the uniform. Now she was seeing everything, and it was... absolutely... glorious...

"Look at me," Celia said breathlessly.

Moxie looked into her eyes. A sound came out of her mouth, a noise she hadn't intended to make and couldn't have identified, and she moved across the pillow. Celia made the same move and then they were kissing, their bodies falling toward the center of the bed as if they'd been pushed, and Moxie hooked her leg over Celia's hip.

"You can touch me if you want," Celia gasped into the kiss.

"Yes," Moxie said.

Celia chuckled. "Wait what?"

"Yes," Moxie was shaking, trying hard to keep her voice steady. "Yes, you can touch me."

"No, I said–" Celia cut herself off with a laugh, shook her head, and kissed Moxie again.

Moxie didn't understand what was so funny, but then there was a hand on top of hers. She gasped and broke the kiss, and Celia shifted her lips to Moxie's chin, her cheek, down to her jaw and then her throat, sucking gently and using her tongue in new and interesting ways. Moxie arched her back and tried to ignore the sensations happening between her legs.

"I think I'm not going to last long, Celia."

"That's okay."

"I want it to go on," Moxie said.

Celia kissed her way back up. "It will. We don't have to stop. It's not an ending."

"But if I finish..."

"Then I finish." She kissed Moxie's lips. "And then you can finish again." She kissed Moxie's chin. "And then I finish..." She tilted her head to kiss Moxie's neck. "And then maybe we finish together."

"Oh..." Moxie's eyelids fluttered shut. "H-how do we know when we're... finished...?"

"I think we can figure that out in the moment."

Moxie licked her lips as Celia's hair tickled her breasts. Making decisions in the moment suddenly appealed very much to her. She pulled Celia with her as she rolled onto her back and shut off the long-term part of her brain for the next little while.

****

Moxie closed the door as quietly as possible, wincing when she heard the latch click against the plate. She knew that no one would think anything of the sound of a door closing in a hotel, but all her nerves were on edge. She was back in her grandmother's dress but she hadn't bothered to put on her shoes. Hopefully that would make the floor creak less. Her hair was a horror show. She looked around to make sure the hallway was empty and then walked quickly to the elevator.

She slumped against the side of the car. She withdrew her wish from earlier about operators. She was extraordinarily grateful no one would be witness to her departure. Except Celia. She smiled and blushed. She was glad Celia knew. Her mind was still trying to process all the sensations and sights she'd just experienced. Looking down to see the top of Celia's head, those wild curls spread across her thighs, as her mouth was~

The elevator dinged on the ground floor. Moxie jumped at the sound and shuffled out into the lobby. If she remembered correctly, there was a side door she could use to make a quick and honorable exit. She didn't know if the party was still going but she didn't want to risk running into anyone who might have questions about where she'd been or why she looked this way.

She rounded a corner and immediately ran into two of her teammates.

The three women jumped away from each other, all of them speaking at once. It took her a few seconds to realize the woman talking the loudest was Marcy, and only a little longer to identify the other woman as Rainy. Moxie stopped her own mouth from babbling. Marcy followed suit and looked Moxie up and down. Moxie also took the opportunity to examine them and realized they were completely drenched from head to toe. Both of them were holding their shoes in their hands, and puddles were growing on the carpet around their bare feet.

Moxie looked at their faces. She took in Marcy's mischievous smile, Rainy's furtive eyes, small smile, and blushing cheeks. Then she stepped to one side and indicated the path she'd just taken.

"Elevators to left, ladies."

Relief washed over Rainy's face. "Thank you, Iona."

"Sure thing."

Marcy looked Moxie over again as she passed her. "I'm glad you had a such good time at the party tonight."

"What party?" Moxie asked.

Marcy squeezed her arm and followed Rainy around the corner. Moxie waited until she heard the elevator bell ding before she shook her head and continued her own escape.

It really had been a great party.

CHAPTER TWENTY-FOUR

MARCY SAT up and leaned to the left, peeking out through the slats to make sure the corridor beyond was still empty. She thought they would've heard anyone arriving, but they'd both been very preoccupied up until a few minutes ago. They were behind a false wall just outside the guest clubhouse of the Brooklyn Breakers' park. It was still a few hours until anyone would show up, but there was always the chance a maintenance worker would happen by or a player would arrive early.

"I think we're in the clear."

Rainy, still lying on the floor next to her, lifted her hips to pull her pants back up. "Good thing, too. This was the riskiest place yet."

Marcy grinned over her shoulder. "I thought you liked risk."

"To a degree." She picked up their shirts, untangled the sleeves, and tossed Marcy's to her. She sat up to put hers on. "But the law of averages says we're bound to get unlucky eventually. And the more we do this, the more opportunity there is for someone to see. Or hear..."

"Hey, you were being just as loud."

"That's not my fault."

Marcy said, "But the fact we have to do it at all *is* your fault. You were the one who cornered me in the equipment room before the first game. You stuck your hand down my pants. You were the one who said you needed me right there."

"*You* were the one who said I never pulled my weight in bed. I'm just making up for lost time."

Marcy sighed. "I remember… but then what happened?"

"You know what happened."

They'd beaten the Breakers 6-2, an unprecedented landslide victory against a team that had previously given them nothing but headaches. Before the second game, Marcy said they had to recreate the exact conditions of their pre-game rituals to guarantee a similar result. Rainy had asked if it had to be the *exact* conditions, and Marcy responded by going down on her in the abandoned men's restroom. They'd won that game by six runs. While the rest of the team was celebrating, Marcy had caught Rainy's eye across the clubhouse and smiled with eager anticipation.

"We're four for four. Now we've got the fifth out of the way." Marcy chuckled and leaned over to brush a kiss over Rainy's cheek. "Today's game is in the bag."

"Don't get cocky," Rainy said.

"I can't help it. I do my best work when I'm cocky."

"So you think."

Marcy stood and held her hand out. Rainy took it and allowed herself to be pulled to her feet. Marcy faced Rainy and started straightening her clothes for her.

"We'll go out there. We'll win the pennant. And then we'll play San Fran. It'll be fantastic. I've always wanted to see California."

Rainy cupped Marcy's face. "Don't jinx anything."

"No jinxing. Kiss for luck?"

Rainy leaned in and kissed her. Marcy loosely wrapped her arms around Rainy's waist and pressed against her. Rainy made a noise of protest against Marcy's mouth, but she didn't end the kiss until a few seconds later.

"Don't start anything you can't finish."

"I can finish."

The sound of an opening door finally made Rainy pull away. "Even you're not that good, Mars."

Marcy sighed and touched her hair to make sure it wasn't too mussed. Rainy peeked to make sure the hall was empty before she left their nook. Marcy waited a few seconds before she followed, walking casually toward the clubhouse so she wouldn't arrive immediately after Rainy.

She really did believe in superstition, and she was trying to keep herself from thinking too far ahead. The Breakers had come into this series thinking they wouldn't have to try. By the time they realized the Shrikes were a force to be reckoned with, it was too late to turn the tide. All they had to do now was win this game and they'd have the pennant.

Rosalind looked up when Marcy entered the clubhouse. She smiled and held out her hand to Moxie. "Told you," she said. "Under two minutes."

Moxie dropped a dollar into Rosalind's hand, then glared at Marcy. "You couldn't have lingered a little bit?"

"What was your bet?" Marcy asked.

Rosalind tucked the money into her cubby. "How long it would take for you to show up after Rainy appeared. Moxie said five minutes. I knew it never takes a shadow that long to appear."

Rainy, at her own cubby, ducked her head and turned away to hide her blush as she finished putting her hair into the now-signature braids.

"It's not that strange we'd get here at the same time, Ros," Marcy said. "We're all staying in the same hotel. And not all of us can run like you."

"Uh-huh," Rosalind said, continuing to gear up. "Just make sure you stay predictable. I'll have Moxie buying my lunch for the rest of the season."

The rest of the team drifted in over the next few minutes, which prompted Marcy to ask Rosalind if there were any bets about anyone else. Rosalind laughed. "I only make bets on the sure things."

Soon everyone was too distracted by thoughts of the game to bother teasing. They didn't want to make the same mistake the Breakers did and let their confidence get the better of them.

The teams took the field at two-fifteen. The bleachers were full to busting with fans, some of whom were Shrike fans who had made the trip from Chicago to see the team in action. Rosalind, Marcy, Ida, and Moxie left the dugout and shielded their eyes from the sun to gaze up at the sea of faces, everyone chattering and laughing and jostling peanut and popcorn containers as they waited for the game to begin.

Two boys wearing Cubs hats saw the players and waved them over. Marcy went to see what they wanted, noticing immediately that they both had a half-dozen Cracker Jack cards fanned out in their hands. She pushed up the brim of her cap with one knuckle and smiled up at them.

"Did you boys come all the way to New York to see us play?"

"Sure did!" One of them stretched his arm out through the rails. He had the card pinched between his thumb and forefinger, and a pen was tucked between his second and third fingers. "You're Marcy Neal, right? Will you sign that?"

Marcy grinned and plucked the card and pen from his fingers. "Sure thing, kid." She pointed at the rest of their deck. "Who else you got up there?"

The boys shuffled and examined, listing off the names. Marcy twisted at the waist and whistled. "Ros, Ida, Lorna, Hildy, Moxie. We got some business to take care of before we take care of the other business." She faced the boys again. "What's your name, kid?"

"I'm Benny. He's Daniel."

"Hiya, Benny and Daniel. Thanks for coming down to support the team." She wrote her name across the red background of her card. Rosalind had arrived, and Marcy handed her the pen. "We're signing cards for these boys. Benny and Daniel."

Rosalind looked at the card, then looked up at the boys, then looked at Marcy. "What's this?"

"Fans, Ros," Marcy said with a wide grin. "Sure as shootin'. We've got fans."

One of the boys, Daniel, had crawled halfway through the railing to deliver his cards. He hung on to the rail with one hand, hanging from it like a monkey at the zoo.

"We ain't got a Caroline Rainy card yet," he said, "but we've been lookin'. Can she sign one of your cards for us, too?"

"I'll do you one better. Hold on a second." Marcy jogged back to the dugout.

Rainy had come out and was watching the autograph session with her arms crossed and a bemused expression on her face.

"What in tarnation is going on over there?"

"The first meeting of the Chicago Shrikes fan club." She crouched down and fished a ball from the bag next to the dugout steps. She tossed it to Rainy. "They don't have a Rainy card. So you're gonna sign that for them."

Rainy looked like she wanted to argue, but then she smiled and tossed the ball up. She caught it easily and started walking.

"What are their names?"

Both boys almost jumped out of their skin when they saw Rainy approaching, and Benny actually shrieked when he saw her sign the baseball. She tossed it to him in a gentle, easily-caught arc, and the boys were so overjoyed that they almost forgot to get their cards back from the other players.

Rainy stepped back and watched, laughing quietly before she turned her attention to the rest of the crowd. Men and women were watching the autograph seekers like they were the pre-game entertainment. But a few people waved when they saw her looking. She waved back, touched the brim of her hat, and nodded to show her gratitude for their presence.

"Did you ever imagine?" she asked.

"What, a crowd like this? For women? Absolutely." She put her hands on her hips. "It's a bit unfortunate that we had to eliminate all their other options before they were willing to buy a ticket. But they've seen what we can do now. We're established. We can play the game and make it worth watching. Do you think those boys are going to forget us just because the male players come back from the war?"

Benny was already running back into the stands, taking the steps three at a time, his signed baseball extended out for anyone who wanted to take a look at it.

"I hope not," Rainy said. "But I've learned not to make too many predictions about things like that." She breathed in deep and exhaled, turning to look out onto the field. "Fresh-cut grass. God, I love that smell."

"It's good." Marcy looked into the park as well. Most of the Breakers were already in position. "So nothing is guaranteed except this game. Right here, right now. And the chance to be the first champions in this division of our new league. We could go down in history today, Caro."

"It's definitely a possibility."

Marcy slapped Rainy's arm. "Then let's stop lollygagging around and get it done."

She jogged back to the dugout, lifting her arm to wave at the visiting crowd. The other players, having returned Daniel's cards to him, were also running along the baseline so they'd be ready when the game began. She knew it had done everyone a world of good to see their efforts were appreciated, that people were actually paying attention to their hard work, but they were done playing to the crowd.

It was time to play some ball.

***

Moxie had spent the time before the game scouring the

newspaper, reading any article that mentioned Europe. She knew more about the geography of France than she'd ever expected to learn. There were battles that had been going on for months, and she could barely figure out how to pronounce any of the names. Verdin? Verdoon? Some? Som-me? As far as she could tell, armies were standing on opposite sides of a field shooting at each other day and night.

"How do you know when a war is over?" she asked, not really expecting an answer.

Hildy overheard and gave one anyway. "There's a treaty."

"Sure, but... how does... Look." She folded the paper. "Everyone is fighting all over Europe. Some of these people have been fighting since February. Is one side suddenly going to say 'okay, that's enough, let's go home now'? Are there going to be signs that it's about to happen? And what if the bad guys say 'okay, we give up,' and it's just a trick so everyone lowers their guard? Because I keep looking and it just keeps looking like it's the way life is going to be now."

Ida said, "It has to end eventually."

"You think?" Moxie asked.

"I mean, sure. Eventually one side is gonna run out of soldiers to send."

It was almost an hour later and Moxie was still shaken by how casually Ida had said that. It would be hard to celebrate the end of a war if it meant wiping out an entire fighting force. But given how many men had already died, they were already past the point of celebration. At least she hoped they were. There couldn't be any winners after everything both sides had done.

Moxie shook her head to clear it of those thoughts. She couldn't let herself think about that. She wouldn't let it distract her from the game.

She was crouched in position behind home plate. They'd already had their first turn at bat and gotten two runs. Now it was their job to keep the Breakers from squaring things up.

She hooked her fingers in the metal grill of her mask and bent her knees to drop into a crouch. She swept her hand through the dirt between her feet and then rubbed the grit into her fingertips with her thumb. New York dirt, a Brooklyn field. There were people who would say it didn't matter, that every park was the same, but they were wrong. The air was different, the soil was different, even the shape of the park could be vastly different from one city to the next. Pitching mounds were always the same height. First base was always the same distance from second. But the outfield...? That was a crapshoot.

Directly ahead of her, Rainy had taken position on the mound. It was no wonder she'd become such a favorite of the fans. She exuded confidence and control before she even pitched a single ball. In the first half, she'd gotten tagged out on her way home, but she'd given it her all.

Moxie adjusted her stance as the first Breaker approached the plate. She was blonde, short and wide, with curls that exploded out from underneath her cap. GRAHAM was stitched along the shoulders of her uniform. Moxie remembered her from their previous face-offs against the Breakers. She was a strong hitter and it made sense the Breakers would put her out in front. They were trying to start things off and get on base immediately. Moxie figured Graham's purpose was to get someone in place that the next hitters could turn into a double- or triple-play.

Moxie dropped her hand between her legs and signaled to Rainy. *Fast, in.*

Rainy nodded. She remembered Graham, too. She pitched the fastball straight over the plate. Graham swung for it, but she couldn't get the angle. Moxie came out of her crouch to chase the ball and lobbed it back to the mound. She got back into position and pounded her mitt back into shape, then signaled to Rainy again.

Fast, in.

Rainy shook her head. Moxie thought it would throw Graham off, but she would defer to Rainy's judgement on that. She made a fist with her free hand, then extended three fingers with her forefinger and thumb curled into a circle. Rainy nodded. A few seconds later, the ball cut through the air at a lazy curve and landed gently in Moxie's glove as easily as if they were playing catch.

Two down. Graham stomped one foot and then swung the bat back up. She held it straight in the air in front of her, standing with her butt out. It looked awkward as hell, but Moxie had seen it work in the past, so she wasn't going to say boo about it. Moxie signaled.

Fast, in.

Rainy tilted her head to the side.

Moxie signaled more emphatically. *Fast. In.*

After a second or two, Rainy nodded. Graham adjusted her grip on the neck of the bat. She leaned her weight on the inside leg and lowered her chin as she waited for the pitch. Rainy through an inside fastball, and this time it cracked off Graham's bat before Moxie could touch it. Graham took off running for first base. Moxie rose out of her crouch and watched as it arced up through the air.

Rosalind and Hildy both raced after it. Graham rounded first. Hildy dropped back to give Rosalind space. The ball hit the ground and bounced neatly into Rosalind's hand. Graham stomped on second base and kept going. Rosalind pivoted, eyed Graham's progress, and threw straight to home with the same movement.

Moxie was ready. It was clear she'd been wrong, both about the pitch and the Breakers' plan to load the bases. Graham passed Lorna Lowell on third, a streak of grey in the corner of Moxie's eye, charging down the third base line. The ball landed in Moxie's glove with a heavy SOCK!, she turned and, still in a crouch, stuck her arm out and tagged it against Graham's shoulder in a fairly hard slap. Graham stumbled but remained upright as the speed drained out of her and she finished her attempted home run in a defeated trot.

One out. Moxie straightened and faced Rainy, offering her an apologetic shrug. Rainy smiled and held up her hand, asking for the ball back. Moxie tossed it to her. Getting Graham out was a small victory but they had a lot of game left to play.

She dropped back into position, tugged on her mask, and waited for the next batter.

After two grueling hours, Marcy led the Shrikes back into the clubhouse. There was no celebration, not yet, because they were all too shell-shocked by how close they'd come to losing everything. They ended the first inning all tied up. By the fifth inning, they were still neck-and-neck but the Breakers had pulled ahead, leading five runs to three. The Shrikes rallied and made up the difference by the seventh inning. Rosalind, Patty, and Ida broke the tie and pushed them into the lead. They forced the Breakers to play in the bottom of the ninth to try and regain their lead and take the win.

Their lead shrank from three to two. And then from two to one. Marcy couldn't remember breathing as she looked out at the field and saw two Breakers poised on base and ready to run as a third prepared to bat. If one player crossed home, it would force an extra inning. If two of them crossed, it was all over. Rainy had pitched the whole game. Marcy could see the exhaustion in her stance, the way she shifted her weight from one foot to the other, the droop of her head as she considered pitches.

Before Rainy took the mound for the last inning, Marcy had leaned in close to whisper in her ear. "Let Lulu take this inning."

"No. I'm bringing this one home."

"Are you absolutely sure?"

Rainy nodded without hesitation. "I wouldn't risk this for pride. We win now, we win as a team. We lose now, it's because of me. I understand that. And I'm telling you I'm up for it."

Marcy nodded. "Okay. I'll have a backrub ready for you at the hotel regardless of what happens."

"And a warm bath?"

"That depends on whether we win or not. I have to give you *some* incentive."

Rainy had smiled and touched her cap.

Marcy dropped onto the bench in front of her cubby. Rainy had somehow found a little remaining strength, some reserve of power she hadn't yet tapped dry, and she took out the last batter with little hesitation or delay. When the third ball zipped past her and bounced past Moxie, the Breaker fans had let out a collective roar of dismay as their batter tossed her bat to the ground like a spike.

The Shrikes had just won the pennant by a single run.

Marcy looked down at her hands. They were shaking. It wasn't some minor tremor that she had to stare to notice; it was a violent quake that didn't even stop when she folded her fingers into her palm and squeezed. Her breathing was rough and slow, and she turned around to see the other players were also looking around for someone to break the tension.

Rainy took it upon herself. She stood on a bench and clapped her hands together. The murmur of conversation stopped.

"Ladies, take a look around yourselves. Say hello to the Chicago Shrikes, the *first-ever* Eastern Division pennant winners of the Women's National League!"

The cheer that rose up could have been heard from the street.

Marcy got to her feet to clap and cheer with everyone else. Rainy hopped down and was immediately enfolded in a hug by Rosalind and Ida. Marcy caught her eye and they smiled at each other, silently acknowledging how they would rather be celebrating the win.

They had planned to get a bottle of champagne or some beer to celebrate the win, but Rainy had convinced her buying it would be tempting fate. Now Marcy wished she hadn't listened. But this was a ballpark, and there had to be something alcoholic they could use for a toast.

She slipped out of the clubhouse with the intention of raiding the concession stand. She barely made it ten steps before a boy called out to her.

"Marcy Neal! Just a sec! Hey, Marcy Neal!"

His voice had echoed off the corridor walls but she pinpointed where it came from and waited for him to close the distance between them. She prepared herself to sign another autograph even though his hands were empty and he was wearing a cap with the Breakers logo.

"Hiya, kid."

"Hey! Hey." He stopped and panted to catch his breath. "There's a guy here. He wants to talk to you."

"A reporter?"

"I don't think so." He hooked a thumb over his shoulder. "He's out in the bandstands. He said 'go tell number seven I'd like to talk with her' and he gave me a silver dollar. I think he wanted you to sign something for him."

Marcy raised an eyebrow. "Golly. Thanks for passing along the message, kid."

"Sure thing." He turned around and ran back the way he'd come. "You played good ball out there!" he called before he disappeared out of sight.

Marcy chuckled.

There was an access door leading to the bandstand not far from where she was standing. She immediately spotted the man who had summoned her. He was the only person still there, standing at the railing and looking out over the field.

She crunched peanuts, pretzels, and popcorn with every step, creating a sticky mess under her cleats as she made her way up to the bleachers. The crowd had cleared out quickly, but she could hear them in the streets outside as they slowly dispersed back out into the city. The cheers of the Chicago visitors still echoed in her ears.

"I hear you wanted an autograph."

"Oh, that won't be necessary." He turned around and smiled. "You've signed your name on enough things for me over the years, Marcy."

She stopped, grateful she was still outside of arm's reach. "David? What the hell are you doing here?"

"A man is allowed to watch a ball game, right?" He smiled and put his hands in his pockets. He'd always had a beard, but he had been neglecting it. The sides were shaggy and unkempt, and the front was long enough that she couldn't see his neck. "I may have had the team stolen from me, but I still like to see how you ladies are doing. You did good out there, Marcy. A really fantastic game."

"Thanks." She started to turn away from him. "I'm sure you can find your way out."

David said, "I need to talk with you about something important."

She sighed. "We have nothing to talk about."

"Oh, yes we do. Because none of this would be happening without me. You would have been stuck in that Podunk police station for a couple more days. Rosalind wouldn't have signed on anywhere. Rainy would probably have ended up on the Breakers or the Pros. Moxie would still be babysitting her cousin or nephew or whoever that little toddler is. The Shrikes wouldn't exist without me, and you just left me out in the cold before I could start reaping the benefits."

Marcy rolled her eyes. "Is that all this is about? You want money? Name your price. I'll talk to Mrs. Waldron and see if it's worth the reward of never seeing you again."

"Oh, I want money. But not from her. I want a lot more than she would give me." He moved closer to her. Marcy resisted the urge to retreat; she didn't want him to think she was scared. "You booted me for no reason."

"I booted you because you *assaulted a player.* I booted you before you could go after someone who was too scared to stand up to your advances. I defended you every time someone accused you of shady shit, and I can never take that back. But I can absolutely stand my ground now."

"Are you sure about that?"

Marcy said, "Oh, I'm a hundred percent positive."

He looked away from her, facing the field again as he took a deep breath and let it out slowly.

"Here's what's going to happen, Marcy. You're going to throw the World's Series. You can win one game, maybe two, just to make it look good, but the Shrikes are going to lose. I'm going to make a bet on that outcome and I'll win enough to make up for you cutting me off the way you did."

She laughed and crossed her arms over her chest. "Okay. Sure. You're delusion if you think--"

"I'm not done. When you drag yourself to Lorraine Waldron to explain your loss, you're going to explain that it was hopeless without my guidance. You're going to beg her to hire me back to act as the Shrikes manager for next season."

"What on God's green earth would ever make me do *any* of that insanity?"

He smiled. "Because if you don't, I'm going to tell every newspaper that will listen that you and Caroline Rainy are queer."

Marcy's entire body went cold. "No one will run something like that without proof." She struggled to keep her voice steady.

"Someone will," he said. "Probably quite a few places. You're both fairly attractive women, unattached, athletic, playing a man's sport in men's clothes. Lots of traveling and hotels. I'm sure it would be easy as pie to find someone to verify you've shared a room at some point on the road. But I don't need evidence. There's more than enough just looking at the two of you to raise eyebrows."

Her panic ebbed a little as she realized he didn't actually know anything or have any proof. He had no idea his attempt at blackmail was hitting so close to reality.

"Do you think those little boys would have been as excited if they knew you're a couple of deviants? Their parents will probably burn the cards you signed. You thought it was bad when the anti-soldier quote happened? This will be a hundred times worse. There's no coming back from that, Marcy. You'd be done. You'd never play again. Neither would Rainy, probably."

Marcy shook her head. "You would destroy this team just to get revenge?"

"I didn't *do* anything. You kicked me out because of rumors and bad feelings."

"You know exactly what you did."

"I never touched any of those girls."

"You touched Rainy!"

They were almost nose to nose now. She saw the rage in his eyes and was suddenly worried he was going to hit her. But instead, and almost more worryingly, she saw it fade away to be replaced by a serene smile. He backed up a step.

"I would never have touched Caroline Rainy, Marcy. See, I've always suspected she was playing for a different team. If you'll excuse the confusing turn of phrase. I already talked to that would-be groom of hers, and he told me that she never really seemed all that interested in sex with men. And come to think of it, I can't think of *ever* seeing *you* with a fella. Seems odd, given how long we've known each other.

Wouldn't you say? All you'd have to do to prove me wrong is hand over a list of your old beaus. But I don't think you're going to do that, are you?"

She looked away. He chuckled.

"Yeah. I didn't think so. That's the problem with giving everything to a game, Marcy. It doesn't leave much room for a social life."

He stepped around her to leave.

"How am I supposed to convince those women down there to throw away the biggest game they've ever played?"

"That's not my problem, Marcy. I won't be a paid employee of the Shrikes until next season. But whatever you decide, do it quick. You can win one game. Maybe two. But if I get the impression you're backing out of the deal, if you win a third game, then I'm going to start calling newspapers. Good luck, Marcy. See you next season."

She dropped down onto one of the benches and put her head in her hands.

IV.
WORLD'S SERIES

"Cynics may contend that on the diamond as elsewhere it is *place aux dames*. Perhaps Miss Jackie (Cooper) hasn't quite enough on the ball yet to bewilder (Babe) Ruth and (Lou) Gehrig in a serious game. But there are no sluggers in the Southern Association, and she may win laurels this season which cannot be ascribed to mere gallantry. The prospect grows gloomier for misogynists."

- "A Pearl Among Pitchers," Editorial. *The New York Times*, 4 Apr 1931

Chapter Twenty-Five

"Does he know?"

"He absolutely does not know."

"But he could."

"He *can't*."

"But he suspects."

Marcy stopped pacing. She wanted to deny it, wanted to assure Rainy that David was just desperate and grasping at straws. But she couldn't say that, not for sure. This wasn't the sort of thing he would have just plucked out of thin air.

"He might suspect," she admitted.

Rainy leaned forward and put her hands on top of her head and grabbed her hair with both hands. Marcy crossed her arms over her chest and resumed pacing. The hotel room didn't provide much of a track for her; she had to change direction every five steps. But she couldn't bring herself to sit down and remain still, not while David and his threat were still out there, hanging over them. Everyone else was out celebrating the pennant win, but Marcy had begged off claiming a headache and Rainy said her shoulder was too sore. They'd gotten a few knowing glances from Moxie and Rosalind, but the dread had been too prevalent to even acknowledge the insinuation.

"Maybe you can ask Lorraine for help," Rainy suggested. "I'm sure she's friends with half the people who own the papers. She can ask them to ignore whatever David sends them."

"Like she stopped that stupid comment I made about hoping the war keeps going? Besides, I don't know if the Waldrons are exactly keen to do any favors for me right now."

Rainy winced. "Have... have you spoken to Lillian since..."

"We haven't even been in the same room."

"That's probably going to change very soon," Rainy said. "I assume Lorraine and Lillian both will want to have another big to-do in honor of winning the pennant."

"Don't remind me."

Marcy sighed and stopped pacing. She sat down next to Rainy on the bed. There were a dozen reasons she didn't really want to have a conversation with Lillian Waldron. She didn't even know if Lillian was aware Marcy and Rainy were together again. She knew whatever they'd been building together ended in the ballroom. Lillian hadn't reached out to her in the aftermath, which Marcy took as a message in and of itself.

"Would he really do it?"

"We have to assume he will."

Rainy thought about that. "He really cared about you, Mars."

"He didn't care about me. He *wanted* me. There's a difference. As soon as he realized I wasn't going to sleep with him, I lost all value in his eyes."

"You think he just changed overnight like that?"

Marcy looked at Rainy with a raised eyebrow. "Come on. You've known men like that. As soon as they realize they'll never get you into bed, they don't see any point in talking to you anymore. I saw that today, looking at David. He was like a whole different person."

"So he might actually do it."

"Yes. He might." She looked down and swallowed hard. "I'll understand if you want to pull back. I just mean I won't hold it against you. It's scary. And if you want to close off, I'll know it's not because of me or how you feel about me, or..."

Rainy reached out and took Marcy's hand. She turned it over, lined up their palms, and threaded her fingers with Marcy's.

"I'm done running away from you, Mars. Whatever happens, I'm right here."

Marcy's eyes stung. She brought their joined hands up and kissed Rainy's fingers. "Thank you."

"I love you."

"I love you, too. Whatever happens."

Rainy looked over her shoulder to confirm there were two pillows on the bed. "Come here." She scooted back, keeping her hand tightly clasped with Marcy's. They moved up the mattress and rolled so they were facing each other.

"So here are the facts." Rainy reached up with her free hand to gently brush some stray hairs away from Marcy's face. "David doesn't know a damn thing about us. He's just throwing out some rampant speculation because he knows it will cause a scandal when it comes out. He's trying to scare us into reacting to a bluff."

"Right. But he's not wrong about the hell it will raise. Lorraine might bench both of us."

"For the Series?" Rainy said. "I can't see her doing that. Not with this much on the line."

Marcy shrugged. "It's a possibility."

"Okay. It's a possibility. But it's a certainty that you can't talk him out of this stupid plan of his."

"I don't know if it's a certainty," Marcy said. "But it seems highly unlikely he'd back down. We don't have anything to offer him in exchange for being reasonable. I could give it a shot. Appeal to whatever feelings he might still have for me. But I think we're way past that now. He wants revenge. He wants to be vindicated."

Rainy sighed. "Okay. So if we can't talk him out of it, and we can't ask the Waldrons to throw their weight around to block any stories he might sell, then the only other option is to ask the girls to tank the Series. We can ask Rosalind, Moxie, Ida, and all those wonderful ladies to give up the biggest game any of us have ever played in. Do you think they'd even go along with it?"

"I think Rosalind would break both my legs with a bat if I even asked."

Rainy laughed. "And Moxie would hold you down."

Marcy reached up and touched Rainy's forehead. She dragged her finger down between her eyebrows, to the tip of her nose, which she lightly pinched between her first two fingers. Rainy squeezed her eyes shut and rolled her head back to escape the assault. Marcy chuckled and kissed Rainy's nose.

"So those are our options," Rainy said.

"I don't remember hearing any options."

"Exactly." Rainy let go of Marcy's hand, pulled her closer. "Lorraine Waldron can't help us, David Buckner won't see reason, and the girls would never agree to lose on purpose. We can't do anything to change what happens in the next few weeks. So I'm not going to waste any energy stressed about it. Everyone is going to do what everyone is going to do, and all *we* can do is focus on getting ready for the game. The rest will take care of itself."

Marcy smiled. "Smart, attractive, and good at baseball. I'm damned glad you were my next door neighbor, Caroline Rainy."

"I'd have found you eventually," Rainy said.

Marcy leaned in and kissed Rainy's lips. "I love you."

"I love you, too. Keep kissing me..."

Marcy did as she was told. She surrendered to the kiss, to lying next to Rainy like this, and felt the weight of David's ultimatum lifting off her shoulders. It felt good to admit things were out of their control. Whatever was going to happen, they would just have to deal with the fallout.

For the time being, they had a World's Series to prepare for.

Moxie was drunk. She was elated, she was so giddy that she kept laughing every time she took a drink, and she still managed to get blotto. She found this fact hilarious. She was even more amused by the fact that she was able to operate the crank telephone and speak coherently enough to the operator that she was connected to the correct number. She lifted her bottle and discovered it was empty, laughed, and dropped down onto the stool next to the phone table to wait for her call to be answered.

She was in the hotel, and the doors to five rooms had been propped open. The Shrikes had taken over the whole hallway for their celebration. She'd heard Lorraine Waldron paid the staff in advance for any complaints or messes that were made in the aftermath of their win. Some of the girls were still in their uniforms, others had only taken off their jerseys to party in undershirts, while others had taken the time to change into their normal clothes.

Rosalind, one of the partiers in an undershirt and uniform pants, came out of one room with an arm slung around Ida Coe's shoulders. Both women were barefoot, and Ida was wearing a men's dress shirt she'd acquired from somewhere.

"Have you seen Marcy or Rainy?" Rosalind asked when she spotted Moxie.

"Not lately," Moxie said. "I think Rainy probably wanted to ice her shoulder. Marcy's probably helping her out."

"Oh I bet she is."

Moxie glanced at Ida to see if she noticed the innuendo. The younger girl's face was flushed pink and she seemed distracted by everything else happening in the party.

There was a fumbling noise on the other end of the line, which drew Moxie's attention back to the phone she was holding to her ear.

"Hello?" Celia sounded like she'd been asleep.

Moxie suddenly wondered what time it was. The game had ended at five o'clock, and it was dark outside. She couldn't remember eating anything. She was suddenly ravenous, and she realized she probably shouldn't have had so much to drink with an empty~

"Is anyone there?"

"Yes, I am," Moxie blurted. She laughed. "Sorry. Hi. I mean, hello. It's me. Iona Moccia." She over-enunciated her name and then said, "My name has so many *vowels*."

Celia said, "Yes, it certainly does. Are you okay, Miss Moccia?"

"I'm hungry."

"Well, did you have anything to eat before you got completely sotted?"

She squinted one eye shut. "I remember... peanuts. Maybe popcorn."

Celia chuckled. "Go eat something, Moxie."

"No, no, wait. Wait. I called for a reason." She sat up straighter and cleared her throat. "We won the pennant."

"I had a feeling you would. Congratulations."

"Thank you. We're going home on the train tomorrow. It's going to go through Detroit. And I was thinking that when we stopped there, I could hop off and go home the day after. Maybe we could, um, celebrate or something."

"You know we're not on the same team, right? I'm happy for you, but not to the point in celebrating a rival. You understand that, don't you?"

Moxie slumped. "I guess. I-I thought maybe you'd want to..." She shook her head. "No, never mind. I understand."

"But," Celia said slowly. "If you got off the train in Detroit and needed a place to stay, I know a place you could wait for the next train."

"Yeah...?"

Celia said, "Sure. Like I said, Moxie, I really am happy for you. I can't wait to hear about your games. Did you do anything great?"

"I tagged someone out right before she got a home run. Saved the day."

"Good girl," Celia said.

Moxie beamed proudly. She turned so she was mostly facing the wall. She lowered her voice and held the receiver close to her mouth. "Can I really come and see you?"

"I would really like it if you did."

Moxie grinned. "Okay." She pushed her hair out of her face. "I should let you get back to sleep. I don't even know what time it is. I'm sorry."

"Don't be sorry. Promise me you'll get something to eat and get some rest soon."

"I will. Okay. Love you." Her eyes widened. "I mean. I mean. I'm... I... I d-d-don't talk on the, I only talk to my mother on the phone, and I-I-I just end calls with~"

Celia laughed. "I won't hold you to anything you say while drunk and celebrating."

"Okay. Thank you." Her face was burning hot, and she pushed up her glasses and rubbed her eyes. "I think I should just go to sleep."

"I think that's smart. Do you know what time your train gets into Detroit tomorrow?"

"Sometime in the afternoon."

"I'll check the schedule and be there to meet you."

Moxie hung up the phone and slumped against the wall. She closed her eyes just for a second, then startled awake when someone bumped her foot. She chuckled at herself and forced herself to her feet so she could go find a bed to sleep off her stupor before she told anyone else she loved them.

Ida wanted to go up to the roof of the hotel so she could see all of New York, but she didn't want to go alone. Men had appeared from somewhere, probably hotel staff or delivery men from the bar that had provided all the liquor currently making the Shrikes loud and obnoxious. Rosalind didn't know how much Ida had been drinking, and she didn't want any of the men getting the wrong idea about the buxom girl who kept trying to take off her clothes, so she stayed close to her side. When the roof idea cropped up, Rosalind agreed to go with her because it seemed like the safest place for her. She also hoped the cold night air would help sober her up a bit.

They found the stairs with roof access and a door that was

fortunately unlocked. Rosalind pushed it open and escorted Ida out into the cold.

"Oh gosh!" Ida's breath plumed out in front of her when she spoke. The buildings around them were too high to see much of the skyline, but Ida didn't seem to care. She walked to the edge and rested her hands on the concrete lip.

Rosalind had to admit the sight was pretty amazing. The hotel was completely enclosed by taller buildings that rose up on every side like stone walls. The walls were crisscrossed by black metal skeletons of fire escapes, and each building had a dozen golden windows which gave glimpses of kitchens, parlors, bedrooms. People passed by without a glance out at the world, engrossed in their own lives. Rosalind wondered if any of the people she could spy on had been at the game earlier.

"I've never been up this high before," Ida said from the parapet.

"I don't know if I have, either," Rosalind admitted, moving to stand next to Ida. She leaned over and looked down at the street. She whistled. "Yeah, we're pretty high up."

Ida pointed at the building across from them. "And they're even higher."

"There are taller buildings downtown."

"Gosh," Ida said again, shaking her head. "Who'd have ever thought. Little Ida Coe, top of the world. Champion baseball player."

Rosalind smiled. "Well, you earned it."

Ida turned around and rested her elbows on the wall behind her. "Not as much as you. Or Marcy, or Caroline. Sometimes I felt like I was just along for the ride."

"We won this last game by a single run." Rosalind leaned against the wall next to Ida. "That ought to prove that every single player matters. You got us where we are now. Enjoy it."

"I guess you're right." She ran her hand through her hair and then pulled it forward so it fell into her eyes. "Did you know I only tried out for the Lady Yankees 'cause I overheard a guy making fun of them. He said it was just silly, like a bunch of cats and dogs playing dress-up."

"Well, he's not laughing now, I'll bet."

Ida scoffed and waved her hand as if she was erasing the unnamed man. "Who cares what he thinks. I'm a pennant winner. What the hell's he ever done, besides get hired as manager at the company his daddy owns?"

Rosalind laughed. "I wish I had a drink to toast to that."

Ida mimed raising a glass to Rosalind. "How about you? Why'd you sign up?"

Rosalind thought about Daisy. "I wanted to travel. There's a whole world out there, and I'd only seen about fifty miles of it. I wanted to say I'd seen more than other people."

"Where are you from?"

"Originally? Little place called Oswego, Illinois."

"Well," Ida said, raising both hands to the buildings around them. "I don't think there are many people in Oswego who can say they've seen this view."

Rosalind took a second to appreciate the sight. "You know, I think you're right."

Ida rolled her head back and took a deep breath, then let it out with a huge plume of white smoke. "I think it's going to take a while for this summer to sink in. I earned money playing baseball. I mean, sure, I got paid as a Lady Yankee, but this is *real* money. This is a real team! I got a Cracker Jack card! And I was on a team that *won*! It feels like any second now, I'm going to wake up and Bobby Coffell is going to be groping me in his little brother's treehouse."

Rosalind laughed. "You want me to pinch you? Make sure you're really awake?"

"Depends. Where would you pinch me?"

"Where...?" Rosalind looked sideways at her. "Your *arm*."

Ida shrugged. "Just making sure. Usually when people offer to pinch me, they have other places in mind."

"Well, those are men."

"Well, rumor has it, you and men sometimes have similar thinking."

Rosalind's smile faded. "Rumors don't mean nothing."

"Yeah? You sure? 'Cause you sure have been attached to my hip all night. Acting all jealous-like if anyone even looks at me."

"I'm not..." Rosalind furrowed her brow and shook her head. "I'm trying to protect you, Ida. You're young—"

"I'm not that young."

"—and those men will pounce on anyone they see as vulnerable."

"I can take care of myself."

"I know. But sometimes everyone could use a little help."

Ida looked down. "I hear that. And... look... it would be easy for me to go down there and find a man I find appealing, and tell him to go for it. But anyone I chose would make it about *him*. Just tonight, I want to make it about *me*. I deserve that."

"You certainly do."

"And I can get tired of helping myself out. Sometimes it's nice to have someone do it for you."

They fell into silence. Rosalind kept her eyes straight ahead, very aware that Ida had lifted her head to look at her.

"I do, sometimes," Rosalind said. "Think like a man, I mean."

"Oh yeah? Like what, for instance?"

Rosalind pointed to a darker corner of the roof. "Like how if we went over there, we could hear the door if someone else came up. And it might give us a little privacy."

"Privacy?" Ida asked.

Rosalind pushed away from the wall and walked over to where she had pointed. Ida followed her. They faced each other in the dark. Ida's face was almost ghostly in the light cast off from the moon and the apartment windows all around them. Rosalind cupped her face and leaned in slowly. Ida didn't move to meet her, but she also didn't pull away when their lips met. Her hands remained at her sides for a long time before she brought them up and rested them lightly on Rosalind's hips.

"You okay?" Rosalind asked when the kiss finally ended.

"Uh huh." Ida's voice was shaking. "What happens now?"

Rosalind gently guided Ida to lean against the wall. She moved her hands to the front of Ida's uniform pants and felt around until she found the button.

"Now I take care of you," Rosalind said.

"Oh..."

Rosalind kissed her again as she slid the pants down Ida's hips. She took a step back and found Ida's eyes in the darkness.

"What I'm about to do doesn't have to mean anything. It doesn't have to be anything but one friend helping out another. You don't have to do anything for me if you don't feel comfortable with it. Okay?"

"Mm-hmm."

Rosalind kissed Ida again and then got down on her knees.

CHAPTER TWENTY-SIX

THE FIRST two games of the World's Series were scheduled to be played in Chicago, at the Shrikes home park. Marcy considered that to be a gift, but she was extremely nervous about the third and fourth games they'd have to play in California. A whole new park, in a state she'd never even visited, against a team they'd never played. She'd gotten as many Bay Area newspapers as she could find and read everything about the San Fran Phoenix. She wanted to know them inside and out before she ever saw them in person.

The morning before the first game, she was sitting at her dinner table with two different papers spread out in front of her. She didn't just focus on the box scores. She read everything, all the articles, anything that would give her a sense of the city. She currently was in the middle of reading about the Panama-Pacific International Exposition that had been held in the city a year earlier.

Rainy came in with the groceries and went straight to the kitchen. Marcy got up and took one of the papers to her.

"We're the bad guys."

"What?" Rainy paused with a box of cereal halfway to the cabinet. "How do you mean?"

Marcy spread the paper out on the counter. "You know San Francisco burned down ten years ago, right? The huge earthquake, the city was basically wiped off the map. Massive fires, countless lives lost, complete devastation."

Rainy nodded. "I've heard something about it, sure. But they've been rebuilding, right?"

"Exactly." Marcy poked the paper. "Last year they had a big exposition to show the world how they've bounced back. They had a four-hundred foot tower that was covered with a hundred thousand jewels. They had the Liberty Bell brought out by train. They, they put in a telephone line that stretched all the way across the country and let people in New York hear the Pacific Ocean."

"That's amazing," Rainy said, continuing to store the groceries. "I'm not sure what a fair from last year has to do with us. How does it make us bad guys?"

"The San Francisco *Phoenix*." She stressed the team name. "The bird that rises from the ashes. The fair was symbolic of their recovery and now their first female ball team has won the pennant and they're going to the World's Series. This story has to end with them winning everything. We're absolutely the last obstacle they have to overcome before they get their happy ending."

Rainy cupped Marcy's face. "This isn't a story, Mars. This is a game. And a game can go either way. The only thing we can do is play it."

"But..." Marcy looked down at the paper. Rainy forced her to make eye contact again. "It feels like a story to me. *My* story. About how... how I finally got everything I wanted. I got my team. My game. My girl." She smiled and turned her head to kiss Rainy's palm. "I thought I was going to win because that's the ending the hero is supposed to get."

"What are you doing here?" Rainy asked. "Are you actually panicking? Or are you just trying to find an excuse to take David's offer and throw the game?"

Marcy frowned. "What? No. We already decided we're ignoring that ass-hat."

"Ahh, okay. So actual panic. Well, what about Moxie? She's discovered something about herself that she never knew, and she's happy. And Rosalind has something going on since we left New York. I don't know what it is, but she looks like she's been reborn. And... you and I found each other again. It wasn't a normal courtship, but nothing about us has ever been normal. But now here we are, basically living together, in love. Wouldn't you call that a happy ending?"

Marcy smiled. "Definitely a happy ending."

Rainy pulled her into a hug and kissed her hair. "Our happy ending has nothing to do with the next few games. It'll be great if we win. But we've already won the pennant and we're on the right path. Whatever happens in the Series, whichever story gets to have its happy ending, we're not going to be sad. Right?"

"Right." Marcy rested her head on Rainy's chest. "I love you, Caro."

"I love you, too." After a moment, she said, "Besides, who cares if their dumb fair had some stupid bell? *Our* fair gave the world electricity. Top that, San Fran."

Marcy laughed and held Rainy tighter.

"Tomorrow is just another game. We've played over a hundred and fifty of them, and we've won a lot more than we lost. That's why we get to play again tomorrow. We won more than the Pros. We won more than the Breakers. We won more than the Hawks and the Pinks combined."

Marcy laughed. "True. But the Phoenix have won just as many."

"Right. So it won't be an embarrassment to lose to them."

"That's one way to look at it."

"It's the only way to look at it." She stepped back. "Do you feel better?"

Marcy nodded and kissed Rainy's chin, then her cheek. "Yes. Thank you." She turned to the paper which was still spread out on the counter. "I'll clean all this up."

"No. I'll do that. You'll just get swept up in some story or another." She put her hands on Marcy's shoulders and guided her toward the bedroom. "Go in there. It's been months of constantly going from one game to the next to the next. Take advantage of having today off and get some rest. I want you nice and refreshed tomorrow."

"You need some rest, too."

"I'll be right in after I clean up a little." She kissed Marcy's cheek and patted her on the rear. "Go. Relax. Don't worry about anything but rest."

"Rest. Right."

Marcy let herself be deposited in the bedroom and went to the bed. She sat on the edge of the mattress and looked over at the side that had become Rainy's. They hadn't had many quality nights in the bed. Usually they came back to the apartment after practice or a game and they were too exhausted to do anything but sleep. But sleep was good, too. Sleeping next to someone she loved as much as Rainy was just as exciting as sex. Although sex was good, too. Sex was really good. Just as good as a rest, in fact.

She unbuttoned her blouse and kicked off her shoes. She would wait for Rainy to come in and then they would take each other's minds off the Series.

At some point between taking off her blouse and loosening her belt, she decided to put her head on the pillow just for a second. And sometime after that, she was vaguely aware of the bedroom door opening and closing. She felt the bed sag when Rainy climbed in the other side. She rolled onto her back and reached for her.

"Hm... surprise..."

"What?" Rainy asked softly.

Marcy started to answer but her lips didn't work properly. She thought she heard Rainy chuckling as she drifted off to sleep, but she couldn't be positive.

***

Moxie spent an hour trying to figure out where to put the ticket. It would take too long for her to notice it on the dinner table. Propping it up against the lamp next to her chair was too obvious. She didn't want to make it a presentation. She just wanted to make sure her mother saw it as soon as possible. She supposed she could just hand it to her. But that lacked any element of surprise. Maybe if she wrapped it...?

She was still trying to decide when the apartment door opened and Bettina Moccia came in. She looked like a shorter, broader version of Moxie with much longer hair and no glasses. The boy waddling like a duck behind her was Moxie's cousin Ike. Bettina had two bags of groceries, one in each hand, while the boy was too busy pressing his fists into his armpits and waving his elbows like wings. Bettina saw Moxie and gave a sigh of relief.

"Iona. There you are. Come take one of these."

"The duck could have given you a hand," Moxie said as she took one of the bags. The duck in question was already halfway down the hall to his borrowed room.

Bettina sighed. "And if he dropped it and smashed the bottles? What then, hm? Easier to just take them both myself."

Moxie said, "That's a great lesson you're teaching him."

"What lesson?"

"Lowered expectations. If no one thinks he can do something, he'll never be asked to do anything. People will do everything for him."

"He's a child, Iona."

"He has to learn some time."

Bettina said, "I'll remind you of that when I let him carry the groceries and you don't have milk in your cereal that week."

Moxie closed her eyes and breathed in slowly to center herself. All the excitement from earlier was being eroded away with every second.

"Ma, before you get started on dinner, there's something I wanted to give you."

She slipped the ticket out of her shirt pocket and held it out. Bettina turned, looked at it, and shook her head before she went back to unloading the groceries.

"What is *that?*"

"It's a ticket to the World's Series, Ma. Game 1, tomorrow night."

Bettina clucked her tongue against her teeth. "Oh, I'm not going to a baseball game."

Moxie tried not to despair. "You know my team is in it, right?"

"Yes." Another weary sigh. "I'm well aware that while all of the other teams are back to their regular lives, you're still out there playing your little game. And next week you get a free trip to California! Hah! Must be nice. Meanwhile I'll be here trying to wrangle that little monster by myself."

"Wrangle?" Moxie said. "You let him do whatever the hell he wants and leave me to clean up the mess."

"Language!"

"I want you to see at least one of my games, Ma. I want you to see what I do for a living."

Bettina laughed. "A living? Oh! It's a career now! Iona, you know as well as I do that when this silly war ends, all the boys are going to come home and pat you on the head for keeping their parks warm and send you away."

"We... we're proving that we can play the game just as well as~"

"You're not proving anything by playing against other women. Maybe if you were playing the boys' teams, maybe that would be different. It's all just a distraction. Something to keep people's minds off the horrible news. I hope you didn't waste too much money on that ticket."

Moxie worked her jaw. "It's my money to waste. And I gave you the cash for these groceries too, didn't I? Every week this season, in fact. I've made sure Ike has cereal and lunches and got those new shoes when school started up."

"And you think that makes this a real job? Playing your games?"

"It is a real job."

Bettina held her hands up and muttered something under her breath. It was either a prayer or a curse, and Moxie honestly couldn't tell which was most likely.

"I put up with this for the past few months because I knew you had to get it out of your system. But enough is enough, Iona. Are you going to spend your whole life crouching down in the dirt and catching a ball? You're wasting your prime years on something that doesn't matter. You need to think about the future. A career."

"I have a career."

"A husband."

"I have..." *Celia.*

She pressed her lips together and looked down at the floor. Her job fulfilled her in ways her mother could never understand. And Celia made her happier than she'd ever been, had ever known she could be. All the things she dreaded about a relationship, the things that made her balk at accepting invitations to dinner with men, suddenly didn't matter as much. The night they had after the Shrikes won the pennant had been one of the best nights of her life, and she couldn't even hint to her mother about it.

"I have everything I need," she finally said, her voice weak.

Bettina cupped Moxie's cheek. "Baseball is giving you the same thing it's giving everyone else in this country. A distraction. I'm doing this for you, Iona. A few years down the road you're going to look around and you'll see an empty apartment and men playing baseball, and you'll realize it's too late to change anything."

"I know what I'm doing, momma."

"I know you think you do."

Moxie pulled away from her mother's hand. She looked at the ticket, then placed it on the counter.

"There's one for Ike, too. I spent ten bucks on those. You can use them, give them away, throw them out. I don't care at this point."

She turned and headed for the door.

"Where do you think you're going, young lady?"

Moxie held her hands out to either side. "I don't know. You mentioned an empty apartment and that seemed real appealing to me all of a sudden. So I'm going to go see if I can find one."

"Iona...!"

She slammed the door behind her.

CHAPTER TWENTY-SEVEN

Game One - Weeghman Park, Chicago

RAINY PAUSED on the top step of the dugout to put on her cap. It was a perfect fall day, with a cool breeze coming in off the lake and perfectly clear skies. She stepped out into the sunlight and the cheers of the crowd drowned out the rumble of the L train speeding past a few blocks away. The flags mounted along the edge of the bandstand waved lazily in the breeze. She was halfway to the mound when she noticed another sound, a new sound, almost like a storm had suddenly rolled in. She squinted up to confirm there wasn't a single cloud overhead, but the sound continued.

Rosalind, jogging past her to get into position, stopped next to Rainy and hooked a thumb over her shoulder. "It's your public."

Rainy lowered her gaze to the bandstand. She saw groups of people who, instead of applauding, were holding wooden tubes and slowly spinning them clockwise.

"Rain sticks," Rosalind explained. "It's a Native American thing. Pebbles or beans in a hollow tube, turning it sounds like rain. For Rainy. Lorraine Waldron mentioned it to Marcy. Apparently security didn't want to let them in, because they could be used as weapons, but apparently someone convinced them it was a show of support."

"Marcy didn't say anything."

"She wanted it to be a surprise."

"Huh. Okay..." She lifted her hand, waved to the crowd, and continued to the mound.

It was just another game. San Francisco was a great team, but they'd played great teams before and come out on top. Part of her still couldn't believe they'd beaten both the Pros and the Breakers. Some games required talent, some required skill, and the rest needed luck. She had a feeling they were going to need all three for this series.

She took her position on the mound. The park where she and Marcy first played wasn't very far away. The first time they played, it had just been them and a bunch of boys. It had never even occurred to them to make a team of girls. Her dreams had always involved being the only woman on the Cubs or the Whales, or whatever team would take her. Leave it to Marcy Neal to see opportunity and grab it with both hands.

Rainy turned to Marcy at shortstop. She was shifting her weight from one foot to the other, scanning the Phoenix dugout as she warmed up. She felt Rainy's eyes on her and turned, smiled, and touched the brim of her cap. Rainy repeated the gesture and then brushed the same two fingers across her lips. Marcy laughed and shook her head, then tapped her lips with two fingers.

If anyone asked, they would claim it was a signal that they were going to get a cigarette after the game. In reality, it was a signal they'd come up with while tangled in Marcy's sheets. It was a promise, but it had nothing to do with tobacco.

She slipped her hand into her pocket and faced home plate. Moxie was in position, her eyeglasses reflecting the sky so it looked like two shining mirrors behind the mask.

Rainy nodded to her. Moxie returned the nod and smacked her fist into her glove.

"*Play ball!*"

Moxie tried not to count any more than necessary. She kept track of the numbers she had no choice about, the strikes and balls and errors. But through force of will, she stopped a cumulative number from building up. She never even glanced toward the scoreboard in the outfield.

In the first inning, she knew that Rainy struck out a lot of Phoenix players but she also knew two of them had crossed home plate. She also knew that in the bottom of the first, the Shrikes got three runs of their own. It was a solid start but she didn't let herself think about that. She didn't let the information they were up by one sink in. She just focused on the current batter, the current pitch.

Both teams went two innings without scoring another run, a streak broken by the Phoenix when they scored three runs in the fourth. The Shrikes weren't able to regain their lead or even tie things up, so they went into the fifth trailing their opponents.

Moxie worked her jaw back and forth as she waited for Rainy's pitch. If she focused all her attention on numbers and the not counting of them, she wouldn't think of the seats just over her shoulder and a few rows up. The seats that should have been occupied by Bettina and Isaac Moccia. So far she'd managed to avoid not looking, and the crowd was thick enough that it would take more than a quick glance to tell if the seats were empty. She thanked the fifteen thousand Chicagoans who had made that possible.

The ball sank into her glove, and the Phoenix player named Stites slumped away from the plate as another strike-out.

Moxie tossed the ball back to Rainy. People in the crowd were still spinning the things Marcy had called a rain stick. It was a very clever way to show support to the pitcher and she found the noise was quite soothing. A rainstorm without the inconvenience of getting soaked to the skin. She hoped the fans kept it up throughout the series.

Another Phoenix approached the plate, this one named Darnielle. Rainy pitched, Darnielle swung, and the crack of bat against ball sounded like a gunshot in Moxie's ears. Darnielle ran, the 5 on her back disappearing in a plume of dirt as she charged for first. Moxie rose up out of her crouch and watched as Rosalind charged toward the fence, corrected directions, backed up, and caught the ball on an errant bounce. She spun and threw to second, but too late to tag her out. She planted herself on the base and tugged at her belt as she waited for her next chance to run.

Moxie released the breath she'd been holding since the ball made contact. She lifted her mask and pushed up her glasses to rub her eyes before she got back into position for the next batter.

Marcy was their fourth batter in the seventh inning. Patty Frett and Lorna Lowell were ironically in their normal positions, on second and third base respectively. The score was currently seven to four in favor of the Phoenix. But if she hit a home run right now, she could even things up going into the last two innings. But they also had two outs. If she struck out, they would be up the creek without a paddle. She eyed the pitcher as she approached the plate.

Before the game, Lillian Waldron had come into the clubhouse to wish them luck. She hadn't spoken directly to Marcy, but she had found her on the bench. She seemed to take note of the fact she was sitting next to Rainy and understood something from their body language. She pressed her lips together, nodded once, and then planted the cheery smile back on her face before she resumed her pep talk to the rest of the team.

"You didn't talk to her yet, I guess," Rainy whispered once Lillian left.

"I figured there's no point to it now. Besides, in a couple of days, we're going to be on a train for two days going to San Francisco."

"She's coming with us?"

Marcy shrugged. "Mama Waldron wants a representative of the store in the bandstand. Besides, Lillian is a fan. She probably just wants to see the game for the sake of seeing it."

Rainy shook her head. "I hope she's still cheering for us when we get to California."

Marcy took her position at the plate. She raised her bat and held it just above her right shoulder. She eyed the Phoenix pitcher. Flora Tepper, a string bean whose chin-length blonde hair stuck out from under her cap and made her look like a scarecrow. She spun the ball in her hand, then hurled it with no hesitation or warning. Marcy was caught off guard and didn't even have a chance to swing, turning to look down at the catcher whose glove was already closed around the ball.

The crowd was noisy but not boisterous. They were energized, which was good. Marcy flexed her fingers around her bat and watched Tepper.

Another unexpected pitch, and Marcy swung for it, marking her strike. She clenched her teeth and resisted the urge to kick the dirt. She flexed her shoulders and raised her bat again. The scarecrow had to have a tell. Some indication she was about to pitch. She'd been watching from the dugout but hadn't noticed anything. She narrowed her eyes and focused on Tepper's face. Her brow was furrowed. The tip of her tongue was sticking out between her lips. She lifted her chin slightly.

Marcy smiled.

This time when Tepper pitched, Marcy was ready. She timed the swing perfectly and sent the ball flying to left field. The crowd cheered, the Phoenix players all turned to look into the outfield to track the ball's disappearance, and Marcy lazily ran the bases with one eye toward home. Lorna crossed, that was one. Patty crossed, that was two. And a few seconds later, Marcy casually crossed for their third run of the inning. The game was officially tied up.

Marcy took off her cap and waved it to the crowd.

Hildy was next up in the batter's box, and Marcy crossed close to her. "She relaxes her face when she's about to pitch."

"Hm?"

"She's squinting to see the catcher's signals. When she decides on a pitch, her face relaxes." She patted Hildy on the shoulder. "The woman needs glasses."

Hildy smiled. "That's good information. Thanks."

Marcy nodded to her and headed into the dugout.

Rosalind kept her eye on home plate and the batter's box. It was the bottom of the ninth, the Shrikes were ahead by two, and the Phoenix already had one out. There was a very real chance the game could end in the next few minutes.

She had spent the game clocking all the Phoenix players and trying to keep a mental list of their power hitters. Darnielle was a real threat, as were Amos, Garcia, and Ramirez. The others were fine but didn't seem capable of reaching center field. One of the middling players - number 6, Slater - was approaching the plate, so Rosalind let her mind drift. And just like every other time she'd let her mind drift since that night on a New York rooftop, it went directly to Ida Coe.

Ida was absolutely nothing like any of the women Rosalind had gone for in the past. She was a social butterfly, she liked to go out dancing and drinking, hanging out with the gals. Rosalind liked staying at home and she preferred it if home was somewhere as close to the middle of nowhere as possible. Rosalind didn't like perky blondes, and Ida... well, Ida had never been with a woman before.

She knew their relationship, or whatever it was, hadn't been tested yet. They hadn't had a true moment to themselves since that first night. Not counting the train back to Chicago, of course, which they had taken full advantage of. And not counting stolen hours where they frantically and enthusiastically explored one another in new and exciting ways. There was a chance they would discover they couldn't stand each other in day-to-day life.

For now, though… whatever they had was fucking amazing.

Ida sensed Rosalind's attention on her. She looked over, smiled, and then casually straightened her posture. She planted her feet shoulder-width apart, laced her fingers together, and stretched her arms high over her head. The material of her jersey pulled taut over her ample breasts as she twisted her hips one way, then the other. Rosalind licked her lips and tried to think of ways to punish the naughty girl.

She was shaken from her fantasies by the crack of the bat. She watched the ball's long, low arc to first base, where Ida was waiting for it. She scooped it up in her glove, hopped on one foot to change direction, and ran back to first where she tagged Slater out before she could safely touch base.

The crowd roared as Slater jogged back to the Phoenix dugout. The game was 9-7, with the Shrikes in the lead. Now they had two outs, and Amos was headed to the plate. All the Shrike players seemed to shift at the same moment, realizing how close they were to starting the series with a win. It wouldn't mean anything in the long run, of course, but it was certainly a good omen.

Rosalind ran her bare palm over the thigh of her uniform pants to dry the sweat on it. She flexed the fingers of her other hand inside her glove.

Two balls and one strike later, Amos made contact. She sent the ball straight up the middle. Rosalind backpedaled with her head tilted back, glove raised, watching the ball as it seemed to come right toward her. There was no need to rush. No need to change direction or reposition herself, she just had to get where it was going and put her glove under it. She raised her hand.

The ball landed perfectly in the palm of the glove.

Amos was out, and the Shrikes had just won the first game of the World's Series.

Rosalind dropped her arm and tucked the ball into the back pocket of her pants as she ran toward the center of the field to celebrate with the rest of their team.

***

Rainy threw both arms in the air when Rosalind made her beautiful catch. Both her shoulders ached, a pain that stretched across her upper back like a yoke was lying across it, but at the moment she could ignore the burn. When she dropped her arms, she looked over to shortstop and saw Marcy watching her. Marcy was clapping, she was smiling, but there was worry in her eyes. Rainy knew exactly what she was thinking.

David Buckner had given them a little wiggle room with his blackmail. They could win "one, maybe two" games before he would assume they weren't going along with his plan. Then he would leak the information about them to the papers.

Rainy shrugged. Marcy tilted her head to the side, reluctantly accepting the dismissal.

Their silent exchange finished, Rainy jogged after Rosalind to congratulate her on the catch.

CHAPTER TWENTY-EIGHT

Game Two - Weeghman Park, Chicago

BACK TO back games had a surreal quality that Marcy doubted she would ever get used to. On Thursday, she woke up and got dressed in her uniform and went to the park to play the Phoenix. On Friday, she did the same thing against the same people. The only difference now was that they were no longer on equal footing. If it was a true repeat, and the Shrikes chalked up another win, the Phoenix would be on their back foot for the rest of the Series. It would also give the Shrikes a cushion, room to make mistakes, and that could be a very valuable thing in a game that relied so heavily on chance.

Rainy was still in the bath when Marcy left the apartment. Her shoulder had taken the beating during Game One, so she was going to let Lulu take the first few innings of Game Two. Rainy would come in later if they needed her.

Marcy walked to the game in her street clothes, but several fans outside Weeghman recognized her anyway. She had to stop to sign their Cracker Jack cards, ticket stubs, and programs. She made achingly slow progress toward the players entrance and was grateful she'd left early. At one point she kept someone's pen and used it for every autograph. As she inched closer to the iron gates, she stopped looking at the faces and just took whatever was handed to her. She took a newspaper from someone who thrust it at her with annoying insistence.

"Hi, what's your name?"

"After everything we've been through, you have to ask?"

Marcy clenched her jaw and looked up into David Buckner's smirking face. "What are you doing here?"

"No rules against seeing a game. Half of Chicago is coming out!" He winked. "Besides, I have money riding on this game."

Marcy shoved the newspaper back at him and walked toward the gate. David followed her.

"You're not allowed back here," she said.

He grabbed her arm. "I just wanted to congratulate you on the win yesterday. It was a real nail-biter, but you gals were giving it your all."

She tried to pull away from him, but his grip tightened. "Let go."

"You were *all* playing your best yesterday. Really great to see, as a fan." He looked around, tried to keep it subtle. He was still smiling. "I thought we had an agreement."

"I thought you said one or two wins wouldn't affect your scheme. Have to make it look good, right?"

"I'm starting to worry you didn't even tell the other girls about the plan."

"Doesn't sound like me."

He pulled her closer. "There are other ways for the Shrikes to lose the Series, you know. Maybe if a couple of your best players had to sit out for the rest of the season..."

"You'd honestly resort to hurting the players?"

His eyes flashed, his brows knitting together. "You took away my life, Marcy. My career. My future. I am just trying to salvage something."

"And who cares if a couple of girls get hurt in the process, right?"

"I'm sure they'd still be able to do jobs that are *proper* for women."

Marcy said, "Cook dinner, raise babies, sweep the house."

"Being a homemaker isn't a death sentence."

"I agree. So *you* do it, and I'll keep doing what I'm good at."

David crowded her again. "Lose today's game. Call it a gesture of goodwill, to show me you're playing along. Otherwise..."

Marcy stared into his eyes, unblinking. "Let go of my arm."

"Don't let her go, David," Rosalind said from right behind him. Her voice was low and unwavering. "If you don't let her go, I'll have an excuse to do something I've been wanting to do for a very long time."

He closed his eyes and exhaled sharply. "Fuckin' nightmare..."

Marcy hadn't realized how close he was to her face until the burst of hot, stinking air washed over her. She winced and stepped back. David let her go and turned to face Rosalind.

She was in a dress shirt under a tweed vest, pageboy cap pulled low over her brows. Her arms were crossed over her chest, the sleeves of her shirt rolled up to reveal the tight muscles from her wrist to her elbows. Marcy knew she had her thumbs tucked under her biceps to push them up and make them look bigger, but she didn't think David knew it.

"What are you gonna do, O'Brien? Punch me?"

"Can I, Marcy?" Rosalind asked, eyes never straying from David.

Marcy said, "No, you probably shouldn't."

Rosalind tilted her head to the side. "One day I won't listen to her."

"You just try it."

Rosalind twitched toward him, feigning a punch, and David flinched hard enough that he skittered back two steps. Rosalind smirked, and Marcy had to cover her mouth so she wouldn't make things worse. David straightened his collar, glared at them both, and stormed off without another word.

"Sorry," Rosalind said once he was gone. "I know you could probably have handled him yourself."

"No need to apologize. Intervention was greatly appreciated."

They started walking together toward the clubhouse. "I couldn't help but overhear," Rosalind said. "Why did that garbage bag think he could tell you to lose the game? As a show you were 'playing along'? With what? What's going on?"

Marcy sighed. She took Rosalind's arm and pulled her closer to the wall.

"He blames Rainy and me for getting him fired. He thinks if we lose the Series, he can convince the Mrs. Waldron that he was vital to our success and get hired as our official manager next season."

"Why would you ever agree to that?" Rosalind said. "You're the one who finally got his ass kicked out."

Marcy checked again to make sure they were alone. "If we don't, he's going to leak that Rainy and I are deviant."

Rosalind furrowed her brow. "How'd he find out?"

"What?"

"You didn't just tell him, did you?"

Marcy hissed, "Ros, he made it up."

"But it's true."

"No it... I... it's..."

Rosalind laughed. "Oh. Oh, I see! He made it up. Honey, you have to realize he didn't just pluck the idea out of thin air. He may not realize how close he hit to the truth, but there's a reason he named you and Rainy instead of you and me."

"H-he just wants to punish Rainy."

"And he doesn't want to punish me?" Rosalind laughed and lightly socked Marcy on the shoulder. "Okay. Don't worry. He's not the kind of guy who would ever make the leap. He doesn't really think any women would ever be that way when they could have a fella like him."

Marcy rolled her eyes and started walking toward the clubhouse. "Who else knows about this little arrangement?"

"There's no arrangement," Marcy said. "I told Rainy, since she's involved, but we decided we weren't going to put the rest of you in the position of making a choice. I figure a couple of you might do something stupid like decide trying to protect me and Rainy. Drop a ball here, run a little slower there, before long we've got a loss on our record thanks to good intentions."

Rosalind said, "Makes sense. But you know that if he *does* follow through with it, Waldron is probably going to pull both of you, and then we might as well hand the Series to the Phoenix anyway."

"This team is more than the two of us."

"Sure, sure, of course. But having our two stars taken away at a time like this won't do any good to our morale."

Marcy's shoulders sagged. "Right."

"Right."

"So the bottom line," Marcy said, "is that we're going to ignore what just happened back there. David was throwing his weight around, but since he doesn't have any weight, it doesn't matter. We're going to focus on the game. Getting a second win and giving ourselves a cushion going forward."

Rosalind nodded. "Sounds good to me, boss."

Marcy started to go into the clubhouse, but Rosalind out a hand on her stomach to stop her. She gently pushed Marcy back to where she'd just been standing.

"I woke up in Ida Coe's bed this morning."

"What?" Marcy said. "Why?"

"Because that's where I went to sleep last night. Eventually."

Marcy tilted her head to the side, then raised her eyebrows, then dropped her jaw. "Oh! Really? Ida is...?"

"No. Well, she wasn't. Maybe she isn't. Not for sure. But she's... definitely a tourist."

Marcy's shocked expression relaxed into a grin. "Yeah...? How'd that happen?"

"I swear to Heaven, I don't know. One minute we're having a conversation in New York, and the next I was on my knees in front of her with~"

"Whoa, whoa, I don't need that much." She waved her hands in front of her face to stop the words from reaching her brain. "But as long as you're both discreet, and you're both willing participants in, um, whatever it is you're doing, it's fine."

Rosalind said, "I'm keeping my mouth shut. But I wanted to tell you, since you had to tell me about, you know. Rainy."

"Oh. Oh, I get it. Thank you, Ros. I appreciate it."

"Sure." She coughed lightly. "Come on, let's go get ready. Time's wasting."

"Yeah," Marcy said. "We've got a game to win."

They were not going to win this game.

Rainy asked Marcy to pull Lulu out after the fifth inning. Marcy agreed, voice tight and face carved in stone. The score was eight to two, and the mood among everyone on the bench proved that she wasn't alone in foreseeing their doom. Halfway through the fourth inning, before the Shrikes had gotten their two runs, the crowd had started spinning their rain sticks. The hollow rattle echoed off the fences and the eaves of the park. It had to sound like a swarm of bees to poor Lulu.

When the other pitcher arrived in the dugout, she shook her head and went immediately to Rainy.

"I'm sorry," Lulu said. "I'm really muffing things up out there."

"You did no such thing," Rainy said. "None of those runs were because of your pitching. And you didn't do anything I wouldn't have done in your place."

Lulu said, "Then why are you pulling me out?"

"Because if I don't, some fuckwit with a typewriter is going to put the blame on you anyway. And there's no way you can focus with those stupid beans rattling around. It's my fault for hogging the mound for so many games. I don't want us to lose with you on the mound and make it look like there's a connection."

"You're taking my loss?" Lulu said.

Rainy shook her head. "Our loss. You did everything you could. And now I'm going to go out there and do the same thing for four innings, and it's not going to make a lick of difference to the end result. Rest and relax your arm."

"Thanks, Rainy."

"No problem."

Rainy slapped her on the shoulder and jogged out onto the field. Someone in the crowd spotted her braids and sent up a whistle, which turned into a cheer, and then a huge section of the bandstand got to their feet and started chanting her name complete with handclaps. She kept her chin down but waved her hand above her head to acknowledge them. Lucille had done a damn good job, but it hadn't mattered because every single Phoenix player was giving a hundred and fifty percent.

If the crowd thought Rainy had some kind of superpower to hold off this beast, she was more than willing to prove them wrong.

The cruel reality of professional sports was that if this was a friendly neighborhood game, both teams would have called it quits at the start of the eighth inning. The score was 13-2, and the Phoenix showed no signs of lagging. The Shrikes, meanwhile, could see the writing on the wall clearly enough that the pep had gone out of their step. She doubted they would get any more runs in this game, let alone enough to force extra innings. But they had to go through the process and play through to the end, no matter how humiliating it might be.

The rain sticks that had been so deafening in the middle part of the game had all gone silent. Rainy was a monolith on the mound, head heavy and arms hanging at her sides like her glove weighed a hundred pounds. Her pitches were still solid, but Rosalind couldn't help but feel like maybe she was holding back. It was ridiculous, of course. Rainy would pitch to the best of her ability no matter what the score might be. And sure, she might hold back a little. At this point there was no incentive to give a hundred percent, just to lose by a little less.

But she couldn't help think of David Buckner and his blackmail scheme.

No. No, it was ridiculous. Rainy couldn't have thrown the game, not when Lucille was the one pitching the first five innings. She was just paranoid and overthinking, trying to find an excuse for the loss that didn't involve accepting the San Francisco Phoenix might be better than them.

A hit echoed off the park fences. It was an infield ground ball that went straight to Ida, who caught it with both hands and tagged the runner.

Rosalind smiled. *That's my girl.*

Only a few more plays like that, and this game would be over. Then they'd get a couple of days to rest while they traveled to California, and they'd start a new game on totally even footing.

This game was not an ending. It was just the beginning.

***

Moxie wasn't going to cry. Not in front of the team, at least. She stayed close to her cubby, head down, ignoring the muted conversations going on around her as she changed out of her uniform. Her eyes felt swollen and they were stinging, but she refused to give in to the urge to cry. She sniffed, blinked hard, and wiped her hand under her nose as she stuffed her things into a bag and slung the strap over her shoulder. She hurried from the clubhouse quickly so no one would try and stop her.

She rounded a corner and nearly collided with Marcy and Rainy. They were deep in conversation, and both jumped when she appeared. Marcy had stopped midsentence - "...swear to me that you didn't~" - and was staring at her like she'd never seen her before.

"Sorry," Moxie murmured, stepping around them and continuing her retreat.

"Moxie...?" When she didn't stop, Marcy said, "Iona, hey."

She slowed down and looked over her shoulder.

"You okay?" Marcy asked.

Moxie nodded, which threatened to shake free her tears. "Fine."

"If you want to talk..." Rainy said.

"No thanks. Gotta run."

15-3. They'd lost the game by twelve runs, which was absolutely unacceptable. By the last few innings, Moxie hadn't even known what signals to send Rainy. Should they go with standard pitches, or try out new, experimental pitches since it didn't seem to matter? Every

Phoenix who came up to the plate could hit. Even though a few were either struck out or got tagged before reaching home, it was no surprise they'd racked up such a huge lead.

She wished she lived far enough from the park to justify taking the L. She considered climbing aboard and just riding it around for a few hours to get her head on straight. It would be better than going home and facing her mother.

They'd barely spoken since Moxie presented her with the ticket, which had gone unused in the end. Bettina was still cooking her meals, but there was no conversation at the dinner table. Ike requested and was given permission to eat in his bedroom to escape the awkward tension between the two women. The very last thing Moxie needed after this humiliating loss was to deal with her mother.

She walked home as slowly as possible, eyes on the ground in front of her. The park had always been like a church to her, and now she could feel it like a weight on her back. She hated it. She hated this horrible feeling when the team lost. Everyone contributed to the wins, so why did she feel like so much of losing rested on her shoulders? If she'd given better signals, if she'd been faster or hit better... the Phoenix pitcher had struck her out twice. *Twice*. She could have helped the team but instead...

"Hey."

Moxie reflexively flinched from the voice, desperate to avoid any fan interactions, but something in her brain registered the voice and made her look up. Celia was walking toward her, hands in the pockets of her slacks, smiling brightly. She looked as if she'd just been strolling down the street and their paths happened to cross.

"Celia? What are you doing here?"

"I happened to be in the neighborhood." Celia stopped in front of her. "I'm guessing by the storm over your head that it wasn't your best game ever."

Moxie's lower lip trembled and she looked away.

Celia put a hand on her shoulder, squeezed, and then let it slide down to her elbow. "Do you want to go somewhere and talk about it?"

"Talk about it? No." She sniffled and composed herself. "But going somewhere sounds like a great idea. But I don't... I-I can't take you home."

"I know." Celia stepped forward to stand next to Celia and slipped one arm across her shoulders. "I had a place in mind. I actually got a hotel room not far from here."

"Oh. Okay." She sniffled again. "Did you not go to the game? You came all this way."

Celia nodded. "This is actually just a pit stop on my real journey. I'm going to California. I've got tickets to a couple of ball games out there."

Moxie smiled. "You're going to come see us?"

"I can't wait to see you. Win or lose."

Moxie pressed tighter against Celia's side. "I think you being there is going to make all the difference."

"Yeah?"

"Yeah. You've already made a difference today."

Celia kissed the side of Moxie's head. "Good. I'm really glad."

Moxie glanced in the direction of home as Celia led her toward the L station. She could run in for a quick second, leave a note to let her mother know where she would be, save her some worry.

Instead, she tightened her arm around Celia's waist and focused on what would happen when they got to the hotel.

CHAPTER TWENTY-NINE

Union Pacific, Chicago to San Francisco

BEFORE THEY left Union Station, Marcy found Rosalind and Moxie and asked them to meet her and Rainy in their berth once the trip was underway. The Waldrons were willing to pay for a private Pullman car that would accommodate the entire team, but everyone would still have to double up on the staterooms. Rainy and Marcy volunteered to share, as did Rosalind and Ida, while Moxie had made arrangements to travel with a private passenger. Everyone else had been scrambling in the station to find a "berth buddy."

The first knock came an hour outside of Chicago. Marcy opened the door and stepped aside to let Rosalind join them. Moxie showed up a few minutes later and took a seat next to Rosalind on one of the plush couches.

Moxie was the only one who didn't know about David's scheme, so Marcy leaned against the door and got her up to speed. Moxie listened with her brow furrowed and then leaned back.

"Huh. Okay. So I assume the reason you didn't tell anyone is because you're not going to go along with it."

"No. We lost yesterday fair and square."

Moxie nodded. "Okay."

"And one more thing," Rainy said. "Just between the four of us, so we have all the information out on the table. David is just making up a rumor here, but he... he accidentally hit on the truth. Marcy and I really are in a relationship."

Moxie's eyes widened behind her glasses. "Oh. I knew you were, uh... but I didn't know it was, um..."

"It's a pretty recent development," Marcy said. "No one knew."

Rosalind cleared her throat.

"No one did *for sure*," Marcy kicked Rosalind's foot. "Now, if it was just a rumor he wanted to spread, it wouldn't be that big a deal. It might ruffle a few feathers and be forgotten by the start of next season. But, since it's true, there's a risk of someone confirming it, or some evidence coming out, or someone will see us..."

"It could be bad," Moxie said.

"Yeah," Rainy said.

Marcy held her hands up, helpless. "I don't know what to do here. I know we can't throw the games. And maybe there's a chance we'll be crushed in California and none of this will matter. But I intend to play to the best of my ability. I expect all of you to do the same. So there's a chance we could pull ahead again."

"And if we win, David will know you're not going with his plan," Rosalind said. "He might release the rumor early."

"Exactly."

"And if that happens," Marcy said, "Lorraine might pull us from the lineup. Lucille is a fine pitcher, and I'm sure any number of our reserve players would fill my spot admirably. But this team deserves to have the best players for this Series. Not to sound too full of myself, I think it's the only way we're going to have a chance of winning."

Rosalind shook her head. "No, I definitely agree. You, Marcy, you might be replaceable in a pinch. But Rainy? We need her on the mound."

Rainy looked down at her feet, clearly uncomfortable with the praise.

"Maybe we could get out ahead of it," Moxie said. "If we're agreeing Marcy is expendable, then maybe she could admit the rumors are true as soon as they come out. But she could say that her lover is someone else instead of Rainy."

"Who would you put on the chopping block?" Rainy said. "Because I'm not comfortable throwing anyone else to the wolves just to save my own bacon."

Rosalind said, "Someone might be willing to volunteer if it means keeping you in the game. Like hitting to the outfielder so the person on third can score. It's a sacrifice fly."

"We can think of a different way," Rainy insisted. "We have two days until the next game. That's plenty of time to come up with a solution."

They fell silent, all four of them swaying with the movement of the train over the tracks. Marcy hadn't noticed any of them raising their voices to be heard, but now the rattle and clank seemed to flood into the room.

"I've been spending the night with Celia Torres from the Pros."

Everyone looked at Moxie. She shrunk in on herself and shrugged.

"I figured since Marcy and Rainy revealed a big secret, I might as well put us on equal footing, right? We've seen each other a couple of times. She's on the train now, actually. She's got a ticket to Game 3, and we're gonna split the cost on a hotel room when we get there." Her face was bright red, and she wasn't looking at anyone.

"Ida said she saw one of the Pros at Union Station," Rosalind said. "I told her she was just seeing things. I guess I owe her an apology."

"Guess so," Moxie said quietly.

Marcy looked at Rosalind. Rosalind looked back. Marcy nodded at Moxie. Rosalind furrowed her brow, feigning confusion. Marcy raised her eyebrows, insistent. Rosalind rolled her eyes.

"There's a reason I'm sharing my room with Ida Coe. We're sharing the bed."

Rainy's jaw dropped, and Moxie leaned forward.

"You're *kidding*," Moxie gasped, moving her hand to cover her mouth. Her eyes darted to Marcy and Rainy. "Five of us on one team? What are the odds?"

Marcy said, "It's not that crazy seeing as I chose Rainy because I'm in love with her. And I knew about Ros years ago. You and Ida are a surprise, though."

"Well, it's early days for me, at least." Moxie pushed her glasses up higher on her nose. "I wonder if there's anyone else like-minded on the team. I mean, can you imagine Lorna~"

Rainy, Marcy, and Rosalind all said, "No," at the same time. They looked at each other, then laughed. Marcy ran a hand over her face and held up her hand to mark the importance of what she was about to say.

"We're not going to bow to David Buckner and his

manipulations. And we're not going to sacrifice any other player to save any of us. We've got a couple of days and a few thousand miles to figure out a better way. A way that we can win this title without putting our heads on any chopping blocks. I don't know what next year is going to bring, but if the Women's League is still around, I damn sure intend to be on it with the rest of you. As champions. So go back out there and start thinking."

Rainy nodded. "We've come this far. We're not going to throw it away just because a man told us to. There's a way out of this. It's our job to find it."

Rosalind and Moxie left the stateroom together. Moxie started toward the front of the train, but Rosalind stopped her with a hand on her arm. She touched a finger to her lips to keep her quiet, then led her to the back of the train. Moxie followed, confused. They passed through a dining room, a galley, and a pantry, and Moxie was left wondering just how much money the Waldrons had shelled out to get them across the country. Some of the other players had said they could "get used to this," but Moxie didn't think she'd ever feel anything but uncomfortable in this kind of luxury.

They ended up on an observation deck where they could see the countryside speeding by. The noise was almost unbearable and Moxie winced, hunching her shoulders as if that could protect her from the clanging and rattling of the train banging over the tracks.

"There is a way we can make sure David Buckner keeps his mouth shut." Rosalind had to raise her voice to be heard, but she wasn't quite shouting. "I didn't want to bring it up in front of them because I didn't know how they'd react."

"Okay," Moxie said, wary. "What makes you think I'll react well?"

"I don't. But I have to run it by someone so it isn't just in my head. I trust you."

Moxie nodded. "Okay. What's the idea?"

Rosalind checked the way they'd come to make sure no one had wandered close. "We could make sure he can't tell anyone anything."

It took Moxie a second to cotton to what she meant. "Criminy. No wonder you were worried about how they'd react. You're talking about..." She couldn't even bring herself to say the word.

"How is it any different than what he's threatening? Rainy and Marcy's lives would essentially be over if he follows through on his threat. I'm not saying I want to do it or that I even know how we'd go about pulling it off, but it's an option. And I think we need to at least discuss the possibility."

Moxie chewed on her bottom lip and crossed her arms. "I don't like it. I'll say that right now. And I don't see any situation where I'll change my mind about that. So I don't think it *is* an option. And I don't think Marcy or Rainy would want us to go to that extreme to protect them. Or for any reason."

Rosalind nodded thoughtfully. "You're probably right. But I think we need to consider the very real chance that anything less won't be enough to stop him."

"Be honest," Moxie said. "Can we win without Rainy?"

Rosalind looked out the window and thought for a full minute before she answered. "Against any other team? Maybe. There are two or three teams we played where I wouldn't have put any money on us if Rainy wasn't pitching. But given what we've seen of the Phoenix? Lucille doesn't have what it takes. We need Rainy on the mound or we might as well turn around and go home now."

"Two days to figure out a way to stop him, then," Moxie said.

"Two days during which we'll be half a continent away from him," Rosalind reminded her.

Moxie exhaled sharply and sagged against the wall. "Piece of cake."

"Yep..."

The train made frequent stops, wheezing up to a station and billowing smoke as it swapped one group of anonymous passengers for different strangers. Rainy watched a group climb down onto the platform, pausing to check their bags or adjust their coats and hats. She wondered where they were all going, if they were on their way home or at the start of a trip.

She was dressed in a man's suit, which she'd packed just in case she wanted to be a bit more anonymous in California. Her hair was tucked up underneath a cap so it wouldn't be quite as noticeable. She waited until the new passengers started boarding before she slipped off the train and tried to blend into the crowd. She didn't know anyone in Omaha, but that just meant no one in Omaha knew her. It would be easy to slip into the crowd and hide until she figured out what her next move was going to be.

She hated abandoning the girls like this. She especially hated leaving Marcy without so much as a note to explain herself. But this was the only option. It had to be her decision and no one else's. If they were going to screw the whole team, she would take all the blame. Marcy would be absolved because she hadn't been asked to vote.

Rainy was almost inside the station when the door flew open and a tiny projectile shaped like a child slammed hard into her. The girl let out a "woof!", rebounded, and ducked around Rainy's hip with a tossed off "'scuse me, sir!" before she ran out onto the platform.

"Patricia!" A woman appeared in the doorway looking after the little girl, then gave Rainy an apologetic shrug. "I'm sorry. She's very excitable on a normal day, and this is like tenfold. Are you hurt?"

"No, no," Rainy smiled. "It's fine. I was an excitable girl myself."

The mother looked at Rainy's face again. "Oh! I'm sorry. It's just the clothes." She chuckled and shook her head. "We're going to a baseball game."

Rainy's smile wavered. "Oh. In California?"

"Mm-hmm, that's the one. Her daddy is from Chicago so she's been following all the Shrike games in the paper." She shrugged. "Getting her a paper every day is cheaper than buying dolls, even if I don't understand all the numbers they put in. I told her that if they made the Series we would go see a game in person. I never thought they'd actually make it! But a promise is a promise, and we can use this trip to see my parents as well, so..." She sighed. "Are you going to the game, too?"

Rainy looked at the little girl, Patricia, who had come to a stop at the edge of the platform. Her head was tilted back to look up at the train.

"Yeah," Rainy said. "Yes, I am. Let me help you with your luggage."

She picked up the bag and escorted Patricia's mother through the crowd to the train. The porter checked their tickets, then tried to stop Rainy from getting back on board without hers. Rainy took off her cap and let her hair down.

"I'm Caroline Rainy. I'm traveling with the team. I just stepped off to get some fresh air."

"My apologies, ma'am."

Rainy boarded, then turned to see Patricia and her mother staring after her with mouths wide open in shock. She smiled at them, nodded, and headed down the aisle.

Marcy was waiting for her outside their stateroom. She smiled and tilted her head to the side. "Changed your mind, huh?"

"You knew?"

"I followed you," Marcy said. "I figured I could drag you back aboard, but then you'd just try again at the next stop. You needed to make the decision for yourself."

"What if the train had left before I got back on board?"

Marcy shrugged. "We'd make do with Lucille. I would be sore at you for a while, but I also understand why you did it. So I wouldn't make you suffer too much. Lucky that little girl came along."

"It wasn't her. Not really."

"Oh?"

Rainy leaned against the wall, her arm pressing against Marcy's. "I got to thinking about our options."

"There aren't many," Marcy admitted.

"Nope. But there's no shame in losing. And I'm not going to let anybody make me ashamed of being in love with you. Whatever happens, the only choice I would regret is quitting. I've quit on teams before. I've quit on *you* before. I'm done doing that. Whatever happens, it'll happen to us both. Together."

"Well, that makes me feel good." Marcy put her head down on Rainy's shoulder. "Whatever happens. Together."

Rainy nodded.

That, she could live with.

CHAPTER THIRTY

Game Three - Recreation Park, San Francisco

ROSALIND STARED out at the field, or as much of it as she could see, and opened her mouth wide to breathe out. She couldn't see her breath but had a feeling it would only take another degree or two before that changed. Half the bandstand was erased by a heavy coat of white fog. It was a cottony blanket that stretched its fingers along the benches and seemed to drip down the walls, it filled the dugouts like it was made of some thick liquid. Centerfield was just a hazy suggestion somewhere in the distance.

"You've got to be kidding me," Rainy said from Rosalind's side.

"They said it will burn off by game time," Marcy said, appearing from behind them. "The temperature should be in the mid-fifties by then, too."

Rainy said, "Good, because I haven't practiced throwing in my heavy coat."

"I didn't even bring a heavy coat." Moxie rubbed the lenses of her glasses and put them back on. "Can anyone even *see* right field?"

Marcy cleared her throat. "The, um, fog lifting is the good news."

Rainy, Rosalind, and Moxie all turned to face her.

"The bad news is that they're expecting showers all day." The other women groaned, and Marcy shrugged. "It could be heavy enough to cause a rain delay."

"So best case scenario," Moxie said, "is that we get a whole extra day to worry, and then we play the Phoenixes *twice* in the *same day*."

"I think the plural of Phoenix is just Phoenix," Rosalind said.

"There isn't a plural for Phoenix," Moxie said. "There was only one of them in the myth."

"Like Medusas."

Rainy held up her hand to stop them. "Okay. We can play in the rain. We can play in the cold. We can do this. As long as we don't have to play in *that*." She pointed at the fog. "I won't even be able to see Moxie's signals in this soup."

Marcy said, "The bright side is that the Phoenixes... Phoe... the Ph... the other team would be in the same pickle. They might be more accustomed to this kind of nonsense, but they don't have magic eyes or any unique ability that will make this less of a headache for them."

Rosalind sighed and looked up at the sky. It was an unbroken blanket of white. "I'm not what you would call confident about this situation."

"Neither am I," Marcy admitted. "But it's the hand we were dealt. So we might as well make the best of it. Come on, let's go get ready."

Rosalind swung her hand out into the fog and closed her hand, looking down at the palm as if she expected to have caught some of it. She brushed her hands off and pressed her lips together, giving the weather one last warning look before she turned around and followed the others back to the clubhouse.

The silver lining, Marcy decided in the seventh inning, was that they had an extra day to figure out what they were going to do about David.

They were trailing again, three runs to the seven for the Phoenix. They weren't playing like themselves. Rosalind slammed into the back fence while chasing a ball, Moxie missed a catch and allowed two players to cross home, and Rainy had been throwing stinkers all game. The clouds had remained stationed overhead and produced just enough rain to make the afternoon gray and miserable. Rain dripped off the brim of Marcy's cap as she hovered near second base and watched Ida strike out. She grimaced and relaxed, knowing she wasn't going to try stealing third.

"You're pretty good."

Marcy glanced at their second baseperson. Her name was McIntosh, McIntire, something like that.

"Sarcasm?" Marcy guessed.

McSomething snickered and shook her head. "No. You actually beat us. That was a surprise. When these leagues were announced~"

She paused as Lorna Lowell swung at a pitch. Strike one.

"~some rich prick with Forty-Niner money handpicked all the best players in the Bay Area. Hell, maybe even the whole state. Every decent player within a train ride of the city got an offer they couldn't refuse. The deck was stacked in our favor all season. You~"

Lorna got a ball.

"You Chicago gals are the first real threat we've faced. You're making us work for it. I appreciate that."

Marcy bared her teeth in a fake smile. "Well, if there's anything we can do to make your victory sweeter, you just let me know."

McSomething laughed and started to say something else, but Lorna hit the next pitch.

Marcy was running before her brain really registered the hit, pumping her arms and planting her feet down hard on every step so she wouldn't slip in the mud as she rounded third. The catcher held both arms out toward centerfield. Marcy was almost close enough to home plate to begin her slide when something hit her in the back just between the shoulders. The blow threw her forward and sent her sprawling in the mud, which splattered over her face and down the front of her uniform.

The point of impact throbbed like a second heartbeat at the base of her neck. She was too stunned to move at first, and then she became aware of people crowding around her.

"Mars? Baby, talk to me."

She lifted her head out of the mud and let herself be carefully rolled over. Someone wiped the mud from her eyes and cheeks, and she blinked up at her rescuer. The raindrops and fog combined to make a halo around Rainy's head, giving her an otherworldly glow.

"Mars? Do you know where you are?"

"Uh-huh, I'm on the ground."

"Be serious, Marcy," Rainy scolded.

"Recruitment... no. Re... Re... Recreation Park. I'm fine. It didn't hit me in my head."

Rainy said, "You still should get checked out."

"No. I'm fine. Help me up."

Rainy took her hand. She sat up and Rainy pulled her back onto her feet. She swayed and leaned heavily against Rainy's side until she trusted herself not to fall. Once she was standing she realized Rosalind, Ida, Moxie, and Hildy had all gathered around her. She smiled awkwardly, embarrassed to be the center of attention for this, and let the team escort her back to the dugout.

"Hussy was aiming for your head," Ida mumbled once they were back to the bench.

"I'm sure she was just throwing for the catcher," Marcy said.

Rainy shook her head. "Then she's got shit aim. And I think we've seen that no one on this team is shit at anything."

"Who threw it?"

"Second base," Rosalind and Rainy both said.

Marcy snorted. "McSomething. And here I thought we were bonding."

Someone handed her a towel wrapped around ice, and she tried to place it on her injury. Rainy quickly stepped in and sat down next to her, holding the pack against Marcy's shoulders. Marcy smiled her gratitude and offered her hand. Rainy took it, linking their fingers.

Rosalind looked down at their hands, then looked to see who was still paying attention. Ida was in the room, but she had told her everything back on the train.

"Maybe it'll be a good thing," Rainy said. "We could get enough stories like that, and it'll drown out whatever David Buckner tries to say."

"Shortstop Stopped Short by Bean Ball," Ida said.

Rainy laughed. Marcy smiled, but something about what Rosalind had said stuck in her mind. "We would need a lot."

"A lot of what?" Rainy said.

"A lot of stories. To make people ignore David's gossip."

Rosalind's smile faded. "I wasn't serious. Don't go out there trying to get hurt or anything."

"No, not hurt." Marcy looked past her, staring at nothing as she thought. "How many stories do you think it would take before David's rumor didn't get any traction?"

Rainy looked at Rosalind. "I don't know what you're talking about."

"He doesn't have any evidence. He just has a story and he's threatening to blab it. Now, if he *did* call all the papers and imply deviant behavior between me and Caro, they'd probably run it just because... well, that sort of thing sells papers. But what do you reckon would happen if his story was just one of... I don't know... five? Five stories they got about us. Or ten. What if David Buckner was the tenth person to call with an unfounded rumor? Do you think the papers would just ignore him?"

"Where are all these rumors coming from?" Moxie asked.

"Us," Rainy said. "They'd come from us."

Rosalind said, "They might listen to one or two. But if there really *was* a flood, there's a chance they would just get ignored."

"Do you think it would work?" Marcy asked.

"It would have to be a lot," Rosalind said. "And they would all have to be different, or else one rumor would just corroborate another."

Moxie said, "Wait, can the newspaper find out where the calls are coming from? It would be kind of suspicious if all the rumors about us were coming from the hotel where we're staying."

Rosalind's shoulders slumped. "Even if they can't, there would be a record of long distance calls from the hotel. It would lead straight back to us."

"Not if we used pay telephones. There was a booth not far from here, I saw it. You put coins in to pay for the call."

"Can they call all the way to Chicago?"

"They had a fair last year showing that they could call from here to New York," Marcy said. "Chicago should be no problem."

"Girls, we don't have to call anywhere." They all looked at Ida. "The reporters are all here. At least the ones who will care about Buckner's rumor. They were on the train with us. Every last one of them tracked me down and asked for an interview."

"And probably a photo shoot," Rosalind said with a wink.

"I have to give the public what they want," Ida said, winking back. "We don't even have to call. We could just leave notes for the reporters at the front desk of the hotels where they're staying. I've got all the cards back at my room."

Marcy said, "Okay. So what~" She clapped her mouth shut as Edith passed by to take her turn at bat. Marcy had completely lost track of the game, but it seemed as if Lorna was on third base now. "So what would the rumors be?"

"One should be about me and Ida," Rosalind said. "It's only fair, after all. No reason you and Rainy should take all the heat."

"You sure?" Rainy asked. "That's a lot to ask."

"You're not asking. If you and Marcy are in danger of being ratted out, then we should be, too." She looked at Ida. "You okay with that?"

Ida nodded hesitantly. "I'm terrified. But yes. I wouldn't feel right if it was just the two of you."

"We might as well mix it up, too," Rainy said. "Rumors about me and Ida, or Marcy and Rosalind."

Moxie raised a hand. "I'll take a hit, if anyone wants to pretend they're dating me."

"We'll let you know if we get that desperate," Marcy said, winking at her. "We can work out the details after this game. If we win, we may have to move fast to start planting the seeds. But if we lose, then we've got at least one more day to plan."

The crowd roared. Moxie, Rosalind, and Rainy turned to watch Lorna cross home plate, followed quickly by Edith. The score was 7-5 now, with two innings left.

Rainy looked at Marcy. "We've come back from worse."

"Against worse teams," Marcy pointed out.

Rainy nodded and went to the front of the dugout to watch the rest of the inning.

The rain never got bad enough to delay the game. Moxie was grateful, because they caught their stride in the last inning. The score was 8-8, against all odds. They could force extra innings if they stopped the Phoenix from scoring in the next few minutes. She was conflicted about that, knowing what she did about David Buckner and his threat. But damn, it would be nice to win. To pull ahead of their opponents, to have a nice lead going into the next game. And to beat them in their own stadium would just be icing on the cake.

She was thinking about their plan to flood the Chicago papers with rumors. Rosalind and Ida putting themselves on the chopping block was courageous as hell. Moxie didn't think she had it in her. Not that she could have offered, at least without running it by Celia first, but even so she couldn't imagine saying it out loud to a stranger. What if that was the one rumor they ran with? She couldn't risk it and that made her feel like a coward.

The ball socked into her glove. That was two outs, and she tossed the ball back to Rainy. One more and they'd go into a tenth inning. The thought made her skin prickly.

She needed to be helpful to the cause somehow, even if she wasn't the one taking the risk. She might not be the same thing Marcy and Rainy were, because a part of her still believed she might still like men, but she was definitely planning to stick with a woman for the time being. And if they could lose everything for doing the exact same thing *she* was doing, then she needed to help them out. Because she knew they would help her if she was the one with the noose around her neck.

The next Phoenix at bat, Mason, made contact on the first pitch. Moxie rose out of her crouch and watched the ball soar. Rosalind and Hildy chased after it. Mason was a streak along the chalked baseline, arms pumping as she rounded first, charging toward second. The ball hit the grass in far right field. Rosalind caught it on the rebound, spun around in a balletic move, swung her arm like it was made of rubber. The ball sailed back to the diamond, moving parallel to Mason as she stomped on third base and headed for home.

Moxie kept one foot on home and stretched her body to its limits, her glove out as far as it could reach. She felt the impact of the ball all the way up to her shoulder. She retreated back toward the plate. Mason flew into a slide. Moxie twisted her body around, foot staying right where it was, and smacked Mason on the shoulder as hard as she could. Payback for what they'd done to Marcy earlier.

"Out!"

Mason slapped home plate hard with the palm of her hand. Moxie dropped the ball and rolled onto her back, laughing as the rain pelted her face. They were going into another inning. They had another chance.

Rainy bent down over her. "Mox? You planning to get up any time soon?"

"I'd love to," Moxie said, "but I think I just popped my goddamn knee."

Rainy looked down and saw how Moxie's leg was twisted. "Oh. Oh shit."

Moxie laughed again as Rainy called for help. She stayed right where she was, letting the rain wash the smut and grime from her face, and waited for someone to come check on her.

She stopped laughing a few minutes later when the pain started to cut through the adrenaline.

***

The rain truly started falling in the bottom of the tenth as the Shrikes took the field. Rainy walked to the mound with her head down but her back straight, already soaked to the skin by the time the first batter approached the plate. Rainy didn't stretch. She didn't swing her arm, roll her shoulders, or kick at the mud under her feet. She just stood ramrod straight and stared at the woman raising her bat. The leather of the ball was slick in Rainy's hand as she danced her fingers over the laces.

Katie Harp was crouched in Moxie's position. Kate was an okay catcher, but there was a reason they used Moxie whenever possible. But now Moxie was in the clubhouse resting her leg. They'd found a doctor in the crowd and brought him down to examine her leg. The kneecap had "adjusted" itself in the time it took him to get down from the bandstand, but he still suggested splinting and icing the leg to ensure there wouldn't be further damage. On top of that, she was to keep off the leg for at least six weeks.

Six weeks. Moxie's season was over.

The Phoenix player was ready. Rainy stared at her and thought about how it felt when Marcy was hit by the ball. She'd gone down hard. For a split second, Rainy thought the ball had hit her in the head. For a brief moment, a handful of seconds that seemed to last an hour, Rainy had existed in a world where Marcy was dead. The relief she felt when Marcy finally moved had felt like ice being injected into her veins, and she'd had to fight the urge to kiss her in front of everybody.

Her hand tightened around the ball. She clenched her teeth and narrowed her eyes.

These Bay Area Bitches may want to symbolize their city's rebirth, but they were trying to do it at the expense of Rainy's family.

She would not allow them to get away with that.

The rest of the Shrikes felt the same. In the top of the tenth, every woman wearing tan and orange hit harder, ran faster, and took more chances. They scored two runs immediately, and Hildy brought it home with a third before Edith was tagged out. Everyone had done their part. Now it was Rainy's turn. She was going to do her damnedest to make sure they stayed ahead.

The rain dripping off the brim of her cap was distracting, so she pulled it off and flipped it backward. Now the rain was in her face, but she could handle that. She blinked it away and conjured up the image of the ball streaking toward Marcy, the muffled thud as it made contact, the way her whole body had jerked as she went down hard.

She put all her fear and anger into the pitch, sinking it into Katie's glove with such force that she was rocked back and almost fell down. She actually pulled her hand out of the glove and shook it, flexing the fingers as if making sure they still worked. She lobbed the ball back to Rainy.

This time she imagined Moxie's face as she was carried into the clubhouse, Rosalind under one arm and Rainy under the other. Moxie hopping on one foot, hissing through her teeth, asking the doctor if he had anything for the pain. Moxie, who might not play another game if the war ended in the off-season.

This time she succeeded in knocking Katie on her ass. She stayed down, eyes so wide they were visible even through the mask. Rainy shrugged an apology and held out her hand for the ball, which Katie returned. She resumed her position behind the plate. Rainy could see tension in her shoulders as she brought her glove up.

No Phoenix was going to get on base. Not again, not in this game. Rainy hurled the ball, the player swung, Katie cringed, and they had their first out of the tenth inning.

The crowd had thinned out due to the weather, but those Shrike supporters who remained were on their feet. Rainy ignored their chanting - *Rai-ny! Rai-ny! Rai-ny!* - and focused everything on her duty to the team and winning the game. It would piss off David Buckner and potentially trigger his damn story, but she was confident their plan would work.

She thought about Marcy's face splattered with mud, eyes unfocused. Strike one.

Moxie's face relaxing when she got her morphine. Strike two.

David Buckner trying to manipulate them by threatening their love. Strike three. Out.

Number 5 walked up to the plate, and Rainy tensed when she realized the woman's name. McIntosh. The one who had actually thrown the ball that knocked Marcy down. If she'd been just a few inches higher... Rainy rubbed the ball against her hip. She switched it to her weak hand, flexed her fingers. She planted one foot, then the other, bent her knees. She put her hands behind her back. She checked Katie's signals.

She ignored them all and threw the ball directly at McIntosh's right leg. She straightened, went stiff, and twisted, but it was too late. The ball smacked hard into her thigh. Her leg collapsed under her and she planted the bat in the ground to keep herself from falling over completely. The umpire waved his arms and gestured, shouting, but Rainy kept her eyes on McIntosh.

The Phoenix bared her teeth as she massaged her injured leg and finally looked up to meet Rainy's gaze.

Rainy didn't blink. She just took her cap off, turned it around, and pulled the brim back low over her eyes.

The umpire patted McIntosh on the arm and pointed for her to walk. McIntosh got to her feet, painfully, and proceeded a slow limp to first base. She cast another look at Rainy, and this time she just gave a quick but unmistakable nod.

We're even.

Rainy nodded back. She could live with letting one of them get on base.

Five minutes later, the game was over. The Shrikes had won, 11-8, and the visiting crowd was cheering as loud as thunder. The team ran out onto the field and surrounded Rainy in a crush, slapping her on the back and massaging her shoulders and arms as they escorted her from the field like she was a knight who had just taken down a dragon.

In the clubhouse, she quickly stripped out of her sodden uniform and sat on the bench in her underclothes. She took her time unbraiding her hair so that by the time she was done, the rest of the team had moved on either to the showers or were discussing the game among themselves. She ran her fingers through the waves of her hair, tugging on the tangles until they were a bit more manageable.

Marcy stepped over the bench and sat down next to her. "I'm okay, Caro."

"I know."

"I saw how you were pitching out there," Marcy said. "I know exactly what you were thinking. And then you hit that cow who hit me. Come on. I know that was intentional. You're lucky the ump didn't eject you from the game."

"Lulu could have handled it."

Marcy bumped Rainy's leg with hers. Rainy looked up and met her eye.

"I can take care of myself, Caroline. But thank you for looking out for me."

"Always."

Marcy took a deep breath and blew it out. "Well. We won."

"Yeah, and what did it cost us? What's it *going* to cost us?"

"We'll deal with that later. For now, let's just enjoy the fact we're one game closer to winning this whole damn thing."

Marcy put her hand palm-up on Rainy's thigh. Rainy took it in hers and squeezed. Marcy put her head down on Rainy's shoulder.

"Whatever happens, we'll know that we didn't back down. We gave it everything we had."

"We did."

They sat like that for a long time, the hum of conversation all around them. Rainy heard laughter and whooping that echoed down the halls, wishing she could join in the celebration. But her mind was focused on how it had taken an extra inning, had taken Moxie being eliminated from the lineup, and they still had to win two more games. Their best might not be good enough, not against this team. Second place, in this instance, would be a crushing blow.

She couldn't help but worry how Marcy would react if they sacrificed everything and still came up short in the end.

CHAPTER THIRTY-ONE

ONCE THE painkillers wore off, Moxie had to fight off a dark cloud of bitter anger and depression. They got her to a hospital after the game. The doctor who saw her confirmed the diagnosis of the man from the crowd. Four to six weeks in a splint, crutches, no strenuous activity. No sports. No World's Series. If the war ended in the next few months, her baseball career was over.

When the doctor released her, the whole team pitched in to hire a car to take her back to the hotel. Rainy offered to escort her back and held her crutches when she climbed into the backseat.

During the right, Moxie tried not to think of what happened as a disaster. She'd inspired the others to come back and win the game. If nothing else, that proved how the rest of the team felt about her, and that was a warm feeling. It lifted her heart to know everyone had gone back out on the field with vengeance in their minds. Someone had hurt her, and all these amazing ladies rose up and punched back.

Tears filled her eyes at the thought. Rainy saw her push up her glasses to wipe the tears away.

"Hey, it'll be all right. You're still part of this team even if you can't play."

"No, I know that." She sniffled, smiled. "That's actually what I was crying about. I've always loved baseball. But I was always outside of it. I would cut the box scores out of the newspaper and then imagine the games in my head. This whole season I've been so caught up with living it that I never took a second to realize I was... I *am* living it. I've got a team."

Rainy nodded. "Yes, you do."

At the hotel, she went to the room Rainy was sharing with Marcy. Rosalind and Ida were also there, sitting on one of the beds with a handful of business cards spread out between them. Marcy got up and hugged Moxie and asked if she was okay.

"My pride is hurt worse than anything else," Moxie said. "But that might just be the painkillers talking. We'll see how I feel when they totally wear off." She scanned the business cards. "Sakes alive, Ida. It looks like every reporter in the state wanted an interview with you."

"I think they were mostly interested in getting photos," Ida said, shrugging her shoulders. "These are the ones that wrote down where they'd be staying, so it makes sense to focus on them."

"Do we have a plan yet?" Rainy asked.

Rosalind nodded. "Marcy thought it would help divert suspicion from us if some of the rumors were delivered while the game was still being played. Some of these hotels are pretty close to the field. Within a mile, definitely inside running distance for me."

Marcy said, "We're thinking Ros could go into the clubhouse, change out of her uniform, run to the nearest hotel, then run back and change in time for our next inning. We'll put her at the back of the lineup so there's very little chance she'll be called upon to bat."

Rainy said, "That's awful strenuous, Ros. Running a mile and then immediately playing centerfield for an inning? You wouldn't get any time to rest."

Rosalind said, "I've run farther, for longer. I wouldn't want to do it every single time we play, but for one game? Yeah, It'll be fine."

"And she'll have two days to rest up when we head back to Chicago for the rest of the Series," Marcy said. "I don't like it, either, but we don't have anyone else as fast as her. She's the only one who can pull it off in the time we've got."

"True." Rainy rubbed her chin thoughtfully. "All right. What about the reporters who are staying too far away?"

"I've got their numbers," Ida said. "Someone can call the hotels anonymously and leave messages. Moxie?"

"Sure, it'll be nice to be useful in some capacity."

Marcy stood and went to the desk, searching the drawers until she found some stationary. She retrieved a pen and brought it all back to the bed.

"Is it smart to use hotel stationary for this?" Rosalind asked.

"There's nothing to identify where it came from." She held up the blank sheet to the light to make sure there wasn't a watermark. She handed the pad to Rosalind. "We can run out and get some notebook paper if it would make you feel more comfortable."

Rosalind examined the pad, then gave it back to Marcy with a shrug. "I think this is fine. So what rumors are we going to make up?"

Ida said, "You and I are having an affair. Like you said, it's only fair."

Marcy nodded and marked it down. "We have to think like men, since that's who we're framing for the rumors. What are some things the crowds have yelled at us?"

"I try not to pay attention to any of that," Rainy said. "It doesn't register."

Rosalind said, "But some of it still gets through. I've heard people shout that I'm really a man. You can go ahead and write that down."

Marcy added it to the list. "I've seen a couple of flyers that claim we're German infiltrators. Trying to feminize the most American institution."

"Good God." Rosalind rolled her eyes. "Someone called me a Kraut and I didn't even connect the dots. The things people will believe."

Rainy snapped her fingers. "The games are scripted and we're just going through the motions."

"Oh!" Ida said. "Yes! I've heard that one! They think we're all dancers!"

Marcy raised an eyebrow as she wrote it down. "Wow. I'll take that as a compliment. No one has ever mistaken me for a dancer."

Moxie said, "We're actually traveling prostitutes. The games are just a cover to bang men in every town."

Rosalind laughed. "So we're gay *and* we're sluts?"

"The two aren't mutually exclusive," Rainy said, giving Marcy a pointed look.

"What does *that* mean?" Marcy asked.

Rainy held up her hands, refusing to comment further. Marcy playfully kicked her foot.

"Okay, how many more of these do we need?"

Rosalind stood up and started pacing. "The more, the better.

And we can't double up. They might assume a rumor that gets repeated is more likely to be true."

"And we can't say anything specific about anyone who isn't in this room," Rainy added. "It wouldn't be fair without their consent, and they can't give it unless we tell them exactly what's going on. So we have to stick to the five of us."

"And David."

Everyone looked at Marcy. Rainy said, "Are you sure that's a good idea?"

Marcy nodded. "He's the one who started this mess. It's only fair to sling some mud back at him. We can say that he didn't get drafted because he... he's got a..."

"Traumatic physical injury," Ida said. "Poor guy got emasculated in a freak automobile accident."

Moxie whistled. "That's a little rough."

Rosalind shook her head. "The man deserves it. He was right on the edge of doing something horrific. Got damn close to doing it to Rainy. I think a rumor like this would be poetic justice. But I'll leave it up to Marcy."

"Emasculation seems appropriate," Marcy agreed. "I'm writing it down. We should all take turns writing the actual messages, by the way. Just in case any of the reporters decide to compare notes."

"Smart," Rainy said.

They kept brainstorming for another hour before Marcy declared they had enough. She tore off pages from the stationary pad and they each took turns writing notes to the reporters. Rainy sat down to write the first note.

"Dear Mister..." Marcy read one of the business cards. "Rutledge. I am writing to you as a fan of the great game of baseball and of America. All caps on America."

"And underline baseball," Moxie suggested.

"Good. It has come to my attention that the Chicago Shrikes are made up of deviant harpies engaging in the most sordid of... of, um..."

"Deviant behavior," Rosalind said.

"We just said deviant," Rainy said.

Rosalind shrugged. "You think the fictional 'concerned citizen' writing this will take the time to critique their dialogue?"

"You have a point," Rainy said. "And my handwriting should be a bit more emotional than this. They would be scribbling quickly. Let me start over." She got another piece of paper and moved the original aside. "Dear Mr. Rutledge…"

They wrote their letters, occasionally starting over to change the handwriting or the tone so it wouldn't seem like all the notes came from the same source. Marcy ventured down to the front desk and borrowed any pens they had, expressing a preference for multiple colors. The clerk smiled knowingly and winked at her.

"Signing autographs, right?"

"The curse of the celebrity," Marcy said, thanking her for the pens as she returned upstairs.

When she got back to the room, Rainy had just finished one of the notes and held out her hand for another pen. Marcy skimmed the letter to make sure it looked different enough from the others. Letters were bigger, more jagged, more cramped together, and the lines slanted down and to the left.

"Impressive work," she said.

"I just tilted the page," Rainy said. "Do you really think this will work?"

Marcy shook her head. "I don't know. But I know it has a better chance than not doing anything. At least this way we're fighting back." She tapped the paper with her pen. "It'll be enough. It has to be."

Rainy nodded, seemingly convinced.

Marcy hoped she was right and wasn't just putting on blinders. Because if this didn't work, they were all going to be finished.

After they finished the notes, and the others returned to their own rooms, Marcy changed into a button-down sleep shirt and pajama pants, then climbed into bed. Rainy pulled back the blankets on her bed and rearranged the pillows, faking her presence there, and then climbed into Marcy's bed to spoon her. There was an ugly bruise on her neck peeking above the collar of her shirt. Rainy bent down and kissed the edge of the discoloration, then nuzzled Marcy's neck.

"I was so scared," she said, keeping her mouth against Marcy's skin. Warm and alive.

"I'm sorry."

Rainy shook her head. "It wasn't your… I just… The way you fell. I don't think I breathed the whole time I was running out to help you."

Marcy brushed her hand over Rainy's arm, crossed over her stomach. She didn't say what Rainy knew she was thinking, what

Rainy herself was thinking. That it could have easily been so much worse. She knew Marcy was probably thinking about what happened to Moxie.

"I can't imagine my life without you," Rainy said into Marcy's hair. "I know that I actually... th-that the years we didn't see each other~"

"Sh," Marcy said. "I know. It's okay." She rolled over onto her back and touched Rainy's cheek. "The truth is, I think it had to happen. We've been a part of each other's lives since we were kids. One of us had to take a step back and make sure this was what we really wanted and not just what was convenient. Some people spend their entire lives looking for their soulmate. What are the odds that ours would be across the alley?"

Rainy smiled and kissed Marcy's lips. "We're women playing baseball in the World's Series, Mars. I don't think the odds apply to us."

Marcy laughed and kissed Rainy back. "I love you, Caro."

"I love you, too." She bumped her nose against Marcy's. "Roll back onto your side."

Marcy did as she was told. Rainy slid her hand down Marcy's stomach to the waistband of her pajama pants. She nibbled on Marcy's earlobe as her hand slipped into the cotton. Marcy inhaled and pressed back against her, craning her neck.

"Kiss me," she said.

Rainy found her lips and moved her hand lower. Marcy arched her back and whimpered, nodded, and reached out. Rainy spread her legs and helped Marcy's hand find its target. They both moaned with pleasure as they moved against each other. The bed creaked underneath them, the corner of the headboard tapping a steady rhythm against the wall.

"Rainy..."

She grunted and nipped at Marcy's bottom lip. "Uh-uh. That's what *they* call me..."

Marcy opened her eyes. "Caroline."

Rainy closed her eyes and kissed Marcy hard, thrusting against her hand as she slipped two fingers inside of her. Marcy cried out, then turned her head to bury her face against Rainy's shoulder as she bucked her hips.

"Caroline... yes, Caroline... Caroline..."

The sound of it echoed in Rainy's ears louder than anything the crowd had ever shouted for her.

CHAPTER THIRTY-TWO

Game Four - Recreation Park, San Francisco

MARCY AND Rainy warned the other players before the game that Rosalind was going to be acting "odd" during the game. Everyone was assured that her behavior did have a purpose, but it wasn't something they could explain. "Just ignore her and everything will work out," Marcy assured them. The others seemed confused but were willing to go along with it. At least that was what they were supposed to say. Rosalind didn't know for certain because she wasn't there.

When the game commenced at three-fifteen, Rosalind was three blocks south and five blocks west in the lobby of the Dolores Hotel. She had borrowed another of Ida's dresses for the occasion, and she felt more inconspicuous than if she'd been wearing her full baseball gear. Her shoes were flats, and the lace gloves she wore felt like spiderwebs on her fingertips.

She checked her watch to make sure the timing was perfect, then stepped up to the desk and rang the bell. A proper young man with slicked-back blonde hair stepped out of the back room with a smile.

"Good afternoon, miss. Checking in?"

"No, I just need to deliver a message to Mr. Arthur Nash. He's in Room 13." Her voice was pitched higher than usual, and she gave herself a sweeter-than-honey accent to go with it. She placed the envelope on the desk. "It's imperative he gets this as soon as possible."

"Of course!" The clerk took the envelope. "May I tell him who left it?"

She smiled and batted her eyelashes. "It's all in the note. Thank you so much."

"We're happy to help, miss."

She laughed, a lightweight and bird-like sound, and waved goodbye with her fingers. She walked to the door and stepped out into the sunlight. She checked her watch again.

3:16:47.

She turned east and took off like a shot from a gun.

The streets were mostly empty, which she was grateful for. She passed a grocers and heard him shout, "Whoa!" as she sped past. Her dress flapped behind her, molded to her thighs from the speed. The street was luckily not as steep as it could've been. They hadn't had time to scout the locations so they had been a chance she would be running uphill. It wasn't the case this time, but they had a lot of hotels left to hit before the day was out.

She charged up the street to the first turn, feet slapping the pavement, arms slicing through the air like blades. She was used to running on grass, on dirt roads. City streets were a completely different track. She was already feeling the impact of each step in her shins. But she recognized the sensation and knew her body would adjust as needed.

The park was three quarters of a mile from the first hotel. She was an incredibly fast runner for long distances. She had the stamina and lower body strength to go for miles. But sprinting was where her talents really were. The relatively short distance around a baseball diamond required quick bursts of speed for just a few seconds. No one had ever tried to gauge her speed on the diamond, but she figured she could maintain thirty feet per second under the right circumstances.

Two minutes after she left the hotel, she burst into the clubhouse and slammed her shoulder into the wall to stop next to her cubby. She undid the top button on her dress and shrugged her arms from the sleeves, pushed the material down her arms, stepped out of it. She pulled on her uniform with the same efficiency, doing the last button as she walked into the dugout.

Marcy was waiting for her by the bench. "Everything go okay?" Marcy asked.

Rosalind nodded, too winded to speak, scanning the field for clues about how the game might be going.

"Two outs," Marcy said. "Rainy and Lorna both scored runs. Edith is at bat now."

"Okay," Rosalind said, breathing out sharply as she sat down on the bench.

Marcy sat down next to her. "Are you going to be okay for all the rest? We can bench you for the game, if you need us to. We just need to prove you're here in case anyone comes asking questions."

Rosalind shook her head. "No, I'm good. I'll be great. It's the first leg of a marathon."

"Don't burn yourself out on this. If you feel yourself hitting the wall, this part of the plan can be thrown out. We'll get the notes to the hotels some other way."

"I appreciate that. Really, though. I'm good."

Marcy nodded. "I'll keep checking in."

Edith got to second base, but Hildy was struck out right after her. The Shrikes took the field, and Rosalind jogged out to centerfield to take her position.

The next hotel was half a mile away. But this time she would have to run there and back, including dressing and undressing in the clubhouse on both ends. It would be incredibly tight even if the Shrikes dragged things out by getting on base and blocking outs. She was figuring ten minutes for each half of the inning. To the hotel and back would take her about eight minutes at full speed. That left her two minutes to change clothes.

She could do it.

She'd have to.

Rainy looked out to centerfield to check on Rosalind's status. She was sweating, but looked solid as ever. She couldn't imagine the stress they were putting her under. She was running all over this damn peninsula just to cover their asses if anyone checked when the notes were delivered. She doubted any of the reporters would compare notes that closely. Hell, she doubted the hotels would keep accurate enough records to make it worthwhile. But it was an extra layer of protection, one more way the Shrikes couldn't possibly have been the source of the misinformation.

It was an awful lot to ask from Rosalind. The least Rainy could do was try buying her a little time. She shuffled her feet in the dirt. She stretched her arms back. She shook off three of Katie's suggested pitches. She rubbed the ball against her hip and tilted her head back to look into the sky. Then, finally, she lazily threw a pitch that the umpire rightfully declared a ball. Then she threw another ball. Then a strike. She kicked at the dirt again.

The Phoenix pitcher was standing in their dugout, arms crossed, jaw set tight, eyes narrowed. Rainy resisted the urge to toss a salute to her. She could almost see the gears working in the woman's mind. *If this Illinois bitch is going to waste my time, wait 'til she sees how much time I can waste against her batters.*

The corner of Rainy's mouth twitched up in a smile that she quickly covered. She threw another ball, then a strike. She could hear the crowd getting restless. Another ball would lead to a walk, so she stopped wasting time and threw a third strike. The player's entire at-bat took almost three minutes.

The Phoenix pitcher shook her head and turned away in disgust. Rainy smiled.

This was going to be a very long game.

Moxie was missing a World's Series game. One of the biggest games of her entire life. And she was stuck back at the hotel, despite Marcy's insistence that she could still gear up and sit in the dugout. She would have felt in the way. A distraction. She could almost see the other girls looking at her with 'there but for the grace of God...' written all over their faces. She didn't need their pity. She stared at the ceiling of her hotel room aware that she should be depressed, that she'd be perfectly within her rights to be a sobbing mess at this moment.

But it turned out the beautiful woman curled up asleep next to her was a powerful mood-lifter.

The knock on her door had come just a few minutes after Moxie left Rainy and Marcy's room. She had just put down her crutches and muttered her favorite off-color words as she got back up and limped over to answer.

Celia had been standing in the hall with a fake stern expression on her face. "Do you know how many hoops I had to go through just to find out which room you were in?"

"What are you doing here?" Moxie asked, any surprise in her voice filtered by her smile.

"I saw you got hurt and thought you might need help changing clothes, taking a bath, doing all kinds of things." Something passed over her face and her voice changed. "And... and I... w-wanted to... make sure you were okay. The papers said you were okay. But I wanted to..."

Moxie had invited her in, waiting until the door was closed before she gave Celia a kiss. She'd let her crutches fall and leaned her weight against Celia, who took her back to the bed.

And that was where they'd remained. She had gotten up to tell Marcy she wasn't going to join them at the park, then returned to the bed and fell back to sleep.

Now the game was probably in the fourth or fifth inning. She had no idea how the Shrikes were doing, and she didn't particularly care. She was dangerously close to spending the whole day in bed. She looked down at Celia's naked body. The wild curls of her hair falling across her face, the curve of her breast, and the line of her hip and thigh.

She smiled. She couldn't think of a better use of a day.

Marcy was in the clubhouse in the seventh inning when Rosalind burst in, dripping sweat and panting for breath as she slumped down onto the bench and reached for her uniform. The game had been static for the past two innings, hovering at 7-8 with the Phoenix leading. Rosalind unbuttoned her dress and starting pulling it off, and Marcy went to her and put a hand on her shoulder.

"Are you okay?"

"Tired," Rosalind said. "But I'm okay."

"I think you've done enough, Ros."

Rosalind shook her head. "I'm fine. I run like this all the time. Back home. I run... everywhere. Home, work. This is nothing." She looked up and met Marcy's eyes. "I'm fine. I swear. I'd tell you if I was about to hit a wall."

"It's not about the wall, Ros. It's about not forcing you to give everything you've got. You've done enough. We can deliver the rest later."

Rosalind stood up and finished putting on her gear. "I appreciate your concern, but I can handle it. I promise you. I've got to be up soon, right?"

"Yeah, you're supposed to be next. But Rosalind..."

She walked past Marcy and headed to the dugout.

Marcy chased after her. She waited until they were on the grass before she shouted, "You're out of here, O'Brien!"

Rosalind turned to face her. "What?"

Marcy closed the distance between them. "You can't talk to me like that. You're benched for the rest of the game."

"What the hell are you talking about?" Rosalind asked, her face twisted in confusion.

"You want to make it two games?" Marcy shouted. She dropped her voice to a whisper, keeping her lips stiff. "You've done more than enough. We just needed people to know you were here. So I'm making your presence memorable." She stepped back and pointed at the dugout. She shouted again. "The bench, or back to Chicago early! It's your choice!"

Rosalind sighed and took off her cap. She wiped it across her face, looked down to see how wet it was, and shook her head.

"Okay. You might be right. Sitting down sounds amazing right now."

"I am right."

Rosalind shouted, "You can be a real bitch, Neal!" She shoved her shoulder against Marcy's as she passed her.

Marcy stumbled and then followed her back to the dugout. They sat next to each other on the bench. Marcy reached up and rubbed her shoulder as if it was actually sore.

"Ow," Marcy said pointedly.

"Hey, you should count yourself lucky. I wanted to punch you." She gestured at the field. "You know, for the realism."

Marcy grinned. "Sure."

Rosalind sighed. "You better hit a home run in my honor."

Marcy put an arm across Rosalind's shoulders. "For everything you've done today? I'll hit two."

She made good on her promise, and Ida threw in an extra run for good measure. Rainy continued keeping the Phoenix from scoring when they were at bat, and the game ended two innings later with the Shrikes on top, 10-8.

After celebrating on the field, while the rest of the team was singing in the clubhouse, Rainy took Marcy's hand, guiding her to a dark corridor leading to the restrooms. She pressed Marcy against the wall and gave her a kiss that made her knees give out. She gripped Rainy's belt with both hands and accepted the kiss passively, letting go of all her thoughts and worries and concerns so she could focus entirely on Rainy's lips and tongue and breath. This close, she smelled like sweat and grass, and Marcy couldn't get enough of it.

The kiss finally ended, and Rainy kept hold of her until she could stand on her own.

"We're one game away from winning the World's Series."

Marcy grinned. "Yes, we are."

"That means David is probably pulling the trigger right now."

"If he hasn't already."

Rainy nodded. "Rosalind told me she got most of the notes to the hotels. She was unbelievable today. If this plan works, it will be because of her."

"Agreed." She smoothed her hands over the front of Rainy's jersey. "God, you look good in this uniform."

"I'll leave it on tonight when we go to bed."

"Mm-mm," Marcy said, shaking her head. "I like you better out of it. All those freckles…"

Rainy laughed and kissed Marcy's cheek. "Come on. Let's go celebrate with the rest of the team. Whatever happens, it's out of our hands now. All we can do is play the game as best we can. Everything else, we'll deal with when the time comes. For now…" She kissed Marcy's hair and pulled her away from the wall. "Let's go enjoy the moment with our girls."

Marcy slung her arm around Rainy's waist and let herself be led back to the clubhouse.

CHAPTER THIRTY-THREE

Union Station, Chicago

WHEN THEY arrived in Chicago two days later, Rainy and Marcy went immediately to the newsstand to check for stories. They paid their dime and stood on the platform to scour the pages. There was coverage of the Series, of course, and a preview of the upcoming game with information about tickets. Nothing about scandals, rumors, no gossip shared in the editorial, not even a whisper of anything they had brainstormed in the California hotel room. Marcy thumbed through the entire paper she had just bought and breathed a sigh of relief, then craned her neck to look at the paper Rainy had bought.

"Anything?"

Rainy shook her head. "This one barely even covers the game. 'It was raining.' We almost drowned and this guy just says 'it was raining.' Unbelievable."

Rosalind came up with a paper of her own. Moxie was with her, limping along on her crutches. The train that had just delivered them home blew its whistle and loudly churned forward, continuing its journey to wherever was next on its itinerary.

"It makes everything you did look meaningless," Rainy said to Rosalind.

"Not at all," Rosalind said. "This was the point of all that running. Total silence from journalists. I consider it time well spent."

She rolled up her paper and slapped Marcy's arm with it. "And I didn't have a chance to tell you on the train, but thank you for making me stop. I spent the whole first day of the trip home sorer than I've ever been. I could barely get out of bed."

Rainy nodded. "Ida said you were stiff as a board."

"A few massages and I was good as new." She winked and smiled. "But if I'd kept going, who knows what shape I would be in today."

Marcy cleared her throat. "And, um, what shape would that be? We need you out in center, but if you need time to recover…"

Rosalind shook her head. "I'm still a little stiff. But a nice long bath and a night in my own bed will cure what ails me. I'll be ready tomorrow."

"Works for me," Marcy said. "But we're not out of the woods yet. David might be waiting for tomorrow's edition to stoke up anger on a game day. The journalists we targeted might have waited until they got home to write the stories instead of sending them over the wire. We need to stay prepared for the worst to happen tomorrow."

"We'll be ready," Moxie said. "And speaking of ready… I hope you are, Marcy."

They turned in the direction Moxie nodded. Lillian Waldron had appeared on the platform, wearing a suit jacket, tie, and skirt. She had clearly seen them but was hanging back while they were talking. When she realized she'd been seen, she cautiously advanced.

Rainy cleared her throat. "Mox, let me help you with your bags."

"I'll help too," Rosalind said.

Moxie said, "I don't have that many bags."

Rainy put a hand on Moxie's shoulder and gave her a gentle shove. Moxie rolled her eyes, hopped in a circle, and followed them to where the porter had gathered all the luggage from the now-departed train. Lillian watched them go and smiled nervously when she was alone with Marcy.

"I see Miss Moccia seems to be recovering nicely."

"She's a tough one," Marcy said.

Lillian nodded. "You all seem to be quite tough. And, um, h-how is Caroline?"

Marcy looked down at her shoes. "She's good. Lillian… about us, and what–"

"We weren't anything, Marcy. I mean." She coughed into her hand, an attempt to end her sentence more than anything else. "We could have been, maybe. Under other circumstances. In a world where Caroline Rainy was... less... who she is." She chuckled softly and shrugged. "I'm not going to hold your feelings against you, Marcy. I'll just take comfort in knowing I was a runner-up."

Marcy winced. "You weren't~"

Lillian stopped her with a wave of her hand. "There's no shame in being second best. Your history, and your present, it's an impossible fight to win. I'm proud of how far I got."

"Thank you," Marcy said.

Lillian waved her off. "There's no need for that. I'm just being a sensible grown-up. And sometimes that is painful, but that's how we learn." She adjusted the knot of her necktie and lifted her chin. "Now. There *is* business we need to discuss."

"Oh boy," Marcy said.

"It's nothing bad. Nothing terrible, anyway. But it would seem David Buckner has been busy."

Marcy tensed. "Oh?"

"Mother was contacted by a friend who works at the *Herald*. It seems that Mr. Buckner tried to submit a plethora of lurid stories about the team while you were in San Francisco. Some of them were even hand-delivered to the hotels where reporters were staying."

Marcy raised her eyebrows. "Hand-delivered? How in the world did he pull that off?"

Lillian shrugged. "Who knows. Friends? Calling in favors? I doubt he has the kind of money that would be required to buy manpower. But however he did it, it sounds like every sports reporter Chicago sent to California received some kind of rumor about the team. Some of them were obviously hogwash. Rosalind O'Brien was really a man in disguise, the games are all scripted, things like that. Some of them were... potentially true." She held Marcy's gaze for a moment, then moved on. "Mother explained who Buckner is, and what his possible motivation might have been."

"She stopped the stories."

"No, no, no. Of course not. Mother is a staunch believer in the free press, and she would never stand in the way of it." She toyed with the cuffs of her jacket. "She... *may* have simply insinuated the risk inherent with printing unsubstantiated rumors. The potential for libel lawsuits could have been brought up. And when the victims are a baseball team preparing to play one of the most important games of their careers, well, the damages a judge may award for such a thing..."

"Just common sense," Marcy said. "I suppose we got lucky, then.

With a little help from your mother, of course."

"Mm-hmm." Lillian said. "I wanted to tell you as quickly as possible, just in case you were concerned about Mr. Buckner. He's officially been banned from Weeghman Park so there's little chance you'll see him tomorrow."

Marcy felt another knot of tension between her shoulders release. "That's fantastic news. Thank you."

"Of course. We're here to look out for you. All *you* have to do is focus on the game." She leaned in and pecked Marcy's cheek. "Go get 'em, Marcy."

"Thank you, Lillian."

"There are cars waiting outside to take all you ladies home. Get some rest."

She waved goodbye to Rainy, who was failing to look inconspicuous a few feet away. Rainy awkwardly waved back.

Rainy waited until Lillian was gone before coming over. "Is everything okay? With the two of you, I mean?"

Marcy tilted her head and cocked an eyebrow. "Jealous?"

"She's beautiful," Rainy said. "And she came close to winning you away from me."

Marcy laughed and slipped her arm around Rainy's. "Everything's peachy. She and her mother helped make sure our plan worked. They're the ones who stopped any stories from slipping through the cracks. It's amazing what a legal threat will do to a newspaper."

"I still don't like standing in the way of the press," Rainy said.

"Oh, hush," Marcy said. "We stopped them from printing rumors with literally no basis in reality. All Lorraine Waldron did was remind them that they should wait until there's evidence to back up their claims before they print a story. They should know that already anyway. And the fact they followed through means what actually gets in the paper is somewhat trustworthy."

Rainy didn't look convinced. "It's still a rich person deciding what gets printed."

"I'll grant you that," Marcy conceded. "But since it worked out for us in this case, let's agree to just ignore the implications, hm?"

"I suppose I can agree to that." Rainy looked around the crowded platform. "As soon as we're someplace private, I am going to give you such a kiss..."

"Oh really?"

"Oh yes."

"Come on," Marcy said. "Lillian has cars waiting for us. I'll tell the driver to go slow and you can whisper in my ear all about this kiss you have planned."

Moxie hesitated outside her apartment door, staring at the knob. She could hear Ike babbling inside, the hum of music from the record player, the clatter of dishes being washed. Real life. The life that had been perfectly fine for her just a few months ago. Now she was used to traveling around the country, playing baseball, signing little pictures of herself for strangers, making love to beautiful women with coffee-colored skin in hotel rooms and private train cars.

Her hands tightened around the grips of her crutches. That life might be over, and she might be shoved back into the old life, which suddenly seemed excruciatingly small. The thought of going back to her old routine made her choke.

There was nothing she could do about it now. She just had to embrace whatever fate threw at her. She took a breath, turned the knob, and pushed the door open.

She had hobbled over the threshold, reached back to drag her suitcase inside, and pushed the door shut. She faced forward and saw Bettina standing in front of the sink, half-turned and frozen, her eyes locked on Moxie's leg.

"What happened?"

"I..." Moxie mentally flipped through the past few days, the telegram she'd composed in her mind but never actually written because she was too preoccupied with Celia. "I sent a letter," she lied. "It must have gotten lost somewhere between here and California. It's not as bad as it looks."

Bettina came out of the kitchen, her hands still dripping from the dishwater. "You're on crutches!"

"It's just my knee. I can't put weight on it for a while..."

"This is just perfect," Bettina snapped. "You were finally going to be useful around here again and now you pull this."

Moxie said, "I dislocated my knee, Ma. I helped my team win. We're leading the World's Series! We could actually win the whole damn thing tomorrow."

"What good does that do me?" Bettina said.

Moxie's face burned, and she had to look away from her mother to keep from saying anything she would regret. She pressed her lips together and nodded, then turned around and opened the door.

"Where are you going?"

"I'm going to stay with my family."

The stairs were going to be a pain in the ass to go down, and then the L station stairs would be an extra nightmare. And she hated the idea of just dropping in on Marcy, but it would be worth it. She couldn't stay in this house a second longer.

"Wait just a minute. Iona!"

If there'd been a hint of actual worry or apology in Bettina's tone, Moxie might have stopped. But she sounded angry, offended, and Moxie knew that staying would only trap her in the rut she'd just been dreading.

"I'll send you some money for Ike."

"Iona, *you get back here.*"

Moxie slammed the door on her mother.

She began her slow descent down the stairs. In a way, the crutches were a godsend. They slowed her down and gave Bettina the chance to rethink her attitude. She could change her mind and very easily catch up with Moxie before she had gotten very far. But by the time she reached the ground floor, out of breath and starting to sweat, she looked back to see that the stairway behind her remained empty.

Maybe she'd go to Detroit. Find Celia.

God knew there wasn't much reason for her to stick around Chicago anymore.

Rosalind bought Ida a sandwich before they took the L up to Rogers Park. They left their luggage in Rosalind's apartment and took a meandering walk through the neighborhood, ending up at a small beach looking out over Lake Michigan. They sat on the rocks and watched the waves, Rosalind silent while Ida took her time eating the sandwich. She offered Rosalind the pickle.

"Sorry I'm not being very entertaining," Ida said.

"You don't need to entertain me," Rosalind said. "I'm happy to just sit here. And eat a pickle."

Ida chuckled, then sighed. "God, I'm tired. Who knew it would be exhausting to just ride a train for two days?"

"Traveling can drain you, for sure. And given how much we've been traveling, I'm surprised any of us can hold our heads up right now."

"For sure." Ida laughed softly and then furrowed her brow thoughtfully. "Huh. You know what? You and I have slept together in

New York, California, and Chicago. And if you count the train trips, we've got most of the country covered."

Rosalind said, "I suppose that's true. Seems significant."

Ida nodded. "It does." She glanced over her shoulder at the apartment buildings crowding up against the beach, with all the windows looking down on them. "I wish I could kiss you right now."

"Then hell, let's get out of here," Rosalind said. "The lake will still be here tomorrow."

Ida laughed and held out her hand. Rosalind stood and helped her up.

They retraced their route back through the neighborhood. Rosalind wanted to hold Ida's hand, wanted to be pressed tightly against her, and she hated that they had to have even a few inches distance between them. She stuffed her hands into the pockets of her coat so they wouldn't do anything without her permission.

"You moved here after Marcy put the team together, right?"

"That's right," Rosalind said. "I still have the house in Aurora, but I didn't want to live in a hotel for the whole season. I could afford to get an apartment for a few months."

Ida said, "That's a big risk."

"It seems to have paid off."

"Sure." Ida chuckled. "I wish I could be that risky. Just take a chance. Let go of the rope and be sure there's a net underneath. I know it would be scary but at the same time... how thrilling."

Rosalind said, "It's easier if you have someone to catch you."

Ida smiled at her and then looked at the ground. "I'm glad I took a chance with you in New York. I was so scared."

"You did not seem scared."

"I hide scared well. I'm very practiced. No one wants to see the pretty girl with the nice figure being scared. Or upset. Angry. Well, they really don't like anything but happy, you know?"

Rosalind took her hand from her pocket, then reached out and took Ida's hand.

"Someone will see."

"I know," Rosalind said. "Scary, huh?"

Ida beamed brightly and squeezed Rosalind's hand.

Rosalind's apartment was nestled right beside the L station, one of the reasons she'd gotten such a good deal on it. The passing train rattled her windows and every frame on the wall like clockwork. The landlord had told her she'd get used to it, but she was still waiting for that to happen. She heard its clatter on the rails as she escorted Ida up the stairs.

If her mind hadn't already been focused on what she planned to do behind closed doors, the man leaning against her door wouldn't have caught her by surprise. As it was, she didn't realize he was blocking her apartment until he pushed away from the wall and moved to stand in front of her.

"Rosalind, the fucking nightmare."

"David." Her hand relaxed just as Ida pulled hers away. "What the hell are you doing here?"

He looked terrible. His beard hadn't been trimmed in days, wild hairs sticking out in every direction, and the bags under his eyes revealed he hadn't been sleeping. He also looked as if he'd slept in his clothes.

"Three wins," he said. "Damn good record. One to go."

"Are you here to congratulate us?" Rosalind said.

He smirked. "I'm here because Marcy Neal and I had an arrangement. One that she *clearly* didn't share with the rest of you. You were supposed to lose this Series."

"The Phoenix thought the same thing," Rosalind said. "We're proving them wrong tomorrow."

David shook his head. "No, you're not. If Marcy won't cooperate, then maybe the rest of the team will be smart."

Rosalind's eyes widened. "Oh, and you came to *me* for help? Oh, David, you must be positively doomed if you're this far down on the roster."

He grabbed her arm. Rosalind looked down at his fingers pressing into her skin, then slowly raised her eyes to meet his.

"You're gonna want to let go of me, David."

He bared his teeth. "Marcy Neal ruined my life for *no reason*. I put this team together. I'm the only reason you bitches are in the World's Series. *I* found the money. *I* made the agreement to let you play in Weeghman. And then that harridan Waldron comes swooping in an- and she... she just takes over after I do all the hard work, and she throws her money around, and now she gets the credit for what *I* created. I just want my due."

"Oh for crying out loud!" Ida snapped. "I am so sick of you, Mr. Buckner!"

Rosalind and David both looked at her, surprised at her outburst.

"First, before anything else, you didn't get kicked off the team for no reason. You were kicked off because you were making all of us uncomfortable. Did you even notice how hard we tried not to be in the same room alone with you?"

"Because of the lies~"

Ida snapped her fingers in front of his face until he stopped talking. "You made a move on Rainy. We all know about that. But that doesn't even matter, because you didn't *have* to do anything. The very fact we felt uncomfortable around you should have been enough to make you change your behavior. But you didn't, and that's why Marcy finally decided to bounce you like a bad check."

David's grip had relaxed enough that Rosalind could slip her arm free. She took a step back, moving to stand behind Ida.

"As for ruining your life? Hah! I wish. But the fact is that you could probably put it on your resume and you could still get hired at a hundred different places. Because men will be the ones hiring, and men will just wink and shake your hand." She demonstrated by nudging Rosalind. "I wouldn't have been able to control myself around all them dames, either! Hah hah."

Rosalind smirked.

"Stop blaming us for your consequences, Mr. Buckner. It's over. You're done with the Shrikes. Forget you ever knew us."

She stepped around him and went to Rosalind's apartment door.

David looked at Rosalind, stunned into silence. Rosalind shrugged and went to unlock the door to let Ida in. She looked back at him.

"I sincerely hope you don't get hired anywhere else. Because I know you'd just do the same thing to the women on any other team you work for. But Ida is right. You probably will. You should start looking now, before the war ends, or else you might miss your chance. But whatever happens, Mr. Buckner, the Shrikes are done with you."

She slammed the door in his face.

CHAPTER THIRTY-FOUR

Game Five - Weeghman Park, Chicago

MARCY WOKE up with a dry mouth, which she tried to remedy by smacking her lips. Her tongue was also dry, so she resigned herself to opening her eyes to get a drink of water. When she did, she discovered Rainy propped up on one elbow next to her, staring down at her. Rainy's hair was a wild tangle on one side of her head and a flattened slate on the other. Marcy smiled, forgetting about her dry mouth as she reached up to try and remedy the mess.

"Why're you looking at me," Marcy muttered.

"Because I missed too many mornings by being stupid." She turned her head and kissed Marcy's forearm. "Do you remember that time you said my face was always dirty and I needed to take more baths?"

"*What?*" Marcy was more awake now. "When did I say that?"

Rainy's smile widened. "I think we were six. Maybe five. Really young. We were playing in your bedroom and we got into a fight about something stupid. You said I was ugly because my face was always dirty."

Marcy laughed. "Because of your freckles. Oh, wow." She covered her face. "Did I ever say I was sorry for that?"

"Not that I can remember."

"Well, I'm very sorry." She sat up and kissed Rainy's lips, then both of her cheeks. "I love your freckles now. I love *all* your freckles." She bent down and began kissing Rainy's chest above the scoop of her sleep shirt, burrowing lower to her cleavage.

Rainy laughed, a sound like chirping, and ran her fingers through Marcy's hair. "Shh. We have a guest, remember?"

Marcy had actually forgotten poor Moxie out on their couch. She pulled back from Rainy's chest and kissed her lips instead.

"What made you think about that fight?"

Rainy kept her hands in Marcy's hair, playing with the strands. "That particular fight ended with me storming out of your apartment, stomping all the way down to the street, up to my own apartment. I went in my room, opened my window, and shouted across the alley, *you're not my friend anymooore!*"

Marcy laughed. "Oh. Oh wow, I do remember that part." She put her hand on Rainy's chest. "I'm glad I came to my senses eventually, even if I didn't apologize at the time."

"That's okay. You more than made up for it. Come here."

They moved closer together in the center of the bed. Marcy hooked her leg over Rainy's hip under the blanket. Neither of them made a move to carry things further, and not only because of their guest. They had to conserve their energy for the afternoon.

"Do you remember anyone else we were friends with back then?" Rainy asked.

"Oh gee whiz. Uh." She cast her mind back. "Travis. Eleanor. Who was the girl who had to wear that awful orthodontic headgear? She always wore overalls. Blonde, I think..."

"Oh. I know who you mean. Uh..." Rainy squeezed her eyes shut and tapped her finger on Marcy's shoulder. "Beth? Bessie!"

"Bessie!" Marcy confirmed. "Whatever happened to her?"

Rainy said, "Probably got rid of the headgear at some point."

"One would hope." Marcy chuckled.

Rainy pulled back and looked down into Marcy's face. Her smile was still there, but Marcy saw something serious in her eyes.

"All these years, and you're still..." She shook her head and pressed her lips to Marcy's forehead. "I'm sorry I ran away."

Marcy said, "That's not important. You came back. That's what counts."

"Yeah. I've spent my entire life with you, Mars. Give or take a few stupid years here and there. And look at where it's gotten us."

"Two miles from the apartment where we grew up?"

Rainy chuckled and pulled back so she could look into Marcy's eyes. "You know what I mean. I know I can't ask you in the way people usually ask this question. But I want to spend the rest of my life with you. Whatever happens today, whatever happens with the war and the team, I want to you in my life from now on."

"Aw, Caro." Marcy brushed the back of her hand across Rainy's cheek. "I've always been yours. You know that."

"So... yes?"

"Yes," Marcy said, laughing when Rainy bent down to seal their agreement with a kiss.

Rainy shifted her weight and rolled on top of Marcy, straddling her before she sat up and cupped Marcy's face with both hands. She brushed away the tears that had fallen from the corners of Marcy's eyes and smiled down at her. Her hair, backlit by the window, looked like it was on fire.

"So what do you want to do now?" Marcy asked, her hands resting on Rainy's thighs.

"Now?" Rainy raised her eyebrows. "Now I want to go win the World's Series with you."

The entire city of Chicago seemed to have turned out for the Shrikes' return game.

When the team took the field, the roar that came up from the bandstand could have been heard by boats on Lake Michigan. An entire storm worth of rain sticks began sounding, their rattling hum echoing in Rainy's ears as she waved to acknowledge the fans. It had been a war just to get into the park when they first arrived. The door to the clubhouse was blocked by people who wanted players to autograph Cracker Jack cards, baseball caps, shirts, anything that could be written on was offered for their pens. Two police officers had finally been summoned to help break up the congestion.

It was a perfect Chicago autumn afternoon. Rainy walked slow to the mound, casually tossing the ball into the pocket of her glove. She could almost smell the lake as she took her post. She looked toward the visitor dugout and saw a dozen furious faces glaring back at her. Half of them were standing, arms crossed, and the rest were sat hunched on the bench like gargoyles.

Rainy smiled at them and touched the brim of her cap in greeting.

Nothing could bring her down today. Not even their glowering mugs could dampen her spirits. Not even the fact Moxie wasn't in the park. She knew she was more than welcome to suit up and sit in the dugout with the rest of the team, but she said she would rather stay in and rest her knee. Marcy was worried she was just depressed about not being able to participate in such a potentially vital game. Rainy could see why that might be true. To come all this way just to sit on the bench for the final stretch would bring anybody down.

But not Rainy. Not today. Today, Rainy had confirmed that she was going to spend the rest of her life at Marcy's side. She didn't need a trophy. She didn't need to win some silly game. She had everything she needed.

She looked to Marcy at the shortstop position. Marcy caught her looking and shaded her eyes with one hand. Rainy smiled and faced home plate. The batter was in position.

Rainy loosened her stance. She dragged her foot through the dirt. They were back home, in their own park, and the breeze pushed against her back like it was welcoming her home.

She threw the first pitch.

Moxie considered going to a pool hall, somewhere she could at least get some idea of how the game was going without actually going to the park. But she was worried about being recognized. And even worse, what if she *wasn't* recognized? She was already fighting the sensation she'd been left behind by the team. She didn't need a whole room of fans ignoring her presence to drive the final nail in the coffin.

The part of her that had grown up on baseball was screaming at her. It was potentially the last game of the first Women's League World's Series, and she was going to miss it? She was going to sit on the couch pouting instead of cheering on her family? But she couldn't bring herself to be a spectator anymore. Before she had always spent games imagining what it would be like on the field. Now she knew all too well exactly what it felt like, and knowing she couldn't run out and join them would hurt too much.

So she stayed on the couch in Marcy's apartment and stared at the ceiling. Her knee didn't hurt, so she couldn't even pass the time with a pain pill. The park was just a train ride away. She could suit up, hop on the L, and get there before the third inning started. Marcy and Rainy had sworn up and down that everyone would love to see her. And she knew that was true. She knew Rosalind liked her, for sure, and Lorna and Hildy...

No. She rearranged the pillow under her head and tried to nap. She hadn't gotten much sleep the night before. Marcy and Rainy probably thought they were being quiet, bless their hearts, but the stifled moans and shushed laughter had echoed down the hall and kept Moxie wide awake for most of the pre-dawn hours.

She had almost dozed off when she heard something scrape the front door lock. She opened her eyes and looked down at her watch. There was no way the game could already be over. The scratching continued and she lifted up to peek over the back of the couch. The knob jiggled, some more scraping, and then the latch clicked. A second later the knob turned and the door slowly opened.

"Hello?" A pause. "Anyone home?"

Moxie dropped back down out of sight. She recognized David Buckner's voice, just as surely as she knew he had no business being in Marcy's apartment while she was gone.

She heard him step inside and close the door behind him. She held her breath and waited for him to realize she was there. But he continued forward into the combined dining room-kitchen. He kept his back to her as he passed through the living room, disappearing down the hall to the bedroom.

"Okay," Moxie whispered, letting out the breath she'd been holding. She slipped off the couch, keeping her weight on her good leg as she retrieved her crutch from the floor. She used it like a cane instead of getting it under her arm and hopped as quietly as possible to press her back against the wall next to the hall door.

"Marcy?"

His voice was wary. Moxie held her breath again. The floor creaked under his footsteps, and she knew he was creeping back down the hall to investigate the noise she'd just made. Moxie scanned for something to defend herself with, then realized she was already holding the perfect weapon. She repositioned her grip on it and pressed herself harder against the wall.

"I thought the game would last~"

He stepped into the living room. He saw Moxie, not who he had expected, and much closer than he had expected, and he recoiled in surprise. Then he cringed and brought both hands up to protect his face. The defense didn't matter, because that wasn't where she aimed.

Balanced on her good leg, Moxie swung her crutch like a lumberjack trying to fell a tree. The wooden rod cracked hard against his kneecap. In the small space it echoed like a home run. He screamed in pain and collapsed into the hallway. Moxie also screamed, as the motion of swinging caused her to lose balance and sent her to the floor where she landed on her bad knee.

"You awful woman!" David cried. "You broke my leg!"

Moxie ignored him and crawled to the door. It took all her strength to ignore the pain as she climbed the wall and twisted the knob. She leaned out into the hall and shouted.

"Someone call the police! A man just broke into this apartment!"

David had crawled after her. He grabbed her good ankle and yanked. Moxie managed to grab hold of the door frame but her bad leg shot out to support her. Pain shot from her ankle to her hip. She cried out and decided if she was going to hurt, she might as well get something out of it. So leaning hard against the wall, she pulled her foot free and kicked David in the head, then stomped hard on his shoulder for good measure. She thought she felt something snap under the ball of her foot. She wished she'd been wearing cleats.

David yelped and rolled away from her. Moxie dropped her good foot to the floor and sagged against the wall, grateful that baseball had given her enough upper body strength to basically hang off the jamb the way she was.

"Miss?"

She twisted to look into the hall. An older man, balding above a face more weather-beaten than her glove, was craning his neck to look into the apartment.

"Are you all right, miss?"

"I'm fine," she said breathlessly. "I just need~"

"Police are on the way," he said. "What did he do to your leg?"

She shook her head. "That wasn't him."

"Then what'd you do to *him?*"

Moxie grimaced and looked down at where David was still writhing, clutching his shoulder.

"Nothing he didn't deserve," she assured the old man.
***

Rosalind split her fingers around the neck of a bat and lifted it. Marcy was suddenly next to her, a hand on her shoulder.

"There are a lot of ways this can go," she said. "Even if we lose, we get another chance to win tomorrow. There's no pressure on you here at all."

Rosalind raised an eyebrow at her. "Yeah. I understand."

"I just wanted to make sure you *knew*," Marcy said. "Whatever happens out there, it's not on your shoulders."

"I appreciate that. But I'm good."

Marcy nodded.

Rosalind looked at the other Shrikes. Not one of them was on the bench. They were all crowded at the front of the dugout, some watching her nervously but most looking out at the field. It was the bottom of the ninth. The score was 11-12, with the Phoenix leading. The Shrikes had two outs. Ida was on second base. Rosalind walked out to home plate with the bat on her shoulder as she considered the possibilities.

She could get to first, Ida could score a run, they would tie. Tenth inning again.

She could strike out, the Phoenix win. The Series would be three games to two, and they would play another game tomorrow.

Or she could hit a home run, she and Ida would both score, and the Shrikes would win the first Women's League World's Series in history.

She took her position. She examined the bat as if she'd never seen one before. She looked out at the pitcher, and then looked past her.

Rosalind looked at Ida.

Ida had her left foot on second base, hunkered down and knees bent, her right foot stretched out as far as she dared. She saw Rosalind watching her and smiled, dipped her head in a single nod. Rosalind flexed her fingers on the neck of the bat. She remembered Daisy's words when they were recovering from their sweet goodbye on the floor of Daisy's bedroom.

"Why did you marry him?"

"He could give me a home."

The pitcher looked at Ida, almost daring her to try and steal. If she did, and the pitcher tagged her, that would also end the inning. The pitcher bowed her head as if she was daring Ida to try.

"I'll give you a home, Ida," Rosalind said under her breath, so quietly even the catcher couldn't have heard what she said. "If you want a home, I'll give you a home."

Ida nodded as if she understood.

The Phoenix pitcher hurled the ball to Rosalind.

Rosalind swung and made solid contact, the bat cracking like a firecracker that set off the whole crowd.

A stiff lake breeze rolled over the walls, through the bandstand and swept across Weeghman Park to right field. It picked up Rosalind's ball and carried it higher, farther. Rosalind, the fastest woman in Chicago, watched it fly and knew she didn't have to push herself. The Phoenix players knew as well, and so did the rest of the Shrikes. They stormed the field and surrounded Ida as she crossed home plate to tie the game. A few seconds later when Rosalind scored the winning run, she was pulled into the swarm as well. She accepted quick hugs, back pats, hand shakes, as she made her way to the center of the team to find Ida.

Ida saw her coming and grabbed her, hugged her around the neck, and pressed tightly against her. Rosalind put her hand in the small of Ida's back and lifted her off her feet, spinning her as the rest of the team celebrated around them.

"I love you, Ros!" Ida shouted in Rosalind's ear.

The crowd cheered and stomped their feet, and the rain sticks were being shaken so hard it sounded like a hurricane had formed over the park, but none of the noise mattered. It all faded to silence in the face of what Ida had just whisper-screamed to her. She held the blonde tighter and spun her in a circle, surrounded by their friends who would have just assumed her smile and happy tears were due to the game they'd just won.

EPILOGUE

"WHEN YOU *come to the end of a perfect day, and you sit alone with your thought...*"

Marcy wondered if David would remember the song that had been playing the last time he bailed her out of jail. She didn't particularly care if he did. She was singing it to amuse herself, so she could actually enjoy some fragment of this process. She wore tweed pants and a matching vest, the collar of her shirt unbuttoned and the sleeves rolled up past her elbows. She didn't quite look like a respectable lady, what with the trousers and all, but the desk sergeant had called her 'ma'am' when she walked in. She must have done something right.

David was sitting on a bench with his back against a cinder block wall. His right leg was extended out in front of him, enclosed in a plaster cast. Moxie had intended to duplicate her injury on him, but she'd done far worse. He had required surgery, and there was a chance he would walk with a limp for the rest of his life.

Marcy stopped in front of the cell and put her hands in her pockets. "I suppose he deserved it," she said.

He opened his eyes, saw her, and flinched as if she'd thrown something at him. "I don't have anything to say to you."

"Really? Well, hell. I expected you'd have a lot to say after you got arrested breaking into my apartment. What were you even looking for?"

"I don't know. Something. Something I could use. Something..." He gestured vaguely at the air in front of him. "Who is he, Marcy?"

She furrowed her brow. "What? Who?"

"The bed. Two pillows. Both sides of the bed slept in."

"So you were looking for something in my *bedroom*? You really ought to be ashamed of yourself, David."

He rested his head against the wall, rocking it back and forth. "I never should have told you about the Women's League. I should have just let you stew in that jail 'til all the teams were filled up. Everything was going so well before you got all these ideas of being a real ballplayer in your head."

"I've always been a real ballplayer, David. You only miss the days when I had to rely on you to play the game I love. I thought you were my friend when really you were just trying to buy me a little at a time. But I never needed you. I just needed people to see me and give me a chance. They see me now."

He took a deep breath and let it out slowly. "I don't suppose you're here to bail me out."

"No, I don't know what would make me do that, David. You have harassed me, harassed my friends, invaded my privacy... I'm not eager to find out what your next step would be. So no. I'm not bailing you out. And I am pressing charges. I'm sorry but it has to be done."

He didn't say anything to that.

"Goodbye, David," she said, her voice as firm as she could make it. "If you do manage to stay out of prison, it might be a good idea to leave Chicago. Find somewhere else to call home."

She started to leave.

"Who is he? Can you just give me that?" He opened his eyes and looked at her. "Just tell me it's not some... fucking fan or something like that. Who are you sleeping with?"

Marcy couldn't help smiling. "The love of my life, David. You never stood a chance."

She rapped her knuckle against the bar of his cell and walked away, leaving him alone to consider her answer.

Two weeks after the World's Series, the Shrikes returned to Weeghman Park and geared up again, this time for an official team photo and be presented with a banner to celebrate their win. Lillian invited Marcy and Rainy to see it in the park's main office before the official unveiling. Marcy was worried she might have an ulterior motive in asking to see them alone, but she greeted them warmly and led them to the conference room where a roll of fabric was waiting on the table.

"Mother had them do a rush order. I think it turned out beautifully. I wanted to point out you were the *first* champions, but we decided it wouldn't be necessary. People will know you're the first. But anyway, enough blathering..."

She had Marcy hold the bottom as she unrolled it down the length of the table. It was shaped like home plate, with gold lettering on a field of blue.

**CHICAGO SHRIKES
WOMEN'S NATIONAL LEAGUE
WORLD'S SERIES CHAMPIONS
1916**

Underneath in smaller lettering, each player was named in alphabetical order with their position. At the very bottom, in script that wouldn't be seen except by someone standing very close, Waldron Department Stores was listed as the team sponsor.

Marcy smiled and touched the material. "It's beautiful."

"Isn't it?" Lillian sighed. "Hopefully the first of many, but it's definitely a good start for the franchise. The only team with a championship under their belt. It's going to do wonders for the ticket sales next season."

Both Marcy and Rainy looked at her. "So there *is* going to be a next season?" Marcy asked.

"We weren't entirely sure what was going to happen," Rainy said.

Lillian nodded. "As far as Mother is concerned, absolutely. She's completely invested in keeping the Shrikes around for another year. It depends on the war, of course. We won't be able to use this park if the Cubs or the Whales come home to play in it. But you know Mother. She's likely to have something or other up her sleeve."

Marcy looked at Rainy. "I guess that's kind of a relief."

"Come on, I'll walk you down to the field." Lillian rolled the banner up and tucked it under her arm, then led them out of the conference room. "Mother would like to meet with all the players individually over the next few weeks. Whatever schedule works best for them. They can call her secretary and work out when they can come in. But she wants to make sure they know they're all welcome back for another year, *with* a pay increase to reflect the championship status." She winked over her shoulder. "If you want to keep the best, you have to pay them what they're worth."

"That's very generous," Marcy said. "And she wants to meet with... everyone? That includes Moxie?"

Lillian stopped on the stairs and turned to look back at her. "Well, sure. Why wouldn't it? Oh no, she's not thinking of leaving, is she?"

"No. But with her injury, and the fact she missed the last game..."

"Oh, bosh," Lillian said, continuing down. "That wouldn't have been the last game if Moxie hadn't given a hundred and ten percent of herself. We'd be idiots to give up someone who literally put her body on the line for this team. Assuming her knee heals up well, which I've heard it will, Iona Moccia has a place on this team for as long as she wants it."

Marcy said, "She'll be very glad to hear that."

"Mother also wants to talk to you all about Liberty Bonds. Now that it's the off-season, you'll have to pull your weight to stay on the payroll. What better way than to help out the war effort? It will help quiet down the people who think you're all capitalizing off the war and the men being away. It shows you support the war and that you know it will end soon."

"We'd be happy to help out however she needs us," Rainy said.

"Super!" Lillian clapped her hands once.

They walked out onto the field. They had invited members of the public to sit in the bleachers for the background of the photo. Marcy was surprised to see how big the turnout was. The entire section behind home plate was full, with a few more groups scattered out to either side. It was a bigger crowd than they'd had for their first handful of home games at the start of the season.

"They know there's not an actual game, right?" Rainy said.

"Mm-hmm," Lillian said. "They're just excited to support the team. And they'll be in the photo, which will be saved for posterity in the front hall of the park. They'll be part of Shrike history. Part of Weeghman history! Part of *baseball* history!" She laughed and clapped her hands. "Oh, ladies, we're at the start of something fantastic."

She hurried off, shouting to get Rosalind's attention about something.

Marcy looked at Rainy. "Another season," she said quietly.

"*Maybe* another season," Rainy corrected her. "I know it doesn't seem like the war is going to end any time soon. But spring is a long ways away. Anything could happen between now and then."

"Okay," Marcy said. "But whatever happens, it will be good news."

"How do you figure?"

Marcy stopped walking and stepped in front of Rainy. She held up her thumb. "Option one, the war ends and the men come home. That's good news because it means the war is over. Objectively a good thing." She held up her forefinger. "Option two, the war keeps going and we get to defend our championship. That's good news for us, especially since we know Lorraine Waldron is definitely going to sponsor us for next season. And the best news is that we can't affect which of those options happens."

"That doesn't make you feel absolutely helpless?" Rainy asked.

"No." She reached up and took Rainy's braids in her hands. "It makes me feel like I'm on a boat, and all I can do is steer it and keep an eye on the weather."

Rainy sighed. "You might have to help me with that."

"Sure thing." She winked and let go of Rainy's braids. "Come on, let's go get our picture taken."

They linked arms and went over to where Lillian had started arranging players around home plate.

"Your team is never going to forgive you for this."

Celia waved off Moxie's concern and shook her curls out of her face. "I'll sit somewhere the camera can't see me."

They were walking down Addison toward the park, having just disembarked from the train. Moxie's new apartment was a few blocks away, and she wasn't happy about the time it added to her commute to the park. Although any method of getting anywhere was taking longer than she would like since she was still on crutches. Her doctor had scolded her for the added strain she'd put on the leg when she hit David Buckner.

"You can go ahead if you want," she told Celia. "You don't have to wait for me."

Celia sighed and then laughed. "You're the whole point of going. I'll wait for you as long as I have to."

Moxie blushed. "I'm really glad you came back to town."

"It's a good town. I might look around, see if there's a job worth sticking around for."

"You'd move to Chicago?" Moxie asked, shocked. "If I gave you the impression we needed a second basewoman..."

Celia laughed and shook her head. "You didn't. Don't worry. I have no intention of forcing Lorna Lowell off the team. Baseball is a lot of fun, but lord it's exhausting. All that traveling really took it from me. The only time I was ever home was to sleep. I'd like to see the place I'm paying rent on. I'd like to relax for a day, take a whole weekend off. I'd like to get a cat."

Moxie considered that. "I like cats," she said softly. "And it would help to have someone paying half the rent on my new place."

"You'd be okay with that?" Celia asked, looking sideways at her. The tone was casual, but the question was anything but.

"I think so, yeah. I've never lived alone before. I might get lonely."

"Oh, well, we can't have that."

They had arrived at the entrance of the park. Celia stopped and put a hand on Moxie's arm.

"I'm thinking about moving regardless. I want you to know that. No pressure, no expectations. I want to be here because that would make it easier for... this..." She motioned between them. "For this to become something else. But you don't have to feel obligated in any way. If you~"

"Celia," Moxie interrupted, giving her a warm smile. "Open the door for me, please."

Celia pulled the handle and ushered Moxie inside. Moxie was grateful to be in the lead, because it meant that Celia couldn't see the goofy smile on her face or the happy tears in her eyes as she crutched over the threshold.

***

The photographer had set up a camera tripod a few feet in front of home plate. Lillian Waldron was running back and forth, trying to arrange the players in the most aesthetically-pleasing fashion. Marcy and Rainy were instructed to stand shoulder-to-shoulder in the center. "We'll build out from the two of you," Lillian said, then she had Ida and Rosalind stand next to each other to see if they were the same height.

"She's a few inches shorter than me," Rosalind said, as she slung an arm across Ida's shoulders. "But most times you can hardly notice it."

Ida blushed, but no one seemed to get the innuendo except for Marcy, who twisted at the waist to look up at the bandstand until she could control her silent laughter. Rainy nudged her, but she was also smirking. Rosalind was put next to Marcy, and Ida was told to kneel down in front of her. Rosalind started to say something else but a sharp jab to her ribs from Marcy kept her quiet.

Moxie was, of course, allowed to sit on home plate. Her chest protector and catcher's mask were artfully arranged against her leg to block the brace she still wore, and her crutches were spirited out of sight so they wouldn't be in the photo.

Patty Frett and Lorna Lowell were placed to Rainy's left, while Hildy Koenig was at Rosalind's side. Edith Mortimer, Lulu Martin, and the rest of the reserve players were told to kneel or sit with their legs crossed spreading out from Moxie and Ida.

Once everyone was positioned, Lillian had the banner hung from the backstop. Props were handed out. They were told they could either hold a bat, a ball, or put on their gloves. Marcy chose a bat, Rainy took a ball. Most of the others who were standing chose the glove, while the sitting and the kneeling opted to be empty-handed.

Lillian stepped back and held her hands up to frame the team, then smiled brightly. "Beautiful! Fantastic!" She whistled to get the crowd's attention. "Okay, everybody! We don't need you to look like this is an actual game, but we need smiling faces and excited energy, okay! We need laughter!"

Marcy cleared her throat and spoke in a voice loud enough to carry. "There once was a lawyer who hung out a shingle with his name and first initial on it. A. Swindler, it said. A passerby saw it and told the lawyer that he would be better off using his whole name even if it made for a very long sign. Even if it was Ambrose or Alexander, it had to look better than that. The lawyer said, 'I think that would make it worse, sir. My first name is Adam.'"

There was a pause, and then the crowd began to snicker.

Rosalind shook her head. "What color is the wind off Lake Michigan? Blew."

The laughter continued, this time combined with a few groans.

Rainy laughed and squeezed her eyes shut. "Oh god. If a man tries to tell you no woman has ever created anything of value, I challenge you to ask him how he was born."

The team laughed at that, with Marcy slugging Rainy on the arm. "You've never told me that one before. That's a good one."

Rainy shrugged.

Ida said, "Two men, both on their honeymoon, met up in the hotel bar. One man asked the other where his wife was. 'Upstairs, smoking,' said the second man. The first man whistled and said, 'I'm good, but I don't think I've ever caught one on fire before!'"

At some point during the jokes, Lillian had motioned for the photographer to get under the sheet and take the photo. The crowd was still laughing when he gave the thumbs up, and Lillian clapped her hands.

"Thank you, ladies! People of Chicago, thank you for coming out today! Let's have a round of applause for your champion Shrikes!" The crowd dutifully applauded. "To the team. If you'd like to arrange your meeting with Mrs. Waldron now, you can come talk to me. Otherwise please make arrangements through her secretary."

Rainy relaxed and looked up into the bandstand. She saw large groups of women, some with men but most of them seemed to be alone. She wondered if any of them had grown up with dreams of being an athlete but had given up because it wasn't allowed, wasn't done. There were women of all ages; grandmothers, new mothers, teenagers, children. All of them had found time to come out to the ballpark on a Saturday afternoon just to sit in the background of a photograph. She suddenly understood that wasn't the only reason they'd come.

She looked at Lillian. "Miss Waldron, how long do we have the park?"

Lillian looked confused. "Well, the landscapers want to get in here at five..."

"Plenty of time." Rainy faced the crowd again and whistled to get their attention. "Any of you ladies want to learn how to play? I can show you how to pitch."

Rosalind smiled brightly. "And any of you who want to race me around the diamond, I'll take all comers. Don't be embarrassed when you lose, though. I've yet to meet anyone who can outrun me."

The crowd murmured amongst themselves, and Marcy could see their interests had been piqued.

"No rush." Rainy broke away from the group and headed out to the mound. "Come on down when you're ready. You heard the lady. We're here until five."

Marcy laughed and jogged to catch up with Rainy. "What are you doing?"

"Playing," Rainy said, smiling like a kid. "The way we used to. When we were kids. For the love of the game and no other reason." She nodded back at the bandstand. "Those ladies might not have been as lucky as us when we were kids. We owe it to them to share our wisdom."

Marcy looked back and saw the women were starting to come down onto the field. Lillian had hurried to open the gate to let them out into the normally off-limit grass.

"Why the hell not," Marcy said. "Let's teach the women of Chicago how to play our game."

The Shrikes spread out across the field, armed with bats, balls, and gloves, and waited for the women of Chicago to choose where they wanted to go first.